Praise for *The Queen of*

“Howell has created a fasc
compassionate, kick-ass he
uses wit and agility to survi

—*Booklist*

“Every once in a while, a novel comes along with a character that I absolutely love. [Dar] is such a character. She is fierce, protective, passionate, scarred, loyal, and wise. . . . I truly loved *King’s Property* and I highly recommend it.”

—Fantasy Debut

“Author Morgan Howell has created an outstanding foundation for the next two books to build upon. . . . Be warned, you will NOT want to put down this story.”

—huntressreviews.com

“An unusual tale . . . Howell’s depiction of orc culture is fascinating—these orcs are as big, strong, and dangerous as any in fantasy, but they also have moral and ethical issues of importance. This is not a book to read for fun on a rainy night—it’s a book to think about.”

—Elizabeth Moon, Nebula Award–winning author of *The Deed of Paksenarrion*

“Dar never loses our admiration and compassion—qualities at the heart of any struggling hero. *King’s Property* tests your own presumptions of ‘the other’ and brings to mind the cultural prejudices and wars born from betrayal that are so sadly evident throughout our own history.”

—Karin Lowachee, author of *Warchild*

“In a crowded field, Howell has succeeded in creating an original and vivid fantasy. The characters display unexpected depths of humanity—even when they’re not human. I was captivated by Dar. Highly recommended.”

—Nancy Kress, Nebula Award–winning author of *Beggars in Spain*

By Morgan Howell

THE SHADOWED PATH
A Woman Worth Ten Coppers
Candle in the Storm

THE QUEEN OF THE ORCS TRILOGY
King's Property
Clan Daughter
Royal Destiny

Candle In The Storm

The Shadowed Path
Book 2

MORGAN HOWELL

BALLANTINE BOOKS • NEW YORK

Candle in the Storm is a work of fiction. Names, characters, places, and incidents are the products of the author's imagination or are used fictitiously. Any resemblance to actual events, locales, or persons, living or dead, is entirely coincidental.

A Del Rey Mass Market Original

Published in the United States by Del Rey, an imprint of The Random House Publishing Group, a division of Random House, Inc., New York.

Del Rey is a registered trademark and the Del Rey colophon is a trademark of Random House, Inc.

ISBN 978-0-345-50397-8

Printed in the United States of America

www.delreybooks.com

9 8 7 6 5 4 3 2 1

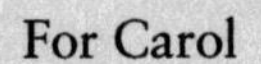
For Carol

The true path is neither wide nor straight,
and on either side lies the abyss.

—*The Scroll of Karm*

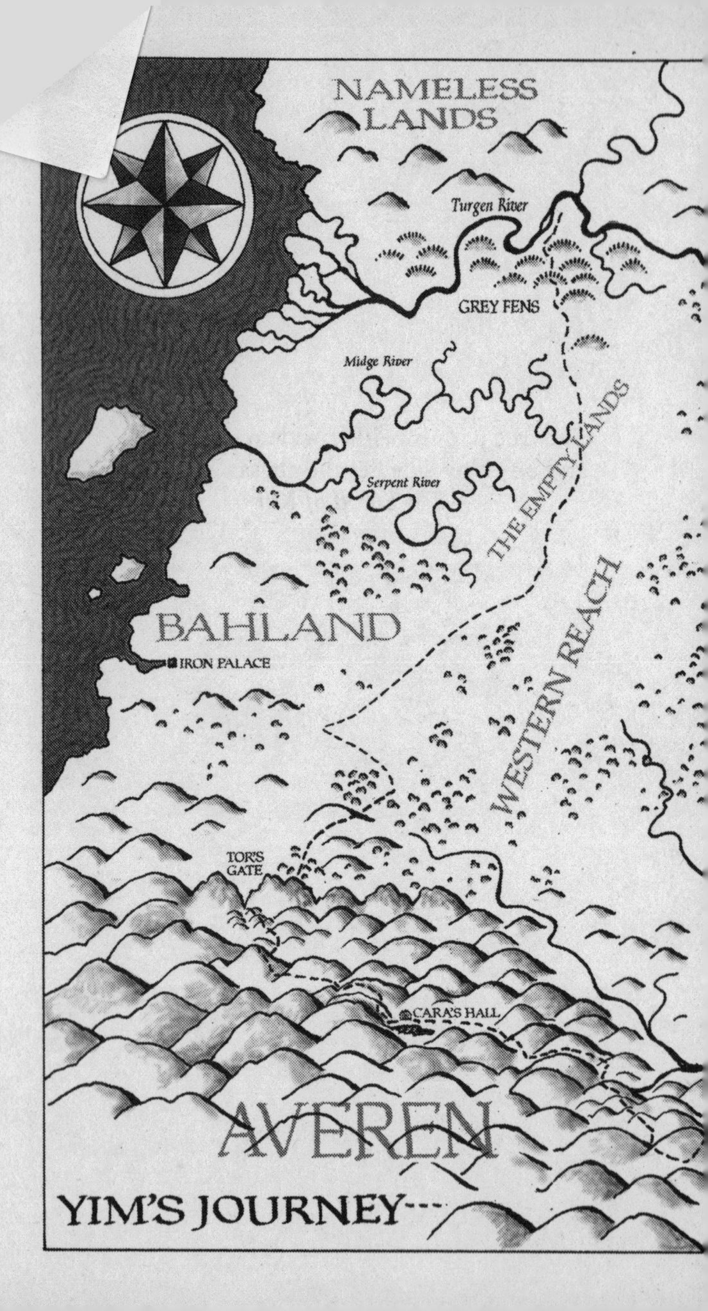
NAMELESS LANDS
Turgen River
GREY FENS
Midge River
Serpent River
THE EMPTY LANDS
BAHLAND
IRON PALACE
WESTERN REACH
TOR'S GATE
CARA'S HALL
AVEREN
YIM'S JOURNEY

CLOUD MOUNTAINS
Lurven River
HIGHLANDS
NORTHERN REACH
LURWIC
LURWIC
CASTLE
FALSTEN
BASTHEM
TURMGEIST
FOREST
DURKIN
WALSTUR
LUVEIN
KARVAKKEN
PASS
LARRESH
DARK MAN'S
CASTLE
ARGENOR
Horse River
EASTERN
REACH
Finlur River
KAMBUL
Yorvern River
BRIDGE
INN
BREMVEN
VINDEN

TOR'S
GATE
WESTERN REACH
River Twayen
Horst Rive
LUVEIN
Spirit River
Little Yorvern River
Finlur River
CARA'S HALL
Yorvern River
STARLIT LAKE
PROVINCE OF
AVEREN
Beware of faerie dells
YIM'S JOURNEY

ONE

SUMMER'S HEAT had settled on Bremven, and the air was stultifying. When the sun rose high in the clear sky, the guards at the city's gate retreated into the shade beneath its archway. From there, they checked all who entered. One unlucky soldier stood in the sun to warn his comrades if a Sarf approached. Sweltering in his armor, he gazed down the length of the bridge, looking for any man with a tattooed face. Sarfs were deadly, and after the destruction of Karm's temple, the guards had cause to be wary of the goddess's servants. Only six days earlier, a Sarf had slain an entire squad when they tried to bar his entry. Thus, despite the heat, fear kept the soldier alert.

A diverse throng crossed the bridge leading to the empire's capital. There were merchants driving wagons, farmers with their oxcarts, the rich on horseback, and the poor afoot. Nowhere was a blue face that signaled trouble. Then one horseman stood out in the crowd. He rode a magnificent black steed. His robe was a similar shade, marking him as a priest of the Devourer. All his kind were officially welcome.

While the priest posed no threat, the soldier couldn't take his gaze from him. The dark rider looked young, barely into his twenties, and he had the sandy hair and gray eyes of someone from Averen. The deep tan of his clean-shaven face set off those pale eyes, and even from a distance they drew the soldier's attention. The guard had the disturbing impression that those gray orbs didn't belong in a young face. The priest seemed aware of the man's scrutiny, for he formed his lips into a cold smile and made the sign of the circle with a casual twist of his wrist. The soldier respectfully bowed his head, relieved for a reason to look away. The black-robed man entered the city and disappeared into its crowded streets.

As he rode through his birthplace, the More Holy Daijen noted many changes. The respect the guard had shown him was but the first. When he had fled Bremven eighty years ago, followers of the Devourer were in disrepute. *Now everyone bows*, he thought. *It marks how we've risen in the world.* Through ruthlessness and cunning, Daijen had risen similarly within the cult. He was the More Holy One, second only to the Most Holy Gorm in gifts and powers. Reflecting upon his rise, Daijen was tempted to visit the squalid alley where he had grown up. He thought how amazed his former neighbors would be to see him young and strong while age had withered them. Daijen quickly dismissed the idea. *There'd be no point. Everyone I knew is likely dead.*

Daijen's eyes lifted from the ancient street and the stone buildings that flanked it until they gazed on the Temple Mount. Karm's temple crowned its heights with stonework cunningly blended with the mountain's natural form. Daijen smiled when he thought how the centuries-old edifice stood empty. The Most Holy Gorm, undoubtedly informed by sorcery, had told him of the massacre there. All who resided within the sanctuary had been slain—the Seers who divined the goddess's will; those training to be Bearers, the holy persons who spread Karm's word; and the young men who trained to be Sarfs, the deadly servants and protectors of Bearers. The temple's destruction hadn't eradicated the worship of the goddess, but it had been a fatal blow. Bearers and Sarfs still roamed the countryside, but they were like worker bees whose hive had been destroyed. They had nowhere to return, and when they perished, they would not be replaced.

Daijen directed his horse toward Karm's temple, eager to

visit the site of his cult's triumph. As the road neared his destination, Daijen paused to view the city and appreciate how the Devourer's temple dominated it. Lord Bahl—the cult's patron—had spared no expense, and the massive black stone temple with its seven pointed spires was an impressive sight. Yet Daijen imagined the day when that structure would be dwarfed by another one that stabbed the sky from atop the mount he was ascending. He envisioned a forest of black spires supplanting Karm's ruined sanctuary and long lines of prisoners being led up the road for sacrifice. It was a stirring vision and one that Daijen was dedicated to realize.

The recent triumph, however glorious, was not the reason for the More Holy One's visit. A far more serious matter had caused him to ride far and fast. Soon after the massacre, an enemy had thwarted the Devourer within Karm's temple. The nature of the deed and its perpetrator were a mystery. The only certain thing was that Daijen must discover and destroy that enemy. The assignment was a perilous one. Ever suspicious, Daijen assumed that was why the Most Holy One had chosen him for the task. The Devourer was a harsh god that punished failure, and Daijen feared his true age would swiftly overtake him if he was unsuccessful. It was a fate he'd do anything to avoid.

Daijen entered Karm's temple, a place he hadn't seen since he was a teenager. He was mildly surprised that he remembered it after so many decades and was pleased to find its outer courtyard stained with blood. It was evident that many had been slain there and their bodies dragged deeper into the temple. Daijen followed a reddish brown trail across the courtyard, through a building with a huge shattered basin, across a second courtyard, and into a huge building with irregularly spaced stone columns carved to resemble trees. He passed through that building and arrived at the remains of a pyre in a central garden.

Blackened bones were piled waist-high, and gray ash

tainted the surrounding landscape. The multitude of violent deaths had weakened the boundary between the living world and the Dark Path, allowing Daijen to feel strongly the Devourer's presence. The trees were gone from the ruined garden, and the remaining plantings were succumbing to a malign influence. Nettles, toadstools, and thorny vines were everywhere, choking generations of careful nurture. The garden was becoming harsh and hurtful. It reminded Daijen of Karvakken Pass, another place where the barrier that restrained his master had been worn thin by slaughter.

This site is conducive to sorcery, thought Daijen. *Here I can learn what has disturbed my master.* Daijen knew he could do nothing without taking the necessary precautions, and he'd need help with that. Contacting the Devourer was always perilous; doing so without a sacrifice was suicidal. *A slave will do. I'll have those at the Black Temple get me one.*

Since he could do nothing more at present, Daijen headed back. He was walking through the dim interior of the colonnaded building when he heard a tapping sound. Daijen stopped and listened, but the noise ceased. He waited for it to return, and soon his patience was rewarded. When the tapping resumed, Daijen traced the sounds to their source—a ragged old man. He was standing on a rickety ladder to chip tiles from a huge mosaic depicting Karm standing on a mountaintop. Much of the lower portion of the artwork had been marred. Although the tiles that formed the white robe of the goddess were untouched, as were the more drably shaded tiles, most of the other colors had been removed. When Daijen entered the room, the man was at work chipping a blue tile from the sky. His only tools were a battered knife and a rock.

"You're a cheeky thief," Daijen said in a loud voice.

Startled, the man nearly lost his balance. He dropped his rock and climbed down the ladder to point his knife at Daijen with trembling hands. "Stay back, or I'll cut you! These are mine."

Daijen flashed an easy smile. "Do you think I care what you do here? I've no love for Karm."

The man eyed Daijen's robe. "I guess not," he said. "Then what brings you?"

"Curiosity," replied Daijen. "Why so nervous? You must have a parade of gawkers."

"You're wrong there. It's lonely work. Everyone's afraid of this place."

"And you're not?"

"It makes me uneasy," admitted the old man, "and I have dreams, bad ones."

"But you still come."

"The tiles fetch a few coppers, and there's not much work for the likes of me." Daijen's amiable manner reassured the old man. He picked up his rock and ascended the ladder to resume his pounding.

Daijen watched awhile before asking in a friendly tone, "Has anyone else come here?"

"Only a Bearer, and that was many days ago."

"What did he say about your enterprise?"

"She," corrected the man. "The Bearer was just a girl."

"A girl? That's unusual. I trust her Sarf was a man."

"Don't know. She was alone."

"No Sarf? Lucky for you, old man."

"I wouldn't have been scared of her, even if she had one."

Daijen smiled. "I see I'm in the presence of a brave man." He sauntered over to the ladder and suddenly kicked it. The ladder toppled and the man fell with it, striking the floor with a heavy thud. Daijen leaned over the man, who lay moaning in pain, and grinned. "Still feeling brave?"

The old man hadn't lost his knife, and he stabbed at Daijen. When the blade touched the priest's flesh, a brilliant blue-white flash illuminated the room. Daijen's assailant fell back, stunned into unconsciousness by the priest's spell against iron weapons. His knife, which glowed eerily, fell from his nerveless hand. Daijen's grin broadened as he hoisted his victim upon his shoulders and carried him to the pyre. He laid the old man on the ashy ground, took a bronze dagger from the folds of his black robe, and slit the man's throat. Blood flowed, forming a puddle. Daijen tore some fabric from the dead man's tattered robe, dipped it in the blood, and used it as a crude brush to paint a large circle on the dirt. He took special care to insure that there were no gaps in the design. Only when he was completely satisfied that the circle was unbroken did he step into it. He sat down in a cross-legged position, closed his eyes, and began to trance.

It was impossible to summon the Devourer without feeling fear. Daijen had no illusions that his master cared for him. The Devourer thrived on slaughter, and the priest knew that his death would satisfy it as well as any other's. Still, the Devourer needed earthly servants, and he rewarded them with unnatural powers. The knowledge that he was needed and the protection afforded by the bloody circle gave Daijen the nerve to continue.

Within Daijen's mind formed a nightmare image of a black sun. It radiated cold instead of warmth and needed life to fuel its frigid fire. The black void was also a conscious being, and when it became aware of Daijen, it turned its thoughts toward him. Malice and insatiable hunger invaded the priest's consciousness as he asked what disturbed his master.

The Devourer answered in an inarticulate way with vague dreamlike images that formed in Daijen's mind. Daijen saw Karm's temple at night. It was hazy and dim, as if viewed from above through a fog. In its center was the faint form of a lone man. He sat on a rock near the edge of a pool. Daijen couldn't discern his face or clothing, for the Devourer distinguished individuals in ways it was unable to communicate. However, Daijen could perceive the man's emotions. He was steeling himself to slay a multitude. Daijen felt his master's eager anticipation of the imminent bloodshed.

Then a woman entered the temple. Unlike the man, her

feelings were hidden from Daijen, but he sensed the enemy guided her. The Devourer sent horrific visions to shatter her sanity. Somehow, she resisted them. She found the man and caused him to abandon his plans. Daijen experienced a surge of frustration and rage as his master communicated the depths of its enmity. It was all directed toward the woman. At any cost, she must be identified, found, and destroyed.

The priest emerged from his trance to find the blood around him boiling. His hands trembled and his head throbbed. He slumped down as he tried to collect his thoughts. His vision had presented a disjointed and nebulous puzzle, but one that was urgent to solve. He dared not disappoint his master.

Daijen began to piece together what he had learned. *Clearly, the woman was one of Karm's servants, for she was guided by the enemy.* Knowing this, Daijen regretted that he hadn't obtained a description of the Bearer from the old man before killing him. *Perhaps she's not the one I seek, but it's likely. The man could have been her Sarf.* Daijen saw logic in this, for Sarfs were lethal and only a Bearer possessed the authority to stop one. It all made sense, and Daijen was encouraged by how far his deductions had taken him. If they were correct, he'd soon find his quarry. As the More Holy One, Daijen commanded all the resources of the Black Temple. A female Bearer would be conspicuous, and Bremven was full of the Devourer's spies.

TWO

DAIJEN WAITED until dark before he went to the Black Temple. The huge building was a windowless basalt hulk with unadorned walls that sloped inward. There was no subtlety or grace to it, only mass and knife-sharp spires. Beside it, the emperor's palace seemed delicate and frail. The temple's massive iron doors were shut for the night, and Daijen had to pound on them with the pommel of his dagger before someone opened them. The wrinkled-faced priest at the door scowled until he saw the emblem of Daijen's rank, an elaborate silver chain that suspended a ring-shaped pendant made of iron. Then he turned obsequious and bowed low. "Welcome, welcome. We're honored, More Holy One."

Daijen hurried in the door. "I'm here secretly," he said. "I want to see the head priest."

"He's at his meat in the order hall, More Holy One. Would you care to join him?"

"Are you deaf?" snapped Daijen. "I said this is a secret visit. I want a private meeting."

The elderly priest bowed. "I'll take you to his chambers and inform him that you're there."

"Tell him to come at once."

"As you wish, More Holy One." The walls of the entrance hall were paneled with gold reliefs, and the priest walked over to one that depicted a battle. He pressed one of the shields in the relief and twisted it. The panel swung inward to reveal a narrow stairway. "This goes directly to the head priest's chambers," he said. Then, taking a candle from a wall sconce, he led the way.

The head priest's chambers were gaudy and lavish, with furnishings that seemed more for display than comfort. Daijen eyed the carved, gilded chairs and decided to stand. He didn't stand long before the head priest rushed in, his fleshy face red from exertion. He bowed low toward Daijen. "Welcome, More Holy One. How may I serve you?"

"Are you aware that the Devourer is displeased?"

The head priest paled. "How can that be? We've reaped many souls for our master. Karm's temple is destroyed."

"Our god is never sated," replied Daijen.

"We've remained diligent," said the head priest in a nervous voice. "Throughout Vinden, we've stirred the folk. Karm's servants are hunted people."

"Nevertheless, someone in Bremven has cheated our master of its due."

"Who? When?"

"That's what I'm here to learn."

"We'll assist you in every way possible. You need only tell me your requirements."

"Secrecy, first of all. Who met me at the door?"

"That would be Grune."

"Sacrifice him," said Daijen. "Immediately."

The head priest bowed low. "It will be done, More Holy One."

"This is the last time you'll see me. I require gold and clothes in the Averen style that would befit a common merchant. I'll be staying at the Blue Mountain Inn under the name of Rangar. Find someone to serve as messenger, someone who can't be traced to here. I need to know about every Sarf, Seer, and Bearer who was in Bremven, however briefly, after the fall of Karm's temple."

The head priest bowed again. "All this will be accomplished, More Holy One. May I do anything else? Perhaps you'd like refreshment."

"I'll have meat and wine. Red wine. Bring it yourself along with Grune's head."

Daijen watched the color leave the head priest's face. *Living in Bremven has made him soft*, he thought. *He wouldn't last long in Lord Bahl's court.*

Three days after Daijen's arrival, winds from the north eased the heat in Bremven. By then, he had received a promising lead and ventured out to pursue it. Standing near a merchant's lavish home, he observed a young woman leave. Dressed as a house slave, she was carrying a large bundle toward the docks. Daijen followed at a distance, but as the woman neared a trading vessel he hurried to catch her. When she turned at the sound of his rapid footsteps, Daijen called to her in an Averen accent. "Mistress? Mistress, could you help me?"

As soon as the woman's eyes met his, Daijen sensed that she was attracted to him. He was a handsome man, and his pale gray eyes would have been appealing even without their supernatural powers. Daijen smiled and watched the woman blush. "Are you speaking to me?" she asked.

"I'm so sorry to disturb you," said Daijen in a timid voice. "You look like you're from my homeland and . . . and I do na know where to turn. I was hoping you might help me."

"How?"

"My name's Rangar, Mistress. I came to join my older brother. He served in Karm's temple and . . ." Daijen's voice choked off, and his eyes filled with tears.

"Your brother's dead, isn't he?" asked the woman in a gentle voice.

Daijen let out a sob. "Aye, Mistress."

"Call me Gurdy. I'm no one's mistress, just a house slave."

"I see na slave, only a kindly face." Daijen wiped his eyes and gazed at Gurdy with a look of hope and trust. "I'm a stranger here, and the place is thick with the Devourer's followers."

"How can I help you?" asked Gurdy, clearly eager to be of some service.

"I seek to work for someone who still respects the Balance."

Gurdy beamed. "You're in luck! My master still honors Karm. He's a cloth merchant, the richest one in Bremven. He always needs men for his caravans. His name's Commodus."

"But would he dare hire someone with ties to Karm's temple?"

"My master's unafraid of the black-robed ones. Until just recently, a Sarf lived with us. My own mistress became his Bearer."

"It's a comfort to know na everyone's forsaken the goddess. But how could a woman become a Bearer after the temple had fallen?"

"I've no idea," replied Gurdy. "I didn't understand it then, and I don't now. I've no idea why Yim would even want to be a Bearer. She gave up a lot."

"Yim?"

"That was my mistress's name. Actually, she was my mistress for only a day. She was a slave before then. When she became my master's ward, I was to attend her. She left the very first night, and when she came back with Honus, she was a Bearer. I don't know how it happened, it just did."

"Who's Honus?"

"Her Sarf. He became her Sarf when she became a Bearer." Gurdy sighed. "Then it was back to being a house slave for me. Yim gave up her lovely room and slept in humble quarters, though she and Honus dined with the master."

"Your tale seems proof that Karm has na forsaken Bremven." Daijen gazed affectionately at Gurdy, then lowered his voice to a more intimate tone. "As does your kindness."

Gurdy flushed. "It's nothing."

"It means everything to me," said Daijen. "Can I carry your bundle? It looks heavy."

"I can manage. The boat's right ahead."

As Daijen watched Gurdy rush off to deliver her package, he was satisfied that he had learned everything of use from her. Nevertheless, he didn't depart. Daijen disliked leaving loose ends.

When Gurdy returned to the wharf, she was pleased to find her new acquaintance waiting. "Would you say Commodus is an understanding man?" he asked.

"He's very kind."

"Then surely he will na begrudge you a little rest. It's pleasant on the riverbank." The man Gurdy knew as Rangar held out a small golden-brown pastry. "I've a berry tart. Will you share it with me?"

Gurdy needed no persuasion. She followed Rangar away from the busy wharf to a quiet stretch of river and a sunwarmed stone on its shore. There she removed her sandals and dangled her feet in the clear flowing water. Her companion did likewise and handed her the tart. Its sweetness complemented Gurdy's mood. "Oh Rangar, this is so good! You must taste it!"

Rangar didn't look at the tart. Instead, he gazed lovingly into her eyes as he touched a finger to the corner of her mouth and drew it away bearing a drop of berry juice. Delicately and slowly, he licked his fingertip. In a soulful voice he said, "It's luscious."

Gurdy felt she was in a romantic tale. She was no longer plain, or even a slave. Everything faded compared to the enchanting eyes that fixed on hers. She bit into the tart, smearing her lips with red sweetness. "Would you like another taste?"

Rangar's hand gently brushed Gurdy's cheek, then traveled to caress the back of her neck. With exquisite slowness, his lips moved toward hers. Gurdy was transfixed with anticipation. She felt the warmth of his breath, then the softness of his lips. Then a stab of pain broke the spell. "Ow!" she cried.

Rangar's gaze seemed to follow something in the sky. "A hornet!" he said. "Did it sting you?"

"I'm afraid so," said Gurdy, touching the back of her neck.

"It must have been drawn by the tart. Are you all right?"

"I think so, but it hurts."

Rangar bent over to wave his hand in the water. For an instant, Gurdy thought she saw something shiny fall from his fingertips and tumble into the depths. Then Rangar withdrew his wet hand to rub her neck. His touch was not only cool and soothing but also tender, and Gurdy became convinced that her eyes had been tricked. *I saw only a reflection*, she thought. "Oh Rangar, that feels good."

"I'm glad," he replied. "But you should get out of the sun."

"Maybe I should. I feel a little woozy."

Rangar stood and helped Gurdy rise. "I'd walk you back to your master's house, but perhaps we should na be seen together."

"Why?" asked Gurdy, not bothering to hide her disappointment.

"Your master may na hire me if he knows I care for you. It'd be better if people think we're strangers when we meet again."

"I'll keep your secret," said Gurdy. She touched Rangar's cheek as she moved closer to him, berry juice still coloring her pursed lips.

Rangar bent down to fasten his sandals. "Then I'll see you tomorrow."

"Yes," replied Gurdy with a sigh. "We'll meet again tomorrow." She put on her sandals.

While Rangar remained on the riverbank, Gurdy headed

back to her master's house. There she kept her delicious secret as she worked the rest of the day polishing the huge dining hall table. It seemed to her that the day had turned hot, and the heat made her dizzy. She went to bed without eating dinner and lay upon her straw-filled mattress, drenched in sweat. When she fell into a fitful sleep, heat entered her dream.

Gurdy stood alone on a featureless plain where the sun beat down from an empty sky. It was oppressively hot. "Come into the shade," said a voice. Gurdy turned and saw Rangar standing in a patch of shadow. Neither had been there before. As Gurdy walked toward him, she realized that she was naked and the heat didn't radiate from the sun, but from Rangar's eyes. She stepped into the shade, and it turned cold. Rangar's mouth was smeared with red. *Berry juice*, Gurdy thought. She moved to kiss it away.

THREE

THE FOLLOWING morning found Commodus in his counting room. He stared listlessly out the window, for the news of Gurdy's death had made him melancholy. Jev, his steward, had been terse in reporting her demise, remarking that Gurdy "looked ill" last evening and her mattress was soaked with sweat when they found her. With dry eyes, Jev had supposed she died of a fever and let the matter rest.

Commodus couldn't let it rest so easily. He mourned the young woman, not because he cared for her especially, but because it seemed that nobody did. The more Commodus thought of Gurdy's lonely death, the more he thought of

Yim's sentiments on slavery. She had wanted him to free Gurdy. Despite his respect for Yim, he had scoffed at the idea and said Gurdy was happy, with all her needs met. Upon recalling his arguments, Commodus felt they rang hollow. The silken robe that Gurdy would wear upon her funeral pyre had cost him more than she did.

A knock interrupted his musings. "Yes," said Commodus.

Jev's voice came from behind the door. "Sire, a young trader wishes to speak with you."

"I told you I'd see no one."

"It's about gold brocade, sire. He wants to order two dozen bolts."

"Did you say two *dozen*?"

"Yes, sire. Two dozen."

Commodus opened the door. "Do you know him?"

"No, sire," replied Jev. "He says his name is Rangar and that he comes from Averen."

"They don't wear such finery in Averen," said Commodus with puzzlement. "Still, two dozen bolts. I guess I'll see him."

Jev ushered in a stranger carrying a parchment-wrapped bundle and then departed. Commodus met his visitor suspiciously, for he didn't like the man's eyes. "My steward says you're interested in gold brocade."

"Yes," replied the man. "My name's Rangar, sire, and I'm new to Bremven. I'd like to commission a pattern. The client will provide the gold."

"That's not the common practice," said Commodus, glancing at the bundle. "I think your client's overtrusting." When he looked up and saw that Rangar was regarding him with a piercing gaze, he grew angry and glanced away. "I know that look! And I can defeat it!"

"I needed assurance that you're honest."

"That's one use for that trick, but only one."

"Please, sire. I beg your pardon. I've been cheated so often, I probe thoughts out of caution. You possess the same ability, otherwise you wouldn't have detected me."

"If you had asked around, you'd know my reputation."

"I did, sire. And forsooth, it sounded too good to be true. I've even heard tell that you sheltered a Bearer and her Sarf when most now lack the courage to honor the goddess."

Commodus looked at Rangar sharply. "Who told you that?"

"A slave girl. She babbled on and on about it."

"You've questioned one of my slaves?"

"Of course not. I merely asked directions. She volunteered the rest."

"Well, you shouldn't listen to a slave girl's prattle. I sheltered no one." Commodus glanced at his visitor, saw that he wasn't deceived, and quickly changed the subject. Pointing to the parchment-covered bundle, he asked, "Is that a sample of the pattern?"

"Yes," replied Rangar as he unfolded its wrapping.

Commodus frowned when he saw the elaborately embroidered black cloth it contained. "This is for vestments worn by the Devourer's priests."

"So? They'll pay well."

"I detest the Black Temple. I'll not garb its priests."

"I've no love for the Devourer either. But profit and religion are separate spheres."

"Perhaps to you. I feel differently. Find another source for your brocade."

"At least give me the benefit of your expertise. I worry that I've been cheated again. Could you tell me if the gold thread in this sample is full weight? It's supposed to be three grains an ell."

"You shouldn't be dealing in brocades if you can't tell that," said Commodus. Nevertheless, he decided to oblige the man in order to get rid of him more quickly. Taking the sample, he ran his fingers over the cloth to feel its gold thread. Suddenly, Commodus jerked back his hand. "Someone left a pin in it." He sucked the dot of blood from his finger, then smiled. "They stuck you, too. The thread's too soft to be full weight."

Rangar looked dejected. "Just as I feared."

"If I were you, son, I wouldn't deal with the Black Temple. You can lose more than money there. Now, since we've no further business, I wish to be alone." Commodus turned to face the window and was glad to hear Rangar leave. The man had left a foul impression, and Commodus was certain that he had been interested in something other than brocade. *The Black Temple draws scoundrels like shit draws flies, and Bremven's the worse for it*, he thought. *Yim was wise to leave when she did*. He rubbed his fingertip, which was still sore where the pin had pricked it. As he did, the room seemed to grow warmer.

Jev entered a little while later. "That was a waste of time," said Commodus. "I'll see no one else today. Send up a boy to fan me. This heat's making me woozy."

The summer's warmth made for quick funerals, and Daijen returned to the counting room only two days after his first visit. "I'm so sorry to hear of your father's demise," he said.

"Thank you," said Dommus. "It was a shock. A sudden fever took him."

"Summer can bring evil vapors," said Daijen. "It's most tragic. I only met him once, but your father impressed me as an honest and principled man. I felt honored to do business with him. He did mention my order? It was a large one."

"No," said Dommus. "He didn't speak of it. Or of you, for that matter. What's your name again?"

"Rangar. Perhaps he didn't mention me because we hadn't sealed our bargain. I had to speak to my client first."

"Well, I know nothing about it. What does this business concern?"

Daijen unwrapped a parchment-covered bundle to reveal

a piece of black brocade, richly woven with gold. "Twenty-four bolts, and that's only the first order."

Dommus's face lit up with excitement. "Two dozen bolts!" He glanced at Daijen, who met his eyes with a piercing stare. Unlike his father, Dommus was easily ensnared. His expression quickly took on the trusting look of one who recognizes a fellow soul. Upon seeing it, Daijen smiled as one worldly man does to another.

Dommus returned the smile. "This is fine work," he said, reaching out to touch the brocade.

Daijen stayed his hand and plucked a needle from the stitching. "I'm sorry, some careless fool left this in the cloth. I wouldn't want you pricked."

Dommus fingered the work appreciatively. "Expensive stuff," he said. "Why go through me? It's more common to deal directly with the weavers."

"I'm seldom in Bremven," replied Daijen. "I need someone to insure the quality. That concerns my client more than price."

"And your client's the Black Temple?"

"Yes. Is that a problem?"

"I'm a merchant," said Dommus. "Gold is gold."

"So religion presents no difficulties?"

"The only problem I have with religion concerns an overstock of dark blue cloth. With Karm's temple destroyed, I can't give it away."

"Yes, it's worth your life to go about in blue," said Daijen with an air of sympathy. "Beatings and worse. You'd think the emperor would stop such persecutions."

"Morvus is under Lord Bahl's thumb," replied Dommus. "He'll do nothing."

"Then why not dye the blue cloth black and sell it for priests' robes?"

Dommus grinned. "I like that idea." He fingered the gold cloth again. "Two dozen bolts you say?"

"In the first order," replied Daijen. "Just name your price. They'll pay it."

Dommus grinned more broadly. "Would you like some wine while we work out our arrangement?"

"As long as it's chilled."

Dommus was into his second goblet before all the particulars were put into writing. By then, he looked quite pleased with himself. Daijen was equally satisfied. "I'm like you, Dommus," he said. "I might sell to the Black Temple, but to me they're merely customers. Religion doesn't interest me, but I'm sorry I missed meeting Yim."

"Yim?"

"Yes, the woman Bearer. Your father spoke of her."

"Oh yes, *Karmamatus*," said Dommus. "Well, she might be Karm's beloved, but did Father also tell you she was a slave?"

"No," said Daijen feigning surprise. "This sounds like a strange tale."

"You'll never hear one stranger," said Dommus in a confidential tone.

Daijen leaned forward, looking intrigued. "How does one go from slave to Bearer?"

"Well, she came with this Sarf . . ."

"Honus?"

"Yes, Honus," said Dommus. "He freed her and more or less dumped her here. Father took her in as a favor. Not that I minded. As we used to say—she was as pretty as the goddess. Only eighteen winters. Long, walnut hair. Big, dark eyes. She filled out a silk robe quite nicely."

Daijen gave Dommus an earthy look. "Someone worth tupping?"

Dommus grinned back. "I'll say," he said. "Not that I got any. Though, I might have if it weren't for Honus."

"He interfered?"

"Not in the way you might think. He dumped her because

he planned vengeance on the Black Temple. Somehow, Yim found out. I think she forced it from Father, though I can't imagine how. Anyway, she rushed out that very night."

"And?"

"She stopped Honus. Good thing for us she did. Otherwise, you and I would lack some lucrative clients. If any man could wipe out the black priests, it's Honus. He has quite a reputation."

"He must have been furious with her."

"Quite the opposite," said Dommus. "Afterward, he worshipped her, and I mean literally."

"So she became his Bearer?" said Daijen. "In one night? I thought it took years to become one."

Dommus shrugged. "I guess not. Honus certainly believed she was holy. Father did, too. It got tiresome."

"I can imagine," said Daijen. "Bearers are a stiff-necked lot, and their Sarfs are even worse. How'd you get rid of them?"

"They left on their own accord. Just five days ago."

"For where?" asked Daijen casually.

"Averen," replied Dommus. "Something to do with Lord Bahl."

"Bahl?"

"That's what Father said. It worried him."

"I'd think it might," said Daijen. "What did they hope to accomplish?"

"Beats me," said Dommus. "All I know is that it was a waste of a fine-looking woman. She was tuppable, Rangar. *Very* tuppable."

Daijen left Dommus's company confident that he had solved his puzzle. Everything he had learned fitted with his informants' reports and his vision at Karm's temple. *Yim's the one who enraged my master.* Daijen was certain of it. There were no other possibilities. Furthermore, Dommus had not only confirmed the enemy's identity; he had said where she was headed.

As Daijen returned to his lodgings, he didn't reflect on the irony that the blood Yim had denied the Devourer would have been spilled in the Black Temple. As far as his master was concerned, blood was blood. As long as it wasn't Daijen's own, it didn't matter to him either. At the moment, he was particularly pleased with himself, for it had taken just seven days to ferret out Yim. Now that Daijen knew she was his target, he turned his thoughts to her annihilation.

FOUR

IT WAS growing dark, but not quickly enough. There was nowhere for Yim to hide. Though the brush was dense and tangled, it was only waist-high, and a recent flood had stripped its leaves. It wouldn't screen her from sight. Moreover, her tracks stood out on the muddy ground. Yim's only chance was to outrun her pursuer. She slipped the pack from her shoulders, wishing she had abandoned it earlier. She opened its flap and took out the knife. *A puny weapon against a sword.* Then Yim turned her attention to her sandal. Its strap had come loose and examination showed that it had broken. *No time to fix it.* Already, Yim heard boots crunching on loose stone.

Yim removed her sandals and resumed running. From the corner of her eye, she glimpsed the man who had been tracking her. He sheathed his sword and ran also. Yim followed a streambed because it offered the easiest path, its banks having been swept clear of brush by floodwaters. Without the heavy pack, Yim outpaced her pursuer, and it seemed she would escape. She ran until she was winded.

Pausing to catch her breath, Yim listened for the swordsman she had seen only twice. Five men had attacked them on the road, and Honus had taken on all five while she darted for safety. The man pursuing her had been lying in wait. If Yim had run to the opposite side of the lane, she would have fallen into his trap. Instead, he had been forced to reveal himself and chase after her. That was the only reason she still lived.

As Yim listened for sounds of pursuit, she noted her surroundings for the first time and saw that she had entered a valley. Its sides weren't enclosed by sloping ridges, but by low walls of vertical stone. They weren't near, but Yim could see that they drew closer upstream. *I'm in a funnel*, she thought. Yim was considering pushing her way through the dead brush and attempting to scale those walls when she heard her pursuer slogging through the water. Yim panicked and resumed sprinting along the stream bank. Before long, the walls closed in, and she was running inside a ravine with no choice but to continue deeper into it. Either by chance or design, she had become game herded into a trap. Nevertheless, flight seemed her only hope.

The surrounding walls were vertical and composed of thin layers of brittle slate, piled horizontally like knife blades. Yim looked for a place to climb, but saw none. The farther she ran, the higher the walls rose until they towered high above her head. Soon the darkening sky was only a ribbon hemmed by stone. There was no vegetation, only mud and rock. In some places, the stream flowed in a thin sheet over a nearly level slate floor. Elsewhere, jumbled slabs of fallen rock littered the way. Nowhere was there a place to hide. A layer of damp silt coated everything, making the footing treacherous and leaving clear impressions of Yim's footprints.

The ravine followed a twisting course, and every turn seemed to present a new obstacle. After clambering over a pile of loose slate, Yim rounded a corner to find a small waterfall barring her way. Water cascaded over a steep slope that was twice Yim's height. She waded through shallow water to climb it. Close to the ravine wall, the pool was only ankle-deep and no water spilled down the barrier. Yim gripped the knife with her teeth to free both hands to climb the damp slate. She made slow progress, for the holds were precarious and the rock was slippery.

Yim had nearly reached the top when she slipped and bounced against rock all the way down. The blows knocked the breath from her, and the knife tumbled into the silty pool below. Yim was cut and scraped by her fall, but she landed on her feet. Ignoring her injuries, she dropped to her hands and knees to grope for the knife in the cloudy water. Yim was still in that position when she heard a sword being drawn from its sheath.

Turning around, Yim spied a man advancing up the ravine. He was only twenty paces away. Flight was impossible. Yim sat down in the shallow pool as her pursuer approached. Supported by her arms, she inclined her torso as if shrinking from her nemesis. He was a young man with a hefty, work-hardened body. Garbed like a farmer, he wielded his stubby sword more like a pruning hook than a weapon. Yim tried to catch his eye, but he carefully avoided her gaze. "Why are you hunting me?" she called out. "I've done nothing to you."

"We know of yer sorcerous ways," the man said as he advanced. "Ye'll not steal *our* children."

"I serve the Goddess of Compassion," said Yim. "I'd never harm a child. Look me in the eye and see truth."

The man resolutely stared toward Yim's feet. "I've heard of that trick. Ye cannot bewitch me."

Yim's eyes fixed on the advancing blade, which seemed a rusty heirloom. It shook in the man's trembling grasp. Her pursuer halted just a step away, and Yim's gaze shifted to his face. His eyes avoided hers, but she could tell that he was nearly as frightened as she was. "You don't have to kill me."

"I must. There's no other way."

Yim began to sniffle softly, then lifted her left hand from the muddy water. She moved it slowly, so as not to alarm the man, and began to unbutton her shirt. Yim couldn't tell whether her tears or her undressing perplexed her attacker more, but in either case he was transfixed. She opened her shirt to expose her breasts. The young man's gaze went to them. "If you're resolved to slay me, pierce me through the heart," said Yim, her voice vulnerable and frightened. "I'll show you where to strike."

Yim delicately grasped the sword's tip and guided it between her breasts, pulling the swordsman toward her. The blade was such a short one, he was drawn quite close. All this happened with such dreamlike slowness that it had an air of unreality. Then Yim suddenly pushed the blade aside and leaned forward as her right hand flashed upward from the muddy water.

Yim guided the knife as Honus had taught her—under the breastbone and into the heart. Yim's attacker jerked from the blow and his sword swung upward to cut her chin. Then the weapon splashed into the pool. Yim felt the man's heart pulsing at the end of her blade. Hot blood spurted over her hand. Yim's assailant met her gaze only as he died. As their eyes locked for an instant, the man's expression became astonished. Then he collapsed.

Yim lay in the silty water immobilized by shock and the weight of the man atop her. He did not yet seem a corpse. His body was warm and smelled of sweat and hay. Yim wondered who had poisoned his mind and if the children that he feared would be stolen were his. She felt like a murderer, not a victor, and it was awhile before she pushed the inert body off hers. Her knife was still lodged in the man's chest. When Yim bent over to extract the blade, she looked at her assailant's young, still face. She found no malice frozen on its features, only awe.

As Yim closed the dead man's eyelids, her hand began to tremble. Whatever relief she felt at her escape was overwhelmed by trauma. She began to sob. Weeping, Yim washed the blood from her shirt, dragged the body from the pool, and made the Sign of the Balance over it. Then she slumped to the ravine's damp floor and continued sobbing until it grew dark.

When Yim finally departed, the way back seemed longer than she remembered. It was too dark to search for the pack and her sandals by the time she emerged from the ravine. It would be hard even to find the road. As Yim made her way in the gloom, the face of the man she had killed lingered in her thoughts. His final moment haunted her. *What did he see?* Over and over, she wondered if his death could have been avoided.

Yim nearly screamed when a dark figure stepped from the shadows, but she didn't draw her knife.

"Yim," said Honus, "are you all right? Someone was following you."

"He's dead," replied Yim, struggling not to sob again. "I killed him."

Honus rushed to her. Yim knew his impulse was to embrace her, just as she knew he would stifle it. Instead, he touched her bloody chin. "You've been wounded. I should tend it."

"You can't. I left the pack behind, and I don't know where it is."

"I do," replied Honus. "I found it and your sandals, too. I'm sorry I failed you."

"How did you fail me?"

"I didn't see your attacker."

"You were fighting five at once!"

"If you were slain, what good would it have done to fight the five? I'm your Sarf, and I didn't protect you."

"Enough, Honus. I'm alive. And the five you fought?"

"All dead."

"So much killing," said Yim in a mournful tone. "Two attacks in two days."

"The black priests have been busy. Folk are stirred against us."

"The man I . . ." Yim paused to regain her composure. "He said something about stealing children. How could anyone believe such lies?" Yim let out a long sigh that sounded like breathy sobbing. "Five days on the road, and I'm already at my limit!"

"A Bearer's path is often hard," said Honus, his tone tender and concerned.

"But it's supposed to be a holy one," replied Yim. "Honus, I just killed a man. What's holy about that? I tricked him, and I'm ashamed to say how."

"Karmamatus . . ."

"Don't call me that!" said Yim, her voice shrill. "I'm unworthy of the name."

Honus seemed about to disagree, but he bowed his head instead. The two walked silently awhile before Yim spoke. "I'm sorry, Honus. I shouldn't have snapped at you."

"After what you've been through, it's natural to be on edge," said Honus. "The pack's close by. Soon you'll have dry clothes, and I'll find a campsite when the moon rises. You'll feel better after some food and rest."

"I doubt it. I can't forget that man's face. When I stabbed him . . ." Yim's voice trailed off and she shuddered.

"Time will ease the memory."

"You say that because you're a Sarf."

"And used to killing?" replied Honus. "How could it be otherwise? Yet I still remember the first man I slew."

Yim fell silent again as she followed Honus back to the

pack. Yim opened it and removed some dry clothes. After she changed, she sat beside Honus on a rock and waited for the moon to rise.

"Honus, did Theodus ever kill anyone?"

"No."

"Then I want no more lessons with the knife. I should trust Karm to protect me."

"Karm didn't protect Theodus."

"Would a knife have saved him?"

"A knife saved you."

"All the same, I won't kill again."

"Yim, you must protect yourself. Things were different when Theodus was my Bearer."

"That was less than three moons ago," retorted Yim.

"The last time Theodus and I were in Vinden, we were welcome everywhere. But that was three winters ago."

"Then things have certainly changed," said Yim. "Still, it seems wrong for a Bearer to kill."

"The goddess metes out death. As do I in your service."

"So, why should I shrink from doing my part?"

"I didn't say that," replied Honus.

"Tonight, my presence drew six men from their homes. Now they're dead and their blood's on my hands, whether I wielded a blade or not."

"Don't be hard on yourself," said Honus. "I know you wish harm to no one. All I hope is that you'll do what's necessary."

Honus's choice of words startled Yim, for Karm had told her to do "what's necessary" in her last vision. It had been ambiguous guidance then, and it remained so. *Did it mean I should kill?* wondered Yim. Her thoughts were interrupted when Honus gently grasped her hand, "Please, Yim," he whispered. "Protect yourself. Don't lose your life to spare a foe."

"Is that Karm's will or yours?"

"I see no conflict. One need not die because they're not good."

"There may come a time when that won't be true," said Yim. "If so, will you be guided by the goddess or your feelings?"

"Though I love you . . ."

"You promised not to speak of that."

"You asked about my feelings," said Honus, as he meekly released her hand.

Yim sighed. "Oh Honus, how can this work? I can't return your love. I feel I'm tormenting you."

"If I can serve and protect you, I'm content."

"Still . . ."

"My fate's Karm's doing, not yours."

When the moon rose and there was light to find the way, Honus led Yim away from the stream and into a nearby forest. There, he selected a campsite that was both hidden from the road and easy to defend. While Yim hung out her wet clothes, he gathered firewood.

As Yim waited for Honus to return, she was discouraged. The sense of purpose that she had felt upon leaving Bremven had been quickly worn down by hardships on the road, and she was uncertain whether she was following the goddess's path. The incident in the ravine seemed confirmation that she wasn't. The dead man's face continued to haunt her, causing her to question her judgment.

Last winter, when Yim had departed her distant highland home, her goal had seemed simple: She was to have a child, and by doing so, help overcome evil. She had been groomed for that task ever since early childhood when Karm had appeared to her and said that she was "the Chosen." The Wise Woman who became her guardian stated Karm would guide Yim to the father. Instead, she had been ambushed, enslaved, and sold to Honus. Everything that happened afterward, from gaining her freedom to becoming Honus's master, seemed as much happenstance as the goddess's doing.

I felt differently on the night I became Honus's Bearer, thought Yim. Then she had felt cupped in Karm's hands. By assuming the role of Honus's late Bearer, Yim believed that she had finally determined the proper course of action. Resuming Theodus's search for the source of evil gave Yim a destination, and upon her journey, she might find the man who was to father her child. After all, Karm had told her to follow Theodus's footsteps. However, recent events made that decision seem imprudent, and Yim wondered if even becoming a Bearer had been a mistake.

Sitting alone in the dark forest, Yim felt abandoned by Karm. Throughout Yim's life, the goddess seemed the mother she had never known and provided love when her guardian offered none. Yet ever since Yim had left the highlands, she felt that the goddess had grown remote, appearing rarely and behaving cryptically.

The more Yim thought, the more her misgivings grew. The vision directing her to follow the footsteps of Honus's late Bearer could be interpreted in more than one way. *Perhaps I'm supposed to retrace his journey, not resume his quest.* Like most of her visions, its guidance was ambiguous. Others made even less sense. Twice Karm had appeared to Yim covered in blood. Those apparitions were as ominous as they were puzzling. Yim tried to imagine what Honus would think of such bizarre visions. *If he knew what I saw, would he think I was holy or crazy?*

Though Honus seemed unshaken by Yim's uncertainty, she often felt like a charlatan. *He knows I'm the Chosen, but I've never told him what that means. Instead, I play his Bearer because I need him.* Until Karm revealed who would father Yim's child, Honus's protection seemed essential. *And what does he get in return? Nothing, not even the truth.*

Honus returned with a load of wood. Even in the dim light, he moved noiselessly through the undergrowth. Soon he had lit a fire. Its small circle of light made the surrounding forest seem all the darker. Honus took out his healing kit, and set a pot of water to boil. "When the water's ready," he said, "I'll tend your wound."

Yim touched the cut on her chin. "Is it bad?"

Honus peered at it in the firelight. "No, but you'll have a scar."

Yim smiled wryly. "I'm catching up with your collection."

"I'm keeping apace with you," replied Honus.

For the first time, Yim noticed that Honus's shirtsleeve was torn and blood-soaked. She gasped. "Honus! Why didn't you tell me you were hurt?"

"I didn't wish to trouble you. Besides, it's not deep." He rolled up his right sleeve to reveal a bloody gash on his forearm.

When the water boiled, Honus poured some into a wooden bowl and added powder from a vial in his healing kit. After cleaning the blood from Yim's face, he wetted a cloth with the solution in the bowl. "This will sting," he said.

"I remember," replied Yim. She winced as the solution foamed inside her cut. Glimpsing the concern in Honus's eyes, she tried to hide her pain. She took a deep breath and said, "I'm glad that's over."

Honus cleaned the gash on his arm with the same solution, then asked, "Would you stitch my wound closed? I'd rather not do it left-handed."

"I'll try," said Yim, "but I've never done the like before."

"It's not hard, and I'm certain your dainty fingers will do finer work than Theodus's thick ones ever managed."

"Before you malign his stitching, you should compare it to mine," said Yim. "As a girl, I was more adept with goats than needlework."

"Then pretend I'm a goat."

Honus took out a curved needle and a strand of gut from his kit and dipped them in the cleansing solution. He declined Yim's suggestion to prepare a brew for his pain, stating he wanted to stay alert. When Yim nervously sewed his wound, he was absolutely stoic. He guided her stitching calmly, tensing only slightly each time the needle pierced his flesh. The only evidence of his pain was the deep breath he took when Yim was done. Honus gazed at his stitches and smiled. "You underestimate your skill."

"I'm glad you're so easily pleased," Yim replied. "The woman who raised me would've made me tear out the seam and restitch it."

Honus winced. "Let's talk of food, instead," he said quickly. "Perhaps this would be a good night to have that cheese we were saving."

"To celebrate our new scars?'

"To celebrate we're both alive."

FIVE

FAR NORTH of Yim and Honus, Hendric stood in a long line for his ration of porridge. The army had halted its advance only when night fell, and he was hungry, footsore, and distraught. The peasant soldier had been on the march for five days, and each step had taken him farther from his pregnant wife and young family. Hendric had joined the army to prevent their slaughter, but that would neither plant the crop nor harvest it, and he feared that those he loved would starve in his absence.

Hendric's newly issued sword hung by his side. He hated it. It felt ponderous dangling from his hip, and every time it knocked against his legs it reminded him of his forced servitude. He hated everyone who had taken him from home and family, starting with Count Yaun, who made a treaty with

Lord Bahl and emptied his realm of men to fulfill it. Hendric despised the black-robed priests who stirred up men to fight against folk they had never seen. It had been Hendric's neighbors who enforced the count's decree by threatening anyone who refused to go. Hendric could no longer stand the sight of them, so he ate with strangers.

Hendric was able to move freely within the mass of men because it was more of a mob than an army. It had no units or officers. The only real soldiers were Lord Bahl's troops, the Iron Guard. They were the armored men who kept order through ruthless brutality. The peasants quickly learned that disobeying their commands or lagging behind could have deadly consequences and safety lay solely in obedience.

As Hendric waited dutifully—if sullenly—for his meager meal, someone tapped his shoulder and spoke. "Hey there. Ye one of them Falsten lads?"

Hendric turned and beheld a ragged man who appeared to be a peasant, despite his well-worn leather armor and battered metal helm. The man was smiling in a manic way that matched the unsettling look in his eyes. "Aye," replied Hendric tersely, hoping to keep the conversation short.

"Ye have that green look ta ye. So I says ta meself, 'Slasher'—that's what I call meself now—Slasher. 'Slasher,' I says, 'ye need ta show that lad the way of things, him being green and all.' " Slasher bowed. "So at yer service."

"I don't need yer service."

"I know ye think so. I hail from Lurwic and was same as ye. Took ye from yer people did they?"

"Aye."

"Well, they killed all mine, but said they'd spare those that would soldier. So I joined. I wasn't happy 'bout it. I wasn't Slasher then. I was like ye."

"I want to stay like me."

"Ye mean miserable and low? Mayhap 'tis so, but ye'll have no choice when you meet our lord."

"Ye mean Lord Bahl?'

Slasher flashed a wide grin. "Aye, and lordly he is. He'll make ye glad ye're here. 'Twill feel good ta slay."

"Never."

"Oh ho! Sure, ye say that now. I did meself afore my first battle. And what a battle 'twas!" The gleam in Slasher's eyes became more pronounced, and his face began to twitch. "Oh, what we did there! Aye, 'twas a piece of work! Ye wait. Just wait. Bahl will stir yer blood, and that stirring feels wondrous good. Then ye'll care not what ye do. 'Tis so . . . so . . . well, ye'll see fer yerself soon enough."

"Mayhap."

"Oh, there's no mayhap 'bout it. But ye see . . . What's yer name?"

"Hendric."

"But ye see, Hendric, after a bit, that feeling—'tis a good feeling, mind ye—that feeling stays with ye, and ye ferget things. Some things, they be good ta ferget. No use pining, I say. But ye may ferget ta take care of yerself. So be like me and get a helm and armor from some dead bloke who don't need it. Do it while ye still have the sense ta do it."

"I thank ye for yer advice," replied Hendric, hoping the man would shut up.

"And beware of those with the look."

"The look?"

" 'Tis hard ta miss. A gleam in the eye, like the fighting wasn't ended. Stay clear of them that have it. They'll slay ye quick just fer nothing."

"Well, thanks again for that." Hendric faced the other way, but Slasher just tapped his shoulder again.

"A Falsten lad, huh? Yer count's a piece of work. What's his name?"

"Count Yaun."

"Well, he sure likes the lasses. That was some beauty he had last night."

"I wouldn't know."

"Well, I was near his tent. Does he always make them scream like that? 'Tweren't from pleasure. *That's* fer certain!"

"I've heard tales in camp," replied Hendric, his face darkening. "The count be more pig than man, and a cruel one at that."

Slasher grinned in his disturbing way. "By and by, all shall die."

Hendric regarded his unwanted companion and envied his carefree madness. He wondered if Slasher was right about Lord Bahl and hoped that he was. His life had become something he'd gladly forget.

The dim light was reminiscent of dusk on a foggy evening. In its pale illumination, Honus was hard to see. He stood alone and motionless on a barren, rocky hillside that overlooked a dry streambed. He was naked, and Yim realized it was not the man she saw, but his spirit. Though cold mist filled the air, the stony landscape was as dry as ancient bones. Yim cried out. "Honus!" He didn't reply, but turned to gaze at her. Even though he was distant, Yim could feel his longing as if it were hers. Then the mist thickened, and Honus's form grew ever fainter until it vanished altogether.

Yim woke with a start to find Honus asleep beside her. She touched his hand. It was warm. Thus reassured, she tried to go back to sleep. The hard ground and a vague sense of dread made it difficult. When the night sky turned the deep blue of predawn, Yim still lay open-eyed beneath the cloak she shared with Honus. She nestled against him, for the rhythm of his breathing was calming.

The world slowly came alive. Birds began to call, and when the sun's first rays turned the treetops golden, Honus stirred. "I'm sorry I overslept," he said. He rose to light the fire.

Yim rose also. "You needed rest," she replied. "Your wound kept you up most the night."

"Did I disturb you?"

"No, other things did."

"Thoughts of the man you slew?"

"More than that. I shouldn't be your Bearer. I don't know what I'm doing."

"To 'bear' means to carry burdens," said Honus. "Uncertainty is one of them. Theodus taught me that."

"But Theodus trained for years at the temple. What right have I to guide anyone?"

"Training doesn't make a Bearer," replied Honus. "Bearers are chosen by the Seers. You were chosen by Karm herself."

"Not to be a Bearer."

"A Bearer is simply a holy person."

"I feel adrift, not holy."

"On the night we returned from the temple, you said you wanted to assume Theodus's quest."

"I did," said Yim. "Only now I'm not so sure. I'm not sure of anything."

"Do you imagine Theodus always had a sense of purpose?" asked Honus. "Sometimes we wandered aimlessly for moons. I don't need to be guided. My role is to obey. If you choose to go fishing, I'll gather worms."

"Will you also bait my hook?"

"At your command, I'll skewer legions of worms. Only please don't ask me to cook your catch."

"One needs no visions to see the folly in that," said Yim.

"It's good to see you smile."

Yim's smile disappeared. "That doesn't solve my problem."

"When Theodus sought guidance," said Honus, "he studied my runes."

That idea had never occurred to Yim. She recalled that Honus had said his runes told portents that only his Bearer should read. *If I'm truly his Bearer, then they're meant for me.* In her current state of mind, Yim was hesitant to find out if that was true. "Perhaps I'll look at them," she said. "But not now."

Instead, Yim cooked some porridge. After breakfast she resumed their journey to Averen. Yet the runes remained on her mind. She had seen them only twice: on her first night with Honus and when he was under the dark man's spell. On both occasions, she had merely glimpsed the markings, and she wondered what a careful examination would reveal. By midmorning, Yim surrendered to her curiosity. She spoke to Honus, who was walking in front of her, which was the customary position for a Sarf. "Find a quiet place away from the road. I wish to study your runes."

For the past day and a half, the road they followed had hugged the banks of the Yorvern River. Away from the winding river, the land was hilly. Peasants tilled the low areas, but the high places were forested. Honus veered toward a thickly wooded slope and began to climb it. Yim followed. Soon all she could see were tree trunks rising into foliage that dimmed the sunlight and tinted it green. Honus halted by a massive, moss-covered oak that stood near the hill's summit. "Karmamatus, is this spot suitable?"

It seemed a fitting place to delve into secrets, and Yim said so. Honus removed his shirt and sat cross-legged on the ground. Yim knelt behind him with an air of gravity, for it felt like a momentous occasion. The long-hidden runes seemed mysterious, and Yim was aware that Honus believed the tattoos on his back transcribed his fate. *And Theodus's fate*, thought Yim. *Perhaps mine also.*

The skin of Honus's back was far paler than that of his neck and forearms, for he always kept it covered. The small blue letters had been needled there during his childhood, and they had stretched and smeared as he grew. About his broad shoulders they were as blurred as watercolors left in the rain. Three scars slashed the inscriptions, one making a long, jagged trail near his spine.

The runes were oddly formed, but similar to the letters Yim knew. The words they spelled were a different matter. The language was so archaic as to seem foreign. A few words were familiar, and Yim could pick out a phrase or two, but nothing made enough sense to provide guidance. She thought that "Ha sendt Daijen" might mean "He sends Daijen." *But what's a "Daijen"?* The question was unanswerable. Once again, Yim felt inadequate.

"Honus, the runes say . . ."

"Don't speak of them!" cried Honus. "I mustn't know what's written there."

Yim hushed and continued to stare at the marks. Recalling that Honus had said Theodus used to touch his runes, she did the same, although it felt like playacting. As Yim brushed her fingers over the cryptic words, she noted a few names. She found "Theodus" among the misty runes near Honus's shoulders. Strangely, it was written only once. As on her first night with Honus, she spied her own name toward the middle of his back. She also found it written several other places. In the last instance, it marked the base of his spine. It unsettled Yim to realize that her name had been tattooed there before she was born and the Seer who had done it had most likely been slain in the temple massacre.

Though the runes offered no guidance, they spoke to Yim nonetheless. They seemed proof that her life wasn't truly hers. She recalled Honus's words. *"How can I be free if Karm wrote my fate upon my back?"* Yim sensed that her life's course had been preordained likewise and then inscribed in words she couldn't decipher. All they seemed to foretell was that much lay in store for her. Yim brushed her fingers over Honus's tattoos a while longer to give the impression that she was studying them. Then she pronounced, "The runes are vague about our course."

SIX

DAIJEN FOUND the inn at dusk. It was a humble place in a poor section of the city. He entered it and found the dingy common room packed with customers. They were a loud bunch, for the ale was cheap. He scanned the dimly lit room and spotted the Sarf exactly where his informant had said he would be. The Sarf sat alone, nursing a mug of tea. Despite the crowd, everyone kept their distance from him.

Daijen caught the innkeeper's elbow as he bustled by with some empty mugs. "My good man," he said amiably, "I wish to order a feast."

The innkeeper regarded Daijen as if he were drunk. "A feast? You've come to the wrong place."

Daijen held his closed hand near the man's face and briefly lifted his fingers to reveal a gold coin in his palm. Having gained the innkeeper's attention, he said, "Send out for it if you must, just be quick about it. I want roast lamb with all the trimmings and a jug of good red wine, something from the slopes of South Vinden. Buy enough for two. Will this coin cover the cost?"

The innkeeper grinned. "It'll do."

"I want the meal taken to the Sarf."

"The Sarf?"

"Yes," replied Daijen. "I'll be dining with him."

"You know him?"

"Not yet."

"Then take my advice and remain a stranger. There are

women here who'd fancy a good meal and know how to show their appreciation."

Daijen assumed an indignant expression. "I've no interest in whores!"

The innkeeper shrugged. "Suit yourself. But I warn you, that Sarf's touchy. Most likely dangerous, too. A Sarf killed a squad of soldiers when he entered the city." The man gave Daijen a knowing look. "Some say it was him who did it."

Daijen shot the innkeeper an impatient look. "Do you want this coin or not?"

"Aye," said the man as he took it. "I'll send my boy up the street for what you want."

"Tell him to hurry."

Daijen moved to a dark corner of the room and waited for the food to arrive. When the boy returned, the innkeeper took the meat, wine, and other dishes to the Sarf. After he left, the Sarf suspiciously scanned the room. When his eyes met Daijen's, Daijen bowed deeply and then approached. When he stood before the Sarf, he bowed again. "Karmamatus, please allow me to honor Karm with this meal."

"Karm sees your generosity," said the Sarf, "and I'm grateful for the food. However, I don't touch wine."

"Still, it needn't go to waste," said Daijen. He took up the jug, and in a loud voice, addressed the crowded room. "I have good South Vinden wine here! Who will join me in a toast to the goddess? Come friends, lift a cup with me to Karm in hopes that the Balance will be restored."

Daijen's proposal was met by uneasy silence. A few men seemed inclined to drink until they glanced about the room. In the end, there were no comers. Daijen sighed and set the jug down on the table. The Sarf looked up at him and said in a low voice, "That wasn't a wise move. You should watch your back tonight."

"Is there no faith left in Bremven?" asked Daijen. "Have all its citizens turned cowardly?"

"I fear both are true," said the Sarf. "Come, stranger, your generosity exceeds my appetite. Would you care to join me?"

"I ordered enough for your Bearer, too," replied Daijen. "I wouldn't presume to eat his share."

"I have no Bearer," said the Sarf in a cold voice.

"Then I'd be honored to dine with a righteous man."

Daijen sat down and appraised the blue-clad stranger across the table. He was muscular and tall, with the dark coloring typical of the region. The Sarf looked young, perhaps not yet twenty, but he had an air of confidence that bordered on arrogance. The Seer who had tattooed his face must have foreseen that trait, for the lines he needled there gave the impression of inflexible sternness. Daijen briefly peered into the Sarf's dark eyes and was relieved to note they possessed only ordinary perception. Daijen smiled as he made his eyes friendly and reverent. "My name is Rangar, Karmamatus. As you can see, I'm a visitor to Bremven."

"I'm Gatt," said the Sarf.

Gatt was clearly glad for a hearty meal, and Daijen let him eat without interruption. Daijen only nibbled at his dinner as he concentrated on reading the man before him. Like Gatt, he didn't touch the wine, for he needed all his wits. The Sarf was undoubtedly aware that some possessed the power to see other's thoughts and sway them, so Daijen took care to hide his ability. He perceived that Gatt was an angry man who was quick to judge and judged harshly. Recruiting him would be a dangerous game where a misstep would result in a deadly foe. Thus Daijen bided his time, and when Gatt's eating slowed, he politely asked, "Was your Bearer slain at the temple?"

Gatt's voice took on a contemptuous tone. "He was no martyr."

"Some illness or an accident perhaps?"

"The coward who was my Bearer still lives," said Gatt, "though only because I couldn't swim to catch him. He turned his back on Karm and fled."

"Fled what?"

"We traveled among people who had turned from the goddess. He had no stomach for persecution."

"What could he fear with you by his side?"

Gatt stared at Daijen menacingly. "Are you questioning my ability?"

"No," replied Daijen quickly, "just marveling at the depths of your Bearer's cowardice. Yet should he die for it?"

"Why not?" asked Gatt. "He called himself holy. I would have laid down my life for him without a moment's hesitation. He betrayed Karm and me and all he stood for. If he would not follow a righteous path, how can we ask common folk to do so?"

"I see your point," said Daijen. "When so many have died for their faith, why should one live for abandoning it?"

The Sarf gazed at Daijen, seeming pleased by his vindication. "Bremven has become a nest of vipers," he said. "It's no place for me."

Daijen kept his eyes locked on Gatt's as he spoke. "You're a man of action," he said in a quiet voice.

Upon hearing those words, Gatt grew restless and agitated. "Yes!" he said. "By the goddess, I am!"

"Of course you are. It's your role in life, the one for which you've trained over many years."

"But I'm a Sarf. Without a Bearer, how can I serve Karm?"

"I've no doubt the goddess will send you some holy task. She's too wise to waste one such as you."

"I pray you're right."

Daijen rose and bowed. "This has been the first pleasant meal I've eaten in Bremven, Karmamatus. You've restored my hope for the future."

Gatt rose also. "Let me walk you to your inn. I suspect your piety has riled a cur or two, and they grow braver in the dark."

"You honor me," replied Daijen, and he bowed again.

The two men walked through the shadowy streets, pausing only when Daijen gave the untouched wine to a poor woman. When they reached the modest inn where Daijen was staying, Daijen bowed once more. "Karmamatus, it would be an honor if you dined with me tomorrow. I know of an inn that's famous for its spiced duck."

Gatt returned Daijen's bow, though he didn't bend as low. "It'd be good to sup with a virtuous man."

"Then shall we meet in the Golden Drake at, say, one bell before sundown? It's in the Averen quarter on the Street of Feathers."

"I'll see you there," said Gatt, who then strode away and vanished into the darkness.

Daijen visited the Golden Drake the following morning to arrange his dinner with Gatt. While taking care not to appear overly lavish, Daijen ordered ample portions, for he suspected the Sarf had not eaten much of late. Extending hospitality to Karm's servants was no longer fashionable in Bremven. It could even be dangerous. Daijen looked forward to the day when it would be a capital offense.

At the appointed time, Daijen was seated at a corner table in the inn's common room. He rose and bowed when Gatt entered. The other diners grew quiet as the Sarf strode across the room, but after he was seated, the talk resumed. While the two men exchanged courtesies, a waiter brought out a large whole duck. It had been slowly roasted until its spiced skin was brown and crunchy. Gatt breathed in its aroma and smiled, causing his host to smile also. While the Sarf sated his hunger, Daijen conversed sparingly about trivial matters. Only when the fowl was reduced to bones did he speak to his true purpose. "Karmamatus," he said, "would you make me your Bearer?"

Gatt's face immediately reddened beneath his tattoos. "Such talk is blasphemous!"

Daijen shrank back. "You mistake my meaning, Karmamatus."

"Then what is it?"

"I asked the question because today I heard of a Sarf who named his own Bearer."

"Impossible!"

"Do you know of a Sarf named Honus?"

"He's Theodus's Sarf," said Gatt. "We're not acquainted, but I've seen him at the temple. It was years ago. What about him?"

"I've just dealt with a cloth merchant—Dommus is his name—who sheltered Honus when he came to Bremven recently. Honus's Bearer had been slain, but he brought a slave with him, a woman named Yim."

"Sarfs don't own slaves," said Gatt.

"Honus did." Daijen gave his companion a knowing look. "Dommus said she was quite a beauty."

"Are you implying that Honus kept her for pleasure?"

"If he did, it wouldn't make so strange a tale," replied Daijen. "Comely women have their wiles, and men—even pious ones—are their natural prey. What's unnatural is that Honus made Yim his Bearer."

"No Sarf has that authority!"

"Honus acted like he did," replied Daijen. "The whole household witnessed it."

"How could he dare?"

"Dommus was convinced that Yim had bewitched him," said Daijen. "Some people have that power. They do it with their eyes."

"Only weaklings fall for such tricks," said Gatt. "Honus is renown for his strength."

"A man can be mighty in some ways and weak in others. Perhaps Yim didn't use enchantments. She might have merely seduced Honus to lead him astray."

"But why would he name her his Bearer?" asked Gatt.

"Because she made him do it. That's what Dommus said."

Gatt looked perplexed. "Why?"

"What better way for her to seal her conquest?" said Daijen, gazing into the Sarf's eyes. "Some women are leeches. They slither up a man's pants and suck his goodness away."

Gatt's face flushed beneath its tattoos. "So Honus now calls his slut holy?" He slammed his fist on the table. "That profanes Karm!"

"Yes," said Daijen. "Even as we speak, the bawd parades about the countryside . . ." His voice became mesmerizing. ". . . demanding charity and respect in the name of our goddess. Yet people aren't fools. Honus may cow them into calling Yim 'Karmamatus,' but they know a whore when they see one."

Gatt shook his head. "I used to admire Honus."

"Doubtlessly because he was an admirable man," said Daijen. "This Yim has poisoned him. She would have been kinder to cut his throat."

"He'd be better off dead."

"But would that be justice?" asked Daijen. "After all, he's bewitched."

"It's Yim's throat that needs cutting."

"*That* would be a worthy deed!" exclaimed Daijen, as if surprised by the notion. "It would surely honor Karm."

"Yet the whore's left Bremven," said Gatt. "She could be anywhere."

"Yim might not be so hard to find," said Daijen. "She told Dommus that they were going to Averen to visit Lord Bahl. There's only one road they could take."

"Bahl? This slut's more sinister than you think."

"What do you mean?" asked Daijen.

"Can't you see? She's delivering Honus to his enemies. How could he be so blind?"

"Then perhaps Dommus was right when he said Yim worked a spell."

"Such a spell would be no trick of the eyes," stated Gatt, "but some fouler sorcery. This sounds like the work of the enemy."

"Do you think Yim worships the Devourer?"

"It would explain a lot. Honus was a righteous man. His ruin would please the dark priests' god."

"I see your point," said Daijen. "That makes his disgrace all the more tragic."

"So many have fallen," mused Gatt. "But to fall with such dishonor . . ."

"Yet Honus might rise again, if he were free from Yim's sorcery." Daijen fixed his eyes on Gatt's and spoke in a quiet, compelling tone. "His salvation could be your holy task."

Gatt grew excited. "Yes! I'm sure of it!"

"It'll be no easy undertaking," said Daijen. "If Honus is under a spell, you'll only release him by destroying Yim. He'll try to protect her."

"I'm undaunted," said Gatt. "Karm feeds my strength. I cannot fail."

"You may have to kill Honus in order to slay Yim."

"His death would free his soul," said Gatt, "and it's his soul that matters."

"I'm in the presence of a brave and just man." Daijen bowed his head. "I'm honored to know you, Karmamatus. Though I lack the courage and prowess for such a crusade, I possess two things that will aid your quest—a horse, so you may overtake Yim, and this." He took a small glass vial from his shirt.

Gatt picked up the vial. "What's this?"

"Paint this potion on your blade to assure success."

"Only a coward poisons his sword."

"This is no coward's quick-acting venom. It won't save your life in combat. Yet with this, you need only wound the witch to assure her destruction." Daijen gazed at Gatt and used his full powers to bend him to his will. "You're fighting against sorcery, so you'll need a potent weapon. Don't let a warrior's pride interfere with your duty to the goddess. A holy end sanctions all means."

Gatt wavered but a moment before he took the vial. "You're right, my friend. I must be humble and perform Karm's will."

SEVEN

YIM HAD set a hasty pace upon departing Bremven, and she and Honus had been on the road only four days when they reached the Bridge Inn. Built on the Vinden side of the span to Luvein, the inn sat at a once busy crossroads. Even after Luvein's devastation, it remained a major stop on the road to Averen, the last accommodation before entering rugged territory. Recalling her previous reception at the inn, Yim had chosen not to seek hospitality there. Instead, she and Honus camped in the woods, as they had every night since fleeing Bremven.

Over the past three days of travel, the villages along the route had given way to scattered peasant holdings. The farther westward Yim and Honus journeyed, the wilder the surrounding countryside became. Traffic dwindled, and the imperial highway began to show signs of neglect. Its paving stones were often crumbled or heaved by frosts to trip the unwary traveler. It seemed proof of the emperor's waning authority.

Yim's pace was spurred by the sense of menace that had driven her from the city and dogged her on the road. It made her wary, and she avoided people whenever possible. She didn't explain her fears to Honus, for she couldn't explain them to herself. All she knew was that whatever troubled her thoughts seemed as threatening as the hostility she met upon the road. Yim worried that the malevolence she encountered in the ruined temple was still seeking to destroy her. She felt it was watching her, filled with deadly rage. She suspected that Honus was aware of her apprehension, although he didn't presume to speak of it.

As Yim trudged along, bent beneath the heavy pack, she gazed at Honus striding in front of her and felt somewhat reassured. His movements reminded her of a cat's—easy, yet alert. Honus seem prepared to pounce at any instant. She had witnessed his dazzling quickness when they were last attacked. One assailant lay cleaved in two even before Yim darted from the road.

A moon ago he was my master, mused Yim. *Now I'm his.* Yet as Honus's slave, Yim had never served him willingly, whereas ever since the night in the ruined temple, Honus served her utterly. His devotion went beyond the reverence and duty that a Sarf owed his Bearer; Honus was bound to Yim by something that baffled her. It was love. Yim found Honus's feelings perplexing and inexplicable. She couldn't understand why they had arisen. Having never experienced desire, Yim found its passion a mystery.

Yim suspected that the Wise Woman had reared her to be incapable of the emotion. As the Chosen, Yim was to bear the child of whatever man the goddess decreed. Since love might impede that duty, it was a weakness to be avoided. Yim wondered if Honus's love might prove a weakness. It worried her, for she feared that the time was approaching when she would need all his strength.

After Yim had attempted to read Honus's runes, she resumed her journey. Throughout the remainder of the day the landscape continued to change. The hills rose higher and pressed ever closer to the riverbank until there were no places to farm. By late afternoon, the only dwellings they spied hugged the Yorvern's banks. Honus said they were the homes of river folk who made their living by fishing and plying the waterway with cargoes. The houses were so close to the road that Yim couldn't avoid their occupants. To her relief, everyone she encountered was respectful.

After passing a hut where the family paused in its activity to bow, Yim said, "I think the black priests haven't come this way."

"Or perhaps none here have believed their lies," replied Honus. "The river is a chancy road and it teaches folk to heed their instincts."

When sunset neared, Yim decided to seek hospitality for the first time since departing Bremven. Spying a wooden hut perched on the riverbank, she approached it. Like all river dwellings, it sat atop stone pilings to keep it dry during spring floods. A series of large rocks led from the road to the elevated doorway. They rested on dry ground, but Yim saw how they would serve as stepping-stones in wetter times.

Outside the hut, a middle-aged woman was gathering small fish that had been strung on lines above a smoky fire. When she saw Yim leave the road, she stopped what she was doing and bowed. Yim returned her bow and spoke. "Greetings, Mother. We request food and shelter in respect for the goddess."

The woman bowed again. "Ye would honor our house, Karmamatus."

"Please call me Yim, Mother. My Sarf is Honus."

Honus bowed politely.

"Then ye should call me Maryen," said the woman, her sun-creased face emphasizing her smile. "We get few visitors. 'Twill be a treat to hear news."

"Little I could say would be called a treat," replied Yim. "Troubles are abroad. You should be glad they're distant."

"Do you have the means to repair leather?" asked Honus. "My mistress's sandals want a strap."

Maryen looked down at Yim's dusty bare feet. "Gracious! Ye must be footsore. Come in and rest yerself."

"First let me help you finish your task," replied Yim, stepping up to the fire. The fish, which were no longer than Yim's forefinger, had been gutted and strung on cords that threaded through a gill and out the mouth. She imitated Maryen, who slid the smoked fish down their cords until they dropped into a basket. When all the fish were gathered in the basket, the two women went to the river to wash the blackened fish oil from their hands before entering the hut. Honus followed them inside.

The hut's interior consisted of a single room with a ladder leading to a loft above. Its wooden walls were darkened by age and smoke from the hearth. They were mostly covered by clothes, dried herbs, and boating gear that hung from pegs, giving the walls a cluttered look that extended to the rest of the room. It was filled with all sorts of items. There were baskets containing roots, smoked fish, grain, and other edibles lining one wall. A sizable stack of firewood was piled against another. Beside it was a cupboard crammed with crocks, kettles, and wooden plates and bowls. A jumbled pile of bedding and laundry lay close to the ladder. Oars leaned against the walls, and other boating gear was scattered about the floor where it mingled with a collection of stools of varying sizes. A large oaken table covered with a fishing net dominated the room's center.

A young, sandy-haired boy sat at the table mending the net. He looked up when Yim entered, bowed his head, and made an inarticulate noise.

"That's my youngest, Foel," said Maryen. "He hears fine, but he has na spoken since he was six winters. Foel, dear, this lady's sandal wants mending. Go get yer tools."

When the boy scampered up the ladder leading to the loft, Yim turned to his mother. "Did he suffer some mishap?"

"Aye," said Maryen, confirming Yim's intuition. "A wreck upon the river with his father and sister. Only Foel was saved, and he's never been the same. Yet he's a good lad and my comfort when his brothers are away."

When Foel returned, Yim took her sandal from the pack and handed it to him. He set to work while Maryen brewed herb tea. Before she could serve it, her son had repaired the sandal and handed it to Yim. Yim smiled and bowed. She ran her finger along the mended strap. Foel had tapered the splice so that it would feel smooth against her foot.

"This is skillful work, Foel," said Yim. "Each step I take will be easier because of you."

Foel smiled shyly and made a pleasant noise in his throat.

Maryen handed wooden bowls of the herbal brew to Yim and Honus. When Honus received his, he took care to smile, for he had noticed that Foel regarded him fearfully. Yim noticed also. "Those marks on my Sarf's face make him look fierce," she said to the boy. "But if you're clever, you'll look beneath them and see a gentle man."

Foel peered at Honus and relaxed. Then he glanced at Yim. When their eyes met, Yim said, "No, they don't wash off," as if replying to a spoken question.

Dinner was a stew of smoked fish and roots accompanied by more tea. Yim ate with relish and complimented Maryen on her cooking. Afterward, she gave a brief description of the temple's destruction.

Maryen shook her head. "I heard that news, but did na believe it. Too many wild tales fly about seeking fools' ears."

"I wish it were only a tale," said Yim, "but I saw it with my own eyes."

"What will ye do now?" asked Maryen.

"I'm still seeking Karm's guidance," replied Yim. "At the present, we're headed for Averen. There we'll visit General Cronin. He's a good man, and his sister's a friend of mine."

"I'm glad ye have a place among friends," said Maryen.

"As we have tonight," said Yim with a smile. She turned her gaze to Foel, who had been listening to her account. In a gentle voice she said, "The river must look lovely by moonlight. Will you show it to me?"

Maryen started to speak, but she was cut short by a grunt from Foel, who nodded yes to Yim.

"Will you hold my hand?" asked Yim. "I don't know the way."

Foel rose and led Yim from the hut. Maryen turned to Honus in amazement. "He's afraid of the river! He will na go near it!"

Yim held Foel's hand even after they sat down on the riverbank. The moonlight sparkled on the Yorvern like cold fire. "It's pretty," Yim said. Then she shifted her gaze from the river to Foel. The boy briefly fidgeted under her scrutiny, for he was unable to look away. Then he calmed.

"Your house lies between two roads," Yim said in a soothing voice. "One is dry and the other is wet, yet both are the same—on neither road can you know what lies ahead. Karm speaks to me, yet I can't foresee the future. So how could a little boy?" Yim paused, and when she spoke again, it was with the gravity of perfect certainty. "It wasn't your fault."

Foel's eyes welled with tears and his mouth began to quiver. "But . . . But I saw it," he said in a rusty whisper. "I saw the snag and could na speak."

Yim embraced Foel as he began to weep. "Your father saw it, too, and couldn't avoid it. Don't blame yourself."

Yim held Foel until his tears were dry. Then she returned with him to the hut. Honus and Maryen were still sitting at the table. Maryen grew concerned when she saw that her son had been weeping, but Foel ran to embrace her. Then in a voice faint from disuse, he cried out, "Momma!"

EIGHT

On the morning that Yim and Honus bid farewell to Maryen and Foel, Gatt departed from Bremven astride Daijen's huge black horse. Despite his bravery, he felt uneasy. Gatt was unfamiliar with horses, and he sensed that he wasn't entirely in control. The steed was powerful and sometimes ignored Gatt's handling of its reins. Bounced about by his mount's jarring gallop, the Sarf was soon saddle sore. Despite his discomfort, Gatt never considered riding at a slower pace. He accepted his unease and pain as the price of swiftness. If he had any hope of catching Yim, speed was essential.

Gatt was far from Bremven when dusk forced him to look for shelter. He passed several modest cottages before stopping at a prosperous-looking farm. Dismounting his lathered horse, he led it up the path to the residence. A man who appeared to be the farm's owner stepped out from a doorway to watch his approach. After traveling on his own for over three moons, Gatt had developed a knack for discerning which households still adhered to the goddess. Nevertheless, he adopted a demeanor that combined both humility and intimidation when he asked for charity. Placing his hand on his sword hilt, he bowed toward the man. "I serve Karm, Father. Do you honor her?"

The man returned Gatt's bow. "How may I help you, Karmamatus?"

"I require food and shelter for myself and my horse."

"I'd be honored to provide both."

"Karm sees your generosity."

"Tarvus," the man shouted, "come and take the Sarf's horse to the stables."

A boy about twelve winters old emerged from the house and regarded Gatt with undisguised excitement. He bowed very low. "Karmamatus, this is an honor," he said before taking the horse's reins. Gatt smiled slightly and inclined his head.

"Rub him down good," said the man to Tarvus, "he's been ridden hard."

"Yes, Father," said Tarvus. "I'll move Tammor from his stall and stable Karmamatus's horse there."

"That's fine, son," said the man. He watched Tarvus lead the horse away before turning to Gatt. "Sarfs are my boy's heroes," he said, "so this is quite a thrill for him. I hope you'll explain your lot's not all adventure and fighting."

"The path of righteousness demands sacrifice and suffering," said Gatt. "Few are fit for such a life."

"That's what I tell him," said the farmer. "I say he should be thankful that the Seers bypassed our farm."

"You're correct to say so," said Gatt. "A childhood in the temple is no easy one."

"Boys! Full of dreams," said the man, shaking his head. "My name is Garvus, Karmamatus. Would you join me in some ale while we wait for dinner?"

"I don't drink ale," replied Gatt, "but I'd be glad for some tea."

Garvus led Gatt inside, where he introduced his wife, who brewed the Sarf some tea. Gatt drank it standing, for he ached from the day's riding. When Garvus finished his ale, he felt less intimidated by Gatt and ventured to question him. "Your horse is a fine animal, yet you pushed him hard."

"I had need to do so. My task is urgent."

"Urgent enough to risk a valuable steed? If you don't ease up, he could go lame."

"Is a horse worth more than a man?" replied Gatt.

"I don't understand."

"I am trying to save one being led to his doom. I must catch up with him before he's destroyed."

"With all respect, Karmamatus, you won't do that on a lame horse. Is the man a captive?"

"No," replied Gatt. "Just beguiled by a woman."

Garvus grinned, and was about to jest before he caught the Sarf's hard gaze and thought better of it. "Are they traveling afoot?"

"Yes. And the woman's burdened also. They left eight days ago for Averen."

"Do they know of your pursuit?"

"No."

"Then you can ease up on your horse and still catch them easily," said Garvus. "A steady pace and a long day's ride will eat up the distance."

"I pray you're right. It's my holy task to free this man."

"Then how can you fail?" said Garvus. "Karm will aid you."

Garvus refilled Gatt's tea bowl and poured some more ale for himself. After Tarvus returned from the stables accompanied by three farm servants, Garvus's wife brought out the evening meal. All sat down for dinner with the Sarf at the place of honor. While they ate, Gatt spoke of his travels. Mindful of Garvus's request, he emphasized the hardness of his life. The stories didn't affect Tarvus as his father had hoped, for the boy's admiration of the Sarf seemed to grow with each new tale of tribulation. Gatt found himself enjoying the boy's adulation. After dinner, when the Sarf excused himself to look at his horse, he was not displeased when Tarvus followed him.

Although Gatt knew little about grooming horses, he sensed the animal had been well tended. He turned toward Tarvus and smiled. "Karm sees the care you have shown my steed," he said. "When I ride forth tomorrow, take pride that you've aided my quest."

Tarvus beamed at Gatt's words. "Zounds! A quest?"

"Yes," said Gatt, standing tall despite his aches. "It's a perilous undertaking."

"Will you tell me about it?"

"I fear your father wouldn't approve," said Gatt. "He said you think a Sarf's life is all adventure and glory."

"Please," begged Tarvus. "This farm's so dull. Great deeds may not be my fate, but can't I hear of them?"

Gatt smiled indulgently. "I'll speak about it if you keep this from your father."

"I will," said Tarvus. "I swear."

"I'm off to slay a sorceress who has captured a virtuous man. He's a Sarf, like myself."

"She captured a Sarf? How could she do that?"

"With foul enchantments and other wiles you're too young to know about," replied Gatt.

"Aren't you afraid she'll do the same to you?"

"I'll kill her before she has the chance, though I may have to fight the Sarf to do so."

Tarvus's eyes widened. "Fight another Sarf!"

"He's under her spell. Until the evil one is slain, she'll control him."

"Oh Holy Karm!" said Tarvus. "If I had to face a Sarf, I'd shake like grain in a hailstorm."

"Grab a straw and toss it in the air," directed Gatt.

Tarvus stooped to pick up one. Then he threw it. Gatt moved so quickly that the boy couldn't follow his movements. All he saw was the flash of a sword slicing through air and the straw fluttering down, split lengthwise. "Zounds!" said Tarvus as he rushed over to pick up the two pieces.

Gatt sheathed his sword. "I serve Karm's will, so I shall prevail."

"And kill the other Sarf?"

"Kill him? I intend to save him."

"But won't he try to kill you?"

"Most certainly," replied Gatt, "but I'll endeavor to spare

his life. At the very least, I'll save his soul, for when a man dies, his spirit's released from sorcery."

Tarvus gazed at the Sarf, speechless with admiration. Gatt caught the boy's look and felt whole for the first time since his Bearer had deserted him. Joy surged within Gatt, eclipsing his pain and restoring his sense of worth. Once again, he was traveling a holy path.

That night, when Gatt was drifting toward sleep, he saw a misty landscape as viewed from above. From the breadth and vividness of the scene, he knew he wasn't dreaming. Instead, he was being shown the world from a divine perspective. Gatt first saw Bremven and then the road he had taken from the city. Swooping above the highway, he passed over the house where he was resting and continued onward. He viewed an ancient stone bridge that spanned the Yorvern and the sprawling inn built on its nearest shore. Then he followed the road as it hugged the riverbank. He continued onward until he spied two vague figures camping by the river and felt a wave of hatred that arose from an otherworldly source. It was bitter and implacable. Although Gatt had always believed that Karm was stern, the virulence of the enmity startled him. Without seeing the figures distinctly or hearing a single word, he understood that one was Yim. He concluded the other must be Honus.

Then Gatt rose higher until he had a commanding view of the surrounding countryside. He peered over mountains, valleys, rivers, and forests. Upon viewing them, Gatt knew the terrain as intimately as if he had spent his entire life tramping over it. Afterward, the scene dissolved into mist, and Gatt sat up shivering from cold. He was convinced that he had experienced his first vision, for he had foreseen the route that lay ahead and learned where his quarry was resting. The Sarf had the impulse to saddle his horse and ride off into the night to catch Yim. He suppressed the urge, knowing that she was beyond the reach of a single night's journey. Moreover, with the certainty of foresight, Gatt knew that he would find Yim, just as he knew what he must do when he did. Gatt had been hesitant to paint his blade with poison, but the vision assured him that he had done the proper thing. *Rangar was right*, he thought. *The whore's death must be certain. On no account should one whom Karm so thoroughly despises be suffered to live.*

Yim and Honus sat at their campsite and gazed at the moonlit river. Clouds of pale insects flew over the water like animate mist. Occasionally, a fish leapt up to catch one. Honus poked the campfire and its flame grew brighter. "Do you really think that I'm gentle," he asked, "or did you merely say that to humor the boy?"

"You're a killer," replied Yim. "If the Balance is to be maintained, you must be gentle also."

Honus smiled and shook his head. "Spoken like a Bearer."

"Are you teasing me?"

"No," said Honus, "I'm not." He poked the fire again. "I'm still amazed at what you did for that boy."

"You shouldn't be," replied Yim. "I merely looked into his eyes and saw what disturbed him. You have the same ability. You could have done likewise."

"Yet there lies the difference between us," said Honus. "It never occurred to me."

They lapsed into an easy silence and watched the river awhile. There was a small island midstream, and it drew Yim's attention. "That little isle reminds me of Cara's secret place," she said.

"What secret place?"

"Cara found a way to sneak out of the Bridge Inn," replied Yim. "She would swim out to an island in the river. She took me there on our second day. It was a peaceful spot."

Honus smiled. "That sounds like something Cara would do. I take it Cronin had no idea."

"None at all. She spied on you and him while you talked on the bridge."

The smile left Honus's face. "I remember that day. We spoke of grim things."

"Cara knew," said Yim. "She thinks Lord Bahl will overrun Averen."

"Cronin's certain that he'll try," replied Honus.

Yim felt a sudden chill as if it were daytime and a cloud had obscured the sun. She glanced upward, but saw only a starry sky. Still, the impression remained, and she sensed a malign presence. Yim shivered, convinced that she was both fleeing danger and running toward it. She wanted to confess to Honus that she was afraid and didn't know where to turn, but she held her tongue. *As a Sarf, he knows exactly where to turn*, Yim thought, feeling the full weight of her circumstances. *It's wherever I tell him.*

NINE

WHEN GATT departed on his quest at dawn, he was invigorated by the conviction that Karm had blessed him with a vision. It seemed the most certain sign yet that he was traveling the true path. His horse also seemed imbued with divine purpose, for it sped down the highway as if it knew the importance of its master's mission. Gatt passed the Bridge Inn before noon. The sight of it spurred him onward.

Yim moved down the road far more slowly. She was tired after a poor night's sleep. Furthermore, half-remembered dreams troubled her. One was particularly disturbing. It featured Honus lying in an empty clearing. His face was gray beneath its tattoos and his eyes stared skyward without blinking.

"Yim, do you wish to rest?"

"No. I must keep moving," replied Yim. Then she sighed. "Yes. I need to rest."

Honus halted and Yim slipped the pack from her shoulders. The two walked to the riverbank and sat upon a boulder at the water's edge. The sky was clear, and the river sparkled with its light. Closer to the mountains, the Yorvern moved more swiftly. It surged against the small rocky islands that dotted its course, leaving trails of foam behind each obstacle. Yim slipped off her sandals to dangle her feet in the cold water. "This feels good," she said. "You were walking in front of me. How did you know I was weary?"

"By the sound of your footsteps."

Yim regarded Honus and smiled. "What other secrets have you discerned?"

"Very few. You remain a mystery."

"I doubt that."

"I know you were born in the Cloud Mountains and that your father was a peddler. The rest is shadow until I bought you in Durkin."

"My father wasn't a peddler. He herded goats and gave me up when I was very young. My childhood was much like yours. I was raised to serve the goddess. As I told you, I'm the Chosen."

"But I don't know what that means," replied Honus.

"On that night in the temple when I lowered my guard and you peered into my eyes, I thought you understood."

"I couldn't grasp what I saw," said Honus. "I experienced only holiness."

"I'm not holy," replied Yim. "I'm merely dutiful. I'm like a Sarf—a tool in Karm's hands."

Honus said nothing, but he looked unconvinced.

"Do you truly wish to hear my life's story?" asked Yim.

"Well, I'll tell you. My childhood was dreary. A Wise Woman trained me in arts she claimed would be useful. She was a cold woman. Stern, but not cruel. I lived with her until a Seer in the guise of a peddler escorted me south. That was four moons ago. We were ambushed on the road. He was slain and I was enslaved. The rest you know."

"And as the Chosen, Karmamatus, what must you do?"

Yim was so struck by the humility in Honus's voice that she felt the urge to tell him everything. But she suppressed that impulse and said, "Whatever Karm ordains."

Gatt's physical prowess made his second day of riding easier. He adjusted to the rhythm of his steed's motion until man and animal moved as one. Gatt was no longer saddle sore, and those who observed the Sarf on the galloping horse thought him a seasoned rider. The road he traveled conformed to the one he had seen in his vision. He was on the portion that threaded between rocky hills and the Yorvern River when a young boy stepped from a roadside hut. As the Sarf galloped toward him, the lad waved and shouted, "Honus!"

Gatt immediately reined his mount, and the horse halted just a few paces from the boy. Once the rider was motionless, the lad could see the Sarf's tattooed face more clearly. "You're not Honus."

"No," replied Gatt. "I'm a friend of his. Have you seen him?"

The boy smiled. "He stayed with us two nights ago."

Gatt made himself smile also. "I'm pleased to hear that. Then I should find him soon."

The boy nodded.

"And was Yim with him?"

"Oh yes! She . . ."

Gatt spurred his horse and galloped off.

Foel stared at the retreating figure and then completed what he had started to say. "She gave me my voice back."

* * *

As Yim trudged onward, she keenly felt the weight of the pack, which contained Honus's heavy chain-mail shirt in addition to provisions, camping gear, and extra clothes for both of them. It was a warm day, and Yim's shirt was soaked with sweat where her burden pressed against her back and shoulders. Yim, trying not to think about the long trek ahead, felt in need of diversion. "Honus," she said. "We haven't seen another traveler all morning. Forget custom, and walk beside me."

Honus complied, but he looked uncomfortable about it.

"Now," said Yim, "let's talk about cheerful things."

"The weather's fair," said Honus.

Yim regard him with half a smile. "It seems that Sarfs aren't instructed in the art of conversation."

"Do you deem me unskilled?"

"Unpracticed."

"It shall be pleasant to see Cara again," said Honus.

Yim grinned. "*That's* more like it. Yes it will be. Is Cronin's manor grand?"

"I wouldn't use that word for it," replied Honus. "I think 'homey' suits better. And it's Cara's manor, not her brother's."

"*Her* manor? When we met her at the inn, she seemed under Cronin's thumb."

"He's protective, for the times require it. Moreover, he's a general and must act like one. But within his clan, both lands and leadership pass from mother to daughter. In Av-eren, Cara's a chieftain and Cronin's merely a high-ranking soldier."

Yim smiled. "Averen folk sound sensible."

"Other clans have other customs. With them, it's the men who rule."

"Then why is Cara's clan different?"

"Because it was founded by Dar Beard Chin, a woman who bought land with a tree of gold."

Yim laughed. "She had a *beard*? Are you sure Dar was a woman?"

"I believe the beard was a tattoo."

"This sounds like a fine tale."

"Cara tells it best." Honus smiled. "Her version is certainly the longest."

"She's as generous with her words as you are frugal. So where did Dar get her tattoo? Was she a Sarf?"

"No. As to the rest, you'll have to ask Cara. All I remember is Dar founded Clan Urkzimdi, Cara's clan."

"Cara never hinted that she led a clan."

"There's more to Cara than she lets on," said Honus. He fixed his gaze on Yim. "That could be said of others."

Honus's look flustered Yim, and she wished that she possessed Cara's insight on matters of the heart. *She certainly understood Honus better than I did*, she thought, recalling how Cara had first told her of Honus's love. Yim had dismissed the idea. *But Cara was right*. She hoped that Cara could tell her what to do about it.

By late afternoon, Gatt found the remains of Yim and Honus's campfire. It was exactly where he expected it to be, providing final proof that he had received a vision. Examining the ashes, he saw that his quarry had been there that morning. Gatt studied Yim's footprints and concluded she walked laden with a pack. *That means she's still masquerading as a Bearer*. Gatt smiled. *That pack will slow her down and also tire her*. He had no doubt his horse could catch up with the impostor before day's end.

Again, Gatt saw Karm's hand in events, for he would reach his quarry at the perfect moment. Wearied from a day of traveling, Yim would be an easy target. Gatt knew that exhaustion dulled wariness. *If I'm subtle, she won't anticipate my attack. And when she's dead, there'll be no need to fight Honus*. Gatt envisioned the Sarf freed from his sorcerous bounds and returned to righteousness. He exulted at the prospect.

High hills hid the setting sun, so the road was shadowed while daylight lingered in the sky. Yim trod wearily down the road, refusing to halt before dusk. Exhausted, she was largely oblivious of her surroundings. Then Honus's pace altered and alerted her that something had changed. Sensing tension in his movements, she asked, "What is it, Honus?"

"Don't you hear it?"

Yim listened and detected the faint sound of hoofbeats mingling with the noise of the turbulent river. "Someone's coming," she said.

"Someone in a hurry."

Honus and Yim stepped to the roadside to observe whoever raced down the highway. The road twisted with the river, and for a long while the only hint of the approaching rider was the staccato hoofbeats of his mount. When a blue-clad and blue-faced horseman finally rounded the bend in the road he was quite close. "A Sarf!" said Yim. He was the second Sarf that she had ever seen, and despite knowing that he served Karm, she felt the same apprehension as when she first saw Honus.

The Sarf reined his horse to a stop and dismounted before bowing to Yim. "Greetings, Karmamatus."

Yim returned his bow. "Greetings. I'm Yim."

"Honus, do you remember me?" asked the Sarf.

"You were to be Daven's Sarf when I was last at temple. How fares he?"

"Fallen. I'm Gatt."

"What sends you to us, Gatt?" asked Yim.

Gatt ambled toward Yim with an easy manner, smiling more broadly than seemed natural for a Sarf. "Karm sent me."

Yim was about to reply when both Gatt and Honus burst

into action. Their bodies seemed to blur, and the air about them flashed as blades sped through it. There was a metallic clang, and for an instant, Yim saw two crossed swords. The edge of Gatt's blade was aimed toward her neck. Honus's sword blocked its path. Then the blades blurred again as the two men began fighting. Yim stood transfixed by shock until Honus shouted, "Flee, Yim!" Then he turned all his attention to his foe.

Yim retreated a distance, but she didn't run away. She was terrified and confused by what was happening; yet the battle in progress was an engrossing sight. She had seen Honus fight before, but never against such an opponent. Both attacked and parried with dazzling swiftness and mingled their blows with feats of acrobatic skill. The fight had the grace of a vicious dance and the energy of a cyclone. There were no taunts or curses, no words of any kind; both men fought in silent concentration, fully engaged in a deadly game of lightning moves. They were so intent on their contest that neither man's face bore any expression other than the one tattooed upon it: Honus seemed wrathful. Gatt appeared stern and harsh. Yim dared not speak for fear of distracting Honus and causing his death.

The combat dragged on, and after a while, Yim perceived a pattern. Both opponents were evenly matched, but they seemed to have different objectives. Yim saw that Gatt was fighting to reach her while Honus was struggling to bar his way. As soon as she saw that, Yim shed the pack and darted off, for she realized that her presence endangered Honus. As she sped down the road, the clash of swords continued briefly, then stopped. Yim spun around to see what had happened. Gatt was bounding after her, his blade raised to strike. Honus was in pursuit.

Yim knew she couldn't outrun the Sarf. She dashed for the river, and without further thought, jumped in. As she passed through emptiness, she felt a gentle tug on her flowing hair. Then she hit the water. Yim gritted her teeth, fearing she might strike a hidden rock. Instead, cold shocked the breath from her as she plunged beneath the river's turbulent surface. The current gripped her like a huge, icy hand intent on holding her from breath and life. Yim struggled against it, impeded by her sandals and waterlogged garments. She broke through the frothing surface and gasped for air. The Sarf was standing on the bank, his sword still extended. A clump of Yim's severed hair floated down to vanish in the surging current. Then Honus arrived, and the two Sarfs resumed their fight. As the river swept her away, Yim watched their contest. Then a watery curtain obscured the scene as she sank into the depths.

The Yorvern had saved Yim from the Sarf, but it threatened to drown her. She had learned to swim in a highland lake; a raging river was far different. Its current fought her every movement, rushing her downstream and clawing at her clothing. She was at its mercy until she kicked off her sandals and shed her garments. The latter was difficult, but once she was free of them she could move unencumbered and the current had less to grip. Yim swam toward a tiny island, but the river swept her past it. She aimed for another and missed it also.

A boulder loomed downstream. Yim fought toward it. This time, she reached her target only to be slammed against it. It was a bruising collision, and then Yim had to claw at the rock to prevent being pulled from it. Her refuge was wet and slippery; moreover, she was numbed by cold. Climbing onto the rock was a struggle that she almost lost. Twice, she slipped back into the foaming water before reaching safety.

Naked, scraped, and shivering, Yim huddled upon the rock while her fate was being decided. The river had carried her far enough downstream that Honus and Gatt were hidden from view. From the sound of ringing steel Yim knew that their fight continued. The swords made lethal music with an irregular cadence, and as long as Yim could hear it she knew the opponents lived. Thus she both longed for its end and dreaded it, for silence would most likely signal death. *If Honus dies, I will, too.*

The sky darkened, and still the swords rang. The trees on the shore blurred into inky shadows that blended with the hills behind them. Suddenly, the only sounds Yim heard were watery ones. The quiet was ominous, and she strained to hear any hint of the battle's outcome. For a long while, Yim heard nothing. Then hoofbeats broke the stillness. As they faded away, Yim slumped her head and wept.

TEN

A VOICE called from the dark. "Yim!"

Its faintness conjured up images of Honus lying mortally wounded. "Honus?" Yim shouted. "Honus, are you all right?"

After a period of agonizing silence, Yim heard the voice again. This time it was louder. "Yim, where are you?"

"Over here!" she shouted. "On a rock in the river!"

Another spell of silence was broken at last by Honus's voice. It sounded closer. "Yim, where are you?"

"Here! Are you all right?"

"I'm unscathed," called Honus from the shore. "Gatt has fled."

Yim peered at the bank, but the moon had yet to rise, and the shore was only a formless patch of shadow. She wondered if Honus could see her nakedness. Honus called out again. "Can you swim to shore?"

"Bring my cloak first!"

"I will."

While Yim waited on the rock, she steeled herself for another swim. The dark river seemed a gray void with mist flowing over it. Already chilled, Yim dreaded plunging in. Then she heard Honus. "I have it, Yim."

Yim jumped and the river seized her. This time, she swam obliquely toward the shore, rather than opposing the current. The frigid water swept her around one bend and then toward a second one with a gravel beach. Yim swam toward the beach. Nearing it, she could make out Honus's dark form against the gray. The cold turned her limbs leaden as she struggled to reach the shore.

Yim made it. By the time she staggered onto the gravel, she was too cold and exhausted to care that she was nude. Honus rushed forward and covered her with the cloak. Then he wrapped his arms around her trembling torso, pressing his hot cheek again her frigid one. He said nothing, but the erventness of his embrace betrayed his feelings.

As always, Yim felt uncomfortable when Honus showed affection. Yet this time she didn't stop him. *He saved my life*, she thought. *At least, I owe him this*. Eventually, Honus sensed Yim's awkwardness and released her. "Why did that man attack us?" asked Yim.

"I can only guess," replied Honus.

"Didn't he say anything?"

"No more than what you heard."

"But how did you know he'd attack?"

"His manner was wrong," replied Honus. "His bow to you wasn't low, and he spoke to me without your permission. A Sarf would never show such disrespect to a Bearer."

"So he wasn't a Sarf?"

"Oh, Gatt's a Sarf. No question of that. But I doubt he believes you're a Bearer."

"Maybe I'm not," said Yim. "Not really."

"You are by all that's holy."

"How could he know that?"

"Whether he could or not, he had no cause to slay you."

"But that's what he meant to do," said Yim. Then, in a quiet voice, she added, "This isn't over, is it?"

"No," said Honus. "But before you come to harm, he'll have to slay me first."

Yim returned to the pack and put on dry clothes. When the moon rose, she shouldered her burden. There was no question of resting anytime soon. Honus advised getting far from the road by a route that couldn't be followed on horseback. That meant climbing the hills at night. Having lost her sandals, Yim would have to do it barefoot. She felt discouraged by the prospect.

At first, Honus followed the road. When he reached a particularly steep and rocky slope, he left the highway and began to climb, saying, "Follow close behind and place your feet where I do."

Yim did her best, fearing that Gatt was as adept at tracking as Honus. If that were true, then his skills would be formidable. She remembered Honus saying that it was difficult to hide a trail at night, so she was particularly mindful of where she placed her feet. Nevertheless, as time wore on, Yim's exhaustion and the dark worked against her. Whenever possible, Honus walked on stony ground that would leave no footprints. This practice left Yim footsore, despite having trekked through Luvein unshod.

Yim was panting by the time the ground became less steep. Though trees hid the path ahead, Yim assumed they had reached a ridgeline and the way would be easier. "Thank Karm for a level path at last!" she said.

"Your gratitude is premature," said Honus. "An easy path is a likely path. We dare not take it."

"Honus, I don't think I can go much farther."

"Perhaps I should carry the pack awhile."

As soon as Honus made the suggestion, Yim saw why it went against tradition. Honus was her sole protection. Encumbered by a pack or even wearied after bearing one, he would be less effective. "No," said Yim. "But we must rest soon. Pick our way with that in mind." She didn't say that she doubted that they would evade the Sarf for long. *Whatever way we take*, thought Yim, *must end with someone's death*.

Leading the way, Honus headed down the western side of the ridge. He didn't go far, but the route he took was much more difficult than the one he used to reach the ridge's crest. The final leg involved descending a stretch of nearly vertical rock wall. There, Yim relented and let Honus bear the pack. Even climbing down without it, she nearly fell. They camped without the benefit of a fire beneath an overhanging ledge near the top of the cliff. There wasn't enough room to lie down and Yim slept sitting up, leaning against Honus.

Dawn came all too soon. Yim rubbed her eyes wearily, for throughout her short sleep she had kept waking, certain that Gatt was sneaking up on them. Each time she woke, Yim would listen anxiously until fatigue overcame her fear and she dozed off. Honus also stirred with the light. He had been awake every time Yim had been, and she wondered if he had slept at all.

Yim opened the pack and searched for something that could be eaten without cooking. She came up with a leaf-wrapped package of smoked fish that Maryen had given them. She and Honus shared the fish in silence. As Yim ate, she surveyed the countryside. The ledge on which they sat was high up on the ridge's slope. Viewed in daylight, their perch seemed precarious, and Yim grew dizzy when she peered at the drop below.

The ledge afforded a good view, and from its vantage point Yim saw that they had entered the highlands. To the north, she glimpsed a portion of the Yorvern River and Luvein beyond it. Trees hid the road and a nearby ridge hid the rest of the river. That ridge, like the one they were on, snaked southward, rising gradually before joining a small mountain. To the west were higher mountains, their peaks rising like waves on a choppy lake. They faded off in the distance without seeming to end. Yim pointed to them. "Is that Averen?"

"It is."

"I assume we won't use the road to get there."

"Our path is yours to choose," replied Honus.

"But the easiest route to Cara's won't be the safest."

"I think not."

"Then we'll go another way," said Yim. "Can you get us through the mountains?"

"Yes."

"Then find the path that's most likely to lose our pursuer."

When Yim and Honus finished eating, they climbed the cliff and continued their journey. Honus led, walking in a meticulous way to prevent leaving a trail. He avoided soft ground and took care not to snap sticks, tread on plants, or dislodge stones. He also chose the least likely route. That usually meant selecting the hardest one. Although daylight made it easier for Yim to mimic Honus, she lacked his long-honed skill. Moreover, fatigue and the heavy pack made her clumsy. Every time she made a misstep and crushed a plant or left a footprint, she envisioned Gatt discovering her error and hurrying after them.

Noon found Yim and Honus on the mountain they had viewed in the morning. Because its slopes were forested, they seldom had a commanding view. It usually seemed that they were walking in a wood where the stony ground tilted sharply. Yet every once in a while they encountered a stretch of bare limestone and looked out from a lofty viewpoint. Then Yim saw that the country ahead consisted of a series of mountainous ridges, their forms softened by trees. Only the most distant peaks were bare at their tops. Honus pointed into the hazy distance. "That valley belongs to Cara's clan."

Try as she might, Yim couldn't distinguish the place Honus was pointing out. "Is it far?" she asked.

"If we were taking the direct path, I'd say a five-day journey."

"But you plan to climb every mountain on the way."

"That won't be necessary," said Honus, "but there'll be hard walking."

Yim sighed. "I thought as much." She glanced at Honus and caught an expression of tender concern before he could hide it. She forced a smile. "We'll have such grand tales when we greet Cara and Cronin."

By afternoon, Honus and Yim had circumvented the mountaintop and begun the descent down its southern side. Honus seemed familiar with the terrain, for he never hesitated when choosing the route. Halfway down to the valley below, they traversed an immense field of bare rock. Yim had the impression that a giant had carved soil and trees from the mountainside as one might slice into the breast of a roasted fowl to expose a slab of white meat. Honus chose a route that crossed the center of the incline. The slope was steep, but the stone was rough and provided sure footing. They had nearly crossed the open expanse and reached a wooded slope when Yim made a disconcerting discovery.

"Honus! I'm leaving a trail!"

Honus turned and immediately spotted a line of small bloody spots on the pale rock. "How long have your feet been bleeding?"

"I don't know," replied Yim. "They've been sore awhile."

"This is my fault!" said Honus, his voice bitter.

"Oh, so it was you who lost my sandals. I thought I kicked them off in the river."

"I should have chosen a softer path."

"Then we would have left prints of a different kind. Honus, there's such a thing as fate. If it's Karm's will, we'll escape."

"Your right, Karmamatus. I should have more faith."

"But let's try not to leave a trail. The goddess doesn't favor fools."

Honus grinned. "That was Theodus's favorite saying."

The field of barren rock afforded a good view of the valley between the mountain and the next peak. A narrow river meandered through its center. It was so shallow that its bottom was clearly visible. Honus pointed to it. "When we reach the valley, that river will be our pathway. There we'll needn't worry about leaving footprints."

When Honus started off again, Yim detected a change in his tactics. He set a more rapid pace, avoided stony ground, and chose an easy route down to the valley. As a consequence, they soon reached the valley floor and then the river. Unlike the Yorvern, it had a lazy current and was never more than knee-deep. Honus removed his sandals, entered the water, and began to wade downstream. Yim followed. The cool water and sandy riverbed felt good to her sore feet. They progressed westward for a way until they had a good view of the mountainside and the expanse of bare rock that they had traversed only a short while before. Then Honus left the river and sat amid a clump of bushes.

Yim joined him. "Why are we stopping?"

"If Gatt's on our trail, we'll see him when he crosses that open place above."

"Do you think he's following us?"

"I'm certain he's trying. I need to know if he's succeeding."

Yim gazed apprehensively at the mountainside. "I don't see him."

"We had a long head start. Rest. I'll keep watch."

Yim stared at the mountainside briefly before lying down. Soon she slept.

Yim felt Honus's hand gently shake her shoulder. She opened her eyes. It was dusk. "Look at the mountainside," said Honus.

The field of bare rock appeared gray in the failing light. At first, Yim saw nothing. Then a dark speck caught her eye. It resembled a spider scrambling across a rock. Her heart sank. "Gatt!"

"We'll wait until he enters the forest," said Honus. "Then we'll head downstream. We'll be safe, Yim. Even a Sarf can't follow a trail at night."

"Yes. We'll be safe," said Yim in the desperate hope that uttering those words would make them true.

ELEVEN

YIM AND Honus waded downstream as quickly as they could. There was no need to proceed cautiously; the current would erase any trace of their passage. They progressed this way until the moon rose. Then Honus began looking for side streams. When he found one that seemed suitable, he began to walk up it. Yim followed, trying her best to leave no trail. After a while, the ground began to rise. Soon they were climbing the slope of another mountain and Honus abandoned the stream as a path. "There's no point in trying to hide our trail from here on," said Honus. "Our best hope is that Gatt won't spot where we left the river."

The two climbed awhile longer, then stopped for the night at a pile of boulders at the base of a cliff. Yim and Honus nestled between two massive blocks of stone and had their first meal since morning. It was what Honus called "battle porridge," uncooked grain and water. After they ate their gritty meal, they slept huddled together.

The next morning they rose at first light, and Honus led

the way up the mountain and down into the adjacent valley. It was heavily wooded. When Honus encountered a wide brook, it became their pathway. Yim had no idea if it headed toward Cara's lands. By that point, she didn't care, for she was far more concerned with escaping Gatt. When they camped that night, dining again on battle porridge, she prayed that they had succeeded.

When the sun rose, Yim and Honus moved onward without pausing to eat. Throughout the morning they continued wading in the brook, which gradually widened and deepened until the water often reached Yim's calves. As the brook increased in size, the mountain to the north that formed one of the valley's walls diminished in height until it was no more that a chain of low hills. Around noon, the hills ended at the conjunction of the brook and a river. "Is that the river from the first valley?" asked Yim.

"Yes," said Honus, "and beyond this point it heads for the Yorvern. We'll leave it to turn west and slightly northward." He gave Yim a concerned look. "The way will be rugged."

"That's not a problem," replied Yim. "My feet are better."

The land between the two waterways ended in a narrow point that appeared to have been scoured by recent floods. Most of its vegetation had been swept away and only a few scruffy bushes remained. Those grew amid piles of boulders and tangled driftwood. As Yim and Honus neared the point, a blue-faced man rose from the debris. Honus whipped out his sword. "Run, Yim!"

"Where?"

"Back to the campsite. I'll fight him off and join you there."

"Honus . . ."

"Run! Run now!"

Yim saw Gatt splashing through the shallow water and felt a wave of panic. She dashed off. By the time she reached the bank, she heard the clang of swords and turned to see the two Sarfs fighting in knee-deep water. It seemed to her that both fought with less grace and more ferocity than before. Honus gripped his sword hilt with both hands and hewed at Gatt as if he were trying to fell a tree. Gatt attacked with equal energy. The savage desperation of the struggle made it unbearable to watch. Yim turned her eyes from the sight and fled along the bank, heedless of the trail she made. *All our care was pointless*, she thought, wondering how Gatt had found them. She considered abandoning the pack, but it contained all their food, clothes, and essential gear. *Speed won't save me. Only Honus's sword will do that.*

When Yim realized the futility of flight, she slowed to a walk. She didn't even know if she could find the campsite again or where to go if Honus didn't join her. Nevertheless, she continued walking, for she was too anxious to remain still. Yim was considering returning to see how the fight had turned out when she heard the sound of someone running through the woods. Yim halted and waited to learn her fate. It felt like she waited for a long time. At last, someone came into view. It was Honus. As he rushed toward her, Yim noticed that his left hand was bloody.

"You're wounded!"

"Just a nick," said Honus. He reached Yim but didn't halt or even slow his pace. "Follow me. Hurry!"

Yim sped after him. Though she feared that she already knew the answer, she asked anyway. "What of Gatt?"

"He retreated."

So it's not over, thought Yim. Honus's reckless pace and brusque manner were out of character, and it worried her. Moreover, he exercised none of his customary care as he moved among the trees and climbed a rise close to the brook. When he reached a clearing, he halted. "Take off the pack."

Yim slipped it off, and Honus opened it to rummage through its contents. He removed his chain-mail shirt and set it on the ground. At first, Yim thought that he planned to don it in preparation for another battle, but then Honus also removed all his clothing from the pack.

"Honus, what are you doing?"

"Making the pack lighter." Honus grabbed a small stick and squatted over a bare patch of ground. "Come. I must show you this."

As Yim watched, Honus sketched shapes in the dirt. It took a moment for her to realize that the shapes were mountains and he was drawing a map. She was about to ask him why when she glanced at his left hand again. It hung limply and had taken on a grayish hue. Yim peered into Honus's eyes. "You're dying." There was no uncertainty in her voice, only grief and fear.

"My wound is poisoned," replied Honus. "I have but little time."

"So that's why Gatt retreated," said Yim. "To wait for you to die."

"I don't think he'll come after you until he's certain I'm dead. That delay and this map will be my last services to you. I pray to Karm they'll provide you safety."

"Honus, I can't . . ."

"You must try, Karmamatus! *Please*, you must!"

Yim gazed into Honus's moist eyes and saw that he didn't fear his death, only hers. "Of course I will," she said for Honus's benefit. "Tell me what to do."

Using his crude map, Honus showed Yim a route to Cara's. It involved backtracking to deceive Gatt. "Proceed slowly, so you leave no trail," Honus said. "Stealth may save you, but not speed. You can't outrun a Sarf any more than you can outfight him." He grasped Yim's hand with his right one. Its grip was weak and the fingers were cold. "Fly, Karmamatus. I'll die in peace if I know you're heading for safety."

Yim softly stroked Honus's cheek. Then, after a moment's hesitation, she kissed him. Yim had never kissed anyone before, and when her lips pressed Honus's, she felt uncertain what to do next. For a long, awkward moment, she remained virtually still. Then she pulled back. Honus gazed at her sadly, as if he were already missing her. Yim's vision blurred with tears. "Thank you, Honus."

"Go. Don't waste time."

Yim shouldered the pack. It was much lighter. Before she headed off, she turned to bid farewell. Honus was shuffling his feet to rub away the map. She wanted to say something that would put his soul at ease but realized words were incapable of such a feat. In the end, all she uttered was "Goodbye."

Yim made her way to the brook with meticulous care in order to leave no sign of her passage. When she reached the water, she waded into it and began to dash upstream. Counting on the current to wash away her tracks, she ran as fast as possible. Honus had advised her to stay in the water only a brief while, since it was an obvious way to avoid making a trail. "The trick," he had said, "is not to let him know where you left the water. Then climb the southern mountain. Leave no trace for Gatt to follow. When you reach the next valley, head east, not west."

Recalling Honus's instructions made Yim think of him dying alone. The image tore at her heart. *I can't go back to him*, she thought. *He wants me safe*. Yim tried to remember the route that she must take to Cara's. Yet when she attempted to envision Honus's map, her memory of it was confused. She remembered shapes scribed in the dirt, but already she couldn't recall their number or exact position. Her most distinct recollection was that of Honus's hand trembling as he drew the shapes. *He was dying, and all he thought about was me*.

Yim started when she heard a twig snap. She peered anxiously about, expecting Gatt to appear. Then she looked down and realized that she had snapped the twig. *You're not paying attention!* Yim looked behind her and saw the impressions of her bare feet on the damp ground, clear evidence that her mind had been wandering. She wondered how many other traces had she left. *Did I always run where the current will wash away my prints? Was my choice of route too obvious? Can I really outwit Gatt? Honus didn't.*

Yim decided that flight was pointless. Gatt would find her; it was only a matter of time. Having reached that conclusion, Yim pondered what to do with what time remained. *I should be with Honus, not running away.* She resolved to return to Honus's side. Somehow, it didn't feel like giving up. *It's my fate to be with him. Wasn't my name tattooed on his back?*

Yim reversed her course. It was a relief to walk without worrying where she stepped and to be concerned only with moving quickly. Yim had but one goal—to reach Honus before he died. She knew that he'd be distraught when she returned, but she'd say that it was Karm's will that they die together. If need be, she would lie and tell him that his runes had foretold it.

TWELVE

GETTING BACK to Honus took longer than Yim expected. When she did, she found him lying on a mossy patch of ground, his hands clasped and resting on his chest. He was gazing at the sky, and his face was gray beneath its tattoos.

"Honus?" Even as Yim spoke, she knew he wouldn't answer. Yim had envisioned holding Honus as he passed from life, but she had arrived too late. Nevertheless, she rushed over to cradle his body, sobbing as she did. She wept for

Honus. She wept for herself. Yim cried until she was drained of tears, but not of sorrow.

Yim's sole consolation was that Honus had died still hoping that she would live. "That hope died with you," Yim said as she closed Honus's eyes. It seemed a cruel trick that even in death he didn't look peaceful. The marks needled on his face prevented that impression. "Where's the implacable wrath that the Seer foresaw? You were so seldom angry." Yim smiled sadly. "Even though I vexed you often enough."

Yim studied Honus's lifeless face. "The rage I see is merely artistry, a trick of line and shadow." She wished she could wash the expression away, as she had the dark man's magic runes. Yim recalled that night in the sorcerer's castle. On that occasion, Honus had been equally still, for his spirit had left his body. *But that was due to magic, not death.*

Death was an entirely different matter, the ultimate separation. Sitting alone with Honus's corpse, Yim felt torn from much of her life and was surprised to realize how thoroughly Honus had become part of her existence. She had known him for only a few moons and had disliked him in the beginning. Yet she found herself incapable of imagining a future without him. Then she reminded herself that she had no future without Honus; Gatt would see to that.

At that moment, Yim had an idea born from extremity. It came in the form of a question: *Could I recall Honus's spirit and restore it to his body?* The question was absurd, and the answer was surely no. Though she had brought forth Mirien's and Hommy's spirits from the Dark Path, their visits had been only temporary. Resurrecting the dead was far different; Yim had never heard of anyone doing such a thing. Certainly, the Wise Woman had never taught her the skill or even spoken of it. Yet once Yim had the notion, it gripped her imagination. Though snatching a man from death seemed impossible, desperation drove Yim to try.

Yim sat on her heels before Honus's body and began the

meditations for summoning a spirit. She was only partway through them when she realized that they would be insufficient. The souls she had recalled from the Dark Path always returned to it. *Hommy wasn't restored to life after I called her forth*, thought Yim. *Something more than summoning must be necessary.*

Yim ceased meditating and pondered what that something might be. She hadn't a clue. The more she considered the question, the more she suspected that the answer wouldn't be found in the living world. Yim knew that the dead slowly forgot their lives. *That's why Honus tranced, to experience their discarded memories.* Yim wondered if those lost memories bound spirits to the Sunless Way. *But why would missing memories do that?* Yim would have to visit the Dark Path in hope of finding out. To do that, she needed to trance.

Although Yim had witnessed Honus trancing countless times, she had never done it herself. It wasn't a skill that the Wise Woman had taught her, and she had no idea how to go about it. *It can't be too hard*, she thought, *Honus learned it as a child.* Yet Yim knew that arts like trancing involved more than techniques that could be learned. At their core, they were gifts bestowed by Karm. Regardless, Yim imitated Honus and assumed a cross-legged position. Then she closed her eyes and searched for the Dark Path.

Nothing happened, for the living world distracted Yim. She smelled the mossy earth, heard the rustle of leaves, and felt the breeze that moved them. When she tried to make her mind blank, thoughts of Gatt intruded. Concentration became impossible. Yim saw her failure as evidence that her goal was presumption at best and more likely an affront to the goddess. *Karm has always cupped me in her hands. I should submit to her will.* Yim resolved to accept her fate and stopped trying to trance.

Resigned to die, Yim remained motionless in the clearing, with her eyes closed. The world grew quiet. Then, with the suddenness of a fall, it transformed. Yim saw the change through closed eyes. The landscape about her was silent and bereft of life, its empty hills stripped of vegetation and even soil. All that remained was the earth's rocky skeleton. The stone landscape was wrapped in twilight and fog, although there was no sun to set and the frigid air was bone dry. The only thing that moved was mist. Wisps of it slowly flowed over the rocks, alternately hiding and revealing them. Despite the swirling fog, Yim felt no wind. In fact, she felt nothing other than numbing cold.

Without moving her head, Yim gazed down at her body. She was nude and slightly transparent. Her bones were visible as faint shadows beneath her pale skin. She glimpsed her organs also and noted that her heart wasn't beating. For a panicked moment, she thought that she was dead, perhaps decapitated by Gatt in a sudden attack. Then she became aware that her body was sitting upright in the clearing, alive but disconnected from her.

In the dimly lit mist, Honus was hard to spot. When Yim finally saw him, his nude form seemed composed of fog. He stood alone and motionless on a barren hillside. Yim cried Honus's name, but it was only a soundless thought. Honus looked in her direction, but didn't seem to see her. Nevertheless, she suddenly felt his longing.

Yim also sensed Honus right before her. It wasn't his entire being, only a part of it. *A memory*, she thought, *one he's already discarded.* Yim didn't move, but she felt that she was reaching toward the memory. In the realm of the dead, the thought of movement was its equivalent. Yim touched the memory, and it became hers. It was the pulse of a heart. Yim touched another and possessed it. It was the urge to breathe. *Could the first things a soul forgets concern how to live?* With the certainty of insight, Yim knew it was true. Then she proceeded carefully, aware that every memory was vital to Honus. She found the pangs of hunger. The scent of grass. The warmth of sunlight. The tickle of an impending sneeze.

As Yim followed the trail of memories, the closer she drew to Honus, the more complex and vivid they became. Honus seemed oblivious of her, while he became her entire focus. Their spirits touched, and in that instant, Yim was tugged into Honus by the pull of his remembrances. The distinction between them dissolved, so that Yim was both herself and Honus, and she relived his life. She was in Karm's temple, a lonely little boy who was yearning for his mother. He gazed up at the mosaic depicting the goddess, which seemed immense to his young eyes. *My mommy's gone*, he thought. *Only you love me now.*

Memory followed memory, each as real as the actual moment until Yim gazed at herself through Honus's eyes. She was sitting outside Hamin's wagon, warming herself by a campfire as she brushed dried mud from her feet. Then she was seized by an emotion that she had never experienced before—a feeling beyond her imagination. It felt like joy, but it was far more than that. Its power and depth were overwhelming. It was tender yet forceful, sublime yet primal, reverent yet giddy all at once. Until that instant, love had only been a word. Suddenly it was a reality, and Yim experienced its fullness.

The whole of Honus's being washed over and through Yim as she learned his deepest secrets. She felt his longing, his doubt, his pain, and his loneliness as if they were her own. She held his wife as she died in his arms. She endured the horror of battle. She yearned for Honus's absent parents. She adored Theodus and mourned him. She raged. She wept. She made love. She slew.

The final memory was the most powerful. Honus was in the moonlit garden of the ruined temple. Yim viewed her face as Honus had seen it when she let down her guard and unveiled her inner self to him. As Honus probed her, he was torn between longing for her and his duty to the goddess. Then gazing into her eyes, the two reconciled, and he felt washed in holiness. That moment defined Honus. And permeating it, like the clear note of a distant song, was love. Love for her.

Then, embracing the entirety of Honus's soul, Yim returned to the living world. It nearly spent all her strength just to open her eyelids. She stared with astonishment at the clearing, for it seemed too bright and green. Then she forced herself to breathe. The air, rich with the scent of life, felt like thick broth and was as difficult to inhale. Yim smelled dirt, herbs, sweat, and myriad other essences, some fragrant, some pungent.

Then Yim regarded Honus. He remained gray and still, but intuition told her what to do. She pressed her lips against Honus's cold mouth and breathed out. As Yim exhaled, she felt warmth return to him as it departed from her. Life drained from her body, until every part was icy cold. Yim didn't care, even as the world turned black before her open eyes.

Gatt was unsure how long the poison on his blade would take to kill a man. All he knew was that it took a while and he had no wish to fight Honus again. On their first combat, he had possessed the advantage, for Honus had seen the venom painted on Gatt's blade. That caused him to adopt conservative tactics. Nevertheless, Honus had successfully shielded Yim, and she had escaped Karm's justice.

On their second encounter, Honus had fought more aggressively, and Gatt had received several wounds. Although he was loath to admit it even to himself, only Rangar's poison had saved him. *Honus knew he was doomed when I cut his hand*, thought Gatt. *That's why he broke off the fight—to run to his whore*. Gatt shook his head sadly. *Even as he was dying, he remained Yim's slave*. It seemed an ignoble end for a once-worthy man.

Gatt genuinely regretted slaying Honus. Yim would be another matter. As Gatt dressed his wounds, he blamed Yim for them, not Honus. None of his hurts were mortal, though the gash on his left shoulder required stitches, which Gatt sewed stoically. The cut on his nose was the most minor, but also the most irritating, for it wouldn't stop bleeding. As Gatt continued to wipe blood away, he imagined hacking off Yim's nose. That led to thoughts of inflicting slow death by many small slices. *She deserves nothing less*. But after Gatt meditated, he was calm and decided it was Karm's role to punish Yim. He was merely a Sarf. His sole duty was to send Yim to judgment. He resolved to do it mercifully and soon.

When the sun was low, Gatt judged sufficient time had passed, and he began to look for Honus's trail. It was easy to find and easy to follow; so easy that he was able to jog along it. He expected that Yim would have long deserted Honus, but his body would be the starting point for tracking her. With good fortune, he would find the sorceress before nightfall. If not, he doubted it would take more than a day.

After running a while, Gatt was surprised to hear sobbing in the woods. He halted and listened. The sound was deep and low, making him think that Yim had cried herself hoarse. It had never occurred to him that the slut might have feelings for Honus. Then he reconsidered the notion. *She's weeping because she knows she's doomed.*

Gatt hurried onward, determined to finish it. He burst into a clearing and found two blue-clad figures there, one prone and the other slumped and weeping. The sight confounded him, for the ashen-faced figure on the ground was Yim, not Honus. Then Honus looked up and leapt to his feet. His sword was out even before he was erect. The blade flashed about him, a haze of lethal metal, and his face was terrible to behold.

THIRTEEN

FLOATING ALONE in frigid darkness, Yim felt warm raindrops on her face. The sensation of them striking her cheeks and flowing over her skin drew Yim toward their source, the living world. She opened her eyes and saw Honus bent over her. His face was lit by firelight and the warm rain was his falling tears.

For a long moment, all Yim could do was stare at Honus as she relived his passion and devotion. At last, she understood his love and it sparked the same feeling in her. All her discoveries served as kindling for the flame. With the suddenness of a lightning strike, love blossomed and consumed her. Then the mere sight of Honus evoked a surge of joy. He seemed transformed, but Yim knew he hadn't changed. She had. Yim reached up with both hands to touch his face, and the feel of him made her heady with excitement. Stroking Honus's face only heightened Yim's desire, and she pulled him toward her until their lips met.

This time, Yim knew exactly what to do. Instructed by Honus's memories, she pushed her tongue past his parted lips to explore his mouth and relish the warm, wet intimacy of kissing. For an instant, Honus seemed totally surprised, but he quickly responded. Then it felt to Yim that they were two waves colliding, such was the force in their meeting. It shook her like a thunderclap. They embraced, clutching each other as if they could somehow merge into one. Yim's whole existence became Honus. He intoxicated her. He was both lovable and loving. She savored the sight of him, his touch, his smell, his taste, and his every sound from his breathing to the pulse of his pounding heart. *So this is love*, Yim thought. She was certain that it was Karm's gift.

In her weakened state, Yim's passion quickly spent her. Kissing and embracing left her in a state of exhausted bliss. Soon all she desired was to sleep with Honus's arms wrapped around her. Honus seemed to understand, for he pulled his cloak over both of them and held her. Yim sighed like a weary child, murmured "Honus," and closed her eyes. Her last sensation was of Honus nuzzling his face into her hair as he repeated her name. His voice was so soft and tender it sounded as if he were praying. It sent shivers down her spine.

Daijen had maintained his guise as Rangar, but after Gatt had departed from Bremven, he lived luxuriously. He moved to the Palace District, where he rented a suite of rooms close to the Black Temple. As the More Holy One, he commanded the obedience of the temple's priests, who provided him with gold for his purse and virgins for his bed. Daijen had visited the temple only once after his first night in the city. That was to sacrifice a child so he could safely commune with his god. From the session he had learned that events were progressing well. On that particular night, Gatt was within a day's ride of reaching Yim and Honus. Daijen had also learned that Lord Bahl's army was in the Western Reach and marching south toward Averen. Already, priests were sowing discord throughout the mountainous province. Soon Lord Bahl would arrive and reap its harvest.

Daijen expected the matter with Yim to soon be concluded. *Probably this evening*, he thought. Although he was enjoying his stay in the capital, Daijen was eager to rejoin Lord Bahl. An air of expectation had preceded the current year's invasions. The End Times were drawing near, and all the Black Temple was abuzz with talk of the Rising. Better than any priest, Daijen knew the rumors were more than idle hope. A tide of blood would soon wash away the old world. Then the Devourer would burst from its mortal vessel and stride among the living to rule and raise the faithful to glory. Daijen counted himself high among the faithful, and he wanted to be present on that momentous day. If the slaughter in Averen progressed as hoped, it could happen there.

That stirring prospect had lent savor to the evening's sumptuous repast, as did the beauty of his young companion. After Daijen had entered his second century, his taste had turned to ever younger girls. The current night's morsel had barely entered womanhood. Throughout dinner, the More Holy One had thoroughly enjoyed her growing apprehension as the evening's consummation drew near. The little darling had barely touched her food, though she downed three goblets of wine while Daijen stuffed himself. Thus she staggered as she reluctantly followed him into his bedroom.

Daijen lit several candles, closed the door, then sat on the bed. The girl remained standing, her eyes averted. "Look at me!" barked Daijen. The girl obeyed. Daijen gazed into her dark eyes and was excited by her look of fear. He found terror an excellent aphrodisiac.

"Undress for me," he commanded.

The girl's face reddened, but she remained as motionless as a fawn before a tiger.

"Now!"

The girl bent down to take off her sandals, which she did as slowly as possible.

When she was barefoot, Daijen smiled and said, "Now remove your dress."

The dress had a bodice with a long row of buttons in the front. The girl's hand rose to the topmost one, then froze as she began to whimper.

"You heard me," said Daijen in a low, menacing tone. "You know what happens if I'm displeased."

The girl's hand began to tremble, but she started unfastening the buttons. She worked at them slowly. Daijen didn't mind, for it drew out her humiliation. She had undone seven buttons when a gust of cold wind sprang up within the closed room and extinguished all the candles. Before Daijen could react, an icy wave slapped his body and passed through it. The force of its blow knocked his breath away and left him in excruciating pain. He gasped for air as he collapsed to the floor. Every part of him ached. His skin stung, all his muscles cramped at once, and every joint throbbed. As Daijen lay feebly writhing on the floor, the door opened, and light from the outer room spilled over him. The girl stood doorknob in hand, staring at him with terror and disbelief.

"Come here," said Daijen. His voice sounded unnatural to his ears. The girl hesitated for only a moment before she bolted, leaving her sandals behind as she fled. For a while, Daijen lay crumpled on the floor as his pain subsided to a deep ache. He became aware that not only had his voice changed; his hands were altered also. The veins stood out, the knuckles were enlarged, and the skin was no longer tight and smooth. The mere sight of them sent a chill to the pit of his stomach.

Daijen rose slowly, for his joints were stiff and painful. There were no mirrors in his rented rooms, but there was one in the inn's hallway. He headed for it, filled with trepidation. As he approached the sheet of polished bronze, he didn't recognize the reflection at first. For over eighty years, Daijen had appeared as a man in his twenties. Thus the face in the mirror looked ancient to him, though it was that of a man in late middle age. Daijen regarded every wrinkle with horror. He had jowls beneath his chin and bags under his eyes. His hair had thinned and receded, and white strands mingled with the tan ones. An objective observer would have called the mirrored face "hard," yet not unhandsome. But Daijen was accustomed to fresh-faced youth. He was sickened and humiliated by the sight.

With that glance, Daijen knew that his scheme with the Sarf had failed. *This is my punishment*, he thought. Henceforth his flesh would bear the mark of his master's displeasure. It would serve as a reminder and a warning. *I must never fail again*. He had been clever, but cleverness and overconfidence had undone him. Since mercy was alien to the Devourer, the fact that Daijen still lived was proof that he remained charged to kill Yim. Daijen turned all his thought and energy toward that task. His ruthless god demanded nothing less.

Yim woke with a start and sat upright. "Gatt!" She peered wildly about the clearing. In the predawn light, every shadow appeared menacing.

"Rest easy," said Honus, his voice still soft with sleep. "He's slain."

Yim calmed and lay down again, but she was wide awake. The events of yesterday seemed like a vivid dream and possessed a dream's air of unreality. *Did I really kiss Honus?* It seemed a brazen act, but Yim felt certain that she had done it, for she wanted to do it again. As Honus pulled his cloak back over her, she turned so she was face-to-face with him. Honus's closeness was both thrilling and distracting, but Yim felt that she should first learn if he recalled her actions. "Yesterday's all confused," she said in a tone that she hoped conveyed puzzlement. "What happened?"

"Your confusion can't be greater than mine. I recall dying, and . . ." Honus shook his head. "That makes no sense. But then I was alive, and you were beside me, so pale and cold I feared you'd traded your life for mine."

"Don't be silly. How could I do such a thing?"

"But I died. I'm certain of it. And . . ." Honus's voice took on a tone of awe. "I remember now. I felt a presence and . . . Did you . . ."

"What? Snatch you from the Dark Path?" Yim forced herself to laugh. "You only dreamt that. When I returned, you were out of your head."

"I don't recall you coming back. Only my death."

"You would have died for real if I hadn't sucked that poison from your wound."

"But why did you return? You promised you'd flee."

"Since when do Bearers obey their Sarfs? Lucky for you I came to my senses. But that poison sickened me and I swooned."

"And then I awoke. That is, if I indeed dreamt my death."

"Of course you did. Now tell me about Gatt."

"Gatt arrived just after sunset." Honus smiled grimly. "He was surprised to see me."

"So you fought him yet again?"

"I'd hardly call it a fight. I was a man possessed, and it was over with one blow. Then I made a fire. Afterward, you revived."

"I recall what happened next." Yim grinned. "You must have thought I was out of my head. Well, I wasn't." Then she gave Honus a lingering kiss.

Sunrise found Yim and Honus still locked in an embrace. For Yim, her feelings had the wonder of being new and unexpected. As her memories from the Dark Path began to fade, she grew less certain how to behave. She looked to Honus for guidance, and he responded with the patience of a man realizing his greatest hope and savoring each moment. They kissed and touched, nothing more. Yim so thoroughly enjoyed herself that only the pangs of an empty stomach caused her to leave Honus's arms. He went to gather firewood while she searched for herbs to lend flavor to their first meal since the evening before last. As Yim was returning to the clearing, she found Gatt's body in the thicket where Honus had dragged it. The Sarf had been pierced in the heart.

Either due to haste or anger, Honus hadn't closed Gatt's eyes. Thus Yim's nemesis stared at her as might a spirit on the Dark Path. If she ignored its tattoos, the face before her bore the same expression as the man she had killed—a look of astonishment. It caused Yim to wonder if the similarity was more than coincidence, and she was tempted to trance to find out.

Yim yielded to the temptation. Having successfully tranced the previous day, Yim thought she could easily repeat the feat. She sat cross-legged on the ground close to Gatt's corpse, closed her eyes, and meditated to clear her mind. Without the fear of an imminent attack, the feat was quickly accomplished. However, unlike before, nothing happened. Yim remained in the living world. After a while, she gave up and returned to the clearing. There, Honus had a fire going.

Yim mixed grain and water in the small brass pot, added the herbs she had gathered, and set the pot on the fire. While she stirred the porridge, she kept thinking of the dead Sarf in the thicket. "Honus," she said at last. "If we were to give Gatt honorable rites, what needs be done?"

"His body would be burnt at sundown. It would have to be cleansed first. His runes remain holy secrets, so only a Bearer can do it. After the fire is lit, I would break his sword and place it with him. Then you would beg Karm to judge him mercifully."

"Then that's what we'll do, for I don't believe he was truly wicked."

"I'm not fit to judge such matters, Karmamatus."

"Yet you don't agree."

"The matter lies too close to my heart, and I lack your goodness. I'm only your Sarf."

"You're more than that," replied Yim in a voice that was low and shy. "You're my beloved, Honus."

"I've longed to hear those words."

"How could I not love you? You saved my life."

Honus reached out and grasped her hand. He seemed about to say something, but he smiled instead and kissed her cheek.

* * *

Gazing at Yim, Honus knew she had spoken sincerely about her love. He was overjoyed, but also puzzled. He had saved Yim before, and she had failed to become enamored. *Why was yesterday different?* Honus had no clear idea. He was disinclined to ponder the matter, especially since the puzzle paled compared with a far deeper mystery.

Honus had experience with poisoned wounds, for the enemy often used venomed blades. He'd seen many men die from them. There was no cure; sucking the wound did nothing. Moreover, Honus clearly remembered dying. It had taken long enough. The slowly spreading paralysis accompanied by a bone-deep chill left a vivid impression. He recalled staring skyward, unable to blink, and then suddenly being on the Dark Path. Having tranced countless times, he found the place quite familiar.

What happened afterward was less distinct. He recalled a presence that seemed to unite with him. *Could it have been Yim?* He had no way of telling, but Yim had saved him before and denied it. Then he was back in his body, with the chill and paralysis gone. *And Yim was slumped beside me, cold and pale as a corpse.* The memory of that moment tugged at his heart, and he glanced at Yim to reassure himself. She was crouching by the fire and stirring the porridge. Yim was dirty and unkempt, with a large lock of her hair cropped short, but she looked beautiful to him. He was reminded of the mosaic in the temple sanctuary; its image of Karm was no lovelier. Moreover, Yim filled him with the same awe that the mosaic did. And despite Yim's words to the contrary, he felt certain that she had delivered him from death.

The preparations for Gatt's last rites extended well into the morning. Honus carried the dead Sarf's body to the brook and left Yim alone while she cleansed it. As Yim undressed Gatt, she was saddened to see how young he was. She washed the blood from his chest, then turned him over to wash his back. The runes tattooed there formed a short inscription; they didn't even reach the Sarf's shoulder blades. *It seems they foretold a short life*, thought Yim. The language was the same archaic one transcribed on Honus's back, and Yim found its text equally unenlightening. Nevertheless, she studied what was written there, looking for some clue to Gatt's actions. One word caught her eye, for it was unique and she had also seen it on Honus's back. The word was "Daijen." It formed half of the final inscription: "Bewarr Daijen."

Does that mean "Beware Daijen"? Is Daijen someone's name? Yim recalled thinking that a line among Honus's tattoos had spelled out "He sends Daijen." She resolved to look at the runes again to verify her memory.

Yim spoke to the dead man. "Was it Daijen who poisoned your mind? If so, how sad you had no Bearer to warn you." Then she recalled that a Bearer wouldn't speak of the portents on a Sarf's back and realized the warning wasn't meant for Gatt. As Yim stared at the words needled on the corpse, a chilling notion came to her. *This warning is meant for me!*

FOURTEEN

YIM REMAINED by the brook after Honus carried Gatt's body away. The suddenness and the intensity of her feelings had disoriented her, and she needed some quiet time to steady herself. Yim thought bathing in cold water would help. Before she did, she plucked fragrant herbs to use in scrubbing the dirt from her skin so she would be sweetly scented when Honus saw her next. Then Yim shed her clothes and washed them. After she wrung them out and hung them in the sun to dry, Yim turned to washing herself. Bearing a handful of violets, woodruff, and wild lavender, she waded to a place where the water ran clear and deep.

Previously, concern that Honus might view her bathing had always made Yim wash hastily. In her new frame of mind, she thought differently about the prospect. The idea of him seeing her nude was deliciously exciting, and she took her time bathing. As Yim brushed the wet herbs over her skin, she imagined their leaves and blossoms were Honus's fingertips. Cupping her breasts, she recalled the night in Luvein when Honus had touched her there. On that occasion, she had felt only passive and apprehensive. That moment seemed from a different life. As Yim imitated the way Honus had gently kneaded her nipples, she felt a warm, pleasant sensation spread from between her thighs.

When her spirit had joined with Honus's, Yim had relived his memories of passion. It made her crave to experience its ecstasies firsthand. *It'll be so easy*, Yim thought, as her hands roved over her body. *He wants me as much as I want him.* All she needed to do was express her willingness and Honus would make love to her. The mere thought of it made her tingle all over.

Yet as soon as Yim envisioned consummating her desire, a contrary thought arose: *I can't! I'm the Chosen.* She couldn't perform her sacred duty if she wasn't a virgin. There was no middle ground; she could either fulfill her love or her destiny. Torn between the two, Yim found she couldn't forsake Karm. She had revered the goddess since childhood, and she had loved Honus for less than a day. Nonetheless, the strength of her new feelings made the choice a wrenching one. Yim hurriedly dressed in her wet clothes, as if to dampen desire. It remained as strong as ever, but instead of being exhilarating, it became torment. Love transformed into a gnawing hunger with no prospect of satisfaction.

Yim slumped on a rock, chilled by her damp clothes. Her physical discomfort mirrored her anguish as joy hardened into sorrow. For a while, she sought to convince herself that Karm had chosen Honus to father her child. *That's why she helped me save him.* Despite wanting to believe that, Yim sensed it wasn't true. *If I were meant to bear Honus's child, we would've conceived one long ago.* The Wise Woman had been adamant that the goddess would reveal the father, so Karm's silence seemed proof that Yim had yet to meet him. She probably never would if she made love to Honus.

When Yim pondered her dilemma further, she felt that surrendering to desire would not only betray Karm but also Honus. As a Sarf, his life was dedicated to the goddess. Yim recalled Cara's words: "*You need only climb into Honus's bed to thwart Karm.*" Yim couldn't imagine Honus opposing the goddess. To cause him to do so in ignorance would be deceptive and supremely selfish.

I must reveal to Honus what it means to be the Chosen, Yim thought. *There's no other way.* She felt the truth would shatter their happiness, and that thought dispirited her. She recalled with irony how she had thought of love as Karm's gift. It had become Karm's curse instead, a poison—first sweet, then bitter—that burnt without hope of relief. Yim wished that she didn't love Honus, yet couldn't bear the thought of being apart from him. She wondered if her feelings were a trial, a punishment, or the means to some end she couldn't imagine.

Yim remained on the rock a while longer, but her thoughts were caged beasts that ran in circles. She loved both Honus and Karm, and she could have one only by denying the other. Finally wearied of thinking, Yim waded across the brook to find Honus and bare her heart to him.

* * *

In the center of the clearing was a huge pile of branches and dry brush. Gatt lay atop it, looking peaceful in death. Honus was nowhere to be found. Yim waited for him and the passing time compounded her unhappiness. Honus didn't return until midafternoon. He carried three pheasants and was grinning broadly before he caught Yim's anguished look. His smile vanished. "Yim, what's the matter?"

"Honus, I must tell you something." Yim saw the concern in Honus's face and felt that he had never looked more beautiful. Words deserted her for a moment, and she simply stared at him, filled with longing. Honus waited patiently until she regained her composure. "Honus, you know that I'm the Chosen."

"Yes."

"You believe that's something holy. Well, it's not. Karm gave me a task. If I accomplish it, some good will be achieved. My worth lies solely in that. I'm only the vessel, not the wine."

"Karmamatus . . ."

"Please Honus, let me finish. I've kept so much from you." Yim felt her throat constrict, and she struggled not to cry. "I . . . I regret that. I was sworn to secrecy, but now . . . now that things have changed between us and . . . Oh Honus! I need your strength more than ever."

Honus bowed. "You have it, Karmamatus. Be assured of that."

"I'm supposed to bear a child. Karm will reveal who's to be the father. She hasn't done so yet. Until she does, I may tup with no man." Yim noted the surprise on Honus's face. "Yes, I lied to you. I'm a virgin and must remain one."

"And last night . . . this morning . . ."

"Mistakes."

"I see."

"I've never loved a man before. I didn't foresee the path love takes. Yet now that I do, I must think only of my duty."

"If your duty is to bear a child, why take on Theodus's quest?"

"Karm told me to follow his footsteps. For a while I thought they'd lead to the man who's to father my child, but now I'm not sure. My visions seldom make sense. I can't even read your runes. You should leave me. I'm unfit to guide you."

"I'm your Sarf. You needn't guide me."

"But we shouldn't be together!"

"Because you must remain untouched? Yim, one can love chastely. I'm proof of that."

Yim smiled wanly. "Now I understand your torment."

Honus gently enfolded Yim in his arms. "It can be hard, but there are good times, too."

Yim wavered, then returned Honus's embrace. "I worry I'll be weak."

"You've never been that, Karmamatus." Honus kissed Yim's forehead. "And Theodus taught me one thing well: Real love is never weakness."

Deep within the Black Temple was a room that few priests knew about and fewer still had ever entered. It was built deep underground so that daylight never reached its walls of dusky basalt. When the room's iron door was shut and the lamp extinguished, the darkness there was absolute. The rough walls leaned inward; otherwise the chamber was featureless except for a circle carved into the stone floor to form a shallow trough.

Daijen entered the room, throwing back the deep hood that hid his newly aged face. A single oil lamp burned, filling the chill air with pungent smoke. Its pale light revealed a small boy dressed in a slave's tunic who lay shivering on the floor. His wrists were tied, as were his ankles. He stared at the More Holy One in terror, his rapid breath visible in the room's otherworldly coldness.

The surroundings were new to Daijen, but the ritual he

must perform was familiar to him. He drew a dagger from his robe and made quick work of the sacrifice, holding his victim's throat over the trough so the blood flowed into it. When a crimson circle marked the floor, the More Holy One stepped inside its protection. There he knelt and sent his thoughts to the Dark Path to invoke his master. The Devourer overlooked the entire world, and none could hide from its malice. Soon Daijen would know where to find Yim.

The sun's last rays filled the clearing with rosy light when Honus touched Gatt's pyre with a burning branch. Flames rapidly spread from the spot. Before they engulfed the dead Sarf, Honus drove the point of Gatt's sword deep into the ground. He placed his sandaled foot against the middle of the blade, which he had cleansed of poison, and grasped the hilt. Then pulling with both hands and pushing with his foot, he bent the blade until it snapped. Honus placed the broken sword on Gatt's chest, then stepped back from the pyre's growing heat. "Now the Bearer speaks to Karm," he said.

"What should I say?"

"Whatever comes to you."

Yim gazed at the dark shape within the swirling flames awhile before she spoke. "His name was Gatt. He was a Sarf. He tried to kill me. That's all I know about him. I hope you'll show him mercy in your judgment because . . ." Yim paused a long moment, gathering her thoughts. "Because he was probably unable to see how deeds play out. Was he guided by your will? You can tell, but I think it was less easy for him. It can be hard to discern the proper path. Very hard. I know, for in this I'm like Gatt. So please show him mercy if he was wrong, just as I hope that you'll show me mercy."

Honus looked at Yim, wanting to contradict her and say that she was unlike Gatt. But when he saw the tears streaming down her cheeks, he knew her words were heartfelt, and so he held his tongue.

It was nighttime when Daijen finally staggered from the subterranean chamber. His hood hid his face from prying eyes as he rushed from the temple. Thus no priest observed his drawn expression and speculated on what had caused it. Daijen wandered the dark streets awhile, scarcely conscious of where he was. He felt like a sailor cast ashore by a raging storm, but instead of wind and waves, otherworldly forces had battered him while he cowered within the ring of blood. The ordeal had seemed like it could end only with his destruction; yet somehow he had survived. Something had struggled with his master within the dark room, and the contest had nearly shattered Daijen's sanity. The invisible forces were so powerful that they affected his mind like physical blows. Each assault from either side was agony, a clap of pervasive pain that left him reeling and nauseous.

When the combat finally subsided, Daijen felt profoundly disturbed. He had always regarded the Devourer as all-powerful—the world's inevitable overlord. Yet within that dark chamber he had just experienced his master's power being challenged. After the massacre at Karm's temple, he hadn't believed such a thing was possible. To him, Karm was a deity for weaklings, one that bestowed only worthless gifts. None of her followers could cheat death, practice sorcery, or enflame men's minds. Yet some power had stymied his master, and Daijen felt certain that it was the goddess.

Pondering on the import of what had happened, Daijen wondered if Karm was as impotent as he had supposed. It seemed possible that the goddess had been merely biding her time and hiding her power until the proper moment to strike. If that were so, then she had just revealed her hand for the sake of a woman. *This Yim is far more than an irritant,* he thought. *She must somehow threaten my master.* Daijen couldn't imagine how a mortal could do that, but he didn't doubt his conclusion. It made Yim's destruction all the more urgent.

Daijen turned his thoughts to that end. He had learned little of use within the room, for whatever guidance his master had for him had been muddled and obscured. The Devourer's hatred for Yim was vividly apparent, but the vision of her whereabouts had been reduced to jumbled fragments. Daijen recalled mountains as glimpsed through a nighttime fog. He assumed they were in Averen, for that was where Yim had been headed. The other images that formed in his mind had dissolved as quickly as smoke in wind. One scene kept arising and vanishing with such frequency that bits of it stuck in Daijen's memory. Mountains. Buildings. He thought one building might have been walled. The other structures were smaller and clustered about it. And something large and bright lay nearby. *A lake perhaps.* Daijen thought the scene showed either Yim's hiding place or her destination.

It wasn't much to go on, but it was all he had. Daijen headed for the taverns in the Averen quarter. As he walked, he devised his story. It would be about a vision, a gift from the goddess. He would recount the disjointed images he had seen and say they hinted where he might find his long-lost child. A daughter named Yim. *With patience, I'll find someone who'll know of the place I seek.* Already, Daijen envisioned himself astride a new steed and riding forth to regain his master's favor.

FIFTEEN

IT WAS tradition to feast after a Sarf's final ceremony in order to celebrate his deeds. Honus saw the meal of roast pheasant as honoring the form—but not the substance—of that custom. He felt there was nothing to celebrate and couldn't bring himself to forgive Gatt, even if Yim did. He knew it was a fault in him, but that knowledge didn't sway his heart. Honus only pecked at his food, his appetite spoiled by discontent. Ill will toward Gatt wasn't its source: That morning he had felt blessed, and that blessing had been withdrawn.

Honus was angry, but he was unsure where to direct his anger. Certainly not at Yim. She gazed at him with such love and sadness that it was painful to look into her eyes. She who had so handily deceived him had become unable to hide her feelings. They were raw, and Yim seemed tortured by them. Every time she glanced at his face, she acted like a bird stealing grain from a cat—stealthy and hesitant, yet driven by need. Her obvious torment was both pathetic and endearing. Honus wondered how he might soothe her misery but doubted it was possible.

Did Karm do this to her? Is this some trial? And who's being tested? Yim or I? Honus believed that Karm was the goddess of compassion; yet to inflict such an ordeal seemed cruel. *But when has Karm ever smoothed my way?* Honus recalled being taken from his parents, his rigid training, the pain of the tattoo needle, the hard road he traveled with Theodus, and his beloved Bearer's gruesome death. *And now this!* Nevertheless, Honus couldn't rage against the goddess. She was the well of holiness, the same holiness that drew him to Yim.

Honus wondered if he should be angry with himself. If he had caused Yim to love him, then he had also caused her torment. It pained him to think that, but the more he considered the notion, the truer it seemed. But if Yim was a victim of his love, he was also. Despite himself, Honus reached out to grasp Yim's hand, which was greasy from eating pheasant. She didn't pull away. "I'm sorry, Yim."

"There's nothing to be sorry for," she replied.

"Spoken by one who forgives her assassin."

"He wasn't my assassin. He didn't kill me." Yim squeezed Honus's hand. "Thanks to you."

"Still, I regret the pain love brings you."

"That pain is Karm's gift," replied Yim, her voice laced with irony. "Most of her gifts are accompanied by pain. You know that yourself. Many times I've seen you trance and return stricken by another's forgotten grief. Yet you still do it."

"I trance to seek happy memories, not sorrowful ones."

"Then you endure the bitter for the sake of the sweet." Yim smiled. "Your touch gladdens me, though it stirs my yearning."

Honus sighed and released Yim's hand.

"Honus, I'll learn to live with this. I must."

In the Western Reach, the burning village lit the night. The peasant soldiers had finished their slaughter and withdrawn, leaving the Iron Guard to systematically loot and burn. Wearing a dead man's helm and breastplate, Hendric sat close to a campfire and stared at his hand. The encampment was crowded, and the darkness was filled with the sounds of men pushed to extremity. Some cried in pain, while others laughed with a raucousness that bordered on hysteria. A few, still caught up in the battle frenzy, cursed and roared incoherently. Somewhere, a woman screamed. But Hendric shut out the din, fully engaged by the puzzle at the end of his wrist.

When did I lose those fingers? he wondered. He had no recollection of the event. They had been there in the morning, and by night they were gone. The little finger on his sword hand was entirely missing and only parts of the next three fingers remained. The bloody stumps were painful, and it was pain that first alerted Hendric that something had happened to him. He assumed that the fingers had been severed in the assault, but when and how were mysteries to him.

Hendric had been in five battles so far, but he recalled none of them coherently. His recollections seemed like half-remembered dreams suffused with manic glee. Once he had been a tenderhearted man, a peasant who hated butchering his chickens. Nevertheless, Slasher had been right; Hendric had come to relish killing. When Bahl stirred his troops for battle, Hendric was swept up in exultant frenzy. Then nothing mattered except the task at hand. During those times, Hendric was capable of anything, and it was easy to disregard the loss of a few fingers.

The peasant never understood how Lord Bahl incited him. It seemed to be more than the power of words. He seldom recalled what was said; only that Bahl's speech stirred him like music that echoed in his mind for ever-longer periods. While it did, Hendric was transported to an energetic form of oblivion that expunged his longing, misery, and fear. Afterward, he was always exhausted and bloody. Moreover, sickening images would haunt his waking thoughts and disturb his sleep. Hendric feared they were memories of things he had done. Regardless, he had come to crave those frantic spells as a drunkard craves ale. Though the aftermath was hard, forgetfulness was bliss.

The army had been on the march for days, leaving a swath of destruction and slaughter in its wake. Lord Bahl rode at its head, accompanied by the priest, the Most Holy Gorm, and Hendric's own lord, Count Yaun. The peasant despised the count who had taken him from everyone he loved, but he felt differently about Lord Bahl. He feared his cruelty, but he also held him in awe. Lord Bahl seemed more than a man, and thus immune to men's judgment. And with each new round of slaughter, his power over Hendric and the other men grew.

Already, there were men among the troops who were never free from Lord Bahl's spell. They were always eager to kill and dangerous to be around. As the march progressed, their numbers increased, despite losses within the army. When Hendric reflected on it, the battle frenzy lingered ever longer in him also. Existence blurred. He had only a vague idea of where he was, other than far from home. He knew that they were headed for Averen, but he didn't know when they'd get there. Hendric hoped it would be soon, for one thing Lord Bahl had said stuck in his mind: In Averen, misery would be washed from his soul in a bath of blood.

Yim slept wrapped in her cloak, apart from Honus. When she arose the next morning, she scattered Gatt's ashes before resuming her journey to Cara's. They were far enough from the highway that it seemed pointless to return to it, and since Honus knew the country from his travels with Theodus, he proposed another route. "Westward lie the lands of Clan Dolbane," he said. "There we'll find farmsteads and roads."

"And will we be welcome?"

"Theodus and I were in the past," replied Honus. "I don't know how we'll fare now."

"I guess we'll find out," said Yim, hoping that when she reached Cara's lands she wouldn't find folk turned against her.

Honus led the way to where he had fought with Gatt and then headed west. For most of the morning, the land they traveled was wooded and wild. The rocky terrain was rugged, and though they walked within valleys, they usually hiked uphill. Until the midsummer sun rose high, the air had a crispness to it. They found a narrow pathway just before noon, and Yim was glad for some sign that people lived about. A short while later, they encountered a field on a sunny mountainside. At its edge was a dwelling that was half-buried into the slope. Smoke rose from a hole in its roof.

"Let's see how we'll be greeted," said Yim. The two climbed the slope until they reached the house. It was made of stone where it touched the ground, and timber above that. The logs that formed its walls had been squared before they were fitted together, and the spaces between them were chinked with moss. The roof was made of broad wooden shakes, weighted with stones. At the rear of the house, the roof merged with the mountain's slope. The smoke hole was there, surrounded by wide slabs of stone. The only windows were on the structure's front. They were small and their shutters were flung open, as was the dwelling's door. Yim approached the house without seeing anyone and peered inside.

The sunny day made the single room beyond the doorway seem all the darker. Yim saw a dirt floor, a table, benches, a loom, and lines that were strung between the walls. Various shades of twisted wool dangled from the lines. Some of the wool steamed and dripped from recent dyeing. At the far end of the room, Yim spied a fire and a large kettle. A small figure stirred the kettle. It took a moment for Yim's eyes to adjust and discern that the figure was that of a girl, perhaps eleven winters old. Plaid homespun was wrapped about her thin waist to form a skirt that reached midcalf. A second length of plaid was tucked into the top of her skirt. It passed across her chest, over her left shoulder, and down her back to tuck into the skirt's rear. These two items comprised her garments, for she wore no shirt and her feet were bare. Her long, light brown hair was tied back, exposing a face whose sootiness made the girl's wide-eyed stare all the more conspicuous. Concerned that Honus's face might have frightened the child, Yim bowed low and said, "Greetings, dear. We're servants of Karm."

The girl said nothing, but she dropped the wooden stirring paddle and slowly edged toward the table. Yim noted there was a knife upon it. "My companion's face looks grim, but his heart is kind. You need not fear him or me. We bring Karm's blessing."

"Karm's dead," said the girl, laying her hand on the knife hilt, but not grasping it.

Yim smiled and spoke in a light, almost amused tone. "How can a goddess die?"

"Da said she did," stated the girl, as if that assertion explained everything.

"Then I bring good news. Karm still watches over you."

The girl simply stared at Yim with doubt and more than a hint of suspicion. Yim, sensing the futility of speaking further, motioned for Honus to back away. She bowed again and said, "Tell your da that we bestowed our blessing." Then she turned and departed.

Trudging down the slope, Yim observed the girl dash from the house and disappear into the trees that surrounded the field. She wondered what the girl would tell her father and if they should fear another attack. After no one appeared, either friendly or hostile, Yim's thoughts turned to the girl's assertion that Karm was dead. She tried to dismiss it as foolishness, something an ignorant girl repeated without understanding. It might be a lie from a black priest or a mere misunderstanding. Nonetheless, the idea worked on Yim's imagination. It matched her foreboding that something terrible loomed ahead. It also recalled her disturbing visions. The last two times Karm had appeared to her, the goddess had been covered with blood. She had seemed battered, not powerful. And Karm's last visitation had been followed by a disturbing absence that intensified Yim's feelings of abandonment.

Honus walked in front, so he was unaware of Yim's musings. They returned to the trail, which gradually broadened into a narrow dirt road as it snaked through a high valley. There, the southward slopes were cleared wherever the stony ground was level enough to till or use for pasturage. Among the clearings, Yim spotted dwellings, but her encounter with the girl had made her reluctant to approach them. Occasionally, they met people on the road. Both the men and women wore costumes similar to the young girl's, but their attire usually included long-sleeved shirts and boots or sandals. Since everyone greeted her politely—albeit tersely—as they passed, Yim began to think her first encounter was a fluke. Eventually, she decided that it was, and when dusk approached she sought hospitality.

Yim spotted a homestead built of timber and stone and told Honus to head for it. Like the first dwelling they visited, it was partly buried into the mountain's slope. It was more expansive, however, appearing to have been enlarged by several additions. Yim noticed adults and children toiling in a nearby field. About the house, more children were driving sheep into a pen or doing other chores while two boys in their late teens sparred vigorously using wooden swords. Red welts upon their arms and chests proved the earnestness of their practice.

A woman, her blond hair streaked with gray, emerged from the house when Yim and Honus reached it. She was barefoot and her plaids and woolen blouse were soiled and threadbare, but she bore herself with dignity. Yim bowed to her. "Mother, we seek food and shelter in respect for the goddess."

"My husband is lord here," replied the woman. " 'Tis his place to say aye or nay." She pointed to the field. "He's guiding the plow."

Yim bowed to the woman and walked over to the field. There, a gray-haired man was plowing under the stubble of winter grain. A young couple pulled the plow, the woman round with child. Ragged, barefoot children walked behind to scatter grain in the freshly turned furrows. The plowman halted when he saw Yim approach. She bowed to him and repeated her request. The man regarded her with interest. "At first I thought I was seeing spirits," he said without returning Yim's bow, "but you seem solid enough. Aye, you can sup and sleep with us."

Yim bowed. "Karm sees your generosity."

The man smiled. "Does she now? Well, na matter either way; we'll be glad for talk. I'm Devren, lord of this holding." He gestured to the couple pulling the plow. "This is my heir, Folden, and his bride, Kaarkan. We'll join you when 'tis too dark to plow."

As Yim headed back to the house, she turned to Honus and said in a low voice, "So many children!"

"Averen families run large, and children of unmarried daughters are counted as the patriarch's offspring."

"Would there be many of those?"

"Usually quite a few. There's a saying here: 'A man needs land to have a wife, but na a child.' Did you see those lads with wooden swords? Landless sons usually go off soldiering."

"And forsake the mothers of their children?"

"The lucky ones return."

"And what if his love has found another?"

"That's the theme of many Averen ballads."

When Yim and Honus reached the dwelling, Devren's wife introduced herself as Fremma. After Yim slipped the pack from her shoulders, Fremma bade Yim and Honus sit at a bench by the table while she brewed them a hot drink. She did that at a fire pit near the room's far wall. A young woman, barefoot and as ragged as her mother, stood there adding herbs to a bubbling kettle. An infant nestled within her plaid chest wrap, nursing at her breast. A naked toddler played about a loom, where a girl of perhaps nine winters worked the shuttle. The light was so dim, she seemed to be guiding it by feel.

Fremma brought out wooden bowls of herbal tea, served Yim and Honus, then left the room. As Yim sipped her drink, she gazed about. The long table at which she and Honus sat occupied much of the central room. Two looms took up most of the remaining floor space. Skeins of wool, plants for making dye, lengths of plaid cloth, and all manner of implements dangled from the rafters. On either sidewall was an entrance to an adjoining chamber. One chamber seemed for sleeping. The other seemed a storeroom.

While Yim gazed about the central room, it slowly filled with children who curiously regarded her and Honus. Although they whispered among themselves, none spoke to Yim or answered her greetings. They kept their distance until Devren arrived to formally welcome his guests. After Yim gave her and Honus's names, the children crowded around her, although they gave wide berth to Honus. The youngsters remained too shy to speak, but they seemed fascinated by Yim's clothes and foreignness.

There was but a single chair at the long table. It was placed at its head, and Devren took it. Then he invited Yim to sit at the end of the bench closest to his right, apparently the place of honor. Honus was offered the seat on the bench to his left. Once Devren and his guests were seated, the male members of his family took their places at the long benches lining the table, the eldest sons sitting closest to their father. Then Fremma, Kaarkan, and Devren's elder daughters served them food and drink. There was coarse brown bread, ale, and porridge that contained a few roots and even fewer bits of mutton. Only after the men were served did the women serve themselves and the children. They sat crowded at the far ends of the benches.

Herbs made the porridge flavorful, and Yim enjoyed both

it and the bread. The dark ale was strong, and she took only small sips from her bowl. Yim suspected that it was brought out in her honor. Only she and the men drank it. All the men, except for Honus, drank deeply. Devren was cordial to her during the meal, as were his sons, but no one was reverent. When tongues loosened as the ale took hold, Yim attempted to steer the talk toward what concerned her most. "Sir, you seemed surprised to see me. Why was that?"

"I'd heard all Karm's folk were slain," replied Devren.

"Who told you that?"

"The new priests."

"So they've come spreading lies."

"I do na agree," replied Devren. "What they say makes sense."

"Like what?"

"That our clan has too long endured wrongs against us. Because our neighbors crowd us, my sons can na take wives."

"Da speaks true," said one of Devren's sons. "Why soldier for other men when a sword can win you a homestead?"

"By that, you mean another man's homestead," said Yim.

"Strength is the sign of grace," said Devren.

"Not Karm's grace," replied Yim.

"That's why your kind's gone," said Devren. "Meekness may have its place, but 'tis a hard world. 'Tis only common sense to turn to a hard god."

Yim felt a chill pass through her. "So you worship the Devourer?"

Devren smiled and patted Yim's hand. "If you're surprised, then you're unworldly."

"So unlike the priests!" said one of the boys who had been sword fighting. Yim glanced at him and was startled by the intensity of his gaze. "They know how things go. How Clan Mucdoi slew our folk and stole our land."

"Aye," said a brother. "'Twas fine land, too, na all hills and rocks like here."

Honus spoke for the first time the entire evening. "Those battles you speak of took place centuries ago, and tales differ as to who was in the wrong."

"Then hear the true tale," said the boy who had praised the priests. "We were foully betrayed and foully slaughtered. Even now, our dead cry for vengeance."

"The departed forget their lives," replied Yim.

"'Tis na so!" exclaimed the lad. "The priest called forth their voices. I heard their cries with mine own ears and was sorely grieved." He gazed around the firelit room, red-faced and with his fists clenched. "I hear them still!"

"Do others feel like you?" asked Yim.

"Enough," replied the boy.

Yim glanced about and suspected most of the family agreed with him. It made her wonder what tales the black priests were telling the Mucdoi Clan.

"So, lass," said one of the brothers, "why do you travel?"

"To visit a lady friend," replied Yim.

"Where?" said the red-faced boy, his voice laced with suspicion.

"In the hall of Clan Urkzimdi."

"Ha! That's an unnatural lot!" exclaimed one of the brothers. "A woman for a chieftain. What nonsense!"

"'Tis because their land lies nigh to Faerie," said another. "Small wonder they're all strange."

Before Yim could react to that remark, the red-faced boy spoke. "To reach Urkzimdi, you must pass through Mucdoi territory."

"Yes," replied Yim, keeping her voice even.

"'Twould na be wise to go that way," the boy said, fixing his gaze on Yim so she might see his menace. "You've heard too much tonight."

"A Bearer listens to all, but repeats little," replied Yim.

"I'll not recite your speeches. As to what path to take, I'll keep my own counsel."

"Since you're offering advice," said Honus to the boy, "I'll give you some of mine: It's unwise to see a threat where there is none, and safety lies in wisdom."

The room hushed as the boy glared at Honus and the Sarf looked back calmly. Then Devren spoke in a mild tone. "Son, speak more amiably to our guest. She's harmless enough."

"Go where you will," said the boy in a subdued tone. Then he looked away, and the tension dissipated.

By then, the fire was dying down, and children were wandering off to sleep. After clearing the dishes, their mothers joined them, leaving the men to linger about the ale jug. Yim stayed with them, though she was uncomfortable as their talk turned bellicose. Atrocities were recounted as if they had occurred yesterday, though generations had passed since the purported deeds. Mingled with grievances were tales of loss. Lands the men had never seen grew more fair and bountiful as they spoke of them, making their home seem insignificant in comparison. As the ale jug passed back and forth among them, the drinkers' voices became louder and more animated until Yim feared they might seize arms and storm out of the house.

That didn't happen, and eventually the ale made the men sleepy. Then they joined the women and children in the adjacent chamber. Yim and Honus followed them. Straw mattresses covered most of the floor, and sleeping women and children covered most of those. The mattresses of Devren and his heir had curtains hung about them, so they might bed their wives in privacy. The rest of the family slept crowded together and Yim and Honus were given a mattress to share with two toddlers, a boy and a girl.

Yim didn't mind the arrangement, and she liked it when the boy nestled against her. Honus drifted off to sleep, but Yim lay awake in the dark room that was filled with the sounds of slumber. The entire family was united by sleep and by common bonds of blood, hardship, and poverty. The tiny boy against Yim's chest seemed an extension of the whole. Through him, the family touched Yim and roused her compassion. She thought how those about her struggled on the hard edge of want and yet shared what they had with strangers. She loved them all, even the angry lad who spoke of vengeance.

Yim's compassion made the priests seem all the more vile to her. They were poisoning this family to turn it against other families. Yim had sensed a grim future during the drunken talk of retribution. Hate was a burning brand tossed into a dry field. Fanned by want and lies, it was spreading. It had consumed the lad and it was overcoming the others. She feared talk would become action, and each cruel deed would inspire more.

These troubled thoughts kept Yim awake, so she was only drowsing when she heard a noise in the outer room. It was the sound of something striking and splintering wood. Yim raised her head to see if anyone else had heard it. When she did, she saw the light of flames coming from the central room. Before Yim could shout an alarm, men with torches burst in on the sleeping family. They carried farm tools that could serve as weapons. Then they attacked the sleepers.

All was fire, blood, and chaos. The bed-curtains went up in sheets of flame. Devren and Folden were both alight when they staggered through them to be hacked down. Then men pushed the burning curtains aside and made quick work of the screaming women behind them. Meanwhile, other men advanced upon the family that had awakened to a nightmare. The killers, their eyes turned red by reflected firelight, seemed inhuman. They slaughtered their helpless victims without pity as though they were scything grain or threshing it. Women and children received no more mercy than the men.

Yim was immobilized by horror, unable even to cry out. All she could do was grip the boy who had been sleeping next to her and shield his eyes from the sight of butchery. Yim was still clutching the child when a man advanced toward them. The mattock in his hand was dripping with gore. As Yim wondered where Honus was, the man tore the boy from her arms and threw him hard upon the floor. The child lay stunned, able only to whimper as his assailant raised the mattock high to plunge it into his chest. Yim reacted instinctively. As the mattock descended, she threw her body atop the boy's to take the blow. Heavy iron plunged into her, splintering Yim's ribs as it dug toward her heart.

With a cry of pain, Yim's eyes flew open. The room was dark and quiet. Then Honus stirred and touched her wrist. When his hand felt hot against her icy skin, Yim knew that Karm had sent her another vision.

SIXTEEN

YIM'S CRY had awakened the boy who nestled against her. The frightened child pulled away, then quickly fell asleep again. Yim did not. She was thoroughly chilled and her ribs and chest ached terribly. Her only comfort was that Honus wrapped an arm about her. She was glad that he didn't speak, but seemed to know what she had endured without asking. Yim gratefully snuggled against him.

As warmth passed from Honus into her, Yim pondered the meaning of her vision. She wondered if it foretold what was to come, or only warned her of what might be. *I was slain*, she thought, still feeling the blow from the mattock. *Is that to be my fate?* She hoped that the mattock was symbolic.

Of what? She had no idea, but feared it was something horrific.

The vision had so thoroughly drained Yim that sleep stole upon her despite her apprehensions. She slipped into dreamless slumber and didn't wake until Devren's family rose. They were unchanged, but Yim saw them differently. Everyone seemed endangered, with a hold on life so precarious that Yim had to struggle against showing tears. The family went to work without a morning meal, with only the very youngest having no chore to do. Yim and Honus left early in the morning, pausing at the field where Devren plowed to thank him for his hospitality.

Honus didn't speak until they had walked some distance down the road. "You cried out last night. Did something pain you?"

"Karm bestowed another gift."

"A vision?"

"Yes. A vision like the one at Karvakken Pass, only worse. It wasn't about what had happened but about what will happen or may happen, I don't know which." Tears welled in Yim's eyes, and she began to tremble. "I feel now as I did then. Overwhelmed. I'm afraid, Honus, and don't know if I can go on."

Honus held out his arms, and Yim retreated to their refuge. She clasped him tightly, burying her face into his chest. Then she began to sob. They stood embracing in the road for a long time, Honus silent and Yim softly crying. Only when Yim grew quiet did Honus release her.

Yim regarded him and saw a face filled with devotion. His look stirred her love and once more tempted her to seek the solace of intimacy. The urge was so strong that she looked away so as not to reveal her desire. Yet even as Yim cast down her eyes, she envisioned leading Honus to some quiet grove and engaging in lovemaking that would drown her fears in a flood of passion. Moreover, it would release her from Karm's task, for its fulfillment would be impossible. Yim wondered if the consequences of such a surrender would be so terrible. Recalling last night's vision, she doubted that birthing a child could prevent such slaughter.

When Yim glanced at Honus again, he was watching her thoughtfully. "Karmamatus," he said, "remember that evening after your vision at the pass? You would've given yourself to me if had I pressed you. The next morning, did you regret that I hadn't?"

The insight of Honus's question so surprised Yim that she was unable to reply. She simply stared at him in astonishment. Honus smiled ruefully, then lightly kissed her cheek. "I thought not."

In her heart, Yim knew that Honus was right. She would regret such weakness. Already, she felt guilty for having considered it. Yim sighed, and without another word, commenced walking down the road. Ironically, though Honus's remark made her check her impulse, it also made that impulse even stronger. She marveled at Honus's understanding. He seemed to know what she was thinking without a word on her part. Moreover, he hadn't thought of his desire, but lent her strength so she might deny him what he wanted most. She found his self-sacrifice utterly endearing, and once again, desire became exquisite torment.

Honus took his customary position in front until Yim asked him to walk beside her. Then he obeyed and matched his stride to Yim's. He said nothing until Yim asked him about his impressions of Devren's family.

"I'd say they're typical of this region," he replied. "The land's poor, and with so many mouths to feed, its folk are likewise."

"Was their warlike talk also typical?"

"No. That struck me as new. Folk who must pull their own plows are usually too worn down to seek a fight."

"So the priests have stirred them up. How?"

"I suspect by means more powerful than words," replied Honus.

"Sorcery?"

"Perhaps. Theodus and I encountered something similar before."

"Where?"

"In Lurwic."

"The place where Theodus fell?"

"Yes."

Yim felt the blood drain from her face as dread seized her. The idea that she had glimpsed her death suddenly didn't seem far-fetched at all. She caught Honus's alarmed expression and knew she couldn't keep silent about her vision. "Last night I saw all of Devren's family slaughtered," she said. "I died with them."

"I'm only a Sarf. Visions are matters for Bearers and Seers."

"They possess the learning to understand such things," said Yim. "I don't. Karm's supposed to tell me what man to bed so I might bear his child. What did my vision have to do with that? Why must I see my death?"

"Theodus said that Karm never reveals one's fate, so I don't believe you glimpsed your end."

"It seemed so real. I felt the blow. I feel it still."

"At Karvakken Pass, you thought you drowned in blood."

"So this vision of my death was equally unreal?"

"I hope so," said Honus.

"Then what did it mean?"

"I'm not fit to answer that."

"Then what would Theodus say? You spent years with him. Surely you must have some idea."

"I suppose he would have told you to ponder why you died in your vision," replied Honus. "Perhaps some answer lies there."

I died to save a child, thought Yim. As soon as she had

that thought, she felt a chill deep within. Her response had nothing to do with reason; it arose from a subtler form of understanding. Then she knew that no mattock would kill her. She would bear a child, and that child would seal her fate.

Honus had been trained to walk in front of his Bearer, performing the function of a human shield. Thus walking beside Yim on the road made him uneasy, and he made sure to walk on her right so that his sword arm was always free. Despite his unease, he liked walking beside Yim, for it allowed him to gaze at her. What he saw made him heartsore.

Honus recalled an impression of Yim that he had on their second day together. As they were trekking through Luvein, he momentarily thought he saw someone struggling under a terrible burden. After all that had happened, he was convinced that impression had been accurate. The only difference was that he had gained some idea of the nature of the burden and the woman who bore it. With that in mind, Honus marveled at Yim's humility, for he was certain that she was both holy and powerful. It perplexed him that Yim didn't seem to view herself as either. Rather, she sometimes acted as if she were still a slave. Certainly not his slave. *Karm's slave*, he thought.

Honus's musings made him love Yim all the more. He swore to himself that he would help Yim bear her burden, though it meant denying himself the intimacy he craved. *That must take another form*, he told himself. He had no delusions that it would be easy. It hadn't been so far. But he was a Sarf and trained for privation. He felt he would be able to restrain himself, though the thought of that restraint made him melancholy. It seemed his love would never be simple or painless.

Honus smiled at Yim in what he hoped would be a reassuring way, but she seemed preoccupied. They walked quietly for a long while before Yim spoke. "This is a fair, though a harsh place," she said. "Yet I fear I've glimpsed a menace that threatens all its folk. I grieve for them, but what can I do?"

"Only what you're able," replied Honus.

"But what's that?" Yim sighed. "I wish I knew."

The dirt road wound through a mountain valley, passing numerous poor farms along the way. Toward noon, the way began to slope downward. Ahead lay another range of peaks, their steep sides covered with trees. "Do those mountains belong to Clan Mucdoi?" asked Yim.

"No," said Honus, "but the lands beyond them do."

"Are they as bountiful as Devren's family believes?"

"Hardly. Winters are severe there and the ground is even stonier than here."

The valley twisted, and the road that Yim and Honus followed twisted along with it to reveal a meadow that contained a large, solitary tree. Under its shade, a group of men and boys had gathered. A man in a black robe was speaking to them. "Come," said Yim. "I wish to hear what he has to say."

Honus had become wary as soon as he spotted the priest. Yim's command heightened that wariness, but it never occurred to him to question it. He merely accompanied Yim, alert for any threat and prepared to respond to it. As they neared the group, none within it paid them the slightest attention; everyone seemed focused entirely on the speaker. The dark priest seemed equally focused on his audience, so that Yim and Honus's approach was unnoticed. They halted only when the priest's words were audible.

". . . real good dirt. Just throw seeds on it and up come crops. It oughta be yers. Aye, they stole it, them thievin' Clan Mucdoi."

"He's not very eloquent," whispered Yim.

Honus agreed, but the priest's audience appeared enthralled by what he said. Every man and boy stared at the black-robed one with rapt attention. Many seemed roused by him, for they were red-faced with their hands clinched into fists.

"So what ye're gonna do?" asked the priest. "Be like women? Let Mucdoi get away with it?"

"He inflames them with his eyes," whispered Yim. "He's good, too."

After Yim's remark, Honus observed how the priest gazed at his audience, staring at a man or boy awhile, then shifting his gaze to another. Although the priest had not glanced in his direction, Honus caught some of the intensity of the man's gaze and sensed its power. The priest continued goading the assembly, and as he did, his eyes lingered longer on those who were the most agitated. Finally he cried out, "What do them Mucdoi deserve? What?"

"Death!" yelled a barefoot, shirtless man in tattered plaids.

"Kill them!" cried a boy.

Then Yim surprised Honus by striding toward the crowd, forcing him to keep apace with her. "Stop speaking lies!" she shouted.

The crowd turned to look in Yim's direction, and Honus heard angry muttering among them. The priest also gazed at Yim and locked his baleful eyes on her. Yim stared back, and Honus had the impression that the two were engaged in a silent struggle. Then the black-robed man's expression slackened, though he seemed unable to glance away. Yim spoke to him in a normal voice. "Have you ever visited the lands you speak of?"

"Aye," replied the priest in a low, meek voice.

"Describe them," said Yim. "Speak loud enough for all to hear."

" 'Tis poor land," shouted the priest. "Stony and cold."

"Then why send these folk to take it?"

"So they might slay and be slain."

"What does your master truly want?" asked Yim.

"Death," replied the priest in a quiet voice.

"Louder. All must hear."

"Death!" shouted the priest.

"Whose?"

"Anyone's. Dolbane. Mucdoi. It matters not."

Yim looked away, releasing the priest. He continued to gaze at her in astonishment as Yim walked closer to the men and boys. Their expressions resembled those of folk awakening from evil dreams. Gradually, wonder settled on their faces as they regarded Yim. "The priest spoke truly," she said. "This war is a fool's quest where death's the prize. Choose peace instead and go home."

The crowd began to quietly disperse, but a few men lingered. They were those who had been most firmly in the priest's power. One advanced toward him and raised a heavy stick. "This dog would have tricked me to my death."

"Spare him," said Yim. "He deluded you, but he was also deluded."

The man lowered his stick and left with the others. Then Yim regarded the priest. "I've faced your master before," she said. "The Devourer is as eager for your death as those you were swaying. Look me in the eye and see truth."

To Honus's amazement, the priest meekly obeyed. Soon tears welled in his eyes. "Forgive me." He began to sob. "I only wanted . . . wanted something more . . ."

For the first time, Honus noted that the priest's black robe was threadbare and tattered and his sandals were falling apart. The man's face was young, but it seemed worn.

"Nightmares haunt your waking life," said Yim. "You live cut off from human kindness. You're slave to a god of hate and slaughter. Is this what you wanted?"

The priest's sobs began to rack his body like hard blows, and it took a while before he could reply. When his sobs finally diminished to gasps, he was able to slip a "nay" between them.

"Then forsake your wicked path," said Yim. "If you choose peace and life, I'll bless you."

The man dropped to his knees and bowed his head. "Bless me, Mother."

Yim walked over to him and gently laid her fingers upon his forehead. "I forgive and bless you. Go forth and honor the goddess through your goodness."

The priest regarded Yim with such devotion that Honus was touched by his expression. Yim seemed somewhat embarrassed by it, though she returned the man's smile before she headed for the road. "Come, Honus," she said. "We should resume our journey."

Honus was about to follow when he gave one last glance at the kneeling priest. He was still beaming at Yim when his eyes suddenly changed. The transformation was so dramatic that Honus felt he was not looking at the same face. It had become the image of malevolence and rage. The eyes, in particular, were terrifying. They projected malice that, even glimpsed sideways, tore at Honus's sanity. Sensing the peril in that gaze, Honus quickly looked away.

As he did, he caught a flicker of movement. Honus whirled, and saw the priest spring up. He was bounding toward Yim grasping a dagger. Its blade was stained with poison. Honus unsheathed his sword in an instant and severed the man's head. The sound of that decapitation alerted Yim. She turned to see a headless body that spouted blood as it advanced toward her. It swung the blade as purposefully as if a brain still directed it.

Honus's sword flashed again, and the dagger fell to the ground with a hand still gripping it. The dead man continued to advance on Yim, swinging his stump as though it still held a weapon. Yim didn't retreat from the approaching horror. Instead, she stared at the ground behind it. She seemed transfixed and unaware of her surroundings. With a flying kick, Honus sent the body sprawling on the ground, where it finally assumed the stillness of a corpse. Yim didn't move at all.

Honus followed Yim's gaze and saw that she was staring

at the severed head. The head was staring back with eyes that not only betrayed consciousness but also power and malice. There was nothing human about that look, and Honus realized that the earlier contest between the priest and Yim was trivial compared to the ongoing one. He was certain that Yim was fighting for her soul and the outcome was far from assured.

An otherworldly chill settled on the meadow as the silent struggle continued. Yim remained frozen in place as the color gradually left her face. Her lips darkened, acquiring a grayish blue hue. She began to wobble slightly, and Honus feared that she was succumbing to her malign opponent. Honus backed away, sensing the deadliness of the eyes that held Yim. It wasn't until he was completely behind the severed head that he rushed forward and kicked it with all his might. It went flying in a high arc. Falling upon a limestone outcropping, the head smashed apart like a melon.

Yim collapsed, and when Honus rushed over to her, her eyelids were fluttering. Honus kissed her icy lips, lifted her so she was sitting up, and embraced her. Yim's breathing was shallow, and it was a long moment before she returned Honus's embrace.

When she recovered further, Honus asked, "What just happened?"

"I was foolish," replied Yim. "I probed the priest's mind too deeply, and alerted his master." She rose shakily to her feet. "We must leave this road and take another route to Cara's. Honus, find some way that's wild and seldom traveled."

"I know of such a path. It'll be a hard one."

"No matter," replied Yim. "Today I challenged Death, and it'll be looking for me."

SEVENTEEN

As in most of Averen, it was but a short distance from farms and roads to the wild. Honus headed toward a north-facing slope, and soon he and Yim were struggling up its steep, rocky side. Scrubby trees hid them from view, and they saw no sign of humanity. "How fast must we go?" asked Honus. "Do you fear pursuit?"

"I doubt anyone will trail us," replied Yim. "But all the black priests will be on the watch, and they'll turn folk against us like they did in Vinden."

"Then I'll try to avoid people," said Honus. "It should be easy enough on the way we're headed." He slowed his pace and was mindful as he chose their route that Yim bore a heavy pack and had lost her sandals. However, there was no easy way up the steep slope, and the climb eventually had Yim sweating and panting. When they stopped to rest, Honus started to rummage through the pack.

"What are you doing?" asked Yim.

"I'm going to don my chain mail," he said. "You needn't carry it."

"Leave it be. I won't have you tiring yourself. What use is a weary Sarf?"

"Karmamatus . . ."

"Honus, our grain sack's nearly empty. After we travel farther, I intend to laze about while you hunt me up a feast."

"I'll try, but game can be hard to come by."

"What? Will there be no fallen logs?" Yim grinned and

licked her lips. "Surely, they'll be full of wood grubs." She laughed when Honus blanched.

He quickly changed the subject. "When you spoke to that priest, you said you had faced the Devourer before. When?"

"On the night I became your Bearer. Also at Karvakken Pass. But I wasn't certain it was the Devourer until I probed that priest today."

Honus regarded Yim with awe. She caught his look and rolled her eyes. "Oh, stop it, Honus!"

"I'm just . . ." Honus looked elsewhere. ". . . just surprised. I've never heard of anyone facing the Devourer, not in all my years at the temple."

"I guess I'm just lucky," replied Yim in a wry tone.

"And the Devourer wants death?"

"It craves it," replied Yim.

"Yet it bestows power to its followers."

"True, but to what end does it bestow that power? Look at Lord Bahl. He doesn't conquer; he destroys. His master wants only death."

"Why?"

"I don't know the answer," said Yim. "Neither did the priest, or at least, he was restrained from revealing it."

"So when I slew him, I also pleased his god," said Honus. He shook his head. "What kind of god is that?"

" 'God' is but a word," said Yim, "and men are careless how they use it."

"God or no, how can such a thing be fought?"

Yim sighed. "I'm not sure it's possible."

Yim and Honus slowly made their way up the slope, pausing frequently. By early afternoon, they reached the winding ridgeline that comprised the mountain's summit. From there, they could view the land beyond. Another mountain ridge lay so close that Yim could make out individual trees upon its slope. Between the two ridges was a steep-sided and narrow valley. It looked like the sun would reach its floor only while it was directly overhead, and already most of the valley was shaded by the adjacent mountain. From where Yim stood, all she could see were trees and a long lake, its shadowed surface as blue-black as the night sky.

"That place seems far from the beaten track," said Yim, surveying the wild terrain.

"It is," replied Honus, "and I don't gladly take you there."

"We walked through Luvein. This place looks scarcely wilder."

"See that lake?" said Honus. "It lies in Faerie. Even in daytime, its surface reflects starlight."

Yim gazed at the lake with curiosity. She could see no stars twinkling on its dark surface. "Have you seen this yourself, or are you repeating old tales?"

"Not all old tales are false."

"So the starlight's only hearsay," said Yim. "Besides, at Devren's hut they said Faerie lies close to Cara's hall."

"There's more than one dell in Averen where the Ancient Folk still linger, and mortals best stay clear of them."

"And this valley's such a place?"

"In part," said Honus. "I certainly wouldn't venture near that lake."

Yim smiled slightly. "Why? Because of faeries? I've heard tales also. They're tiny folk with dragonfly wings. Mischievous, perhaps, but certainly not perilous."

"Do you have faerie dells in the Cloud Mountains?"

"No," admitted Yim.

"Well they do in Averen, and here tales differ. No tiny sprites dwell in such places, but creatures with little love for our kind."

"How so?"

"If you were present at the world's beginning, would you be pleased with what we've done to it?"

Yim thought of Luvein. "I guess not."

"So we'll follow this ridge west awhile, and enter the valley farther from the lake."

When Yim and Honus finally descended into the valley, the way was steep but not overly long. They reached its shadowed floor by late afternoon. There, the woods seemed already wrapped in twilight. Upon her journey, Yim had passed through many forests, but the one in the valley seemed different from all of them. It took her a while before she decided why. *It's undisturbed*, she thought. The trees appeared ancient and the undergrowth beneath them was unmarked by pathways. The plant life was lush and the air was filled with birdsong and the sounds of creatures rustling among the leaves. There was a sacred quality to the place that made Yim decide against sending Honus out to hunt.

Honus found a game trail and was following its narrow, winding route when he suddenly halted. Yim peered around him and saw a girl of no more than eleven winters standing on the trail. She carried a bark basket filled with cattails and was strangely dressed in a short tunic made from the pelts of various small animals. Leaves and entire plants dangled from a cord that was tied around her waist—so many that they formed a kind of herbal skirt. Both the "skirt" and tunic ended high above the girl's knees, and her feet and long legs were bare.

Despite the girl's unusual garb, it was her face that seized Yim's attention. Her skin was as pale as moonlight and her long red hair was tied back. Both these things emphasized her eyes. They were the lightest shade of blue that Yim had ever seen. The girl gazed at Yim with none of the shyness common to children but with a look that was at once piercing and serene. It made the child seem wise, as did her knowing smile.

The girl paid no attention to Honus, walking past him to reach Yim. Then she knelt on the ground, set down her basket, and seized Yim's right hand with both of hers to kiss it. Only then did she speak. "Welcome, Mother. I'll lead you to food and shelter." She turned to glance at Honus. "He may come also." Then, taking up her basket, she rose and stepped from the trail.

The girl merged so silently into the undergrowth that, for a moment, Yim thought the child had vanished. Then she heard her voice again. "Come, Mother, you know it's safe." Yim, certain that the girl spoke truly, pushed her way into the undergrowth. Twigs snapped and leaves rustled as she followed her guide. Honus trailed behind, moving more quietly, but not matching the perfect silence of the girl. That silence discouraged speech, and Yim refrained from asking any questions.

Yim and Honus's guide took a long and convoluted route through the densest part of the forest, and it wasn't long before Yim lost her sense of direction. All she knew was that they were moving closer to the lake. Suddenly, the girl halted. If it wasn't for the smoke rising from a stone chimney, Yim might have missed the dwelling altogether. It resembled a hillock within the forest, topped by an ancient tree with tangled roots. Only upon closer examination was Yim able to spot a knee-high hole forming an entrance among those roots.

. "This is my home," said the girl. "Na metal may enter it." She gave a sharp glance to Honus. "Especially your killing stick."

When Honus seemed about to protest, Yim said, "Your sword stays outside. I'm in no danger here."

Honus looked perplexed, but he unstrapped his sword and leaned it against the pack, which Yim had unshouldered and set upon the ground. As he did this, a woman crawled out from the entrance to the hillock. Her hair was dazzling white, but her face looked neither young nor old. Like the girl, she was dressed in skins, but had no plants about her waist.

"Mama," said the girl, "Mother has finally come."

The woman immediately knelt and smiled radiantly. "Welcome, Mother. I'm Nyra. Your visit is a long-anticipated honor. Please come inside and rest."

The woman's greeting puzzled Yim, but she smiled and bowed. "Karm sees your generosity and we're grateful for your hospitality. But please call me Yim. My Sarf is Honus."

"Oh, 'Yim' will na do, Mother. Lila insists on proper naming."

"Lila?" said Yim.

"My daughter. She's faerie-kissed."

Yim understood the term as meaning "sunny-natured," and she wasn't sure it applied to the mysterious girl dressed in pelts and leaves. Nevertheless, she smiled pleasantly. "If it pleases you to call me such, then do." Then she followed Nyra toward the hole at the base of the hillock, thinking it looked more like the entrance to an animal's burrow than to a human dwelling. Before she crawled into the opening, Yim glanced back toward Honus. Lila stood behind him, gazing skyward. Yim looked upward also, and saw three large owls, each bearing something in its talons. They were swooping down toward the girl. Then Yim dropped to her hands and knees to crawl through the hole.

The short tunnel that Yim passed through sloped upward and was lined with wood that appeared smoothed by long use. It ended at a chamber that defied Yim's expectations. Instead of squatting in an earthen burrow, she stood in a cozy room with a flagstone floor, wood-paneled walls, and a large stone fireplace. Light came not only from a fire in the hearth, but also from numerous windows. They were covered with some translucent mineral resembling glass. Glancing about, Yim saw that everything was made from plants or other natural materials. A large, flat stone served as a table. It was only knee-high, for there were no chairs or benches. Upon it were wooden plates and bowls, drinking vessels made from gourds, knives chipped from stone, and other utensils made of bone or wood. Lining the walls were large baskets filled with acorns, nuts, faerie arrow and fox sword tubers, dried mushrooms, and other foodstuffs, but nothing that looked like it had been cultivated. Also about the walls were several low openings to adjoining chambers.

An ancient-looking man rose from where he had been stirring a series of clay pots that sat in the hearth. "This is my husband, Fenric," said Nyra. She turned to him. "Fenric, Mother has finally arrived."

Fenric bowed low. Though what little hair he had was the same shade as Lila's, he seemed far too old to be her father. His garb matched that of Averen men, being made of cloth. It seemed ancient and exceedingly worn.

Honus entered, and Yim was introducing him to Fenric when Lila crawled into the room. Along with her basket, she carried three freshly killed hares. Yim noted that they bore wounds from talons on their backs. The girl handed the hares to Fenric. "Here, Da. They're for the feast."

Fenric placed the hares on a board near the hearth and began to skin them using a flake of black, glassy stone. As he did so, Yim turned to Nyra. "You said I was expected."

"Aye, Mother. Lila's talked of little else since the end of winter."

"But how would she know?"

"She speaks to the Old Ones by the lake, as I did afore Fenric came."

"By the Old Ones, do you mean faeries?"

"Some call them that."

"And they know of me?"

"For ages and ages."

Yim felt as disconcerted as when the Seer had said that knowledge of her was "an old secret." She noted that Honus seemed to have the same reaction, and she felt it wisest to speak of something else. "Well, it's been ages and ages since I've eaten. Everything smells delicious. What's cooking in those pots?"

"Acorn porridge with herbs and honey," said Nyra,

pointing to one pot. She gestured to the others in turn. "Summer stew, faerie arrow with garlic scapes, mushroom soup, and this is hot water."

Lila gripped the rim of the water pot using scraps of pelts and emptied it into a wide crockery basin. Then she set the basin before a large rounded rock. "Sit here, Mother," she said pointing to the rock. As Yim sat down, the girl tested the water's temperature and added some of the leaves that hung from her waist. When she stirred them in, a fragrant mist arose. "Place your feet in the water," said Lila, "and I'll wash them."

"I can do that for myself," replied Yim.

"Please let me have that honor," said Lila.

"Only if you'll explain what's going on."

"Na here. Na now. Later."

"All right." Yim lifted her feet and placed them in the warm, herb-scented water. Initially she felt awkward as Lila washed the dirt from her feet and began to massage them. The girl's fingers were strong, and she used them skillfully to ease Yim's soreness. It seemed to Yim that Lila's hands spoke to her, acknowledging her hardships and offering relief. Yim relaxed, and her thoughts turned tranquil. After Lila lifted Yim's feet from the water and dried them using a cattail, she brought out a pair of sandals. "These are yours, Mother."

Yim put them on. After all the strange things that had happened that afternoon, she wasn't surprised that the sandals fit perfectly, down to the impression of her feet on the leather soles. They were oiled but not new, and when she looked down at them, she realized that one of the straps had been repaired. Yim took that sandal off, examined the strap, and recognized Foel's handiwork. "I kicked this off in the Yorvern River!"

Lila smiled, then whispered in Yim's ear. "A token from the Old Ones that you may look to them in times of need."

Yim stared at her sandal, wondering what form of magic

had restored her footwear and what other secrets Lila knew. The girl ignored Yim's amazement and joined her father in cooking the hares. Her mother stirred the other pots. No one spoke, but the silence had a peaceful air that gradually put Yim at ease again. The light coming in from the windows slowly faded, and when dinner was served, it was eaten by firelight. The food was delicious, and Lila and Nyra entertained their guests with stories of the forest and its creatures. Some of it sounded like gossip—a feud between the crows and owls; how a larcenous raccoon tricked a badger; and the laments of voles. They also spoke of the lineage of trees and the spring's surprises. But the topic of faeries never came up until Yim asked, "Does the lake really reflect starlight in the daytime?"

"Aye," said both mother and daughter.

"But the stars are in their old places and hard to recognize," added Lila.

"I'd forgotten that," said Nyra, mostly to herself. " 'Tis been a long time."

"And you meet faeries there?" asked Yim.

Lila silently raised a finger to her lips.

EIGHTEEN

IT WASN'T until the meal was over that Yim finally had a chance to speak privately with Lila. As the table was being cleared, the girl took the remains of the butchered hares outside. Shortly afterward, Yim followed her. When she emerged from the hillock, she saw Lila standing in the darkness with the ghostlike forms of owls feeding near her feet.

The birds remained put as Yim approached. The girl knelt briefly, then rose.

"What's happening here?" asked Yim.

"You're visiting friends."

"Friends I've never met before and who seem to know all about me."

"Na all," replied Lila.

"Then what?"

"That you're the Chosen."

Yim started at the word. "Who told you that? Honus?"

"Na him. 'Tis an old secret."

"I've heard that once before." Yim gazed at Lila. The child's pale skin made her seem ethereal in the dark—almost like a vision—and it didn't feel foolish turning to her for guidance. "What will happen to me?"

"You can na understand your life until the very end."

"Why?" asked Yim. "Earlier, you said you'd explain things."

"I can na explain what is na certain."

"That's babble," said Yim, not bothering to hide her frustration. "You know things, but say nothing."

"Do what's necessary."

Those words again! thought Yim. "I don't know what's necessary."

"You do," said Lila, her voice quiet yet assured. "You've always known."

Lila's reply was so similar to Karm's that it momentarily silenced Yim. Then, despairing of ever getting a direct answer, Yim asked something simple. "How old are you?"

"Twenty-three winters," replied Lila. "But I sleep through them and age slowly."

"You're older then me!"

"And my friends are far older still. Please do na be cross with them or me. We've told you all we know. The end approaches, but we do na know its nature."

Yim saw she was being told the truth. "I'm not angry,

Lila." She stroked the girl's cheek. "It's just that you seemed so knowing. I'd hoped . . . I don't know what I hoped. That you had some answers, I guess."

"You possess the answers, na I. But I can give you food, and speak to your lover about what route to take."

"He's not my lover."

"He loves you. And you him."

"Yes, but . . ." Yim sighed. "You probably already know."

"I do. 'Tis sad."

"It is."

Yim and Lila spoke a while longer, but about nothing of consequence. The girl wouldn't discuss the faeries, and she had given Yim what guidance she could. The owls finished their meal and flew off as Lila and Yim went inside. There, Nyra showed Yim and Honus their sleeping chamber. It lay beyond one of the low openings in the wall and resembled a snug, wooden-walled burrow. Its rounded walls and ceiling formed a space that was too low to stand in and just wide enough for two persons. A thick, soft layer of fragrant dried plants covered its wooden floor. Yim imagined Lila hibernating through the winter in that very place or a similar one. The idea seemed pleasant. She removed her newly recovered sandals, settled into Honus's arms, and fell asleep.

The next morning, Yim awoke to view hordes of mice scampering about the central room. She glanced at the stone table and saw that it was covered with fresh berries. The mice departed when Yim's hosts emerged from their sleeping chambers to invite her and Honus to a breakfast of berries, nuts, and herb-flavored water. Throughout the meal, Lila told more tales of the woods. Although he must have heard them before, Fenric seemed as enthralled as Yim by his daughter's stories. "Do you sleep through the winters also?" Yim asked him.

Fenric's eyes grew melancholy. "Nay. Lila and her mother do, so 'tis a lonely time for me. Only the kiss bestows long sleep, and only girls are kissed."

"This place looks old," said Honus to Nyra. "Have your folk lived here long?"

"Since beyond remembering," replied the woman. "The tree that grows above this house is but the latest of a long line." She gave the Sarf a stern look. "Do na speak ill of the Old Ones. They're wary and protect what they love, but they're na evil."

"Then why do folk fear their dells?" asked Honus.

"Because they should," said Lila. "People are heedless, and the Old Ones never forget." She turned to Yim. "But they love you, Mother. Remember that."

After Yim and Honus had eaten, Nyra gave them provisions for their journey, and then Lila led them from the forest. When she reached its border, a crow flew down and perched upon her shoulder. Then the girl spoke to Honus. "Karmamatus, this is Kwahku. He'll guide Mother to her friend's dwelling. Follow him and no unfriendly eyes will spy you. Anywhere he alights will be safe."

Honus seemed almost as surprised that Lila called him "Karmamatus" as he was to have a crow for a guide, but he said nothing. The crow flew off as the girl knelt before Yim and kissed her hand. "Many hopes go with you, Mother."

Before Yim could thank her, Lila rose and stepped into the undergrowth. Then she seemed to vanish. Kwahku, who had been circling above, gave a "caw" and began to fly northwestward. Honus and Yim followed him.

Throughout the day, Yim and Honus were guided by the crow. The bird would fly a distance—a short one in wooded places and a longer one over more open ground—before perching within view. Honus, with Yim close behind him, would make his way to the bird. As soon as they reached him, he would fly off again. Sometimes he circled high above, seeming to survey the territory ahead before choosing which way to go.

By this means, Yim and Honus traveled through valleys and over slopes without encountering a single soul. As dusk drew nigh, the bird led them to a perfect place to camp. The spot had running water nearby and was so hidden that having a fire didn't seem imprudent. Honus gathered wood and lit one. Afterward, Yim roasted tubers in its embers. When dinner was cooked, Kwahku landed next to Yim and she fed him as she ate.

Honus watched Yim with such reverence that she felt awkward and tried to steer his thoughts to more mundane matters. "Honus," she said, "when do you think we'll reach Cara's hall?"

"I've never followed a bird before. Perhaps you should ask our guide."

Yim stared into Kwahku's black eyes for a moment. "He says five days as the crow flies." Honus appeared awed until Yim laughed. "I'm *teasing*, Honus. You've been looking at me strangely all day. Stop acting so worshipful."

"Said by one who has faeries fetch her sandals."

"The girl did that, not I."

"After seeing what you did with that priest, it seems likely you could view a crow's thoughts."

"Well, I can't. I want to be treated like a woman, not a shrine. If you love me, you will." Yim puckered her lips. "You can start by kissing me."

Honus kissed Yim, but in a restrained way that left her dissatisfied. Later, when they lay down to sleep, Yim reflected on Honus's restraint. It depressed her. *But what should I expect? He must restrain himself.* Nevertheless, it bothered her that he could.

Kwahku led Yim and Honus for six days over a rugged route. The hardships of travel helped distract Yim from her desire for Honus, but it was always present—an ember hidden among ashes. Yim worried it might flare into indiscretion if she let down her guard. Certain that Honus was undergoing the same trial, she felt that love both united and divided them.

Not once in that entire time did they encounter another person, though they sometimes passed through settled places. Honus was often familiar with the terrain, but not always. One night they camped by a high waterfall that he had neither seen nor heard about. That evening, otters brought fresh-caught trout and laid them, still flopping, before the campfire. For a while, Yim worried that Honus would get his worshipful look again. He didn't, and she was glad.

Late in the afternoon of the sixth day, Yim and Honus crested a ridge and gazed upon a sizable lake nestled among the mountains. On a rise overlooking the far shore was a walled stronghold with a tiny village clustered around it. Beyond the village was a broad and disordered expanse of tents, makeshift shelters, and people camping in the open. From a distance, it resembled a blight that had spread over the surrounding fields. Smoke from its numerous fires smudged the sky. As Kwahku flew eastward and disappeared from sight, Honus pointed to the stronghold. "That's Cara's hall," he said.

The sight disheartened Yim. In her mind, Cara's home had seemed a refuge from hostility. Seeing it ringed with people gave Yim pause. She had no idea why they were there. For all she knew, they might be a besieging mob. At the very least, they were likely refuges and fertile ground for the black priests to sow their lies.

Yim made no effort to hide her discouragement from Honus. "So that's where Cara lives," she said in a heavy voice. "It seems we must run a gauntlet to reach her."

NINETEEN

HONUS STUDIED the encampment surrounding the hall and village awhile before he spoke. "Things are less chaotic than they seem. Troops are bivouacked there, and I think folk have camped nearby for safety."

"Why?"

"I'm not certain. Most likely, war's begun."

Honus's words gave Yim a chill, and the sense of dread that she had felt throughout her journey increased. "But you think it's safe to walk through the encampment?"

"Probably," replied Honus, "but I'd rather be cautious. I know a less open way to the hall."

Yim took a deep breath. "Then let's go."

Honus led the way from the mountain ridge, heading for the eastern side of the lake. Despite Yim's initial apprehensions, they encountered no one for a while. At first, they walked down a forested slope that obviously had been tended as a woodlot. Stumps marked where trees had been chopped down, and Honus quickly found a pathway. He followed it to a dirt road that led toward the lake.

Before Honus and Yim reached the shoreline, the trees gave way to an open meadow. There they spied the first people they had seen in six days. They were three shepherds watching a flock of sheep. The men were sitting on the ground, but rose and bowed when they saw Yim.

"That's a good sign," said Yim. "Let's talk with them."

Honus led the way over to the men, who bowed again to Yim. "Greetings, Karmamatus," said a tall, curly-headed fellow. "You're a rare sight. Karm's servants have been scarce of late."

"Small wonder with what's about," said one of his companions. "You're a brave lass to take to the road, Sarf or nay."

"I've come to see your chieftain and her brother," replied Yim. "Are they at the hall?"

"Aye. Been there since shearing time," said the curly-haired man. "But you're lucky, for Cronin's leaving soon to fight."

"And we're going with him," said the second shepherd, "if our chieftain will give us leave."

"Pardon me, Karmamatus," said the third shepherd, "but is your Sarf Honus?"

"He is."

The man turned to his companions. "I told you he was!" Then he spoke to Honus. "You probably don't remember me, but I was with Cronin at Kambul. I'll never forget what you did there."

"It was a hard fight," said Honus.

"Hard? Cronin would be dead if na for you. And the rest of us with him. When you charged . . ."

Honus cut the man short. "My Bearer has urgent business in the hall, but I wonder about the folk surrounding it. Have the black priests mingled among them?"

"Those dogs!" said the man. He spat on the ground. "Cronin slays every one of them he finds. But they're a treacherous lot. 'Tis likely some have shucked their robes to spread their lies in secret."

Yim bowed to the men. "I'm heartened by your greeting and glad for your news. We should be off."

Honus immediately headed for the road, and Yim followed close behind him. "If spies are about," she said, "we should try to avoid their gaze. I don't wish to draw trouble to Cara."

"We won't," said Honus. "We'll arrive through a secret entrance."

Honus followed the road around the lake's eastern end until he reached a grove of trees upon its shore. There he left the pathway and found a place by the water's edge where dense undergrowth screened them from view. "We can wait here until dusk," he said.

Yim took off the pack and sat down. She was glad for the rest, but anxious about what lay ahead. Lila had told her that "the end approaches" and Yim's instincts confirmed it. *It'll begin in Cara's hall*, she thought. Parting the branches, she gazed across the water at her destination. From her closer viewpoint, the "stronghold" didn't look formidable. Its walls were short of two stories high and there were no towers or a keep. It was the smallness of the homes in the surrounding village that made the hall seem large. Viewed more objectively, it was a modest manor protected by an equally modest wall.

"How did you learn about the secret entrance?" asked Yim. "Have you visited here before?"

"Yes. Theodus and I came several times."

"Why? I thought Cronin and Cara lived in Bremven."

"Clan business often brought them here."

"Of course," said Yim. "Cara's clan chieftain."

"She wasn't chieftain until she attained her majority. Before then, a steward served."

Yim smiled and shook her head. "I still can't imagine her as a chieftain."

"Tonight, you won't need your imagination."

After the sun set, Honus and Yim left the grove and walked along the shoreline of the lake. Campfires glowed in the fields surrounding the hall and village, but the grounds near the lake were dark. As Yim and Honus drew nearer to the hall, the land beyond the beach rose up to form a long, sloping field that ended at the village's edge. Near the shore was the roofless ruin of a small stone hut, and Honus headed there. He entered the hut, and Yim followed him.

The hut's floor was made of stone. Honus pointed to the largest block, which was two paces long and half as wide. "That's the entrance to the passageway," he said. "I just hope I remember how to open it." He studied the rough stones forming the wall awhile before he grabbed one and tugged at it. The stone slipped out a palm's width before stopping. "This has to be done in the proper sequence," he said, before pulling on a second stone. After Honus tugged three more, Yim heard a dull, scraping sound beneath her feet. Honus walked over to the block and pushed its narrower edge with his foot. The stone pivoted on its center to reveal an opening.

Honus pushed the stones in the wall back into their original positions before he climbed down the opening. Yim heard him striking an iron with flint before a flame flared in the hole, and she could see him plainly. He was holding a torch that illuminated a stone-lined passageway. Iron rungs were set in one wall to form a ladder to the floor, which was covered with murky water that rose to Honus's knees. Honus called up. "Do you want to toss down the pack?"

"I can manage with it," said Yim. She climbed down to join Honus.

After Honus pushed the entrance stone back in place and reset the locking mechanism, he led the way up the narrow, dank passageway. "This dates back to the clan wars," he said, "but it's kept in repair."

Despite what Honus said, Yim found parts of the tunnel were crumbling, and even after they weren't treading through water, the footing was treacherous. It seemed to her that they walked a long distance before their way was barred by a stout oak door. The walls on either side of it had slots for shooting arrows, and a chain extended from a hole in the ceiling. Honus pulled the chain several times, then waited.

A long time passed before a voice called out the hole from which the chain dangled. "Who's there?"

"Honus and his Bearer, come to see the chieftain and her brother."

After Honus spoke, there was an even longer spell of silence before the oak door flew open and Cronin burst into the tunnel. "Honus!" he shouted, giving him a bear hug. Honus still held the burning torch, which prevented him from returning the hug, but he grinned broadly.

Only when Cronin released Honus did he seem to notice Yim. Then his expression turned both surprised and puzzled. "You said you were with your Bearer," he said to Honus.

"I am," replied Honus.

"But how can this be? She's your slave!"

"No more," replied Honus. "Yim's my master now. As to how this came to be, you should ask her."

Cronin glanced at Honus as if to confirm that he wasn't jesting. Then he bowed to Yim. "Pardon my confusion, Karmamatus."

"It's understandable," replied Yim. "Much has happened since we parted. Do you know the temple's been destroyed?"

"Aye, I heard and feared the worst for Honus. But now you've brought him here in the time of our greatest need. Surely, that's Karm's doing." Yim said nothing, so Cronin spoke. "Well, there's na point tarrying in this dank place. You must want food and drink. And Cara will be delighted to see you both. Come, Karmamatus, I'll show the way."

A small room lay beyond the oak door. When Yim followed Cronin into it, she discovered it was also the bottom of a shaft. Two bowmen stood in it, but they had put away their arrows. Attached to the wall was a wooden ladder, which Yim and the others ascended.

Yim found herself in what appeared to be a small subterranean storeroom, for it was windowless and piled with various goods. Cronin led her and Honus through a succession of such rooms until he reached a set of rough wooden stairs.

They climbed these and entered a pantry. Beyond it was a kitchen, its table piled high with dirty pots and bustling with activity.

Cronin turned to Yim and said, " 'Tis na the grandest of entrances, Karmamatus, but you've come by the back way."

"I'm glad to have come here by any way I could, and please call me Yim."

"You've risen in the world," said Cronin. "I did na wish you to think that I had na noticed."

"She hasn't risen," said Honus, "for she was always holy. But now that holiness has been revealed."

Yim saw Cronin cast Honus a questioning look that quickly disappeared from his face. When he regarded her again, he smiled graciously. "The evening meal is in progress. Would you honor us with your presence, or would you rather refresh yourself before supping?"

"We've traveled hard and look it," replied Yim, "but we'd be glad to dine among friends."

"Then we'd be glad, too," said Cronin. He led the way out of the kitchen into a long room that appeared to be an entrance hall. It had a high ceiling, wood-paneled walls containing several doorways, and a flagstone floor. A pair of large double doors, bolted for the night, lay at the far end. They faced a broad but short stairway leading to another set of double doors carved with hunting scenes. Those doors were open, and beyond them was a banquet hall.

Cronin escorted them there. A meal was in progress, and though most of the hall was empty, the head table was crowded with about a dozen diners. It was raised, and Yim could see Cara seated at its center in a thronelike wooden chair with a high back. The place to her right—Yim assumed that it was Cronin's—was vacant. Cara was the only woman at the table. Yim remembered many of the men there from her stay at the Bridge Inn. *Army officers*, she thought.

Yim's gaze returned to Cara, who had yet to see her. Her friend seemed transformed, at least in appearance. Upon her head was a thin gold circlet. She wore a gray-green gown with a square low-cut neckline and a sash of dark green plaid that was pinned at the shoulder by a brooch in the shape of a tree. Like the circlet, it was golden. Cara's demeanor matched her regal attire. When Yim thought of Cara's face, she recalled it as animated and often impish. Yet the woman at the table appeared dignified and even grave, indeed a chieftain. Yim felt somewhat disappointed.

Cronin preceded Yim up the stairway, and announced in a loud voice, "We are honored tonight by a visit from one of Karm's Bearers, Yim, and her Sarf, Honus."

Cara looked up, and all of her former animation briefly passed over her features. She was in turn surprised, delighted, puzzled, and curious. Then she forced her expression into a semblance of gravity, though she grinned too broadly to seem genuinely grave as she rose and bowed. "Welcome, Karmamatus. You honor us."

Yim returned the bow. "Karm sees your generosity, and we're grateful for your hospitality." It felt strange to speak formally when she wanted to rush up to Cara and hug her, but she sensed formality suited the occasion best.

Cara turned to both her left and right, addressing those who sat there. "Please make places for my guests. They've been much on my mind, and I wish them close."

Only Cara had a chair; the others at the table sat on two long benches, so her guests simply slid down them to make spaces. Most did so graciously, but Yim noted that the middle-aged man to Cara's right seemed annoyed to lose his place. As she made this observation, Honus whispered in her ear. "Call Cara 'Clan Mother,' that's how the Urkzimdi address their chieftain."

When Yim approached the head table, Cara gestured to her right. "Please take the place of honor, Karmamatus."

"Thank you, Clan Mother, but please call me Yim."

"All right, Yim." Cara's eyes twinkled from a suppressed smile. "And you must call me Cara."

When Yim sat down, Cara tightly gripped her hand. "It's good to see you. When I heard about the temple, I feared . . . But what does that matter now? Look at you! A Bearer! And Honus . . ." Cara gazed at him as he took the place to her left, and for a moment she was at a loss for words. She studied him, then turned to study Yim, who felt her face redden as she was being scrutinized. "Zounds!" she exclaimed at last. "You've both changed, and I thought *my* life was eventful." She clapped her hands. "Food and drink for our honored guests." As servants scurried forth with both, Cara said, "You popped in unexpectedly and caught us as we truly live these days, eating porridge and drinking watered ale. Tomorrow we shall feast you properly. By Karm, it'll be good to make merry, or at least pretend to. And while you dine on tonight's poor fare, I'll have a place readied for you." She lowered her voice to an intimate tone. "Well, Yim, will you be needing two beds . . . or one?"

"Two," replied Yim in an even lower voice, "in separate rooms."

Cara appeared disappointed by Yim's reply, but she quickly perked up. "Well, then we can talk all night!"

Yim suspected that Cara wasn't exaggerating.

TWENTY

CARA WASN'T exaggerating about the humbleness of the repast. The main course was porridge mixed with bits of mutton and diced roots. There was also roasted whiteroot and loaves of brown bread, both in quantities that added more variety than substance to the meal. The ale was heavily watered, and the diners were sober in fact as well as demeanor. But Yim guessed that the quality of the food and drink weren't the cause of the table's subdued atmosphere. The mood reminded her of the meal at the Bridge Inn on the night Cronin had told his officers that they were returning home to defend it from invasion.

Yim gazed about the hall as she ate. It was fairly large, but simple in construction and decoration. The walls were paneled with wood that had turned dark brown from smoke and age. A huge stone fireplace took up the center of one wall, but no fire burned in front of its blackened stones. Torches that resembled huge rushlights provided illumination. They were set around the wall in sconces and upon the table in iron holders. The high roof was supported by massive wooden trusses that were festooned with long garlands of flowers. Obviously relics from an earlier occasion, they were dried and brown.

The evening didn't seem fit for small talk, and Yim engaged in none. "Why is this place surrounded by folk living outdoors?"

"Brother has gathered all men who'll fight against Lord Bahl," said Cara. "Many were loath to leave their families because of the feuds, so they've brought them here. The others are folk who've fled from trouble. We provide for them as best we can."

"So feuds have broken out already?" asked Yim.

"Feuds and worse," said Cronin. "Mostly in the west. There, the clans squabble like roosters, all the while ignoring the advancing wolf. 'Tis madness!"

"This comes as no surprise," said Yim. "We've arrived from the east, where the black priests are also stirring trouble."

"Yim met up with one and . . ."

"Honus!" said Yim in a cautionary tone.

Honus immediately bowed his head. "Pardon me, Karmamatus."

Cronin looked at Honus, unable to hide the surprise upon his face. Yim caught the look and said, "I'll speak to you privately of what I've learned."

"There's na need for secrecy here," said Cronin. "Cara's clan mother, and Rodric's clan steward." He gestured to the middle-aged man who had surrendered his place at Cara's right. "The rest here are men who've fought beside me for many winters. Any counsel for me is counsel for us all."

"I've learned Lord Bahl is not your true enemy," said Yim.

Cronin's expression grew incredulous. "Then who is?"

"Bahl's master. The Devourer."

"A god? My enemy's a god?"

"Yes."

"And how can I fight a god?"

"You can't."

Cronin gazed at Yim with fierce eyes. "I make na claim to be holy. I can only use what sense I have. So mayhap what you say is true, and I can na defeat my foe." He slammed his ale goblet down on the table, spattering the brew everywhere. "But, by Karm, I'll try!" Then he rose from the table and strode toward the door.

Cara rose also. "Cronin!" she shouted with a tone of authority that Yim had never heard from her before. "Do na insult our guest!"

Cronin threw up his hands in a gesture that could have signified resignation, fury, apology, or defiance; Yim was unsure which. Whatever its meaning, Cronin didn't turn around as he left the room.

Cara sat down, looking angry. "I apologize for Brother's ill behavior."

"He spoke his heart," replied Yim. "That's not a bad thing in these times." She turned to Honus. "When you've eaten, go to him. Speak with him as you deem best. He needs your friendship."

Honus bowed his head, then quickly finished his porridge. Afterward, he rose to do Yim's bidding.

* * *

The clan hall proved overflowing with people, and many had noted Cronin's passage. They directed Honus to the wall that enclosed the hall. A wooden walkway ran behind its crenellated top. Honus climbed up to it and found Cronin pacing along its length, peering at the campfires in the dark. He turned at the sound of Honus's footsteps. "I thought she'd send you here."

"You sound displeased," replied Honus.

"I've suffered many blows. But to see you unmanned! 'Tis beyond abiding!"

"Is that what you think?"

"What else? The temple's been destroyed, so who invested Yim as your Bearer?"

"Karm herself."

Cronin gave a bitter laugh. "Why look so high to explain her hold on you? 'Twould be wiser to peer below your drawstring."

"Tread lightly, friend," said Honus. "You've not seen what I've seen."

"True enough, although her slave's tunic was revealing. I'm sure she's shown you . . ."

Honus seized Cronin's collar and jerked it until they were nose-to-nose. He glared at his friend for a moment, then just as suddenly released him and stepped back. "I'm sorry. That's not what Yim wanted."

"What *did* she want?" asked Cronin.

"For me to help you."

"Then why did she bring you here only to say there's na point fighting? What does she propose to do? Wait like lambs in a slaughter pen?"

"I lack Yim's wisdom. You should speak with her."

"She's just a pretty lass. What wisdom can she have?"

"Karm guides her. Of that I'm certain."

"And how did you come by that notion?"

"When we reached Bremven and found the temple destroyed, I gave Yim her freedom. As a favor to me, Commodus made her his ward. With Yim safe, I prepared to avenge the massacre by slaying the priests in the Black Temple. Yim stopped me."

"Stopped a Sarf? How could she do that?"

"That night, she forced the truth from Commodus and tracked me down in the temple's ruins. She said killing would displease the goddess. I mocked her and called her deluded. But when I peered into her eyes, she revealed her holiness to me."

"I think you gazed at your lover and found what hope had placed there."

"It wasn't like that at all," said Honus. "You know my powers of perception. And I was steeled for death, not seeking love."

"So what did you see?"

"Indescribable holiness."

"Indescribable?" said Cronin. "I give up. There's na talking to you."

"I've seen miracles, too. Deeds worthy of legendary Seers and Bearers."

"Like what?"

"She raised spirits. She made a black priest confess his lies and renounce his god." Honus lowered his voice to an awed whisper. "When I died, she restored my life."

Cronin simply stared at Honus, dumbfounded.

"Don't tell Yim I said that. She'll deny it."

"As well she might. Such tales are meant for fond ears only."

"She claimed she only sucked poison from my wound. But you know that doesn't work. Besides, I recall my death and resurrection, though she said it was but a dream."

Cronin sighed. "If you believe she's holy, then it does na matter what I think. Yet to replace Theodus with a timid lass . . ."

"She's not timid."

"She talks defeat. 'Tis a fool's counsel."

"So wisdom lies solely in fighting?"

"If one fights wisely," said Cronin. "Hope remains, but we must act soon. Bahl's already in the west and pressing at Averen's outskirts. Word has it he slaughters everyone except those who join him. Thus his army grows even as it ravages, and death breeds more death. But to come this way he must pass through Tor's Gate, and there we can make a stand."

"I've heard of the place," said Honus. "There's a stronghold there, but it's not mighty."

"I do na plan to defend the stronghold," said Cronin. " 'Tis Tor's Gate itself that will aid our cause—a notch between the mountains that squeezes a large force into a long thin one. Within its confines, Bahl's unskilled killers can na overwhelm us with their numbers. We can cut them down as they advance. Help me, Honus! We can prevail."

"Convince Yim, and I'll do her bidding."

"And if I can na convince her?"

"Her word will guide me, not your pleas."

"She must lend our cause your prowess and courage. Think on this: If we fail, Bahl's red-handed men will surely come for her, just as they came for Theodus. And though you'll defend her, she'll share his fate. You've seen it before. Do you want to see it again? Your Bearer torn apart before your eyes?"

Honus failed to answer, for he was reliving the horrific day that Theodus fell. He stared into the dark with tear-rimmed eyes as if he were viewing the carnage Cronin had evoked. Then the scene within his mind underwent an appalling change, and it wasn't Theodus whom the horde ripped apart, but Yim.

TWENTY-ONE

DINNER WAS long over when Honus returned to the banquet hall. Because the clan mother lingered at the table, the other diners did also. "Well, Honus," called out Cara, "did you calm my brother?"

Honus didn't reply at once, and Yim noted that his face was far from calm. Rather, she detected a mask forced on his features to hide the turbulence within. She was alarmed, but at a loss as to what to do. *If we were alone it'd be different*, she thought. But Yim was keenly aware that she had an audience that was watching her every move. She turned to Cara. "My Sarf and I have traveled long and hard, and it's taken a toll. If you would show us where we might rest, we'd be grateful."

Cara rose, and the others at the table rose also. "Good night, gentlemen," she said. "I'll see you tomorrow. Yim and Honus, you're under my special care. Please stay awhile."

The other diners dispersed, but Cara remained behind with Yim and Honus until she had them to herself. "Well, Honus, what did Brother say to you? You've never looked so upset, and you a Sarf. Zounds! What's the world coming to?"

Honus, having regained some of his composure, said, "He expressed concerns."

"Concerns!" said Cara. "Why, I'm sure he did. Zounds, Brother's concerns would overfill a valley. He went on about Yim, I'm certain of it. After what he said at dinner, you can na tell me otherwise. Men! Agree with them, or be called a fool!"

The tiniest of smiles briefly passed over Honus's lips. "I'd never be so rash as to disagree with you."

"Wise choice," said Cara. "We'll talk tomorrow. I've got to put Yim to bed. You, too. Now come." She started walking from the banquet hall, but kept talking without pause. "Yim says you're to have separate rooms. 'Tis a pity, but that's na my concern. So, Honus, you'll have your own room, except you'll have to share it—just na with Yim. It won't be fancy, for we're full up. More than full, with every relation you can imagine. And Brother's officers. A few strays, too. So, Honus, you'll sleep with Brother's serving man. And a third cousin from Karm-knows-where. But at least your room will be close to Yim's." Cara glanced at Yim, who had retrieved the pack from the entrance hall. "Yim, you'll share my bed."

"I couldn't do that!" said Yim.

"Of course you can! And you will. But you must bathe first and tell me what happened to your hair. Who chopped it off?"

"A Sarf," said Yim.

Cara shot Honus an outraged look. "Zounds, Honus! How could you?"

"It wasn't me," said Honus.

"Then who?"

"Ask Yim," replied Honus, "for I'm sure you will, regardless of what I say."

"I will then, and when . . ." Cara spotted a servant and went over to tell him to fetch a tub and hot water to her room. Distracted by the interruption, she started on a new topic upon her return. "Honus, you must talk to Brother about his plan. I'm na fool, I know its prospects are na so good. Brother knows it, too, but will na say it. But a little chance is bigger than none. Oh Karm, to think that . . . Oh, well, here's your room. Sleep tight, Honus. We'll talk about it more tomorrow."

"And where will Yim be sleeping?" asked Honus. "As her Sarf, I need to know."

"Why, in Dar's room, of course," replied Cara, pointing to the door at the end of the hallway. "I'm clan mother now, or have you forgotten?"

Honus smiled and bowed. "That would be impossible."

As soon as the two women were alone, Cara threw her arms around Yim and hugged her close. "Oh Yim, I thought I'd never see you or Honus again. And now that you're here, I'm happy and sad at once. I fear your visit may have doomed you."

"Danger's everywhere," said Yim, "so best to face it with friends. Already you've performed a wonder and cheered up Honus."

"After Brother did just the opposite. Well, Honus was always a brooder. You must know that for sure. But like most men, he can't ponder two things at once, so I just gave him more than he could handle."

"More than I can handle, too."

"Nay, na you. But enough of that. You're in *love*! And Honus is, too! I knew the moment I saw you two, so do na deny it. How truly wonderful! I'm so glad you heeded my advice. So, why separate rooms? Both of you can have this bed. I want you to have it. Who knows where we'll be soon. The Dark Path, most like. So why na grab what happiness you can?"

"You know why, Cara. I'm the Chosen."

"You mean you're still . . ."

"A virgin? Yes."

"Why? I see the way you look at Honus. And the way he looks at you. Why na tup him?"

"And abandon the goddess?"

"It seems to me that she's abandoned you. Why even think you can have a child? There's na time for it. I fear Bahl's fiends will be at our door long before nine moons pass."

"My path was set long ago, and I'll follow it as far as I can."

"But you *do* love Honus?"

"Yes, and it's torment! Every night I waver. And every night it gets harder to ignore my heart."

Cara gazed at Yim sadly and shook her head. "I do na understand you."

A knock on the door interrupted the two women. A voice from behind it said, "Clan Mother, we've brought the bath."

Cara had the servants enter. One carried a small copper tub, while others brought ewers of hot water, soap, and a drying cloth. Yim was glad for the interruption and suspected that Cara sensed her relief, for after the servants left, Cara didn't resume the previous conversation. Instead she asked if a Sarf had really chopped her hair.

"Yes," replied Yim, "but he was aiming for my neck."

"Zounds! And he missed? I thought Sarfs never missed."

"I was leaping into a river when he swung."

"Oh Holy Karm! What a life you've been leading! And where did you get that big scar on your back? That's new. So tell me all. Do na leave out a single thing."

"When you said we'd share a bed, I thought you'd let me sleep in it," said Yim. "I think instead you plan to keep me up all night. Can't I have a little rest? I'm not leaving tomorrow."

"When are you leaving?"

"I don't know. I have no plans. I'll stay until Karm directs me elsewhere, or you tire of me."

"I'll never do that," said Cara. "We'll grow old together." She quickly made the Sign of the Balance. "Karm willing." Then she bounced up and down like an overanxious child. "But zounds, Yim, *please* tell me *something*!"

While Yim washed, she began an abbreviated account of her adventures since she last saw Cara. She continued it after she changed into her old slave's tunic, which still served her as a nightgown, and climbed into bed beside her friend. Yim omitted a great deal in an attempt to seem as unremarkable as possible. She didn't speak of visions, raising spirits, the malign presence in the ruined temple, or her encounter with Lila. Since Yim had once used her powers to force truth from Cara, she did speak of doing the same to the Devourer's priest. However, Yim didn't describe the aftermath. She related the incident with Gatt as a series of combats in which Honus finally triumphed and won her heart.

For her part, Cara kept mostly silent, except for uttering "Zounds!" at dramatic moments and asking a few pertinent questions. She looked thoughtful throughout the narration, and Yim had little doubt that Cara was weighing everything she said and finding much missing.

Yim awoke alone. Sunlight was streaming through the room's tiny windows. By its angle Yim saw that she had slept late into the morning. She glanced about for her clothes and for the first time noticed that the room had once been a cottage. Its front door and some of its windows had been sealed up, but their outlines were still visible, and the ancient wooden floor was most worn around the former doorway. The room's fireplace was hearth-sized and still had pothooks. *Cara called this Dar's room*, thought Yim, suspecting it had been the clan founder's home. She imagined a long line of women living in the space, ruling a growing clan and adding to the cottage until it became a manor house.

Yim continued looking for her clothes, but could find only her sandals. A short-sleeved gown of finely woven wool lay next to them, making Yim think it was intended for her. The gown wasn't dark blue, the appropriate shade for a Bearer, but bluish-gray. Thus she donned the garment reluctantly, feeling that it diminished her standing. After Yim dressed, she opened the door and found a young woman waiting outside. The woman bowed immediately. "Good morning, Karmamatus. Clan Mother says I'm to serve you."

"I have a Sarf for that. Where is he?"

"Waiting for you, Karmamatus. Shall I take you to him?"

"Please. And what happened to my clothes?"

"They're being washed and mended, Karmamatus."

Yim was inclined to ask the servant to call her "Yim," but thought better of it. Cronin seemed to have questioned her sanctity at dinner, and she was currently dressed like an ordinary woman. The servant led Yim to a small room off the kitchen that seemed an informal dining area. Honus was seated but rose immediately when Yim entered. He bowed. "Good morning, Karmamatus."

Honus's formality bothered Yim until she gazed at his face. His loving look was stronger than ever. She had missed his closeness in the night, and she felt certain that he had missed her equally. "Did you sleep well, Honus?"

"The mattress was soft." Honus smiled wryly. "But the company was abundant." Then his voice turned wistful as he gazed into Yim's eyes. "Sleeping outdoors had greater charms."

Yim was about to agree, but said instead, "And greater temptations."

"Yes," said Honus, looking away. "Those also."

"Would Karmamatus like some porridge?" asked the serving woman.

"Yes, please," said Yim.

When the woman left, Yim spoke to Honus in a low voice. "What did Cronin say to you last night? I've seldom seen you in such a state."

"He didn't like what you said, so he was disinclined to believe your authority." Honus paused. "Last night, you said that one can't fight the Devourer. Before, you were only uncertain it was possible."

"Perhaps I spoke too strongly," said Yim. "However, I've begun to think that fighting is futile."

"But you're not certain?" said Honus, his tone betraying hopefulness.

Yim responded to Honus's tone rather than his question. "What went on between you?"

"Cronin has a plan. Perhaps you should hear it."

"It wasn't talk of strategy that left you devastated."

"He spoke of what will happen if that strategy fails. If Bahl comes here, I know what will ensue. I've witnessed it firsthand."

Yim sighed. "He made you recall Theodus's death . . ." She gazed at Honus and saw his eyes begin to glisten. Then her voice became soft and sad. ". . . and imagine mine."

Honus nodded.

"Then I'll speak with Cronin about his plan and judge its wisdom."

Meanwhile, Cara strode through the fields surrounding the hall and village. Rodric, the clan steward, was at her side and two burly serving men followed close behind. Cara spotted what seemed to be a clump of rags amid the barley and headed in its direction.

"They're new this morning," she said to Rodric. As they approached, some of the rags rose and assumed human form. The oldest appeared to be a girl of not more than sixteen winters. Her brownish blond hair was as wild as windblown weeds. She was unshod, her clothes were tattered, and a babe suckled at her breast. A younger boy and girl, equally disheveled, clung to her. Two even younger children dozed at their feet. The girl with the babe regarded Cara with a stare that was nearly vacant except for fear.

"You can na abide among my crops," Cara said, taking care to keep her voice gentle. "Come, I'll take you to a better place."

The girl didn't move, which meant the others didn't move.

"You're safe now," said Cara. "Na one will harm you. Have you any food?"

At the word "food," the girl's eyes displayed some understanding, and she shook her head.

Cara turned to one of the serving men. "Thamus, a loaf." The man handed Cara a small round loaf of brown bread, and she broke off three pieces and handed them to the refugees before looking at the sleeping children. "Are they your kin?"

"Aye," said the oldest girl, her mouth stuffed with bread.

"Wake them, and I'll feed them, too. And when you're resettled, I'll give you more."

The girl knelt and shook the children awake. The youngest seemed only four winters. Her bare feet were so cracked and bleeding that Cara couldn't imagine how she made the journey. "Goden. Hommy. This lady has food fer ye."

Cara gave them bread, then spoke to the eldest girl. "What's your name, dear?"

"Gertha."

"Well, Gertha, did any men come with you?"

Gertha shook her head. "All slain," she said in a haunted, empty voice.

"By whom?"

"Dolbanes."

Cara looked at Rodric. "So now there's feuding in the east." Then she turned again to the girl. "Gertha, there's no feuding here. Anyone who fights is sent away. Anyone who slays is put to death. This is my law, and I see that it's enforced with no exceptions. Understand?"

The girl nodded.

Cara looked at the younger children. "Do you understand?"

They nodded also.

" 'Tis a hard law, but 'twill keep you safe. So no talk of vengeance. Now come with me, and we'll get you settled."

The ragged group picked up meager bundles that contained what few possessions they had, and followed Cara to a field where the ground had been packed hard by many feet. Cara tried to hide her discouragement as she gazed about. Want and desperation were all around her, and the newest arrivals were proving the neediest. She found a vacant spot of bare earth, handed out the remnants of the loaf, then said, "You can stay here. Gertha, see that tree? There's a barrel with drinking water there. Do you have bowls?"

Gertha shook her head.

"Well, you can get one there, but you'll have to share it among yourselves. I have servants by the tree. We're stretched thin, but you can turn to them for aid. This evening, they'll have porridge." Cara sighed. "I must go help others now. Are you all right?"

The girl nodded, but Cara doubted it. Nevertheless, she strode away to find other new arrivals. When Cara glanced back, the girl was still standing, looking lost as the other children clung to her as to a tree in a storm.

"Clan Mother," said Rodric, "this can na go on! More and more arrive each day. They trample our fields and eat our stores. You must be stern, and look first to your own."

"So what do you counsel?" asked Cara. "Send those children into the wild? Or should I be more merciful and drown them in the lake? Who knows when we'll stand before Karm and have our deeds weighed on her scales? Soon, most like. So think upon her judgment before you act."

"It's that girl who's swayed you from your duty."

"What girl?"

"The girl who claims to be a Bearer."

"Yim *is* a Bearer, and I'll na hear you say otherwise. As to where my duty lies, I'll be the judge of that."

Rodric fell silent. When Cara received word that there was a family in the field between the manor and the lake, she headed in that direction. The steward and the two serving men followed, so neither Cara nor they saw the rider who came down the northern road. Otherwise, they probably would have noted his arrival, for few were traveling unless need drove them. The man's horse was heavily laden, but he didn't have the look of a refugee, for his hard but handsome face showed no signs of privation. He appeared to be in his late middle age, and his cold gray eyes bore the satisfied look of one who had found what he was seeking.

TWENTY-TWO

DAIJEN WAS gladdened by the wretchedness about him as he made his way to the village. The Devourer benefited only from violent deaths, and the huddled refugees were like a field of ripened grain ready for scything. Daijen was pleased that some fool was feeding them. Starvation was too peaceful an end, one that cheated his master of anguished souls.

Since the village was tiny, Daijen had little difficulty finding its single inn, even though it lacked a sign. He wrinkled his nose at the sight of it, for it seemed little more than an overgrown hut. *A few crude rooms at most*, he thought, *and a place for peasants to swill.* He dismounted and entered the open door.

Inside the dark common room, he found an elderly man wiping a grimy tabletop with a rag that looked scarcely cleaner. "Good sir," said Daijen, putting on an Averen accent, "would you fetch the innkeep?"

The man rose from his task. "I'm him. What do you want?"

"A place to stay."

"So 'tis a room you're wanting?" The innkeeper smirked. "You and five dozen others. Well, we're three to a bed and full up at that. Our clan mother will let you sleep in a field. If you want a roof, you better have brought a tent with you."

"I know these are hard times," said Daijen. He dipped his hand into a purse that dangled from his belt. Afterward, he touched the table. When he did, his fingers made a metallic *snap* and left a gold coin behind.

The innkeeper's gaze went to the coin, although he said nothing.

"I have goods with me," continued Daijen. Another *snap*. "Goods I'd be foolish to leave in the open, or even in a tent." *Snap*.

Daijen never glanced at the three coins on the table. Instead, he regarded the innkeeper's face. When the man finally lifted his eyes from the gold on the sticky tabletop, they were met by Daijen's gaze. Daijen smiled. "In troubled times, a wise man looks out for himself. You strike me as wise. If so, I'll have a room all for myself, and each of these coins will have a companion."

"*Six* golds for a room?" said the old man, his voice shaky from the thought of it.

"I think that's fair. Do na you?"

"Aye, 'tis fair, sir."

"Call me Rangar," said Daijen, placing three more coins on the table. "I'm just a peddler."

The innkeeper quickly scooped the coins from sight. "And what's worth peddling when everything's so stirred up?"

"Daggers." Daijen smiled. "There are times when a good blade is worth your life, and I think those times are drawing nigh. Do you own one?"

"Nay, just a kitchen knife."

"One moment," said Daijen. "Perhaps we can do some further business." He left the inn and returned bearing two large leather saddlebags. By the way he carried them, they were obviously heavy. He laid them on the table, opened one, and withdrew a sheathed dagger. "This shall be yours if you assist me."

The innkeeper's eyes narrowed. "How?"

"Watch over my goods when I'm out, steer buyers my way, and apprise me about the local manor. It's there I'll most likely find my buyers."

The innkeeper drew the weapon from its sheath to admire its gleaming blade. "I'll do everything I can."

"Good. Then this day has brought good fortune to us both. Before you go and clear a room for me, I have a question. 'Tis my custom to gift some worthy person with a blade. It gains goodwill and helps display my wares. Whom would you suggest?"

"That's easy. Our clan mother, Lady Cara."

"A woman? Nay."

"Then her brother, Cronin."

"*General* Cronin?" Daijen shook his head.

"Rodric, then. He's clan steward, and used to run the manor afore Lady Cara returned."

So he's tumbled down a notch, thought Daijen. "Rodric sounds a perfect choice."

"My wife's nephew serves in the manor," said the innkeeper. " 'Twould be easy to give him a message for the steward."

"Your cunning gladdens me," said Daijen. "It bodes well for my endeavor."

"I'm glad to be of use, Rangar," replied the innkeeper as he felt the weight of the gold in his palm. "Very glad indeed."

Cara returned from her rounds among the refugees in a disheartened state. She directed Rodric to make an inventory of their stores, and then she went to speak to the cook about reducing the portions for all meals. She decided that feasting Yim and Honus's arrival would be too extravagant, but she did request a honey cake for the evening meal. That done, she returned to her room to change from her gown, which had been muddied while tramping the fields. There she found Yim seated on her bed.

"Why, Yim, what are you doing here? I thought you'd be out and about."

"I'm waiting for my clothes."

"What's wrong with that gown? 'Tis better than what you were wearing. Those clothes were filthy. Karm knows when you washed them last."

"I hadn't taken them off since . . ." Yim's expression took on a distant look that intrigued Cara. ". . . the day of Gatt's funeral pyre."

"That was half a moon ago. You mean you've been living in them all that time?"

"We traveled hard, and I lost my other outfit in the river."

"Well, I'll have another set made for you if I can get the proper shade of dye."

"Don't bother, Cara."

"Why? Is something going to happen? You have visions. What has Karm told you?"

"Nothing yet."

"But you know something. I'm certain of it."

"I think the end is drawing near."

Cara's face grew pale. "What end?"

"I don't know."

"Well, it certainly has na made you cheerful." Cara walked over to the head of the bed. A sword belt and sheathed sword hung there. Cara drew the weapon from its scabbard and assumed a fighting stance. "If the end's coming, I'm ready for it."

"Cara! When did you learn to use a sword?"

"I've yet to learn all the strokes and parries, but I will na go down without a fight." As Yim watched, Cara began attacking an imaginary opponent, slicing and thrusting while punctuating each move by shouting "ha!" or "die!" She was grinning when she finally sheathed the weapon.

"Cara, it doesn't feel good to actually kill a man."

"How would you know?" Then Cara's eyes widened. "Zounds! You slew someone! When? Where? Why did na you tell me last night?"

"I wanted some sleep. Remember?"

"Well, you're rested now. So tell me all about it."

After Yim related how she had stabbed her pursuer in the ravine, Cara looked puzzled. "He was going to kill you! Why feel sorry that he died?"

"I keep thinking there might have been another way."

"Yim, there was na other way, so stop torturing yourself. We're na always given a choice, and the day's coming when either our foes will live or us. You should talk with Brother and hear his plan."

"I've already told Honus that I would, and I will."

"Oh thank Karm!" said Cara. "Yim, I do na want to kill. I just want to live."

After Daijen was settled in his room, he decided to take a stroll. A survey of the hall, village, and lake further confirmed that the place was the one his master had shown him. At the moment, Daijen had no idea if Yim was there. It was possible that she had not yet arrived. *Perhaps she's already passed through*, he thought, hoping that wasn't the case. *I must find out without arousing notice.* He was well aware that Averen communities were places where everyone minded their neighbor's business. That was one reason why he had overpaid so extravagantly for his room; the innkeeper would keep mum about his good fortune for fear of provoking ill will.

Once Daijen determined Yim's whereabouts, he would have a second challenge: He needed to recruit assassins. The More Holy One hadn't reached his advanced age by performing his own dirty work. Even the most careful plans could encounter unanticipated twists. When things went wrong, Daijen always insured that others paid the price, not him. Cronin's practice of slaying priests had left Daijen short of resources, but the presence of refugees offered a solution. *All I need is a few desperate men.* Experience had taught him they were easiest to bend to his will. *Each day that they're hungry will make them more pliable.*

Though the task at hand didn't seem particularly difficult, the stakes involved made Daijen anxious. He needed only to glance at his body to realize the price of failure. He had yet to recover from the shock of aging thirty years in an instant. Although he looked less than half his true age, he still mourned his youthful form. Daijen blamed Yim for his reversal, and each time he felt an ache in his joints or a pretty girl ignored him, hatred flared within him. Accordingly, he prepared carefully for Yim's demise. The men he recruited would carry blades dipped in a special poison; one that not only guaranteed death but also insured that it would be excruciating.

Despite his venomous thoughts, Daijen seemed benign as he strolled leisurely about the field. Whenever he paused among the ragged men who had been driven from their homes, he appeared genuinely distressed by their circumstances. Sometimes, he was even moved to give them a few coins. If anyone noted that only the bigger and hardier men benefited from his generosity, they didn't remark on it.

When Cara saw Daijen, she was making her afternoon round among the refugees. She paid him no mind. There were so many strangers about that another one was easily overlooked, especially someone who didn't seem wanting. Moreover, Cara's attention was on Yim. Cara was intrigued by her friend's manner with the children. No one knew she was a Bearer, for she was still dressed in the blue-gray gown. Nonetheless, Yim possessed a quality that calmed even the most troubled child. Cara watched her, trying to decide whether it was the compassion in Yim's voice, the gentleness of her touch, the tenderness in her gaze, all three, or something else that had such a soothing effect. Whatever it was, Cara was glad to have Yim with her.

Daijen paid even less attention to the two women than they did to him. Focused on his particular needs, they held no interest for him. Since Cara wasn't dressed as clan mother, he assumed that she and her companion were merely servants on some errand. His only impression was of the shortness of Yim's hair, which Cara had trimmed to an equal length earlier that afternoon. Still, wishing to project a docile air, he smiled blandly at them before turning away.

As Daijen was returning to the inn, a man caught his eye. At first, there seemed nothing remarkable about him. He was as ragged as the others, though perhaps a little better fed. Then Daijen glanced toward the man's eyes, and felt a wave of relief approaching exultation. From that moment onward, he was certain his enterprise would succeed.

By the time the evening meal was served in the banquet hall, Yim was dressed as a Bearer again in her clean and newly mended clothes. The same small, select company sat at the high table; the rest of the household ate less formally elsewhere. The fare was unchanged also, with the exception of the honey cake. When Yim was seated, Cronin sat beside her and bowed his head low. "Karmamatus, I must apologize for my ill manner last night."

"I think you spoke honestly. I appreciate that."

"But I was overly ardent and did na explain my reasoning."

"You had no need. You command your troops. I have no sway over them."

"You have sway over Honus. In the past, Theodus lent him to our side. I have hope that you might do the same."

"You mean send him away on your campaign?"

"Aye, as Theodus did. 'Twould be but only for a little while."

The suggestion came as a shock, though Yim felt that she should have anticipated it. *Of course I'd stay here.* Nevertheless, even the idea of a separation was upsetting. Yim wondered if Cronin could see it in her face. Trying to make her voice sound casual, she replied. "I'd be pleased to hear your plans."

Cronin smiled. "Then we'll speak after dinner."

Yim tried to return his smile, but a sense of dread froze her lips.

TWENTY-THREE

THE ROOM was small, plain, and tucked under the eaves, so its ceiling sloped. It was furnished with shelves full of scrolls and a single table, which was currently covered with maps. Cronin used his rush candle to light oil lamps above the table. When there was sufficient illumination, he turned to Yim. "I have a temper," he said, "and I regret what I said last night. I'm a soldier with rough soldier's ways."

"But a good heart," said Yim. "Meeting you and Cara changed my life."

"I hope 'twas for the better." Cronin gave Yim a smile, but it was an uneasy one. "Are you sure you do na want Honus here?"

"This is between you and me. Please speak frankly."

"Then tell me this before I talk of tactics and battles: Will I be wasting my time? Last night you said I fight a god and victory's impossible."

"I believe you'll not be truly fighting Bahl, but his master—the Devourer."

"Then it seems to me that Bahl must be fighting Karm."

"That's likely true," said Yim, "but the goddess and the Devourer seek different things. Bahl's master craves death, and cares not who dies. I think that opposing such a foe with arms is like using oil to douse a fire."

"What you say has some sense to it," said Cronin. "If you claim that killing Bahl's men will please his god, I will na disagree. But think upon this: Killing one wolf saves many sheep. Bahl's men will never stop slaying until they're slain. They never tire. They're never sated. A sword can do Karm's work, otherwise she'd have na need for Sarfs."

"What did you say to Honus last night?" asked Yim. "Not that, I think."

"You're right. Honus knows all about Bahl's forces. How they outnumber us and fight on heedless of their wounds. Last night I told him there's but one place where we might overcome them, one place where the terrain favors us."

"Such talk would not leave him distraught." Yim looked Cronin squarely in the eye. "You evoked my death to win him to your cause."

"I did," said Cronin. "And I do na repent it. If we fail, there is na hope. You may flee all the way to Bremven, but 'twill only postpone death. Bahl will come there also. If you can na stop him, you can na escape him. Cara sees that. She's na holding back, but sending every man who's fit to fight."

"So I shouldn't hold Honus back either?"

"He wants to save you, and he can do that only by my side."

Yim lay awake as Cara slept. It was long after her meeting with Cronin, and long after Cara had given up trying to find out what Yim had decided. In truth, Yim was far from a decision; she had only promised to make one. Cronin had done his best to get her to commit Honus to the cause. Using maps, he had shown how a range of mountains worked as a funnel to force an advancing army through Tor's Gate. Yim had peered at the old maps so long that she could recall the shapes of the peaks drawn so carefully there in shades of colored ink.

The peaks had been labeled, as had the valleys, lakes, and rivers, but Yim remembered none of their names. She had been too busy imagining Honus marching through them. Marching away from her. Marching to . . . *What? Everything's so uncertain. If he goes with Cronin, will he be going to his death, or will staying here doom him?* Honus wanted her to live. She wanted him to live. *And what does Karm want?* That hadn't changed: Yim was supposed to bear a child. Yim wondered if Cara had been right and circumstances had made it impossible. *Perhaps the man who was supposed to father my child is dead.* Then again, perhaps the correct decision on Yim's part would save him. Yim could only speculate; she had no way of telling which course to take.

Yim's only hope lay in receiving a vision, and even that seemed a faint hope. Karm's messages were both sporadic and ambiguous. Yim suspected that she would have to make up her mind without guidance. Nevertheless, she resolved to put off making a choice until forced to do so, just in case Karm revealed her will. If Lila was right and the end was approaching, then the goddess had only a short time to express her wishes.

Deciding not to decide calmed Yim a bit, but it also allowed her thoughts to wander in other directions. They quickly focused on Honus. He had been upset to discover that she had been among the refugees with Cara. Yim could tell because he was especially respectful, calling her "Karmamatus" as he pointed out the dangers of venturing forth without a Sarf. "Remember the priest who attacked you?" Honus had asked. "He had a poisoned blade." Yim worried what would happen if she told Honus that he must go with

Cronin. She knew he would obey, but she was fearful of what that obedience would cost him. *And me.*

Yim was seized by the urge to creep into Honus's room and wake him. *What would I say?* The fact that two others were sharing his bed and she was sharing Cara's complicated the matter. It also made her aware that it wasn't conversation she desired. *I just want to be close to him.* Memories of sleeping on the ground, her body pressed against Honus's for warmth, filled her head. Want became need. Nevertheless, Yim fought her desire and remained with Cara.

When Yim finally drifted off to sleep, she dreamed of Honus. He was alone and walking down an empty road. It was nighttime and raining heavily. Honus bore a wooden staff, not a sword. Neither was he dressed as a Sarf. He wore filthy rags instead. Dirty cloths were wrapped about his hands and feet like bandages. A similar cloth had slipped from his face. Honus looked haggard. But his eyes were what disturbed Yim most. They seemed not to be gazing at the living world. They appeared empty and profoundly sad.

When sunlight filled the room, Yim awoke alone and haunted by her dream. Envisioning Honus worn and ragged on a lonely road aroused her compassion. She quickly dressed and hurried to the room off the kitchen. Honus wasn't there. The serving woman who had met Yim the previous morning was. "Where's my Sarf?" asked Yim, trying to sound calm and almost disinterested.

The serving woman bowed. "He said to tell you that he's studying maps."

Yim turned and left without a thought of breakfast. She found Honus alone in the room beneath the eaves. He was bent over one of Cronin's maps, his fingers tracing the contours of a mountain ridge. Honus straightened as soon as he saw Yim, then bowed his head. She rushed over to him before he could speak.

In her dream, Honus's tattooed cheeks had been furrowed with lines. Yim felt the need to erase that image by stroking Honus's face. Her fingertips glided over his smooth, firm skin, and then before she knew it, they guided his head toward hers. Their lips met, and Yim felt as she had on that night when she returned from the Dark Path. She kissed Honus, and the sensation was heightened by pent-up passion. Her feelings had urgency to them, like hunger or the need to breathe. Yim was certain that Honus felt the same.

Seizing Honus's hand, Yim guided it to her breast. He touched her through the fabric of her shirt. His fingers were gentle, exploring her contours before working their way to her nipple. It was rigid when he brushed it. While he touched her, he kissed her also. It felt wonderful, but it spurred Yim's desire rather than satisfied it. Yim's hand went up to her shirt to unfasten its buttons. When she had undone three, Honus's hand slipped past the opening. Then Yim felt the warmth of his fingers on her breast. She was amazed that so delicate a touch could have so strong an effect. A warm tingling was spreading through her, as if Honus's touch had lit a wildfire.

Then Yim heard the tread of boots upon floorboards. At the sound, she and Honus pulled apart. Before Yim could button her shirt, Cronin appeared in the doorway. Yim could feel her face flush red when Cronin saw her unbuttoned shirt and a ghost of a smile crept onto his lips. "You need na say your farewells yet," he said. "We will na leave for three days."

"I haven't reached my decision," said Yim. "I'm waiting for divine guidance."

Yim could see that Cronin was disappointed, although he did his best to hide it. "Of course, you're a Bearer."

"I will say yea or nay before the time comes, whether Karm sends me a sign or not."

Cronin bowed his head slightly. "That's all I can ask. Well, I'll leave you to yourselves."

Yim buttoned her shirt to the sound of Cronin's retreating footsteps before she looked at Honus. "I'm sorry. That was unfair to you."

"It was my fault," said Honus. "I should've been stronger."

"All I want . . ." Yim paused to wipe her eyes. "All I want is a happy ending." She smiled bitterly. "How foolish."

"Karmamatus . . ."

"What a silly name for me. 'Karm's beloved,' indeed! Oh, why did she pick me for this? I was just a little girl. No one special."

"You've become someone special," said Honus. "Cara spoke of how you calmed the children."

"Yet I can't calm myself. What am I to do, Honus? Time's running out, and I must decide."

"You'll decide, and your decision will be wise."

Yim smiled, unsurprised by Honus's confidence in her. Still, it made her feel somewhat better. "Well, I've decided to have some porridge. That is, if they'll serve slugabeds here."

Honus followed Yim to the room off the kitchen where they found Cara. "Good morning, Yim," she said in a perky voice. " 'Tis good to see you about after last night. A troubled mind makes for a restless sleep, and you were tossing and turning like a pup with fleas. But I've just the cure for troubles—an outing. Today, I deliver Dar's Gift."

Yim didn't know what Cara was talking about. "Wherever we go, Honus must accompany us."

"He can ride in the boat if you insist," said Cara. "But he must get off at the far shore, for na man may enter the dell."

"Boat?" said Yim, feeling uneasy at the prospect. "And what dell?"

"Cara intends to take you to Faerie," said Honus.

"Do na fret, Honus," said Cara. "Yim will be perfectly safe. I know. Do na ask me how, but I do, and that's the end of it. So *must* you truly come? There's nathing like a man to spoil a good conversation."

"That's up to Yim," said Honus. He turned to face her. "If I escort you to and from the boat, you should be safe otherwise."

Yim glanced at Cara, who bore such a pleading expression that it made her smile. "Honus, you may stay here if Cara promises not to drown me."

Cara grinned. "I swear you will na drown." She made the Sign of the Balance. "I've never drowned anyone yet, and I promise na to start today."

A while later, Cara, Yim, and Honus made their way to the lakeshore. Yim and Cara wore garlands of sky-blue asters in their hair, and Cara carried a basket containing a huge sphere of cheese. It was three hand-lengths in diameter, and its surface was golden brown with beeswax. There were several boats tied to the dock, but it was obvious which one they were going to take. It was a slender wooden vessel with two seats, a single pair of oars, and a curved prow and stern, both wrapped with cables of asters.

Cara helped Yim into her seat before climbing aboard herself. Then they were off, leaving Honus behind. Yim watched his form appear to grow ever smaller as Cara rowed farther into the lake. It was perfectly calm and each oar stroke left expanding sky-colored ringlets on the dark green water. Cara sighed. "'Tis so peaceful here." She sighed again as if to emphasize the point. "'Tis good to leave the world behind awhile. I used to come with Mother when she brought Dar's Gift. 'Twas always a special day."

"Now will you tell me what we're doing?" asked Yim. "You were so mysterious before."

"That's because 'tis mysterious business we're about. Na man may know, na even Brother." Cara pointed toward a gorge that split the mountains at the western end of the lake. "See that tree with leaves of gold?"

Yim glazed in the direction Cara pointed. The leaves on a single tree had turned bright yellow, making it stand out against the green forest. "Isn't it early for trees to turn color?"

"Na in Averen. Another moon may likely bring the first snow. But that tree always changes first, and it does so overnight. 'Tis the sign that Dar's Gift is due."

"Gift? To whom?"

"The Old Ones in the dell."

"You mean faeries?"

"Aye, faeries. When Dar settled here, she made a pact with them."

Yim was intrigued and knew that Cara would need little encouragement to tell the entire story. "Is this Dar Beard Chin you speak of?"

"Aye, but the beard was only a tattoo. She got it when she became an orc."

Yim smiled. "An orc? Do you mean a goblin?"

" 'Urkzimmuthi' is the proper name, but aye, she became an orc. Na on the outside, but in her spirit. She was a slave before that, like you. But she ran away and was the orcs' queen awhile. Then she came here with an Averen man named Sevren and a golden tree. It looked like my brooch, except my brooch is only gilt silver and hers was solid gold and as big as two hands.

"She and Sevren were seeking land, and this valley was all she could get. A chieftain traded it for her gold only because he believed the ground was cursed. And 'twas, for na one could live here. Folk tried, but they always left. Crops failed overnight, wolves took livestock, game fled, and 'twas worth your life to venture on the lake. But Dar had a vision from the world's mother . . ."

"Do you mean Karm?" asked Yim.

"Dar gave her the Orcish name, 'Muth la,' but I think she must have been Karm. Anyway, Dar went to the dell and spoke with the Old Ones. She promised to always respect the dell and send a gift to its keepers in token of her promise. So every year the clan mother brings a gift when the tree turns gold."

"Have you ever seen a faerie?" asked Yim.

"Nay, but I sense them watching in the dell. Do you have any metal on you?"

"No."

"Good, because they will na abide it, and 'tis perilous to anger them."

Yim gazed at the gorge in the distance. Steep rocky walls shaded its interior, so that it seemed like a sliver of twilight amid a sunny day. An eerie sight, it made Yim respect the woman who first ventured there alone when the valley was all wilderness. *And Cara's her heir*, thought Yim, seeing her in a new light.

Then Yim was seized by a sensation that she could only describe as "otherworldly." She sat in the boat while simultaneously rising aloft to peer down at herself from high above the lake. From that divine perspective, the boat looked tiny and fragile against the dark expanse of water. Nonetheless, Yim knew that she was totally secure and Cara would safely guide her through the unknown. Honus was visible also, left behind and standing on the shore. The moment passed, and Yim saw the world only from inside the boat. Nothing seemed to have changed, but with the certainty that comes from visions, Yim knew that she could let Honus go with Cronin and place her trust in Cara.

TWENTY-FOUR

As THE boat glided over the lake, Cara turned uncharacteristically quiet. The nearer they approached Faerie, the darker the lake became, as if it were bottomless or the evening sky lay beneath its surface. Ahead loomed a gorge where high walls of dark rock squeezed out the light. Cara rowed past the golden tree, its leaves blazing in the sunlight. As she did, a large white owl rose from its branches and flew toward the dell. Yim followed its form, a spot of brightness in the shadows, until it vanished from sight. At that moment, the boat glided from the sunlight into shade. Spruces flanked the waterway and the tall, somber trees enhanced the twilight mood of the place. The still water was a dark mirror. Cara pulled the oars only occasionally, so as to disturb it as little as possible.

The waterway narrowed into a stream, but a seemingly bottomless one. It twisted, and when Cara followed its bend, the sunlit lake was hidden from view. Then all was trees, water, and mossy rock illuminated by a sliver of sky. Yim peered at the water and saw stars reflected on its surface. Cara turned another bend and the waterway ended at a broad circular pool. Its shore was lined with rounded stones and boulders so covered with moss that Yim saw only shades of green. The boat's keel scraped against gravel, and the vessel halted.

"Take off your sandals," said Cara in a voice so hushed that it was scarcely more than a whisper. As Yim removed her footwear, Cara did the same and stepped from the boat. She grabbed the basket with the cheese and said in the same low voice, "Come with me."

Yim stepped into the water. It was icy cold. She followed Cara to the shore, where the mossy stones felt wonderfully soft beneath her feet. They also muffled her footsteps so the only sound she made was her breathing. The moss-covered stones formed a broad, irregular pathway that climbed deeper into the gorge. To Yim, it resembled an alpine brook turned fuzzy green and petrified. Cara climbed it slowly and solemnly, and Yim did the same.

Yim had no sense of time other than the impression that it passed at a different rate. Thus she couldn't tell if it was a short while or a very long one until Cara halted before a large, flat-topped boulder. Cara placed the sphere of cheese on its mossy surface, then knelt on the ground. Yim knelt also. Then Cara called out in a voice that seemed unnaturally loud in the silence. "Vertut Dargu-yat. Fer urak kala ur."

There was a soft sound like that of a breeze in the trees, and a dreamy calmness stole over Yim. Her eyelids grew heavy. She blinked, and the feeling left her. Yim glanced at Cara, who was gazing at her. "We're done here," whispered Cara, rising to her feet.

Yim rose, and when she did, she noticed that the cheese was gone. She followed Cara back to the boat and climbed aboard. Cara pushed the boat free from the gravel, climbed into her seat, and took up the oars. When they turned the bend and could see the lake again, it was sunset. Yim stared at the darkening sky in disbelief. "We were there only a short while."

"Mother used to say that time settles in the dell like sediment in a bottle. Whether 'tis true or nay I can na say, but things move slowly there. That's for sure. I think 'tis why 'tis so peaceful."

"I'm glad you brought me there," said Yim. "I feel like I measured my troubles against all of time. It made them look smaller."

"I hoped it would. I was only nine when Mother died. That year I rowed out alone when the tree turned golden, and in the dell my grief grew bearable at last."

"What did you say before the stone?"

"Those were urkzimmuthi words. They mean 'Remember Dar. She gives this gift.' When I say them, I think of how I'm kneeling on the same spot that Mother did, and Mother's mother did, and all the mothers going back to Dar."

Thinking of what Cara had faced and would face heightened Yim's compassion for her, and that feeling helped Yim resolve her mind. "Cara, I'm going to send Honus to fight beside your brother. I'll stay here and weather the storm with you."

"Yim, are you sure?"

"It feels like the hopeful thing to do."

"Well, you've certainly given *me* hope! I dreaded being left behind. I'll be as glad for your company as Brother will be for Honus's. And I really *do* think Brother's plan's our only chance. But oh my! You'll miss Honus so!" A romantic look crept onto Cara's face. "Would you like me to sleep elsewhere tonight?"

Yim sighed heavily. "No, you must stay put, and perhaps you should tie me up while you're at it."

"I've always wanted to be in love," said Cara. "I mean truly in love, like in the songs the bards sing. But zounds, now that I see what it's done to you, I'm na so sure." Then she grew quiet and put her back into the oars to bring the boat more swiftly to where Honus waited in the gathering gloom.

The banquet hall was draped with fresh garlands of asters and filled with people. All residing in the manor hall were there, along with many of the villagers. Upon the tables were cheeses resembling miniature versions of Dar's Gift. No one was seated, for the clan mother had not yet returned from the dell, and the hall was noisy with talk.

Rodric stood near the high table, showing one of Cronin's officers his new dagger. "So what do you think of it?" asked the steward.

The soldier took the weapon and balanced it in his hand. "I like its look. Na fancy hilt; all the value's in the blade." He felt its edge. "Good steel, well forged, and nicely sharpened. A fine tool for deadly work."

"I acquired it just today from a peddler named Rangar, an Averen man and an affable fellow. He has many more daggers like this one."

"How much is he asking for them?"

"Three silvers, and that includes a sheath and belt."

"A reasonable price. I'll pass the word about."

"Rangar's just arrived at the inn. I told him he was lucky to show up in time."

The officer cast the steward a sharp look. "Why did you tell him that? Did you say we're about to move out?"

Rodric's face paled. "Oh nay! I just said . . . Well, troubled times, you know."

"Aye, times when loose tongues cause mischief." The officer handed the dagger back to the steward. "Here's hoping you'll have na need for this."

Rodric was retreating from the officer just as Cara arrived. She was still crowned with flowers that looked as fresh as they had that morning. All the company noted that her companion also wore flowers in her hair. They seemed to shine like stars against her dark tresses. Rodric was appalled that Yim had received a distinction reserved for the clan mother or her eldest daughter. It made him recall how Rangar had told him that Yim stirred trouble wherever she went.

The steward considered relaying his concerns to the clan mother, but concluded there would be no point to it. *Cara's just a flighty lass*, he thought, *more readily swayed by the lies of a friend than the wisdom of an elder*. He feared what would happen after Cronin left. He watched as the clan mother approached her brother and had a private conversation. Whatever she said improved Cronin's spirits. Rodric wondered what it was and whether he'd ever find out. It galled him to be on the outside after so many years of governing the clan in Cara's name. He attempted to console himself by recalling that tradition required that a woman be chieftain. *But Cara's still young, and these are dangerous times*. He prayed to Karm that the clan would survive them.

The Gift Day Feast was a Clan Urkzimdi tradition that not even the threat of war could wholly dampen. In the inn, locals gathered in the common room for some revelry. Daijen avoided the festivities by staying in his room. As the drinking dragged on, he grew increasingly annoyed, for he wanted to venture out without being noticed, and he couldn't do that until the common room emptied. It was long past midnight when he finally had the opportunity to slip away.

The village was dark and quiet under a moonless sky and the campfires of the refugees had burned out or died to a few red embers. Daijen was only one shadow among many as he quietly made his way to the meeting place. He had chosen it, a roofless hut on the lakeshore that was close enough to reach but sufficiently out of sight. When Daijen neared the structure, it appeared as a black shape against the deep gray of the lake. He halted and listened. He could hear footsteps on a stone floor. Someone was pacing inside the hut.

Daijen approached it noiselessly, and whispered in the doorway. "When our lord comes, what shall wash the temple floor?"

"Blood," answered a whisper.

Daijen stepped into the hut and saw a dark shape move. "Come before me," he said. The shape approached and took the form of a man. Daijen reached out and touched the man's chest until he felt the pendant hidden beneath his shirt. It was in the form of a circle, the emblem of the Devourer. "You wear iron," said Daijen.

"Token of our god whose grace is power," intoned the priest.

Daijen revealed his medallion. It was iron also, but its elaborate silver chain was the emblem of his rank within the cult. "My name is Rangar," he said. "Know that I have been sent by the Most Holy Gorm himself and demand your full obedience."

The priest knelt before Daijen and kissed his hand. "I am Thromec, holy one. You shall command me in all things."

"First tell me why you're here."

"A dream has much troubled me. In it, I am our master. I peer from some dead meat and behold my enemy. Hate scalds me, and I crave this foe's destruction. Yet the vessel that contains me sees imperfectly. I perceive a face, but not its features. There is brownish darkness about it. Then everything vanishes and only hatred remains.

"Others of our brethren have also had this dream. We have spoken together and concluded that the darkness about the face is long dark hair, and our master was viewing a woman. Thus we seek out dark-haired women and slay them. I've killed seven already, yet the dream returns. I've ventured here in hope of finding the one our lord despises."

"And you've succeeded," replied Daijen. "I've learned today that she's staying in the hall. Her name is Yim, and she's a Bearer."

"Then we should kill her at once!" said Thromec.

"Her death must be certain," replied Daijen, "and certainty requires patience."

"Fie on patience! You haven't suffered my dream! It gnaws at me."

"I've suffered also," said Daijen, "and it has tutored me

to be thorough. I've an informant in the hall, a man I'm bending to my will. Already he has told me that the troops about this place will leave the day after tomorrow."

"Then I'll go and incite men to storm the hall. They could be here in seven or eight days."

"I see that assault as augmenting the more stealthy one I'm planning. This woman must die, and a double-pronged attack will assure success."

Thromec bowed. "I see why you've risen high. It's wisest to leave nothing to chance."

"Yes," said Daijen, rubbing his newly aged hands, "our lord brooks no failure."

TWENTY-FIVE

THE FESTIVE spirit of Gift Day didn't linger for long in a hall where men were preparing for a desperate battle. The following day, Cronin and his officers were busy getting ready for the march. Scouts were reporting back from reconnaissance. Emissaries from other clans came and went, a few bearing good tidings and most not. Refugees continued to arrive, and each carried news of feuds and strife. Bahl's invasion loomed as a threat that was yet invisible, but felt by everyone. It drove events and made each action seem urgent.

Cronin found his sister drilling with the arms master in the courtyard. They were using blunted swords to practice thrusts and parries. He noted that Cara's deficient form was partly compensated by her ferocity and that she was holding her own. Nevertheless, the master eventually disarmed her and held his blade against her neck.

Cronin called out in a jocular tone. "Arms Master, a private word with our clan mother before you cut her throat." Cronin's attempt at humor fell flat. It was too close to what he feared, and he regretted his words. After the arms master left, Cara came over to her brother. "I've reconsidered my plan," Cronin said. "Perhaps it'd be wiser to leave some men behind."

"I want to hold nothing back," said Cara.

"Bahl's not our only foe. The black priests have stirred our neighbors. If they know our hall's defended only by women . . ."

"Brother, this is my decision."

"So 'tis, but I can spare those men who'd slow the march—some of the older archers to man the wall, and those with lame legs, but strong arms. I'll fight better knowing you have some defenders." He attempted a smile. "You can na kill all our foes yourself."

"Nay," replied Cara. "For that, I'd need another fortnight of drill. You're right. A small garrison is a wise precaution."

"Then I'll see to it," said Cronin.

With that business done, they stood in the courtyard, not as general and clan mother, but as brother and sister. Both were aware that their positions would restrain their final farewells, and the present moment might be the last to speak their hearts. Yet there was so much to say that they found it difficult to say anything. Cara simply stared at her brother, as if trying to memorize every detail of his face. Cronin spoke first, his voice thickened by his feelings. "We've said goodbyes oft enough before, and I've always returned."

"Aye, 'tis true."

"If I do na this time . . ."

"You will! You must!"

"But if I do na, trust your judgment, Cara. You're wise beyond your years, and you've a noble heart. Mother would be proud."

For once, Cara was speechless, and it made her brother feel awkward. They gazed lovingly at each other until Cronin finally said, "Well, I must be off to confer with Honus about the campaign."

Cara watched him go. Then, wiping the tears from her eyes, she went to find the arms master and resume sword practice.

There was an art to swaying another to one's will, and long practice made Daijen adept at it. He didn't gaze into someone's eyes and force him or her to do his bidding. Although that tactic usually worked, the victim seldom performed satisfactorily. Daijen's method was subtler and more effective. He used his powers to discover weaknesses and employ them to spur the subject toward whatever action he desired. Gatt had fallen under Daijen's power because of his self-righteousness, anger, and lack of purpose. Rodric possessed different flaws, but they would make him no less useful.

Thus Daijen was pleased, but not surprised, when Rodric sought him out at the inn. He was sitting in the common room when the steward entered with an agitated expression on his face. Daijen noted that Rodric was wearing the dagger he had given him, which seemed a promising sign. The steward rushed over to him and whispered, "You were right!"

Daijen put on a concerned expression and replied in an equally low voice. "Shall we talk in my room?'

Rodric nodded and followed Daijen there. It was a small, inelegant space with rough plastered walls, a single unglazed window, and an earthen floor strewn with reeds. A bed and a chamber pot were its sole furnishings. The men sat on the bed and Rodric started talking in a burst of words. "Already she's been honored! Garlanded for the feast like a clan mother or her heir!"

"I presume you're speaking of Yim."

"Aye. And like you said, she's convinced everyone that she's a Bearer."

"Who would doubt her with that Sarf in tow," said Daijen. He shook his head sadly. "She's clever. Moreover, she's practiced this mischief before."

"Where?"

"I know of an instance among the Dolbanes," said Daijen. "She arrived at a holding as a paragon of piety and peace, befriending all and winning their trust. And when they were all beguiled, she loosed her confederates. The home was looted and the family slaughtered."

"But this place is na isolated holding," said Rodric.

Daijen gazed into the steward's eyes and nudged his thoughts in the direction he desired by enflaming Rodric's resentment while deepening his fear. "Nay," he said, "your clan hall is a far greater prize, and one with strangers camped about it."

Alarm spread over the steward's face. "I warned Clan Mother of this!"

"But she did na listen, I suppose," remarked Daijen. He sighed dramatically. "Young headstrong women are oft blind to peril." Then he added in a casual tone, "When she was feeding those beggars the other day, was that Yim with her?"

"Aye, 'twas. Clan Mother ignores me while Yim worms her way in ever deeper. Already, she sleeps in the clan mother's chamber."

"Mark my words. Soon Yim will have it to herself," said Daijen. "Your clan mother has been ensnared, just like that Sarf. There's little hope for her."

"You said little, but you did na say none."

"You can na counsel your chieftain from folly, for Yim's hold is too strong," said Daijen. "Yet Yim has gained her share of enemies. If they could reach her, the impostor would meet with justice." He shrugged. "But Yim's safe within your hall."

"These enemies," said Rodric. "Is their grievance solely against Yim?"

"Aye, only her."

"So they would na harm anyone else?"

"All they want is justice and to save others from Yim's schemes."

Rodric pondered the matter for a moment. "There's a hidden way into the hall."

"And you would show them its secret?"

"Nay, but I'd admit them so they might find whom they seek."

"The Urkzimdi are fortunate to have you as their steward, and when Yim's spell is broken, your clan mother will know this also."

"Then let's do this soon," said Rodric.

"I think Yim will grow less wary when the troops move out. That will be the time to strike."

Honus spent the day with Cronin and his staff, talking strategy and logistics. He had fought alongside the general before, so the role was a familiar one. Only he had faced Bahl in battle and every man was intent on what he said. It was grim talk; yet Honus saw hope in Cronin's plan, and he spent his time refining its details. It was late afternoon when the meeting finished and Honus went to find Yim.

Cara found him instead. "Honus, a word with you."

"Yes, Clan Mother. What do you wish?"

"Zounds, Honus, call me Cara. And what I wish is a private talk with you. Come." She led Honus to a dusty room beneath the eaves that was filled with chests and ancient furniture. The only open space was before a dormer and the two stood there. Its window offered a commanding view of the village and the fields beyond, which were currently filled with refugees. Cara gazed briefly at the scene, then hugged Honus tightly. "Oh, Honus! Take care of Brother. This time I'm really frightened for him."

"I would do that without your asking," replied Honus. "Now I'll be doubly vigilant."

"That's a nice turn of phrase. Quite elegant for you, Honus. I know you're saying that to make me feel better, and I guess it does. But do we have a chance, Honus? Tell me if there's any hope at all."

"Some. We're not marching to certain death. If the invasion's going to be stopped, Tor's Gate is the place to do it."

Cara sighed. "So Brother says. If you agree, then I'm sure he's right. But it feels so horrible being left behind to wait and hope. And I know Yim will be miserable with you away, but zounds, she's miserable with you here! If love makes you that unhappy, I'd rather forget all about it."

"Yim's different from other women," said Honus. "Karm has plans for her."

"I know," said Cara. "Zounds! Some plans! She told me about being the Chosen way back when we first met. I did na understand it then, and I do na understand it now."

"Some things are beyond our understanding."

"That's for sure!"

Honus grasped Cara's hand. "Protect her while I'm away. Yim has a destiny, and I believe her fate may overshadow all we do."

Cara regarded Honus's face. She always had the talent to see beneath his tattoos, and Honus had no doubt that she perceived the depth of his love. "I swear by Karm I'll watch over Yim," said Cara, making the Sign of the Balance. "She'll be like my sister."

"Then my heart shall rest easier."

Cara's gaze shifted to the field beyond the village. Another ragged band was traveling toward it. "More refugees! How will they ever make it through the winter? How will we?"

"I think our troubles will end before then," replied Honus. "Either for good or ill."

* * *

The meal in the banquet hall was subdued, and only the high table was occupied. Yim only vaguely remembered eating. If there was conversation, she didn't notice. Nor did she catch the way Rodric glared at her. Her attention was focused solely on Honus, who sat on the other side of Cara. All she could think about was that he'd soon be leaving. Moreover, she had an ominous feeling about their separation. She could foresee only loneliness. *I've been lonely nearly all my life*, she thought. *I can get used to it again.* Yet having tasted love, she feared that wasn't true.

Never had the urge to forsake Karm been so strong. She yearned to go away with Honus and consummate her desire. The idea was deliciously exciting. *We could go far from here, the Northern Reach or the Cloud Mountains.* Yim knew that all she needed to do was tell Honus they must depart. *He'll obey. He's my Sarf.* Yim wondered if Honus would see such a departure as Karm's will or recognize it as the product of desire. That question led to others: Could she hide from the goddess? Could she keep the truth from Honus? How would he regard her if he learned it? *If only I could decipher the words on his back!* It seemed a cruel irony that the answers could be so close and yet remain unknowable.

The meal concluded when Cara rose. She and the others left, but Yim and Honus lingered behind. "I should get my chain mail and extra clothes from the pack," said Honus.

"Of course," said Yim. "But who will bear your burden? Theodus said you never should."

"A soldier will carry my pack until I return."

"I'm jealous of him." Yim smiled wistfully. "At first, I hated that pack. I hated you."

"I gave you cause."

"That time I ran away, a woman nearly made me into sausage."

"And that improved your opinion of me?"

"A little bit. But it wasn't until . . ." Yim grew silent.

"Until what?"

"Until later when I . . . Oh, Honus, it's best you go with Cronin, but I can't bear the thought of it!"

Each rushed into the other's arms, where they embraced tightly and desperately. They stayed that way a long while, neither speaking, as if only touch could express their feelings. Then Yim whispered. "I can't kiss you because I won't be able to stop."

"That would make for an awkward march," said Honus.

Despite her sadness, Yim smiled at the thought of them marching off with locked lips to face Lord Bahl.

TWENTY-SIX

IT MIGHT have been dusk; Hendric couldn't tell. To his eyes, the days had grown darker until they blended with the nights. On those increasingly rare occasions when he was capable of thought, he wondered if he was marching on the Dark Path. It wasn't the lack of light that gave him that impression; it was his distance from life. He had stopped tasting food, longing for his family, or feeling pain. His severed fingers made his right hand useless, but he noticed only because it forced him to grip his sword with his left. That made killing more difficult, but he managed.

The horrific things that Hendric did no longer troubled him. He was detached from those he slaughtered. Men, women, and children had no more hold on him than the weeds he had plucked from his field in his former life. Their voices didn't reach him, and their suffering washed over him without leaving a trace. Hendric had become an empty vessel that only Bahl could fill, and the only brew he poured was hate.

As the world became darker to Hendric, Lord Bahl seemed to grow brighter. It wasn't truly light that Hendric sensed, for the radiance was invisible. However, he felt it as he used to feel the sun's heat on a cloudy day. He had no word for the brightness, but power or divinity came close. With each death, it grew stronger.

Mountains loomed ahead. They were marching into a place called Averen, though the name no longer possessed meaning for Hendric. He was aware of only one thing: The end was drawing near. He didn't know what would end—the war, his life, the world, or perhaps all three. But with what vestige of desire that Hendric still possessed, he wanted the end to come. And come soon.

The activity was hectic on the last day before the troops departed. Yim saw nothing of Honus after breakfast. Having given him over to the campaign, she spent the day helping pack provisions and joined Honus only during the final dinner. This was not held in the hall, but outside with all the troops. It resembled a feast in that sheep were roasted over fire pits and the ale wasn't watered, but the mood was somber. A table was brought out for the clan mother and the ranking guests, and they ate with the troops surrounding them.

Most of the soldiers were Urkzimdi men, although a few of the other clans had also provided fighters. Yim tried to count the soldiers, but it was dark, and she soon gave up. She guessed the total was somewhere in the hundreds, not the thousands. Cara rose early in the meal, grabbed an ale jug, and wandered among the men to refill their bowls. When the jug was emptied, she had another brought to her, so that she circulated among the soldiers through most of the feast. Cronin watched his sister's gesture with pride in his face, and when she returned at last to her cold food, he said, "Every man will remember how you honored him tonight."

Throughout the meal, Honus fixed his gaze beyond the circle of soldiers. Some men stood there, silhouettes in the fading light. Honus's eyes never left them, and by his alertness, Yim guessed that he found them suspicious. When Cara and her company rose to return to the hall, Honus stayed close by Yim's side. Once she was safely in the hall, he spoke to her. "Yim, will you do something for me?"

"Of course."

"Tomorrow when you wave farewell, do it from the wall. And afterward, please don't venture from its protection."

"You saw something at dinner, didn't you?" asked Yim.

"Does that surprise you?"

"What did you see?"

"Men who would do you harm."

"It was dark. How could you tell?"

"I'm a Sarf and can read a man's carriage."

Yim stroked Honus's face, certain of what he was thinking. "I'll stay safe, Honus. I'll be here when you return." Touching Honus quickly led to kissing him, and Yim had to fight her mounting passion to pull away. She stood gazing at him, her heart pounding. "You're my beloved. You always will be." Then, feeling that she was at the very edge of a precipice, she retreated. Yim backed away, turned, and ran to Cara's room. It was empty when she arrived. Yim threw herself onto the bed and burst out sobbing.

Sunrise found Yim peering over the manor wall at the troops assembled beyond the village. She had arisen before dawn only to discover that Honus had already joined the soldiers. Mindful of her promise not to venture beyond the walls, she didn't go to Honus; though she was sorely tempted to disregard his warning. *If I do that, it'll only add to his worries*, she thought. Thus she stared at the mass of men until there was enough light to discern the blue-clad figure among them. Honus looked tiny in the distance, yet once Yim spotted him she never looked elsewhere. She waved, and eventually he waved back.

Soon afterward, the troops marched off. Everyone in both the hall and village seemed turned out to see them go. Cara and the clan steward stood in the front of a throng that was mostly composed of women, children, and infirm men. The only hardy men comprised the garrison that Cronin left behind and those refugees who declined to fight. Yim noticed that a few of the latter were ignoring the soldiers and were watching her instead. Their gaze made her uneasy, and she worried that she had done Cara no favor in staying behind.

Yim watched the long line of men and pack animals slowly move up the northern road, pass between two low mountains, head westward, and disappear from view. Although Honus marched with Cronin at the column's head, Yim didn't descend from the wall until the last man was out of sight. By then, people were returning to the hall. The atmosphere was somber and anxious, but also chaotic, for Cara had invited many of the villagers to dwell within the safety of the walled manor. Thus there were weeping children and their harried mothers to contend with, as well as the sickly and infirm. Cara had her hands full directing the settling in of so many guests, and Yim was glad to assist her by calming the distraught. The steward was no help in this. His fretting tended to upset those he sought to soothe, and Yim sensed his disapproval of the whole idea.

It was late afternoon before there was some semblance of order, and Yim didn't stop working until the evening meal. This was a crowded affair held in the banquet hall. The room was packed and noisy, and even the high table was crowded. Yim sat at Cara's right, the place of honor, while Rodric was seated to the clan mother's left. Dinner consisted of a reduced ration of porridge mixed with a few bits of salt mutton and boiled roots, which provided more flavor than nourishment. The ale was mostly water.

Throughout the meal, Yim noticed that Rodric avoided looking at her. In their limited dealings he was always stiffly polite, but Yim had the distinct impression that he disliked her. That evening, she sensed that his dislike had blossomed into enmity. After the meal was over and she retired to bed with Cara, Yim suggested that Rodric be given the honored place at the table. "Zounds, do na be silly," replied Cara. "You're a *Bearer*, and he's just a steward. By honoring you, I honor Karm. Besides, Rodric's been out of sorts ever since I assumed my duties as clan mother. I think he rather liked the high seat and misses it. But he'll get over it."

"When did you become clan mother?"

"Just this summer, when I came of age. Until then, I only came here to present Dar's Gift."

"You mean you made the trip every year?"

"Nay, but when I did na come, the tree did na turn yellow. I do na know why."

"It's the Old Ones," said Yim. "They know what happens among us and also seem to know what will happen, at least in part."

Cara stared at Yim, but there was no disbelief in her face. "Zounds! Will you ever stop surprising me? Where did you learn about faeries?"

"On our travels we met a girl who visits them."

Cara's eyes widened with excitement. "She saw the Old Ones! What are they like?"

"She wouldn't say, but she did say that they believe something momentous is about to happen."

"What?"

"I don't think even they know. But I feel it, too."

"A vision! A vision about the father for your child!"

"I don't know," said Yim. "I hope so."

Cara yawned. "Well, I've been up since before dawn and so have you. We should get some sleep. I wish I could sleep through the days ahead until it's over. Then I'd either wake up happy or never wake up at all." With that, Cara blew out the rush candle and darkness filled the room.

The following day was not a busy one for Yim. Honoring Honus's plea to stay within the manor walls limited her activities, especially when Cara went out among the refugees. Yim tried to be useful while Cara was away, but the servants felt uncomfortable having a Bearer share their tasks. Finally, Yim found the same dusty room where Cara had taken Honus. There she gazed out the window, wishing she could view the men marching toward Tor's Gate, discern the army advancing against them, and perceive the threat that lurked outside the manor walls. She knew all were real, and all were hidden from her.

Yim longed for Honus with an intensity she scarcely had imagined possible. She wished she had kept one of his garments, so she might hold it to her nose and smell his essence. If she had thought love was torment before, it had become doubly so. The torture of restraint had been replaced by the chilling fear of loss. Her mind conjured up countless heartrending scenarios, and each one affected her as if it were real. She reminded herself that they weren't, but since they were all possible, she couldn't shut them from her thoughts. When she had joined with Honus's spirit on the Dark Path, she had experienced the horrors that took place in Lurwic. Thus she knew what he faced, and it terrified her.

Nevertheless, Yim suppressed her feelings when she joined Cara at dinner. Throughout the meal, she was the silent image of serenity. If Cara guessed Yim's true feelings, she didn't attempt to pry them out, even when they were alone. Yim wasn't surprised, for her friend had enough troubles of her own.

The following day, Yim grew even more subdued. Frightening dreams had disturbed her sleep, and though they slipped from her memory when she awoke, they left a lingering sense of dread. This combined with her fears for Honus's safety to increase her misery. Throughout the day, Yim felt that matters were coming to a head, despite the goddess's silence. At dinnertime, it was more difficult to hide her anxiety, but she felt that she pulled it off.

The next day was worse yet, for Yim recalled some of her dreams. They were horrific glimpses of slaughter done by men stripped of their humanity. Yim grieved for both the slayer and the slain, for they seemed equally tormented. The images were so vivid and detailed that Yim feared they weren't dreams at all, but visions. If they were, she questioned why Karm would show her atrocities that she was unable to prevent. It seemed pointless and cruel. Yim was so distraught that she retreated to the dusty room and spent the day there alone.

It was dusk when Cara found her. "So there you are! Zounds, Yim, what's the matter?"

"I feel useless and in the way."

"Oh silly me!" said Cara. "And I thought that you were worried about Honus. Well, you won't be in the way at dinner—which is about to be served, by the way—for there's a place for you. And such a feast has been prepared! For a change, we're having porridge and it's so delicious that we're serving only half portions. Ale-flavored water, too! 'Twould be a shame to miss it. Or Rodric's gay banter, for that matter. He'd sorely miss you. So, dust off your clothes and join the fun. And afterward, you can help me with an important task."

"What that?"

"There's something we must kill. But do na pry. You'll learn about it soon enough. Now come along."

Cara's cajoling lightened Yim's mood somewhat, and she was able to seem tranquil during the meal. When it was over, Cara ushered her to her bedroom. "We must be proper attired," said Cara, "before we kill this foe." In response to Yim's puzzled look, she said, "Get in your nightclothes."

While Yim slipped into her old slave's tunic, Cara changed into a short smock that was equally loose. Then she climbed into bed, reached beside it, and produced a dark green bottle. Patting the place beside her on the spacious mattress, she said, "Join me on the field of battle. Tonight we shall kill this bottle."

"What's in it?"

"An old clan recipe. Falfhissi, which means 'laughing water.' You've been moping for three days straight. Tonight, I'm going to get you properly drunk."

TWENTY-SEVEN

YIM EYED the bottle that Cara held. It was covered with dust except where Cara had touched it. The liquid inside appeared to be black, and Yim felt more than a little dubious about drinking it. "I've only been drunk once. Then I cried my eyes out."

"Well, even weeping would be an improvement! You've been acting like a lump ever since Honus left. All right, you're a Bearer and must seem unflappable. But na around me. I'm your *friend*! You can share your sorrow." Cara broke the wax seal about the bottle's top, pulled out the wooden stopper, wiped the dust from the bottle's neck, raised it to her lips, and took a long swig. "And this will help."

Tears welled in Yim's eyes. "In all my life, I've never had a friend," she said in an emotion-choked voice. "My guardian saw to that."

Cara reacted to Yim's tears by hugging her. "Well, you

have one now, and we're going to get drunk together." She released Yim to hand her the bottle. "Take a sip."

Yim took a small swallow. The liquid was sweet, tasting of honey and some spice that she had never encountered before. It was a complex and pleasant flavor, although the liquid burned her throat a bit when she swallowed. She took a second, larger sip. Soon her stomach began to feel pleasantly warm. She handed the bottle to Cara, who took another gulp and handed it back.

"So this is falfhissi," said Yim, taking a large gulp. "I've never heard of it."

"Dar brought the recipe from the north. 'Tis something orcs drank. Mother made this batch herself, so 'tis extra special. I watched her make the stuff many times. You cook up whiteroot and let it sit until it gets bubbly and stinky. Then you heat it in a copper kettle with a thing like a twisty, pointed hat that catches the steam, but 'tis na really steam because it turns into burning water. You mix that water with special black seeds and let it sit. Then pour it seven times through cloth, add honey, and bottle it. The older it gets, the better it tastes."

"So when we finish this bottle," said Yim, taking several additional gulps, "we'll not rush out to make some more?"

Cara held up the bottle, noted how much Yim had drunk, and grinned. "Trust me, Yim, when we're finished, we'll na rush to do *anything*."

Yim flopped backward on the bed. She felt light-headed, and it was a pleasant sensation after the past few days. "Doing nothing sounds lovely." She stretched and yawned.

"Oh nay! Sit up!" said Cara. "Do na go to sleep. We're going to talk. I've seen you take on other's troubles. Now share your own. Do you miss Honus?"

Yim sat up, her mood already altered. "Oh Cara! I love him so much! And I'm terrified for him!" Then she began to sob.

Cara held and comforted her. "There, there. 'Tis frightening for sure, and 'tis sometimes helpful to cry." She let Yim vent her grief before she spoke again. "Let's talk of something cheery. Tell me how you fell in love. That would be a grand tale." Cara took a long drink from the bottle and gave it to Yim, who did the same. "Aye, 'tis a fine thing, love. Na that I've had much success."

"But you will, Cara! You will! You're pretty and wise and good and young and witty and rich . . . *and* you're a *chieftain*!"

"Most men would rather *be* a chieftain than woo one. 'Tis na so easy to find a man who's willing to be ruled. So tell me about *your* love. When did you know you loved Honus? After we talked at the Bridge Inn?"

"Oh no! What you said confused me. I felt . . . Well, I had no idea *what* I felt. Not really. Certainly not in love. Love was just a word to me. It had no meaning."

"Come on, Yim, *everybody* understands love."

"Well, they weren't raised like me! By an old woman with only one purpose—to train me to be the Chosen."

"Train?" Cara laughed. "Zounds! Na woman needs training to have a babe! Really, Yim. You just lie back and let a man have his way with you. When the babe comes out, well, *that's* a different matter. That's why we have Wise Women."

"I was raised by a Wise Woman, so I know all about birthing babies. My training taught me different skills."

"Like what?"

"Oh, stuff," replied Yim, sounding breezy. "Stuff like when I forced the truth from you."

"Zounds! I remember that! I thought you were inside my head! What else can you do? Please tell."

"Just like Honus, I can look into a person's eyes and see things about them. And I can stop others from doing the same to me."

"Oh, zounds! That's so . . . so . . . spooky. So, what else?"

Yim smiled in a silly, almost boastful manner. "I can call forth spirits."

"From the Dark Path? Nay! Really?"

"Yep."

Cara started giggling. "Then call forth Dar, and we'll drink with her!"

Yim shook her head dizzily. "Her spirit would enter one of us, and that's not much fun. Afterward is worse. You're freezing cold. And if a spirit stays too long, even breathing is hard work."

Cara shivered. "Why would you learn *that*?"

"It's proved useful."

Cara rolled her eyes. "Oh, the mysterious one again! But we were talking about love. So you did na understand it. Were you trained to be a stone?"

"Oh, I care for people. I care for them lots. Just not one especially. Not until Honus."

"Zounds, Yim! You're driving me daft! Tell me. Tell me. Tell me! How did you ever fall in love with him?"

Yim's face took on a dreamy look. "Well, I didn't like being his slave. Not at all! Honus scared me at first, and I disliked him. In fact, I ran away. But I quickly learned I was safer with Honus than without him. So I grew used to him, and he became nicer, but so slowly I didn't notice. When he finally told me that he loved me . . ."

"When was that?"

"After we left the Bridge Inn. I had a horrible vision and crawled into bed with him."

"So that's when you fell in love?"

"No. I felt nothing. Well, I felt sorry for him, I guess. And bothered, too. He seemed like an overfriendly dog."

Cara burst out laughing and pounded her heels on the mattress. "Zounds, some men are really like that! Big dogs that keep trying to tup your leg."

Yim laughed, too. "At least Honus never tried to do *that*!

But his love *was* bothersome. It made me hesitate to accept him as my Sarf."

"Well, you're telling me *lots* and *lots* about how you didn't fall in love. But that's na what I want to know. So zounds, Yim, have another drink and get to it!"

Yim took a long sip and continued. "After we left Bremven, we were attacked on the road. The black priests were stirring up folks as they have in Averen, except in Vinden they stirred them against us. The last attack was different. A Sarf found us. He said his name was Gatt, and he acted friendly up to the very moment he tried to kill me."

"Why would he want to kill you?"

"Who knows? He wasn't much for talking."

Cara shook her head. "What Sarf is?"

"Anyway, I jumped into the river. That's when Gatt cut my hair. He was aiming for my neck. Honus fought him off, and he rode away. But Honus knew he'd be back, so we fled into the mountains. What Honus didn't tell me was that Gatt's blade was poisoned."

"Poisoned! Sarfs do na do that!"

"This one did, and the second time Honus fought him, he received a wound. Gatt retreated to let him die before coming after me."

Cara looked baffled. "Wait! Wait! Who was poisoned?"

"Honus."

"But . . ."

Yim's face screwed up with anguish. "He died, Cara! Died alone! And . . . and . . ." She started crying. "All he cared about . . . his last thoughts . . . were of me!" Yim's sobs became more intense, leaving her breathless.

Perplexed, Cara gazed at her weeping friend. It was a long while before Yim regained her composure and resumed the story. When she did, she rushed to finish it. "Honus begged me to escape, so I left him as he was dying. But I changed my mind, and decided to die with him. When I returned, he was already dead. I sat beside him and waited for

Gatt to come. While I did, I had the idea that I might return Honus's spirit to his body. I'd never been able to trance before, nor have I since, but on that day Karm bestowed the gift to me. It's true that spirits shed their memories on the Dark Path. The first thing they forget is how to live. I gathered those memories for Honus. He left a trail of them. I followed that trail, and when I reached Honus, our spirits merged."

Yim's face took on an ecstatic glow as she relived the moment. "Oh, Cara! It was so . . . so . . . so absolutely beautiful! I knew everything. I felt everything. And for the first time, I experienced love! His love became my love. He gave it to me, and it was glorious. It *is* glorious. Then I returned to the living world and breathed life into his dead body. It nearly killed me, but I didn't care. I loved him so! And then everything went black. When I opened my eyes, Honus was weeping over me. I was so happy! I kissed him right away. We kissed and kissed until I fell asleep in his arms."

Tears of joy streamed down Cara's face. "That's so beautiful!" she said, embracing Yim.

"I woke to the happiest morning of my life. I was in love. I believed it was Karm's gift."

"It was!" exclaimed Cara. "It surely was."

Yim sighed. "Perhaps that morning will be my only happy one. We kissed and embraced. Then I bathed alone, imagining Honus's hands on my body. That's when I recalled I was the Chosen and must remain a virgin until Karm tells me who's to father my child."

Cara stared at Yim in disbelief. "But . . ."

"How could I trick Honus into betraying Karm? He loves her as much as I do. I told him the truth, and we've remained chaste. It's been torment for us both." Yim started to sniffle. "Perhaps that's really why I had him join your brother: Because I was afraid I'd be weak."

"Weak?"

"Yes. I can't be that. I'm the Chosen."

"You're na weak. But zounds, you sure are stupid! You've been waiting for a sign to make a babe? Do you know why folks make babes? Well, 'tis na because Karm taps them on the shoulder. They fall in love! So Honus is dead, and Karm sends you to the Dark Path to give him life and fall in love, and you're *still* waiting for a sign? Zounds, Yim! What's the goddess supposed to do? Strip you both naked and toss you in a barrel? You *got* your sign! You had it on that happy morning! If you had tupped Honus then, the child you're supposed to bear would be growing in your belly now. And who knows? Maybe Lord Bahl would have turned to dog poop. At least, for sure, Honus would na be marching off to fight him. He'd be with you, and you'd both be happy."

Yim simply stared at Cara, with a stunned expression on her drunken face. As her friend's words sank in, her expression turned anguished. "I sent him away, Cara! I sent him away!"

Cara sighed. "Aye, you did."

"And he's the father. Of course. Why didn't I see it? Why didn't Karm tell me?"

"She did," replied Cara. "But from what you say, she does na speak plainly." Then sensing that Yim was on the verge of tears again, she quickly added, "But now that you know, we can act! Honus is marching on foot, but there are horses here. We can ride and catch him before he reaches Tor's Gate."

"But you're Clan Mother!"

"Aye, a clan mother with a steward. Besides, I promised Honus I'd watch over you. And I shall, Yim, I shall. This is love and Karm's will all rolled into one!" Cara sighed. "And 'tis *so* romantic!"

TWENTY-EIGHT

RODRIC HAD visited Rangar only once after the troops departed, and the subject of the secret passageway did not come up. He felt relieved about that, for although he was convinced that Yim was a threat, the idea of allowing strangers in the secret way went against his grain. He believed that the deed would be justified, but it still smacked of treason. Moreover, the impostor had grown subdued of late and spent her days sulking. Rodric prayed that Yim's quiescence was a hopeful sign, but he doubted it. As the saying went: "The adder charms the bird before it strikes."

Thus the steward was concerned when word came that the clan mother had not risen, though it was well past her usual time. Instead she had remained with Yim in her bedchamber. It was said that the two had been drinking late into the night. Such behavior was uncharacteristic of Cara. *Yim's influence*, thought Rodric, fearing the worst.

Cara finally appeared shortly before noon, stomping up to Rodric with bloodred eyes and her face a matching shade. "Karm's wrath on it! Where are the maps?"

Rodric bowed. "What maps, Clan Mother?"

"Brother's maps! They were on the table in the scroll room."

"I believe he took them with him."

"Shit! All of them?" Cara slumped in a nearby chair and moaned. "Oh, Karm's aching bunions, my head! I'll never do that again!"

Cara's swearing was out of character, and it made Rodric

timid. His voice was meek when he spoke again. "What maps do you seek, Clan Mother? Mayhap your brother left some behind."

"I need to know the way to Tor's Gate."

Rodric thought that it wasn't the time to ask why. "I'll look myself," he said. Then he hurried off, his mind filled with suspicions and ill-bodings. The scroll room was a shambles. Maps and scrolls were strewn about the table and floor. Rodric unrolled and examined each one before putting it away. It took a while, but his meticulousness paid off when he found what Cara had been seeking. It was an old document, and worse for wear, but it showed the route to Tor's Gate. Rodric rolled it up and finished shelving the scattered scrolls before he left to present the map to Cara.

After searching awhile, he found her in the room off the kitchen. She was seated at the table with Yim, who was pale and gazed queasily at her untouched bowl of porridge with bloodshot eyes. Though Yim was obviously hungover, her physical distress didn't diminish her air of triumph. Rodric was curious about the cause of her mood and more than a little alarmed by it. He did his best to hide his feelings as he gave the map to Cara, who eagerly unrolled it.

"Rodric," Cara said. "You've ridden all over. How long to Tor's Gate by horse?"

"Would this be a leisurely ride or a gallop?"

" 'Twill be a hasty journey, but one of the riders will be inexperienced."

"Then two days should suffice."

Cara turned to Yim. "Brother said the march would take six days. If we leave this afternoon . . ."

"Clan Mother!" said Rodric. "What are you planning?"

"I must take Yim to Honus. 'Tis Karm's will. You'll manage affairs while I'm gone."

"Of course, Clan Mother," said Rodric. "But I fear you're overhasty." He cast Yim a meaningful look. "A green rider with an unsettled stomach will na get far. And such a trip requires preparation. I think an early start tomorrow morn will serve you better."

"A wise counsel," replied Cara, "and I'll heed it. However, I want to leave at sunrise. So see to it."

Rodric bowed. "I will, Clan Mother."

While Cara pored over the map with Yim, Rodric went to the stables and spoke to the horse master's wife about Cara's needs. The woman was in charge during her husband's absence, but the steward didn't worry about her competence. It was irrelevant. Having performed that duty, he headed for the village and the inn. He found whom he was seeking in its common room. "Rangar, I'll be needing another dagger."

Daijen smiled. "Come into my chamber, and I'll show you my wares."

When the two men were behind the closed door, Rodric whispered, "Tonight."

"Tonight? You give me scant time."

" 'Tis tonight or never. Yim will take Clan Mother to her doom. If we do na stop her, she'll leave next morn."

"Then stop her we shall. I have the men if you'll show them the way."

"There's a roofless hut by the lake . . ."

"I know it."

"Have the men gather there after dark. When the moon sets, a door will open. How many will meet me?"

"Three. All good men. Sober and levelheaded."

"And they'll na harm Clan Mother?" asked Rodric.

"Never. They're her true friends."

"You've set my heart at ease. I should go now. Tomorrow will be a better day."

Daijen took Rodric's hand. "Aye, indeed."

After the steward departed, Daijen paced about his room cursing him. "Dawdling prig," he muttered, "but there's no help for it. I can only hope that Thromec's done his part."

Daijen waited awhile before he hung a scrap of red cloth from his dagger belt and went out for what appeared to be a leisurely stroll. He ambled about the refugees' encampment with the aimless manner of a man taking the air before he headed to a copse of trees beyond the farthest field. There, sheltered from view, Daijen waited. It was a while before a man arrived. Sharp-faced with a wispy beard and a wiry frame, he moved with nervous energy. His clothes were ragged, but his boots looked new. The toes of them had been cut off to fit his long feet. He grinned when he saw Daijen. "I saw the cloth. So 'tis tonight?"

"Aye, be in the roofless hut when the moon sets."

" 'Tis just past the first quarter. 'Twill set late."

"That works to your advantage," said Daijen. "Everyone will be asleep. A man will arrive to show you in. Ask him where to find her. You know what to do next."

"Aye, slay the dark-haired one first, the one who waved from the wall."

"That's most important. Then kill the other, open the manor's gates, and . . ." Daijen smiled. ". . . enjoy yourselves."

The man grinned. "We know how to do that."

Daijen opened a bundle that contained three sheathed daggers. "Use these tonight."

The man picked up one and drew the weapon to examine it. Its blade was painted with a brown substance.

"Handle that carefully," said Daijen. "Nick yourself, and you'll die painfully."

The man slid the dagger back into its scabbard. "And ye want her head?"

"It's worth three gold coins to the man who brings it." Then Daijen added, as if he had read the man's thoughts, "The others know that, too."

The wiry man grinned. "Mayhap, but they're na quick like me." He placed the dagger with the others, rolled up the bundle, and put it under his arm. "I'll see ye in the morning, so have yer gold ready." With that, the man hurried off.

Thromec arrived a short while later. "So it's tonight? I'd hoped for more time."

"She's fleeing tomorrow morning. I just found out this afternoon. How many have gathered in the wood?"

"Several dozen when I was there this morning. 'Tis likely more have come since then."

"Fighters or peasants?" asked Daijen.

"Peasants," replied the priest. "But there are some likely lads among them, and all are inflamed. If they find that Bearer, they'll hack her to bits along with anyone who stands in their way. To their eyes, she's to blame for everything."

"Then you've done well, and the Most Holy One will learn of it."

The priest bowed to Daijen. "Our lord has graced me with the power to make it so. Never has it been so easy to bend men to my will."

"Our might increases as the Rising approaches. Soon we'll triumph. Tonight's work will bring that day closer."

"So when should we attack?"

"Wait until the moon sets, then surround the hall. Slay anyone who flees it. If my men succeed within the hall, they'll open its gates, and one will have Yim's head. Give them time to do their work. Attack only if you believe things have gone awry."

"One way or another, Yim will perish," said Thromec, "even if all within the hall must die to assure her death."

By late afternoon, Yim's head and stomach had settled enough for Cara to teach her something about riding. Cara ordered her gelding to be saddled, along with a mare for Yim, and directed that the steeds be brought to the courtyard. The enclosure lacked the space for proper riding, but Cara hoped to acquaint Yim with its basics.

When the horses arrived, Yim proved every bit a novice. She mounted clumsily after falling a half-dozen times. Neither did she know how to sit nor how to use the reins and her feet to guide the horse. However, one thing surprised Cara: Yim had an instant rapport with her mount. Cara had never seen anything like it. The mare, instead of rebelling against Yim's inept handling, seemed to forgive it. *'Tis almost as if she wants Yim to ride her*, thought Cara, amazed by the pair of them. It made her optimistic about the next day's journey.

Before Yim went to dinner, she filled a pack with everything that she had carried on her journey with Honus, adding Cara's things and provisions also. At the evening meal, both women hid their growing excitement. Only Rodric and the horse master's wife knew of their plans, and Cara wanted it kept that way. After eating, the two women retired to bed early.

Rodric stayed up and watched the moon from a dormer window. It moved toward the horizon with maddening slowness, and while it did, he wondered if he was doing the right thing. All afternoon, he had engaged in an internal debate over whether he should warn Cara about Yim. He had nearly done so, only to change his mind at the last instant. As the moon dipped toward the mountains, Rodric began to regret his silence. Then the fear and resentment that Daijen had stirred within him overwhelmed any second thoughts. *What would have been the use of speaking?* he asked himself. *Cara's headstrong, and Yim holds her in her palm. Clan Mother has been bewitched, and only Yim's removal will break the spell.*

When the moon sank from view, Rodric steeled himself for what he must do and headed for the secret entrance. The hall was deathly quiet; the only ones awake beside him were the archers who manned the outer wall, and there were only four of them. Rodric made his way through hallways to the kitchen and then to the pantry. There, he lit a torch and descended into the lower rooms. He passed through these and climbed down the shaft to reach the oak door sealing the passageway to the secret entrance. Then he slipped the door's bolt and entered the dank tunnel.

The tunnel was longer than Rodric remembered, and he was dismayed to find that water had seeped into its lower portion. It was a relief to finally reach its end. There, he stood in knee-deep water in a shaft twice his height. On one side of the shaft was the complex wooden mechanism that allowed the hatch to be opened from above. Opening it from below was easier: all Rodric had to do was pull a lever. He did so, and a large stone pivoted in the ceiling to reveal a patch of night sky. The shadowy shapes of three men emerged from the opening to descend the iron rungs set in the shaft's side. The first to splash into the water was a wiry-looking fellow. The two that followed him were shorter and bulkier. All three men were bearded and ragged, and none bore a look that Rodric would characterize as either "sober" or "levelheaded." Rodric pushed the lever, and the secret entrance closed.

"Greetings, friend," said the wiry man. "So where's the dark-haired sorceress?"

"I'll take you to her," replied Rodric.

"Oh, nay," replied the man. " 'Twould na be wise. Ye might be seen with us. Best ye say the way, and we'll part company."

Rodric saw the wisdom in that and gave the men detailed directions to Cara's room. After they repeated them to his satisfaction, he showed them the lever for opening the hatch. "When you leave with the woman, you must close it from above. I'll show you how to do that."

The wiry man grinned in a disturbing way. "Save yer trouble."

Rodric felt a sharp pain in his thigh. He looked down and saw that the man had pricked him with a dagger. Though the wound was a tiny one, its pain was excruciating. Rodric felt as if a gigantic hornet had stung him and pumped him full of venom. He opened his mouth to scream, but his lungs wouldn't work. What followed was far worse than pain. Rodric needed to gasp for air, but it was impossible. As he suffocated, his silent agony amused the men, and they laughed as if his desperate contortions were entertainment for their behalf. One took the torch from his hand. Its flame was the last thing Rodric saw as the world darkened to black. When the steward toppled into the stagnant water, he was dead before he made a splash.

After the men ceased chuckling, the wiry one pulled the lever to open the hatch. Then he turned to one of his companions. "Get a big rock and smash those wooden works so the hatch can na be shut."

The man departed on his errand and called down a short while later. "Stand back and I'll toss it down." His accomplices retreated into the tunnel, and after they did, a large rock struck Rodric's floating corpse. The man who threw it descended the rungs and studied the mechanism that closed and opened the hatch. "I've figured where to whack it." He groped in the water until he found the rock and lifted it up. It was a heavy, jagged lump of granite that quickly reduced the carefully made apparatus to splinters. Part of the oaken framework toppled against the hatch, jamming it open. The man grinned. "The 'secret way' is na so secret now."

The three men advanced up the tunnel. When they came to the open oak door, they pulled the pins from its hinges. Then they carried the door halfway into the tunnel, dropped it, and threw the pins into the murky water. With that done, they advanced into the sleeping hall to obtain the head that was worth so much gold.

TWENTY-NINE

YIM FELT a searing pain in her shoulder. Her eyes flew open, and she saw a blade lodged there. Whoever grasped it was only a black form in the dark bedchamber. A second blade plunged deep into her bowels. Yim was in agony, but she hadn't the breath to cry out. A third blade bit into her thigh. This assailant stabbed her leg and thigh over and over again in a frenzy of blows.

Yet Yim suffered all of this in silence, with Cara snoring beside her. Unable to speak, Yim tried to wake her friend before she was murdered, too, though Yim was already faint from the lack of air and racked by all-consuming pain. Expending her remaining strength, she managed to shake Cara, who merely moaned and rolled over. Everything went black. Yim felt, but couldn't see, someone place a palm against her chin. The palm pushed her head back, arching her neck. The last thing Yim felt was a blade sawing through her throat.

Then she woke. The room was dark and still, illuminated only by dim starlight coming from the windows. Cara was sleeping peacefully beside her. "Cara! Wake up!"

Cara moaned sleepily.

"Cara, someone's coming!"

Cara stirred only a little. "Who?" she asked in a tired voice.

Instead of replying, Yim crawled over her friend's prone body to reach the sword that hung from the bedpost. She drew the weapon from its scabbard, and still kneeling on the mattress, turned to face the door.

"Watch that blade!" said Cara. "You're like to slice my head off! What's going on?"

"I had a dream . . ."

"What? Put away that sword. Zounds, you've left your senses. A dream indeed!"

"It seemed a vision of my murder." Before Yim could say more, she heard footsteps in the hallway and hushed.

Cara obviously had heard them, too, for she whispered, "Quick! Give me the sword!" Yim did so. Cara leapt out of bed and raised the weapon into the attack position. An instant later, the door quietly opened and the figures of three men stepped into the room. It was too dark to see more than their shadowy shapes and the pale metal of their drawn daggers.

Cara didn't hesitate. She swung at the foremost man, the tallest of the three, and her sword struck muscle and bone. The man's head assumed an odd angle as his blood sprayed over Cara. He made a gurgling sound and toppled forward as she pulled her blade free and stepped back.

Yim saw the man's dagger clatter across the floor, and lacking any means to protect herself, she lunged for it. When she grasped its hilt, she looked up. Two more attackers remained. Apparently, they hadn't expected any resistance, for they stood frozen for a moment, but only a moment. Then both rushed at Cara with blades raised high. Still on her hands and knees, Yim swung wildly at the closest one. She was in no position to deliver a lethal blow, but she was desperate to defend Cara, and wounding one of her opponents seemed her best hope.

Yim's blade merely grazed the man's shin, but the tiny wound stopped him cold. His dagger fell to the floor as he stood wavering on his feet. Yim's attention shifted to Cara, who was swinging her sword to keep her opponent at bay. The man dodged the strokes until he noticed Yim. As soon as he did, he lunged at her. Cara swung and struck the base of his spine. The man's legs buckled, and he tumbled to the floor. As soon as he hit, he used his hands to drag himself toward Yim. Despite his grievous wound, he moved quickly and was nearly within striking distance when Cara splattered his brains.

Then there was silence in the dark room. Yim rose to her feet. Cara stood motionless, the tip of her sword touching the floor, as if the weapon had suddenly become too heavy to hold. Then she began to tremble. Blood flowed from two of the corpses, forming ever-widening pools. They looked black in the dim light.

"Cara, are you all right?"

Silence.

"Cara!"

"Oh Karm! Oh Karm!" Cara said in a shaky voice. "What's happened?"

"It's just as I feared: I've drawn evil to you."

Cara backed away from the spreading blood, then took a deep shuddering breath. "Dress and grab the pack, we can na stay here."

"But this is your hall!"

"Perhaps 'tis, perhaps nay. Who knows what others are sneaking about? Best to get you safe before finding out."

Yim dressed quickly. Then she stowed her tunic in the pack and strapped on her own dagger, discarding the poisoned one. By the time she was ready, Cara had donned her clothes and buckled on the sword belt and scabbard. "I'll take you to the secret passageway," Cara said. "If we can make it there, you should be safe while I rouse the guard. That way, if the hall's overrun, you'll have an escape route."

The two women cautiously entered the dark hallway with Cara in the forefront. Everything was quiet, and they made their way to the pantry without encountering anyone. Only there did Cara risk a light, using a flint and iron to light torches for Yim and herself before descending into the storerooms below. When they reached the shaft leading to the secret passage, Cara said, "Climb down and hide behind the door while I find out what's happened. You can peer through the slots and see the torchlight of anyone coming. If you do na hear my voice, flee through the secret entrance. A lever opens it from below. Hurry, Yim, I'll return soon."

As Cara walked away, Yim gripped her torch with her teeth and descended the ladder into the dark shaft. As she neared its bottom, the torchlight revealed that the door was missing. She called to Cara. "The door's gone!"

Cara returned to look, then climbed down the ladder. Drawing her sword, she advanced into the tunnel. Yim followed her. "Cara," she whispered, "is this a good idea?"

"I must check the secret entrance," Cara replied, picking up her pace. "You can stay behind if you want."

"I'm coming with you."

Soon Yim and Cara were standing knee-deep in water at the tunnel's end. Cara stared at the open hatch with a dismayed expression. "Oh Karm!" she said. "We've got to close it."

"How? It's jammed open."

"I think I can manage if you help," said Cara. "Climb up and move the hatch so I can try to clear the jam. The stone's heavy, but it pivots on its center, so you'll na bear its full weight."

"Of course, I'll help you," said Yim. She was about to ascend the rungs set in the wall when she felt something brush against her leg. Looking down, she thought she glimpsed a hand in the murky water. Then whatever touched her sank from view. "Cara!" she cried. "I think there's a dead body here!"

"Never mind! Climb up the rungs," urged Cara. "If we do na close that hatch, there'll be bodies everywhere."

Yim hurried up the rungs and exited the shaft. As soon as Cara set her torch in a holder, she followed after Yim, halting just beneath the top of the shaft. When Cara stopped climbing, Yim called down to her. "Tell me what to do."

Gripping a rung with one hand, Cara drew her sword

and used it to poke the wooden framework that jammed the hatch. "Pull the stone up a bit," she said. "Hold on tight."

Yim extinguished her torch, then tugged at the stone hatch. She discovered that, while the stone pivoted on its center, it wasn't balanced. Instead, it was inclined to fall to the closed position. Nevertheless, Yim was able to pull the hatch farther open. A chain dangled loosely from a ring set in its far end. Yim wondered if the chain had been attached to a counterweight. If so, that would explain why the hatch felt so heavy.

Beneath her, Cara was pressing against the frame with her sword. Yim heard Cara's voice. "All right. The frame's no longer wedged. Lower the hatch a bit, and I'll push it free."

Concentrating on holding the hatch open, Yim no longer saw what Cara was doing; she simply followed directions. The hatch became increasingly difficult to hold steady. "Lower it some more," said Cara. Yim did so. The more the stone tilted, the heavier it seemed. Despite Yim's resistance, it began to incline further. Then Yim heard a loud crash.

"Cara! Are you all right?"

"Hold the hatch, I'm coming up."

"Hurry Cara, it's slipping!"

Yim saw a hand on the edge of the opening. The stone grew heavier. Cara's torso emerged from the hole. Yim gritted her teeth, fighting against the growing weight that fought to break free from her grasp. "I can't hold it much longer!" Cara was nearly out when Yim's fingers lost their grip. The hatch slammed closed with a crash. Cara stood frozen in a hunched position.

"My cloak's caught," said Cara.

Yim drew her dagger and cut Cara loose. "Oh, thank Karm, I feared I'd crushed you! What now?"

"Sneak into the village, and see if archers still guard the walls. If so, I'll call to them."

"And if not?"

"Well, then we'll do something different. At least na one will sneak in the back way."

The pair headed up the sloping field toward the hall and village, which were only silhouettes against the starry sky. They were halfway there when they spotted torches moving in the dark. The flames illuminated men who seemed to be spreading out around the village's perimeter. Cara halted. Yim did, too. "Could they be your guards?" Yim asked. "Perhaps they're looking for us."

"There are too many of them," replied Cara. "Some mischief is afoot."

Just then, several thatched roofs were set alight. As the fires grew, their red glow reached into the field and illuminated Yim and Cara. A pair of men dashed in their direction. "Run from the light!" said Cara.

Yim raced alongside Cara toward the lake and the greater safety of darkness. She glanced back only once. Their pursuers were barely visible. Other men were running in their direction also, but they were farther away. "Head for the boats," said Cara between gasps. The women were swift, but the men ran with the energy of the possessed. At the lakeshore, the first of them caught up with Yim and swung a hoe at her.

Cara's sword met the tool's descending shaft and splintered it. The hoe's blade spun off into the night, but the remnant of the shaft could still serve as a club, and the man swung at Cara with it. She ducked the blow and stabbed at the man. Her sword pierced his gut and emerged out his back. Cara was pulling it free when the long curved blade of a scythe bit into her upper arm.

Yim had been so focused on the man with the hoe that his companion seemed to have appeared from nowhere. She cried out in horror at the sight of Cara's wound. Then she reacted with animal ferocity, springing at Cara's assailant and burying her dagger deep into his chest. The man fell back, releasing the scythe. It remained embedded in Cara's arm. Then her arm bent where it shouldn't and dangled like an empty sleeve, releasing the blade.

The aftermath was ghastly. Blood spurted from Cara's half-severed arm in time with her rapid pulse, darkening her garments. Even in the dim light, Yim could see her friend was growing deathly pale. Cara's lips appeared as white as her face and her eyes had taken on a vacant gaze.

"I'll take care of you, Cara," said Yim, shaking her friend to get her attention. "I was raised by a Wise Woman. I know what to do." She yanked the drawstring from the dead man's pants and tied it tightly above the wound to stop the blood flow. Then she examined Cara's arm. The blade had completely severed the bone midway above the elbow so that the limb was only partially attached. There was nothing Yim could do but remove it. Yim kissed Cara's clammy cheek. "I'm going to have to cut some more," she said. "I'll do it quickly."

Cara whimpered only once, sat down, and squeezed her eyes shut. Yim pulled her dagger from the dead man's chest, wiped it clean, and sliced through the remaining muscles in Cara's arm. She placed it gently on the ground, as if it were still part of Cara, and touched the hand in a gesture of farewell. It was still warm. Then she returned Cara's sword to its scabbard and helped her friend to her feet. "Come with me," she said, "I'll take you somewhere safe."

Cara didn't reply, but numbly submitted to Yim, who embraced her to hold her upright as they made their way to the dock. Somehow Yim managed to get Cara into the boat they had used to visit Faerie. She untied the vessel and began rowing clumsily into the lake. Initially, she did more splashing than actual rowing, for the oar shafts simply slipped between a pair of upright dowels. Holding their paddles at the proper angle and positioning the shafts so both oars pulled evenly was not as easy as it seemed when Cara had done it. The boat moved both slowly and erratically while Yim got the hang of it.

Cara stirred and moaned. "It hurts. Oh Karm, it hurts."

"I'll do something about the pain soon," said Yim. She

hoped that she wasn't lying. Honus had taken the healing kit with him, so she had no pain-dulling herbs. Her best hope was that Lila had been correct and the Old Ones were her friends. *They'd better be Cara's friends, too*, Yim thought, regarding her wounded comrade. Cara was slumping in her seat and looked about to tumble into the lake. Alarmed, Yim crawled over to her as the small boat rocked unsteadily. Then she eased her friend down so that her back rested against the stern. Cara was no help in this maneuver, for she was listless and seemed almost asleep. Yim knew that wasn't a good sign, but she needed to take up the oars. A glance toward the dock revealed that men were arriving there and climbing into a boat.

Yim rowed for her and Cara's lives, and her rowing gradually improved. Instead of zigzagging about the lake, she guided the boat with more accuracy. The shore grew more distant. Yim's palms began to chafe, but she paused her rowing only to splash water on Cara in an effort to keep her conscious. "Stay awake Cara! Talk to me!"

"Oh Karm! Oh Karm!"

"Cara, you were so brave. You saved my life many times tonight. Be brave now. We'll get through this. Talk! Talk!"

"You were right."

"Right about what?"

"Killing. 'Tis na fun. Sometimes when the men drank and spoke of battles, their deeds seemed glorious and exciting. But I have someone's *brains* splattered over me! And my arm . . . Oh, Karm help me."

"She will, Cara. She will."

Yim looked at the dock. The men had launched the boat. It was difficult to see, a black shape against the dark shore, but it seemed large and bristling with oars. Yim prayed the men who manned them were as inept as she.

Cara spoke again, her voice faint. "Where are we going?"

"To the faerie dell. The Old Ones will shelter us."

"Metal," said Cara, sounding fainter than before. "Na metal. They will na . . ."

Yim waited for her friend to finish, but Cara had closed her eyes. Yim pulled in an oar so she could scoop water with a hand and fling it. Cara didn't stir. Yim flung more water, splashing Cara's face, but she didn't react. "Wake up! Don't die! You can't die! I won't allow it!"

Yim blinked tears from her eyes and glanced at the other boat. It was closer. A voice carried across the dark, still water. "Pull! Pull! Pull!"

Yim grabbed the oars and began to row again. Desperation lent her speed. She moved farther into the lake before thinking about what Cara had said. *Metal! The faeries can't abide it!* She threw Cara's sword into the lake. Her own dagger followed it. Neither weapon would be of use against a boatload of foes. The men needed only to capsize the slender boat to drown Cara. Yim knew she would fare no better. Her and Cara's only hope lay in speed and the goodwill of the Old Ones. Then a thought arose. *There's metal in the pack!* Yim rummaged through it. She flung the pot away, and the knife, and the fire-making iron. *Is there anything else? The needle! No, that was in the healing kit.*

"Pull! Pull! Pull!"

Yim gazed toward the other boat. It was gaining on her. She seized the oars and rowed with all her might. Blisters formed and broke on her hands until they were raw. The oar handles grew slippery with sweat or blood or both; Yim didn't look. Yet despite her efforts, her pursuers drew ever closer.

"Pull! Pull! Pull!"

A man stood on the vessel's deck to shout the count, and the oars moved in perfect unison. Yim thought the standing man must be a black priest who could enthrall others with his voice. Perhaps the oarsmen were only peasants, but they rowed so that their boat sped upon the water with the agility of a giant centipede.

The gorge leading to the faerie dell loomed ahead, a black gash in the dark mountains. But even as Yim neared it, she saw the oncoming vessel would overtake her. She could not keep up her former pace, and even that had been insufficient. Doom drew ever nearer. Soon, she could make out the face of the man who commanded the oarsmen. His mouth looked like a dark gash in a pale orb. It seemed to be grinning with malice and triumph.

THIRTY

YIM WAS panting. Her back ached and her arms were leaden with fatigue as she pulled the oars from the water and set them in the boat. It was a relief to rest while the slender craft glided onward, propelled only by momentum. Glancing at her pursuers, Yim knew that her relief wouldn't last long. If a man could step from the approaching boat and walk on water, he would reach her in fewer than a hundred strides. Yim wondered how many strides equaled an oar stroke. The answer would tell her how long she had to live.

Cara lay unconscious, inclined against the curved stern. Yim was glad that her friend was unaware of approaching doom, and she hoped that when she capsized the boat Cara wouldn't wake. Yim planned to do that just before the men reached them. She would gather Cara in her arms and sink with her into the lake's dark depths, the two of them entwined like loving sisters. Yim watched the oncoming boat to time her final act of defiance.

The larger boat suddenly veered to one side when it was

only fifty paces away. The turn didn't seem intentional, for the standing man began to curse the oarsmen. Their discipline disintegrated as the oars flayed the water to no effect. Then Yim saw that the boat wasn't veering at all, but turning away. Nevertheless, foreboding made her take up the oars again and rower farther from the other boat.

As Yim rowed, she also watched her foes. They were no longer engaged in pursuit, but traveling in a circle. As they moved, they picked up speed. The standing man was still yelling, but his voice had taken on an edge of fear. He and the oarsmen were staring at something in the water. Yim looked at it also. There was a darker spot in the lake, and the men's boat was revolving around it. After Yim peered at it awhile, she realized what it was. *A hole in the water!* she thought, amazed at the sight. It looked like an inverted cone, and with each successive orbit, the other boat was pulled closer to it.

Oars fell from the boat as men abandoned them. They trailed behind the doomed vessel, caught by a current that moved it ever faster in ever tighter circles. Some men jumped into the water and vanished. The standing man's commands grew shrill, and they seemed to lose their power, for the men suddenly surged at him. He disappeared beneath their flaying fists. Yim heard screams, followed by silence. By then, the boat was within the hole and only partly visible. It was moving farther down when the whirlpool collapsed, swallowing the vessel and its remaining occupants. Only a ring of expanding ripples marked the spot. When they dissipated, the lake was still and quiet.

Yim was about to start rowing again when she realized that the boat was moving on its own. Thus, instead of working the oars, Yim pulled them into the boat and dipped her sore hands into the soothing cold water. By the force of the current, she realized that she was moving at a steady but stately pace. As Yim glided toward the gorge, she gazed at the stars reflected in the lake. They looked brighter and different than those in the sky, closer somehow. When the boat entered the gorge, the light grew brighter.

Though it seemed impossible, the water reflected moonlight and uncommon moonlight at that. It had the yellow tint of a full autumn moon, so that the stream Yim sailed upon was a golden mirror winding in the night. Eventually, it turned a bend to reveal the circular pool. Yim slipped off her and Cara's sandals. Standing in the shining water were forms that looked not quite human.

Within the village, all was chaos. It seemed that it was under attack: Several buildings had been set alight. Armed men with torches roamed the fields, killing anyone who tried to flee. News of them drove the villagers to pound upon the manor's gates. While archers watched warily from the walls, the gates were opened and the villagers poured into the safety of the courtyard. There they milled about, fearful of more attacks.

The innkeeper was among them, being too old to march off with Cronin. For a while, he feared that the general's plan had failed and Lord Bahl was descending upon them to mete out gruesome deaths. His fears allayed somewhat when he saw that the archers continued to calmly pace the walkways high upon the walls. From what the innkeeper had heard, Bahl attacked with overwhelming force and his rabid hordes destroyed everyone and everything in their path. Whatever was going on didn't seem like that. The innkeeper felt somewhat relieved, but no less confused.

Everyone about him seemed in the same state. As the villagers stood and anxiously waited, news and rumors spread among them. Some said that the refugees had attacked them, but a widow claimed that most had abandoned the fields and fled. "That proves they were in on it," said the innkeeper's wife.

"Nay," said the widow. "They were afeared na one would shelter them, and I'm afeared they were right."

"Then who are those men if na those beggars camping in our fields?" asked a farmer's wife.

"Could be another clan," said the blacksmith's eldest daughter. "There's been feuding. Mayhap it's spread here."

An archer called from a walkway above. "Who will help douse the fires? We'll send guards to protect anyone who does." When voices called from the crowd to volunteer, the archer told them to advance toward the gates.

After the volunteers had assembled, archers and swordsmen met them and gave them buckets. The gates were opened, and the firefighters rushed out with their protectors. Then the gates were quickly closed. The innkeeper remained in the courtyard, which had become less crowded. When the sky began to lighten, he scanned the crowd for Rangar's face but didn't spot it. Soon afterward, a guard limped out to open the gates, saying it was safe to return home. He also said that a chambermaid had told him the clan mother was missing. That news set tongues abuzz.

Some villagers rushed home, but others like the innkeeper remained in the dirt lane talking about the night's strange events. There was much to talk about, and folk kept arriving with fresh news or baseless rumors. Everyone debated which was which. Those with relations serving in the hall confirmed that Lady Cara's disappearance was no rumor. Her guest, the Bearer, was missing also. Reliable word had it that three corpses had been found in the clan mother's chamber—two slain by weapons and a third killed by magic. There was much speculation about the Bearer's role in the latter death. Some said it was the work of Karm, others claimed it was dark magic.

Three homes had burned down, and a dozen more had suffered damage. The folk who had doused the fires had done so unhampered. The men who had set the blazes had vanished. Some thought they had fled. Others feared they were regrouping for a second attack. A wild-eyed refugee woman claimed they had been carried off by bears and wolves that had descended from the mountains at the western end of the lake. No one believed her.

More news emerged from the manor house. A guardsman's wife said the steward was nowhere to be found. That started a fresh wave of speculation. The cook's niece said Rodric resented the clan mother and had murdered her so he might rule. The brewer's wife called the niece a lying bitch and said the steward had rescued Cara from the clutches of the visiting sorceress.

The women were about to come to blows when someone rushed up to say two boats were missing. Both women claimed the news proved their assertion. That was when the horse master's wife stated that Cara planned to ride off with the Bearer in the morning and it was Rodric himself who had told her of the plan. A few people rushed off to the stables and soon returned saying the clan mother's horse was still there.

Someone found a gnawed foot in a field, which spurred others to investigate. What they discovered seemed to confirm the refugee woman's story. They found wolf and bear tracks, discarded weapons, and blood. However, that single foot was the only sign of the men who attacked the village. There were no signs of the missing boats, including the larger one that was used for hauling timber and should have been easy to spot. Someone suggested that it might have been taken into the gorge, but the idea was ridiculed. The gorge was a fell place, and only a fool would venture there.

"Clan Mother goes," said a child.

"Lady Cara's special," replied her mother. "She bears Dar's Gift to the Old Ones."

"But she took her friend, too."

"Aye, but she's a Bearer, na a common woman. So hush."

The innkeeper eventually tired of the talk and returned to the inn. He still hadn't spotted Rangar, and mindful of his promise to keep an eye on his goods, the innkeeper checked Rangar's room. Rangar wasn't there, but the room wasn't empty. What appeared to be a decayed corpse lay upon the floor.

Then, to the innkeeper's horror, the corpse moved, and proved to be a living man. A wrinkled and venous parchment of yellow skin covered a skull that possessed only a few strands of wispy white hair. The skull turned to face the innkeeper, though the eyes inside the deep sockets were filmed over and seemed incapable of sight. The decayed man feebly waved a skeletal hand and opened a toothless mouth, but the only sound that emerged was a watery hiss. Even from several paces away, his breath was nauseating and the innkeeper felt his stomach rise from the stench.

"Where's Rangar? Why are you wearing his clothes?" Since the man seemed incapable of violence, the innkeeper assumed he had stolen the garments.

The response was a warbling hiss.

Encouraged by the intruder's apparent helplessness and the prospect of a reward, the innkeeper decided to retrieve Rangar's garments. "You stole those boots from a friend of mine," he said, tugging them off.

The putrid smell of the feet he exposed nearly drove the innkeeper back, but he was a hardened man. Mastering his disgust, he began to unbutton the jerkin. When the intruder feebly clawed at him, the innkeeper slapped back, and none too gently. As his hand struck the withered face, he felt its jaw crumble like stale bread. Afterward, the man's hisses took on a higher pitch, and his mouth hung slack and open. The innkeeper removed the jerkin without further resistance. The pants came off easily, for the waist was far too big. He declined to take the undergarment.

Having retrieved Rangar's clothes, the innkeeper seized the intruder and hauled him to his feet. Then he marched him out from the inn and tossed him upon the unpaved street. The man lay upon the dirt as an appalled crowd gathered around him, disgusted but fascinated by what seemed a living skeleton. They drew back when the wretch managed to rise and stagger down the street. Dogs growled, but none dared approach the abomination that slowly made its way out of the village and down the road, a living corpse seeking a lonely grave.

The innkeeper didn't watch it go. Returning to room of the man he knew as "Rangar," he gathered up the missing man's possessions. He searched through everything and was pleased to find a pouch of gold. "Best not leave that here," he said aloud. "I'll keep it safe." Secreting the pouch upon his person, he arranged the clothes he had retrieved from the intruder into a neat pile on the bed, placing the saddlebags beside them. He decided to give his tenant until afternoon before he rented out his room again and stowed his possessions elsewhere. As for the gold, he was inclined to see it as fair recompense for dealing with the foul intruder. The more he considered the notion, the better he liked it. *After all*, thought the innkeeper, *in troubled times, a wise man looks out for himself.*

Yim awoke beneath tree roots and starlight. Before her hosts had entered the den, they raked starlight from the sky and formed it into glowing spheres. These illuminated the subterranean chamber. Yim lay upon a bed of soft, feathery leaves. Cara slept beside her. Both she and Cara were "pelt-clad," which was the Faerie term for "nude." The Old Ones disdained human-made things, though they made an exception for cheese.

Rupeenla sat cross-legged nearby. She was also pelt-clad, but her pelt was glossy fur similar to an otter's. She was the size of a girl of twelve winters and her body possessed a similar shape, with breasts that were no more prominent than a cat's. Aside from a covering of fur, her least human feature was her face. It was hairless, but the upper part sloped to a small, wide nose, giving the impression that she had a snout. A receding chin enhanced the look. Her eyes were much larger than any human's and resembled a cat's in their golden color and slit pupils. Her ears, which were placed like those of a human, were rabbitlike, although more pointed and not as long. Like a rabbit's ears, they twitched frequently, seeming to hear sounds that Yim couldn't. The hair on Rupeenla's scalp was no longer than elsewhere on her body. Despite this and a lack of prominent breasts, her gender was obvious.

Yim turned her attention to Cara and was glad to see that her color had returned and her sleeping face looked peaceful. The stump of Cara's severed arm was covered with what appeared to be spiderwebs that glistened with dewdrops. Yim was surprised to note that the webs weren't bloodstained although they dressed a fresh wound. It made her wonder how long she and Cara had been asleep. Yet when Yim glanced at her palms, her blisters looked recent and were unhealed. Thinking about the passage of time caused Yim to recall how urgent it was to reach Honus. *We were supposed to ride at dawn!* she thought, growing alarmed.

"Fear not, Mother," said Rupeenla. "You yet have time to do what's necessary."

Yim regarded her host, who smiled and bowed her head. It had been Rupeenla who had greeted Yim at the pool and directed that Cara be carried into Faerie. Yim remembered little of the journey to the den, except that she had been requested to leave her pack and her clothing on the same stone where Cara had placed Dar's Gift. The request had been a respectful one, but it also had felt like a command.

"That was not our wish, Mother," said Rupeenla, responding as if Yim had spoken. "In the unchanging realm, things are or they are not. Second pelts are not. Nor is that lump you carried on your back."

Yim wondered why.

"Who made the world, Mother?" replied Rupeenla in an amused tone. "Not I."

Snoff emerged from the den's tunnel-like entrance. He resembled his mate, except his back was striped like a chipmunk's. He bore a glowing sphere that cast the rosy light of dawn. When he released it, the sphere floated up to settle near the ceiling. It made the den brighter, and Yim noticed for the first time that a huge bear slept in one corner. The animal opened its eyes, stretched, rose, and padded over to sniff Yim and Cara. Snoff growled at it in a good-natured way. The bear responded in kind, then squeezed out the entranceway.

The brighter light also allowed Yim to see her hosts better. On the previous night—if her sense of time was accurate—they seemed prominent personages, perhaps rulers among their kind. Yet as far as Yim could determine in better light, they seemed quite young.

"Yes, we die," said Snoff, who, like his spouse, responded to unvoiced thoughts. "But we leave not our lives upon the Dark Path."

"Do you mean memories?" asked Yim.

"What else are memories but life?" replied Snoff. "For us, death is but a rest on a long journey. Rupeenla and I are new-birthed, but we remember the world's beginning."

"You've visited the Sunless Way," said Rupeenla. "Only humankind litters it with woe and terror. And what an evil those memories have wrought! Mother, you know of what I speak. You've met it. And humans call it 'god.' What foolery!"

"The Devourer?"

"Aptly named," said Snoff. "For it will eat all the world, and our journey will end with forever darkness."

"Lose your fear, husband. 'Not yet,' may become 'not so.' Mother brings hope."

Snoff regarded Yim with eyes that seemed old, wise, and sad. "But she brings so little, dearest."

"True. But little is better than none."

THIRTY-ONE

CARA STIRRED. "Yim," she said in a sleepy voice, "I've had the strangest dreams. We . . ." Her eyes opened and immediately widened. They quickly went from Rupeenla, to Snoff, to her stump, and back again. "It was na a . . . You're really . . . The lake . . . The wolves and bears . . ."

Rupeenla smiled. "All true, Dar Child. Your kin are safe. You're safe. And we're well pleased, for you brought Mother to us."

Cara gazed at the stump of her right arm and gingerly felt it. "It does na hurt."

"You may pull the webs away," said Rupeenla.

Cara brushed the covering at the end of her arm to reveal bright pink skin. She gazed at it with amazement. "How?"

"A better question is 'why,'" said Rupeenla, "and I've already answered it. You've earned our honor."

"Thank you," said Cara.

"No, Dar Child, thank *you*."

Then Snoff rose and gathered things to eat from baskets about the den. The four sat on the hard-packed dirt floor and dined on flowers, honey, berries, and nuts. They washed it down with nectar from a hollowed gourd. The meal was the most satisfying that Yim had ever tasted. Everything was perfectly fresh, though some of the flowers blossomed only in early spring, while the nuts ripened in the fall. It made Yim wonder if Cara's arm had healed over many days while she had slept for but one night. Rupeenla responded to that thought. "How long lasts a dream?" she asked.

After their meal, Yim and Cara left the den. They had to crawl up a slanting earthen burrow, a feat that Cara managed with only one hand. The two women emerged into a thick clump of ferns at the base of an immense spruce. From only a few paces away, the burrow was invisible. The air was warm, and everything about them seemed both ancient and new. Yim felt new herself, a naked infant emerging into the world, and felt an infant's sense of wonder. She glanced at Cara, to see if she was experiencing the same.

Cara was gazing at an empty space before her. "Was it just last night that I had a hand there?" she asked in a mournful tone that tore at Yim's heart. "It seems much longer than that."

With Cara's words, all the horror of the previous night returned to Yim. "It was my fault, Cara. I'm so sorry."

"How was it your fault? You saved my life."

"Because those men never would have come if not for me."

"Perhaps that's true. But you were supposed to come," replied Cara. "And I'm glad you did, even though I think those men were supposed to come also. I believe that because my dreams last night were like your dreams. I saw things. True things. That was Rodric's corpse in the tunnel. He was tricked by the Devourer's servant, the same one who convinced the Sarf to kill you." Cara smiled grimly. "Do na worry. That man's powerless now. The only death he seeks is his own."

"So you've had a vision?"

"Na a vision. The Old Ones showed me those things, using dreams as a kind of speech. They're powerful, but also helpless. They know much, but na the future. That's hidden. Even from Karm." Cara sighed. "But they told me this: We'll part today, for you must journey to Honus alone. I've played my role, and my clan needs me. Like the Old Ones, all I can do now is wait and hope."

Then it seemed to Yim that Cara was a changed woman. It wasn't merely the missing arm; she had become someone wiser, quieter, and perhaps more melancholy. Cara's brief stay with the Old Ones had altered her, and seeing that, Yim understood why Faerie was perilous to enter.

The two women walked silently together for a long while among the giant trees. The Old Ones were nowhere to be seen, but Yim sensed their presence. It was a benign one. The ground was soft beneath her feet and a delicate breeze washed over her bare skin. It was a place of innocent pleasures. Under its influence, Cara's mood seemed to lighten, and when a cloud of butterflies fluttered above, she gazed at them with the delight of a child. Then she spoke to Yim at last, sounding more like the exuberant and romantic Cara of old. "You *will* return, Yim. I know you will. And when you do, you must tell me *everything*. Na holding back. And na modesty either. Zounds, especially that! I will na stand for it!"

Yim grinned. "I promise. And if my child's a girl, I'll name her Cara."

At sunset, Yim and Cara returned to the flat-topped stone, accompanied by a throng of Old Ones. There, the faeries gave Yim leaf-wrapped bundles of provisions that could be eaten without cooking, since they were aware that Yim had jettisoned her cooking pot and fire-making iron. Then they departed without ceremony, blending into the forest so quickly and quietly that they seemed to disappear. When the faeries were gone, Yim and Cara dressed.

"I'll walk with you to the boat," said Yim to Cara.

"I wish I were going with you," said Cara. "I so wanted to see Honus's face when he learns he's the one."

"Cara! That will be a private moment!"

"Oh, nay. He'll know the moment he sets eyes on you."

Yim felt that Cara spoke the truth, and it made the lonely journey ahead seem less daunting. When the women reached the boat, they found it draped with flowers. A garland of yellow leaves sat on a seat. Yim took Cara's extra clothes from the pack and waded out to the boat to place them there. When she retrieved her sandals, she noted that the oars were gone. Then Cara waded to the boat, placed the garland on her head, and climbed aboard. As soon as Cara was seated, Yim pushed the boat free from the gravel. As the vessel glided into the stream, Yim waded back to shore. There she slipped on her sandals and hurried along the bank, for an unseen force was quickly pulling the boat to the lake. As she ran, she waved to Cara. "Good-bye, good-bye!" she called out, feeling inexplicably sad.

Cara called and waved back, seeming to be gripped by the same emotion. Eventually, she glided into the lake, stranding Yim on its shore. Cara continued to wave with her remaining hand, growing ever smaller until she was but a speck in a wide expanse of water that glowed with the shades of the evening sky.

As the light began to fade, a crow landed on Yim's shoulder. Yim smiled and said, "Hello, Kwahku. Are you to guide me again?"

The bird cawed and flew to a tree branch in the distance. Despite her greeting to Kwahku, Yim felt hesitant to follow him, for she assumed that by doing so she was placing herself in the Old Ones' power. *Why worry about that now? You've done it before.* Nevertheless, Yim remained put. The faeries seemed aware of her intentions and obviously placed their hopes in her. *But are their goals the same as mine? Or Karm's, for that matter?* Yim had no way of telling. The Old Ones might know much, but they were closemouthed.

After pondering the matter further, Yim felt forced to trust in the faeries' benevolence. With Cara gone, following Kwahku offered her the best hope of reaching Honus. Thus Yim strode toward the waiting bird. Kwahku took off as soon as Yim reached him. He flew a short distance up a wooded slope, perched until Yim caught up with him, and then flew farther. He continued in that manner until it was dark. When Kwahku landed on a stony ledge and didn't fly off again, Yim realized that she was supposed to camp there. She fed the crow some of the porridge grain, and opened a leaf-wrapped bundle for her dinner. It contained fresh spring strawberries and fall hazelnuts.

The ledge provided a commanding view of the lake and the village near its shore. As Yim watched, a line of torches moved from the hall to the dock. Strains of music drifted up, mingled with cheers. *Cara's returned to her people*, Yim thought, *in a flower-filled boat from the realm of Faerie*. She smiled, imagining what songs the bards would weave from such a magic night. Then Yim went to sleep and dreamed of Honus.

Yim rose with the sun, ate a hasty meal with her feathered guide, and the two departed. Kwahku chose a rugged path, but Yim didn't question his judgment. She was unarmed, and Lord Bahl wasn't the only threat. Refugees had brought tales of savage feuding in the west, and more recently it was said that dark-haired women were in special danger. Thus Yim was anxious to travel unseen. The bird seemed to understand that.

By concentrating on her guide, Yim gained little sense of the route she traveled, other than it seemed erratic. Sometimes Kwahku soared high up and disappeared for a long while before returning to show the next leg of the journey. Yim was confident that the bird would keep her safe, but she was less certain that he was aware of her need for speed. It would gain her nothing to arrive alive and find Honus slain. She knew that he would reach Tor's Gate long before she did. Yim had no idea if Lord Bahl would be waiting when Cronin's troops arrived. A battle could be raging at that very moment. The only thing Yim could do was walk as quickly as possible, so she did.

Upon her first day of travel, Yim climbed the mountain above Cara's lake, descended to the wooded valley on the other side, made her way along its length, ascended to a ridge, and followed its crest until sunset. Kwahku led her to a spot that was sheltered from the wind, but it was still cold. After eating, Yim gathered dried leaves. Then, wrapped in her cloak, she burrowed beneath them for warmth. The crow joined her to sleep.

The next day of travel was a blur of anxiety and exhaustion. Descending from the ridge was as hard as climbing to its crest. The valley below was a maze of jumbled boulders, and late in the afternoon, Yim waded across a wide swamp. She wondered if a bird could understand how difficult it was to walk through calf-deep muck. After nearly losing her scandals twice, she ended up carrying them. By the time they stopped for the day, Yim was so tired that she fell asleep while eating.

By the third day of travel, Yim lost any notion of where she was. Life was reduced to a matter of following the crow as her journey became a monotonous routine: Reach the bird, watch where he flew next, reach the bird again, and repeat over and over until it's too dark to see. Yim had no idea of when the routine would end. For all she knew, it would stretch on for days. The following day was like the previous one. The only thing that changed was that the mountains were higher, but that didn't stop Kwahku from leading Yim up one of them. She spent her coldest night yet near its summit.

The following morning, when Yim was descending the mountain's other side, she was able to overlook the northwestern landscape. Below lay an irregular series of ridges, most of them too low to be called mountains. In the distance, beyond the jumble of heights and valleys, rose a range of formidable peaks. A few were so high as to be capped by snow. The mountains formed a solid wall except in one place. There, they were notched by a narrow valley surrounded by steep hills. *Tor's Gate!* Yim thought, recognizing it from the maps.

As Yim climbed down the slope, she was encouraged to have seen her destination, but discouraged by its distance. Although it was hard to estimate how long it would take to reach Honus, she feared it would require several days. When Yim reached the valley floor, walking became easier, and she made better time. In the afternoon, she reached a long, broad valley that was mostly cleared and filled with peasant holdings. Judging from the state of the crops, the land looked fertile.

Up to that point, Kwahku had always avoided open places, but to Yim's surprise he flew across a field and landed on the roof of the nearest dwelling. For a moment, Yim hesitated to follow him. "Don't be silly," she said aloud. "He won't lead me astray now." Yim headed for the house, which was similar to those that she had seen among Clan Dolbane. To reach it, she passed through a field of grain that was ready to harvest.

When Yim arrived at the house, her guide didn't fly off immediately, which was puzzling. Curious why the house was apparently abandoned, Yim entered it. A family awaited her inside. They were lying on the floor. The mother and father had been hacked and stabbed to death. Their seven children lay beside them, arranged in a neat line according to age, from an infant boy on the far left to a girl of thirteen winters on the right. Each had his or her throat slit. Yim burst out sobbing at the sight, distraught by such wanton cruelty. She ran outside, and Kwahku flew off.

The crow soared over homes and abundant fields in a straight line, alighting far away in an apple tree heavy with fruit. Yim had an easy time reaching him, for a well-used road went in that direction. As soon as Yim reached the tree, the bird took off, leading her farther down the road. Though it was a relief to travel easily, Yim was devastated by the certainty that Kwahku chose the route because all the valley's inhabitants were dead.

By the time night fell, Yim had made good progress. Though there were empty homes nearby, Kwahku chose a sleeping spot in the woods. Yim was relieved that he did, marveling over the bird's insight. *How can a creature that kills only from necessity grasp human evil?* Yim saw no reason for the destruction within the valley. *All the crops here will rot and the houses will tumble down, and who will gain from it?* The chilling answer arose in Yim's mind. *The Devourer.* Then it seemed more urgent than ever to reach Honus in time.

The following day, Kwahku continued leading Yim down the open road until midmorning, when he led her back into the wilds. Afterward, the way he took her became wildly irregular, causing Yim to believe that she was skirting danger and it was nearly everywhere. When night fell, the crow didn't stop, but continued to guide Yim. Following a black bird at night wasn't an easy task. Frequently, Kwahku had to call out so Yim could find him, even though he had alighted only a short distance away. It was well past midnight when he finally stopped. Yim gave the crow a few handfuls of grain and dozed off without eating.

Shortly after Yim commenced traveling again, she crossed a barren hilltop and saw mountains. They appeared quite near, and Tor's Gate was near also. It seemed that she would reach it before noon, and the prospect invigorated her. Yim picked up her pace, but when she next viewed the mountains, they seemed only a little closer. She ended up spending the night in the woods and rising at dawn determined to complete her journey before sunset. Throughout the day, Kwahku guided her on a circuitous route that seemed evidence that the countryside was rife with danger. Then at dusk, the bird alighted on a tree branch above the first living man that Yim had seen since leaving Faerie. He was a soldier standing guard.

The soldier spied Yim and drew his sword. "Who goes about?"

Yim advanced as Kwahku flew away. "I'm Yim," she said.

"So what? That means naught to me."

Assuming the soldier was new and wouldn't know Honus either, Yim simplified her reply. "I've come with news for your general. Will you take me to him?"

"I ken na leave my post, so ye must wait awhile." He raised a wooden whistle to his lips and blew a short series of notes that imitated a birdcall. Soon afterward, another soldier appeared. He didn't recognize Yim either. "This lass asks to see the general," said the first soldier. "Says she has news."

The new arrival regarded Yim suspiciously. "Mayhap, ye do. Mayhap nay. Why are ye dressed as a Bearer?"

"Because I am one."

The soldier appeared dubious. "Well, Bearer or nay, drop that pack and hold up yer arms."

Yim did as she was told, and the soldier pushed the pack away with his foot. Then he felt Yim for hidden weapons before shouldering the pack himself. "The countryside's gone mad with feuding. How'd ye get here?"

"Through Karm's grace," replied Yim.

The soldier snorted. "Well, I'll take ye to our general. He's a shrewd one and sees through lies. Fer yer sake, ye best na be bearing one." The soldier drew his sword and led Yim over open ground flanked by steep, wooded hills. As Yim walked, she spied a few soldiers but no encampment until her escort led her into a gap between two hills. There she saw a collection of tents, and also men who seemed to be living in the open. It was dark, but it appeared that there had been fighting already, for Yim spied some wounded men and passed one dead one.

Yim's guide took her to a cluster of large tents, which Yim assumed was Cronin's headquarters. She feared that Cronin would want to talk with her awhile before taking her to Honus. So close to her goal, the thought of a further delay grated her. *Be calm*, she told herself. *Soon I'll be with Honus*. But anticipation was agony, and Yim flushed with nearly unbearable excitement.

Her escort halted before a tent that was flanked by guards. "This lass claims she has a message for the general," he said. "I've checked her. She's unarmed."

"I'll take her from here," said one of the guards. He grabbed Yim by the arm and led her into the tent. Inside was a sort of vestibule, with the far end of the tent shut off by a cloth partition. Yim could hear men's voices behind it.

Unable to contain herself any longer, Yim called out. "General Cronin! It's me, Yim!"

The cloth partition parted and Honus stepped out. "Cronin's dead," he said in a controlled voice. "I'm general now."

THIRTY-TWO

OVER THE past days, Yim had imagined her reunion with Honus in countless variations, but none of them was like the actual moment. Honus struggled to keep his face neutral, but Yim saw a range of emotions pass over it. The first was shock, followed by concern and then sorrow. Suffused through them all was love, but she never caught a glimpse of happiness.

The guard still gripped Yim's arm. "General, do you know this woman?"

"I do."

Yim heard a hint of tenderness in Honus's voice. Then the partition parted further, and a dozen men peered at her. Some she knew as Cronin's officers, but most were strangers. In the presence of those men, Honus's face stiffened, and when he spoke again, his tone was formal. "Why are you here?"

"The clan hall was attacked. Cara was wounded but has recovered."

"You came alone to tell me this?"

"I've come because Karm sent me," said Yim, also conscious of her audience. "The matter is both urgent and personal."

"We're deploying for battle tonight. It's a matter that can't be postponed. I'll speak with you as soon as possible." Honus addressed the guard. "This woman is my Bearer, so honor her. Billet her in General Cronin's tent and see to her comfort." Then he stepped behind the partition and rejoined his officers.

The guard bowed respectfully. "Please come, Karmamatus. I'll see to your needs."

As she was being led away, Yim said, "General Cronin was my friend. Do you know what happened to him?"

"He fell to a traitor with a poisoned blade," said the guard. "The man was a clan chieftain whose mind was twisted by the black priests. He came to offer aid and instead slew the general and over half his staff. He would have killed them all if na for Honus."

"And why is Honus general now?"

"He was made so by acclamation. Na soldier can match his experience or wisdom."

The guard opened the flap of a good-sized tent that was furnished with a folding cot and table. Cronin's possessions were still there, and Yim had the impression that they had been left untouched. Gazing at them, she envisioned Cara's grief upon hearing of her brother's death. That image increased her own grief for the man who had treated her with kindness when she had been only a slave.

"Can I get you anything, Karmamatus?"

"My pack, please," said Yim, "and some water for washing."

After the guard bowed and left, Yim sat on the cot. She was so disappointed and anxious that she feared she might burst out sobbing. However, the presence of strangers within earshot was inhibiting, and she certainly didn't want Honus to find her weeping. So she waited and tried to follow Honus's example by putting on a calm mask. A short while later, the guard returned with her pack, a small cooking pot filled with water, and a reasonably clean rag. After he departed, Yim washed the dirt from her hands, face, and arms before cleaning her legs and feet. Then she waited for Honus.

Time passed with agonizing slowness, and whenever Yim heard footsteps, she thought they were Honus's. As her wait dragged on, Yim's fatigue got the better of her. She grew drowsy and lay down upon the cot. Then without intention, or even awareness that it was happening, she went to sleep.

The delicate touch of fingers upon her cheek woke Yim. A lantern illuminated the tent, and Honus was kneeling beside the cot, his eyes rimmed with tears. "Why did you come?" he asked in a mournful voice. "This is a deadly place."

Yim didn't answer. Instead she seized Honus and kissed him hungrily as pent-up passion overwhelmed her. Honus responded in kind, but after they kissed awhile, Yim sensed that he was fighting to rein his feelings. Then Yim broke off from kissing. "Honus, Karm has sent me here because I'm the Chosen. It's you, Honus! You!"

"What?"

"It's *your* child I'm supposed to bear."

"You've had a vision?"

"I didn't need a vision. When Karm helped me restore

your life, your spirit and mine mingled on the Dark Path. That's when I came to love you. Our love is Karm's gift. It's also her sign. I see that now."

"Yim, I must set the lines tonight. My officers are waiting outside."

"Don't you understand?" said Yim. "I've traveled for days so we could couple. It's important. I believe it'll change everything."

"Shouldn't our child be conceived in tenderness, not haste? Yim, I must leave for a little while."

"Why? Tell me what's so important."

"Five days ago, Lord Bahl seized the fortress before Tor's Gate. He always follows the same pattern. First, he establishes a base to ravage the countryside and gather men to join his forces. Everyone else is butchered. A period ensues while growing madness enrages the recruits. Then Bahl's army bursts forth again, and the rampage begins anew. That time draws nigh. Tomorrow or soon after, Bahl's men will surge through this narrow way. If we're to stop them, here's where it'll be. There'll be no second chances, or hope if we fail."

"Our child will be that hope."

"Not if its mother is hacked to pieces. Oh, Yim, I fear for you!"

"Have faith, not fear. Father our child."

"I will. Tonight, if Karm permits." Honus embraced Yim and tenderly kissed her. "Sleep while I arrange my forces. I'll return before dawn. Then we'll have our time together and hopefully beget a miracle."

As Honus rose, Yim could see that he was torn between love and duty. As his Bearer, she could command him to stay and he would. But that would reduce her time of bliss to a matter of breeding, a quick tup while Honus's officers waited outside. Yim didn't want to settle for that. She rose to give a parting kiss. "Come back as soon as you can," she whispered. "I'll be here, dreaming of you."

When Honus departed into the night, Yim lay down on the cot. Her entire body felt alive with excitement, and she couldn't imagine how she could possibly sleep. Yet somehow she did.

A presence in the dark tent woke Yim. "Honus?" she whispered. But the silhouette was that of a woman, not a man. Yim froze. Then the figure became more visible, glowing with inner light until Yim beheld Karm. As she had been in Yorn's moonlit courtyard and outside Bremven's gate, the goddess was stained by the blood of those she mourned. She regarded Yim with an expression that combined deep love and sadness.

Karm smiled. "I chose well. You've endured and overcome much to reach this moment."

Yim bowed her head. "It was worth it. Thank you, Goddess."

"There's no cause to thank me. You made the choices that brought you here. You might have fled from the Seer and lived your life as a servant girl; or let the dark man steal Honus's soul; or remained Commodus's ward."

Yim smiled. "But you knew I wouldn't abandon my path."

"I never know the future," Karm said. "My children are free to find their way, although I know where each path leads. Even now, I don't know if you'll accept the man who should father your child."

"Accept him? Of course, I will. I love him!"

"No. You love Honus."

Yim felt a sudden, icy shock. Her hands began to tremble, and when she spoke, her quiet voice quivered. "But my love for him was your gift!"

"It was. Everything you've seen and everything you've endured has been for a purpose. You shouldn't choose your path blindly. You had to see everything; what will be gained and what will be lost through your choice."

"The Wise Woman always said that you'd reveal the father. I thought that you had."

"I have not, but I'll do so now."

"Who?"

"Lord Bahl."

Upon hearing those words, the world seemed to fall away for Yim, and she felt suspended over an abyss. There seemed to be no future other than endless despair. For a long time, she couldn't speak; she felt too numb. Then a spark of anger flared in her chest. It grew to resentment approaching rage. "All my life! All my life for *this*!" For a long while, Yim's outrage silenced her. When she spoke again, her voice was taut with bitterness. "If you can foresee where a path ends, how could you think I'd bed a monster?"

"Because you've seen what'll happen if you don't," Karm replied. "Lord Bahl is the Devourer's incarnation, and every violent death heightens his power. Honus can't stop him. He'll be swept away in the wave of slaughter that will overflow the world. You've seen its horrors. No one will be safe."

"I don't understand. How can I do anything about that?"

"If Lord Bahl conceives a child, he'll lose his power."

"But won't it pass to his son? Isn't that why his line waxes and wanes over time? The son always becomes his father."

"But this time there's a chance to break that cycle," Karm said. "Take the child north and raise him apart from strife. Meanwhile, Honus will live and so will Cara and countless others. There'll be hope."

"And if I stay with Honus?"

"You'll have your moment of love. But as you hold Honus in your arms, you'll know he's doomed. He already suspects he is, and you won't be able to hide the truth from him."

"But if I go to Bahl, he'll live?"

"If you conceive a child with Bahl."

"But that's not certain?"

"Nothing's certain."

"Just Honus's death if I fail!" said Yim, not bothering to hide her bitterness. "And how can I get Bahl to tup me? I've no experience in such things."

"You're a clever woman, and a beautiful one. And part of Lord Bahl remains a man. As the Devourer overtakes him, his human part craves earthly pleasures all the more desperately. Bahl's not wholly one thing. He's mostly monster now, but desire can still sway him."

"But the Devourer part will know me for what I am."

"I'll hamper that. I've struggled with the Devourer before. If you're quick, you'll have time to do what's necessary."

Yim began to sob quietly as she realized what she must do, knowing that she would try to do it. She would sacrifice her happiness to give others hope and save Honus's life. *Is it really such a sacrifice?* she asked herself. *My happiness has been mostly an illusion. But I did have that one morning with Honus. That's the treasure I'll bear to the Dark Path.* Yim wiped her eyes and turned to tell the goddess that she would go to Lord Bahl, but the goddess had already vanished.

Yim sat awhile in the dark tent, summoning her courage. She felt that she must do it quickly, for she didn't want to face Honus again. The thought of that was far too painful, and it spurred her into action.

First, Yim rummaged through the pack until she found the slave's tunic that she used as a nightgown. It was her only garment that didn't mark her as a Bearer. Yim shed her clothes and put the tunic on. Then she groped around in the dark until she found Cronin's dagger. She used its blade to cut away the cloth around the flimsy garment's neckline. Working mostly by feel, she cut and tore the fabric until the upper swells of her breasts were exposed. She thought the hemline was short enough, having once been cut to make a bandage. However, she made a slit to provide a glimpse of leg.

Having decided that her outfit was sufficiently provocative, Yim neatly piled her Bearer's clothes on the cot. She wanted to give Honus some message to show that she hadn't abandoned him uncaringly. Knowing that he couldn't read, and not wanting anyone else to read her message to him, she wondered what to do. Then she had an idea, and began rummaging through the pack again. When she found what she was looking for, she placed it atop her Bearer's clothes.

The item was the scrap of embroidered fabric from Mirien's wedding gown. It had been given to Yim on her second morning with Honus, and it seemed a perfect symbol for their fate. Mirien had never worn the gown. Like Yim, Mirien's hope for bliss had been shattered. In the girl's case, death had intervened. Yim felt her fate would be a form of death. *At least it's my choice*, thought Yim. *Mirien didn't have even that.*

Yim clung to that meager bit of solace as she strapped on her sandals. Then she found Cronin's cloak and helm and donned them as a makeshift disguise, hiding her hair beneath the helmet. With that done, Yim slipped into the dark to find Lord Bahl.

THIRTY-THREE

YIM EMERGED from the tent into an encampment that was mostly empty. The few soldiers that remained were caught up in the confusion that precedes a battle. Thus she was able to pass unchallenged. She reached a wooded slope and began to climb it. Yim assumed that Honus would position his men so they could descend from high ground upon Bahl's soldiers as they marched through the narrow gap between the hills. Accordingly, she avoided those places, choosing a route through the hills that stayed far from the gap.

In imagining Honus's strategy, Yim envisioned him choosing ground and placing men for combat. *While he's doing it, is he also thinking of me?* Yim was sure that he was. The idea of Honus returning to Cronin's empty tent tortured her. For a while, she wavered and seriously considered going back. *How much is a moment of love worth?* Yim felt willing to die for it. She imagined that Honus was willing also. *But others would die because of that moment. Too many to count.* Yim sighed and continued onward.

The terrain was rugged and trees blocked the moonlight. Yim made her way cautiously through the shadows, fearful of blundering into soldiers. Yet the soldiers she sought to avoid were friendly. Her goal was to reach the enemy. Yim had no idea what she would do when she encountered her foes. Dying was a possibility, but she believed that if death were certain, Karm wouldn't have urged her to go.

Yim remembered from studying Cronin's maps that hills lined both sides of the passage known as Tor's Gate. The hills merged with the mountains that flanked the Gate's entrance. The maps had also depicted a fortress constructed on one of those mountainsides. Yim assumed that it was the fortress that Honus had spoken about and that Lord Bahl would be found there. When the first light of dawn appeared in the east, Yim reached the last hill. She climbed to its top, but it was wooded, forcing her to descend the other side before she could view what lay ahead.

When Yim passed beyond the trees, she saw that the gap between the peaks did indeed resemble a natural gate. To her left and right were tall mountains that extended into the plain to create a funnel leading to the gap. Hills were visible in the distance, but the nearest ground was flat. To her right was a fortress built near the bottom of a mountain slope. Portions of the structure were blackened, but its outer walls remained intact. Scattered around the captured stronghold were the makeshift encampments of the troops that had taken it. They comprised a chaotic sprawl that extended into the despoiled countryside. Yim glimpsed a few fires with men roving about them. Even from a distance, the men seemed to possess the agitated manner of disturbed ants.

They will be my first obstacle, thought Yim, *my first chance to die*. She pulled off Cronin's helm and cloak. Their purpose was accomplished. After some consideration, she also shed her sandals, reasoning that a barefoot woman seemed more vulnerable. Yim planned to pose as a camp founder willing to betray others to save her neck. By wearing only her flimsy tunic, she hoped to give the impression that she had just fled from some man's bed.

Yim was terrified as she walked toward the men, and her terror grew as she advanced. Her short journey was a descent into a nightmare. The land about her had been fair and populous, but all that had changed. Nothing remained whole. All the houses were in ruins, and their inhabitants slain as if their killers had competed to see who could commit the worst atrocity. Yim turned from one horrific sight only to behold another: Heads hung from branches like fruit. A fence had been constructed using death-stiffened limbs. A burnt child dangled from a doorway. While Yim viewed these horrors, she approached their perpetrators.

The army's encampments seemed flung down haphazardly. Some featured crude tents or makeshift shelters, while others were merely spots where men sprawled in clusters on the ground. One site had a cold cooking fire with a spit that skewered a charred human leg. Because it wasn't yet dawn, most of the men slumbered. By weaving a route between the scattered sleepers and avoiding the few who were awake, Yim penetrated the army's lines a short distance before she was stopped. A huge unkempt man in blood-caked peasant's clothes rose from a sleeping mass of men and strode up to her, a bloody hatchet in one hand.

Yim folded her arms across her chest and squarely looked the advancing man in the eye. "You!" she said in a loud voice that she hoped masked her fear. "Take me to Lord Bahl at once!"

The man halted. "Why ye wanna see the master?"

"Because I'm his."

The man moved forward, his eyes taking in Yim's body. As frightening as that was, it seemed a hopeful sign to her. *At least*, she thought, *he's not a raving killer*. When the man groped at Yim's breasts, she slapped him hard across the face. "I belong to Lord Bahl. Touch what's his and feel his wrath!"

Rage filled the man's face after Yim struck him, and for an instant, she thought that he would slay her on the spot. Then that rage gave way to fear, giving Yim her first glimpse of the terror that Bahl inspired in his men. "I'll take ye ta the master," the man said in a meek tone.

Yim grabbed the man's arm as she walked beside him. By that ploy, she hoped that they would be seen as belonging together. They had made only a little progress toward the fortress when Yim began to sense the same malign presence that she had at Karvakken Pass and the ruins of Karm's temple. *Karm said Lord Bahl is the Devourer's incarnation.* Then Yim realized that she had fulfilled Theodus's quest and found the source of evil. If she fulfilled her own quest, she would mate with it.

The closer Yim and her escort came to the fortress, the more densely packed were the men around it. They were rising with the sun, and Yim could view them better. She thought they scarcely comprised an army, for she associated armies with discipline. What she saw seemed more a mob of armed peasants. An air of madness pervaded them. Wild-eyed men paced about, glancing balefully at their fellows. Savage fights broke out spontaneously. Yim passed a man who repeatedly punched the bloody mush that once had been another man's face. Like the malign aura, the madness increased with each step toward the fortress.

Only when Yim reached the entrance to the stronghold did she encounter some military discipline in the form of armored guards. They barred her and her escort's way. "What's yer purpose here?" asked one.

"She says she belongs ta the master," said Yim's escort.

One of the guards grinned. "That could be said of every bitch. What makes ye so special?"

"I have something he wants," replied Yim.

"Mayhap," said the guard. "That leg will yield some nice filets. And ye'll look comely writhing on a stake."

"I think your master will find other uses for me," said Yim. "Since it's his choice, you'd best take me to him."

"He's not awake yet," said the guard's companion, as he squeezed Yim's buttocks through her tunic. "So we'll just tup until he rises."

"So you'd dare taste your master's meat before he sups? Perhaps I'll let him know."

"Not if I cut yer throat!" replied the guard, drawing his dagger.

"And when he looks for me, just lie to him about what you did," said Yim. She flashed a taunting grin. "I'm *sure* he'll believe you."

The guard scowled. "Ye'll see him soon enough. And when he's done with ye, mayhap he'll toss us what's left." He turned to another guard. "Put her in a box till the master rises."

The third guard grabbed Yim's arm. "Come on, birdie." Then he marched her inside the fortress. Beyond the gatehouse was a cobble-paved courtyard. The men milling about it wore armor or at least items of it, but they seemed more like lunatics than soldiers. Many had vacant expressions, and Yim sensed that the only thoughts within their heads would be those Bahl placed there. Other men glared at her with hate that inspired terror. A few men wept openly.

A large stone keep dominated the fortress's interior, and Yim thought that she would be taken there. Instead, the guard dragged her toward a side of the courtyard where there were several large piles of ashes. In the center of each was a blackened rectangular box that was sized to accommodate a squatting person. One side of each box was a latched door. The other sides had bands of tiny holes.

The guard walked over to one of the boxes, unlatched its door, and swung it open. Then he tilted the box so the charred corpse inside it tumbled out. It was so badly burnt that Yim couldn't tell if it had been a man or a woman. The guard kicked the blackened body, and it crumbled into pieces. Then he grinned at Yim. "Yer room's ready. Get in."

Yim had no idea whether she was passively submitting to an excruciating death, but she seemed to have little choice but to climb inside. A squatting position was the only one she could assume. As she did, the guard closed and latched the door. It was dark inside the iron box and its interior was coated with greasy soot that had a nauseating smell. Yim felt a rush of panic that she had to struggle hard to subdue. *The worst thing that can happen is that I'll die*, she thought. But then she realized that wasn't the worst thing. *If I die, I fail. Then many others will die also, and Honus will be among the first.*

Yim's time in the box stretched on and on. Squatting became agonizing. The box warmed in the sun and grew stultifying. She felt an urgent need to relieve her bladder, and though she fought the urge, eventually she had no choice. Although she heard noises from the courtyard, the holes in the box's walls were positioned so she couldn't view out them. Yim lost all sense of time. It might have been early morning or late afternoon; all she knew was that every moment dragged.

Sometime during that nightmare, Yim heard a woman weeping and the sound of footsteps nearby. Next came the clank of a metal door being shut. More footsteps followed. Yim smelled smoke. Then the screams began. There was no question as to their source or cause. Yim tried to shut them out by covering her ears, but she could still hear them. Moreover, she felt them clawing inside her. They went on and on until Yim feared that she would go mad. Even when the screaming stopped, their terror resounded in Yim's thoughts.

Eventually, the door to Yim's cramped prison opened. The sunlight was blinding, although it was late afternoon, and her aching body could barely move. "Get out!" said a voice. "The master will see ye. Afterward, who knows? Mayhap 'twill be yer turn ta roast." Yim slowly crawled out, moving as stiffly as an old woman. She smelled of burnt flesh and her own sweat and urine. Soot was smeared on her arms, legs, and tunic. *And now I must seduce a stranger.*

An armored man gripped Yim's arm, his gauntlet biting into her flesh as he tugged her toward the keep where the building's interior reflected the malevolence of its master. Everything was vandalized. Doors and windows were smashed. Broken furniture and shattered glass littered the floor. Being barefoot, Yim had to mind her step, which wasn't easy in her escort's iron grip. Besides the destruction, there was the sight and smell of wholesale slaughter. Bloodstains were everywhere, and some victims, or parts of them, still lay about. Armed and dangerous-looking men with mad or vacant eyes roamed the hallways that Yim was hustled through. She was amazed by how many of the men were mutilated, though they seemed oblivious of their injuries. Once again, Yim was glad to be escorted, however roughly.

Beyond a pair of smashed doors was a large hall with a

lofty ceiling. A huge fire burned in a great stone fireplace, and the first thing Yim felt was a wave of heat. The odor of blood was especially strong and the floor felt sticky beneath her feet. A series of upright poles flanked the aisle leading to a raised platform. Each pole impaled a man or woman, transforming him or her into a macabre form of banner. Some of them were still alive. Upon the platform three men sat in ornate chairs. The bearded man seated to the right wore the black robes and iron pendant of a priest. To Yim's surprise, she recognized the gaudily dressed young man seated on the left. He was Yaun, the count's son who had carried Honus's pack.

Yim's gaze quickly shifted to the pale man seated in the center. He was richly dressed in fabrics sewn with gold, and even from across the room, his eyes were compelling. Yim immediately sensed his power. The fortress was a maelstrom of madness and savagery, and he was its center and source. Yim bowed her head low. "Lord Bahl," she said. "My beloved."

THIRTY-FOUR

LORD BAHL'S sardonic laughter echoed across the huge hall. "Your beloved? Did I hear that rightly? Come closer, slut, so I might gaze upon you."

Yim advanced slowly and proudly, as if she were dressed in silken robes and smelling of perfume. It was a tawdry performance, but it seemed to amuse its principal audience. When Yim reached the platform, she kneeled before it and bowed her head.

"Look at me!" commanded Bahl.

Yim faced upward, and Bahl's eyes bore into hers. She felt their force and resisted it by veiling her thoughts so he might see only what she wished. That was fear and awe. She couldn't fabricate desire.

"You told men that I possessed you. What prompted you to say that?"

"Because I wished it so," replied Yim. "Don't you like possessing lovely things?"

"I think I might enjoy your loveliness better if you were skewered naked on yonder pole," replied Bahl.

Yim lowered her voice, but kept her eyes raised. "You're all-powerful, my lord, and can pierce me in any way you wish. But a wooden stake lacks feeling; a different shaft might please you more."

A hint of a smile crossed Bahl's lips. "How droll! A silver-tongued tart."

Yaun leaned toward Lord Bahl. "I know this woman, Your Lordship. A Sarf named Honus owned her as a slave."

"I remember you, too," said Yim. She forced a laugh. "You meekly carried Honus's pack before I took it up. Did he tup you also?"

Yaun flushed red. "This woman's a whore and a spy!"

Yim returned her gaze to Lord Bahl. "True on both counts, my lord. But I'm your spy."

"How so?"

"Honus now commands an army, and I know his plans."

"Why come to me with this?" asked Bahl.

"Because I'm drawn to power. In troubled times, a strong man is a woman's only refuge. Honus could make Yaun heel like a cur, but you, my lord, will make the whole world heel."

"That I will," replied Bahl. "But unfortunately for you, the world's full of women, and whores are especially easy to come by. So tell me something useful if you wish to live. Be quick."

"Honus has massed an army about Tor's Gate. There, he

intends to ambush you. His men are skilled with arms, and he believes they can prevail in a tight place that limits the opponent's numbers."

The priest spoke for the first time. "This whore seems uncommonly versed in tactics. Perhaps she was instructed on what to say. Best kill her."

Yaun grinned. "I know of some amusing ways. We could make a show of it."

As Lord Bahl regarded her, Yim thought she caught a glimmer of interest in his gaze. "I'll send scouts to test this bitch's tale," he said. "If she proves to be my spy, who knows? I might use her as my whore. If she's false, I'll make her death a spectacle. Put her in the dungeon until I decide her fate."

The guard seized Yim with his bruising grip and marched her from the hall. As he led her to the dungeon, he said, "Ye're a wily bitch. Already, ye've lasted longer than most."

A set of winding stone steps ended at a short hallway with seven oak doors. The only light there came from the guard's torch. Judging from her long descent down the stairway, the chill of the air, and the dankness of the walls, Yim judged that she was deep underground. When the guard opened the door to her cell, his torch briefly illuminated it. The stone chamber wasn't long enough for a person to stretch out fully, and it was only half as wide. A leaky wooden bucket served as a toilet. It was nearly full. A second bucket held some water. Some straw had been cast upon the stone floor, quite long ago by the look of it. Then the guard pushed Yim into the chamber and shut the door.

After the guard bolted the door and left with his torch, Yim's cell was absolutely black. She explored it with senses other than sight. The stone walls were rough, cold, damp, and gritty. She could touch both side walls without fully extending her arms. The air smelled of wet stone, excrement, and unwashed bodies rancid with fear. The only sounds

Yim heard were those she made herself. As far as she could tell, she was the only prisoner. Yim groped about until she found the water bucket and drank some of its foul contents.

The chilly stone floor made an uncomfortable bed, and Yim slept only sporadically. She hadn't eaten since the previous day, so hunger also hampered rest. Although the dungeon was an improvement over squatting in an iron box and never knowing if she was about to be burnt alive, it scarcely felt that way. Any number of terrible fates might be awaiting her, and accomplishing her goal didn't seem much better. Yim feared that bedding with Lord Bahl would be different from enduring rape only in that she must pretend to enjoy it. She questioned whether she would be up to the task, worrying that when the crucial time came she would be unable to counterfeit desire when all she felt was revulsion.

There were no meals or human contact, so the continuous darkness quickly rendered time irrelevant. Living in a monotonous void, Yim had no idea whether it was night or day, how long she slept or lay awake, or the length of her confinement. She tried to think of happy things, but every pleasant memory seemed remote, while her fears were fresh and insistent. Yim's sense of reality began to dissipate until she felt that she had fallen into an abyss that swallowed time and hope.

When the cell door opened, it came as an unexpected shock. A man stood in the dank hallway bearing a torch. A large bucket lay close to his feet, and some sheer cloth was draped over one of his arms. "Strip and wash yerself," he said. "Then ye'll see the master."

Yim obeyed, shedding her tunic while the guard watched. She grabbed the rag that floated in the bucket and used it to scrub her grimy body. Flower petals also floated in the water, so although it was cold, it was pleasantly scented. Although she was embarrassed to wash in the presence of a stranger, Yim forced herself to gaze into his eyes. The desire she found there was empowering.

When her spirit had mingled with Honus's, Yim had experienced how men viewed women. Yim knew the sight of her nudity thrilled the guard and stirred longing that she might use to her advantage. It was her only power within the nightmare place. To test it, she smiled at the man and slowed her scrubbing to a more sensual pace. After Yim washed thoroughly and brushed the water from her skin with her hands, the man held out the cloth. "This is for ye," he said in a voice that was warmer than before.

Yim smiled at him and replied in a soft, breathy voice, "Thank you."

The cloth turned out to be a gown made of sheer material that only partly hid her nudity. In the torchlight it appeared to be a rosy shade. Yim slipped it on. It was long and sleeveless with a slit neck, so it covered her body while also revealing it. Yim turned around so her guard might view her. "How do I look?" she asked, smiling as she did so.

The man grinned sheepishly. "Real pretty."

Yim held out her arm for the guard to take. "I hope our master agrees."

As Yim ascended the stairs, practicing doing it gracefully, she recalled Karm's words: *Part of Lord Bahl remains a man.* Yim resolved to find that part, focus on it, and play to it. She formed an image in her mind of a man shackled to a demon. *I must ignore the monster and find sympathy for the man*, she thought. Yim had no illusions that it would be easy, or that all men deserved sympathy. Nevertheless, it seemed a workable strategy, and she was determined to make it succeed.

It wasn't until Yim entered the hall that she discovered that evening was approaching. In addition to the fading daylight coming from smashed windows, the room was lit by numerous torches and a blazing fire in the massive hearth. The flames illuminated the bodies of men and women impaled on the tall wooden stakes that flanked a long banquet table. At its end, Lord Bahl sat in a thronelike chair. The priest sat to his right, but Yaun was seated elsewhere so that the place to Bahl's left was empty. Yim was encouraged by that until she noted that a nearby wooden stake was also vacant.

The other seats at the long table were filled by several dozen men who seemed military types. Yim was the only woman in the room, if she didn't count those on the stakes, and she was very much aware of the men's gazes as she was marched to the table's head. When she halted before Lord Bahl, she dropped to her knees and lowered her head. "Master," she said in a tone that she hoped sounded both submissive and seductive.

"Rise and look at me," commanded Lord Bahl. When Yim obeyed he gave her a smile, but it was a cold one. "I've prepared two places for you at this meal. This stool," he said, patting it, "and yonder stake." Bahl gestured to the empty wooden pole. It was a hand's width in diameter, tall, and bloodstained from its sharp point down to where an iron socket held it upright. Lord Bahl pointed elsewhere. "Look at that blonde."

Yim obeyed and regarded the nude woman upon a nearby stake. She gazed back with eyes filled with agony.

"That's Count Yaun's handiwork," said Bahl in a breezy manner. "His style's obscene, but he's a skilled craftsman. That bitch has endured one night so far, and some have wagered she'll last another. Do you think you can beat that mark?"

"If it would please Your Lordship, I'd try," replied Yim in a shaky voice. "But I'd prefer the stool."

"So you would, but your preference doesn't count." Lord Bahl glanced at a man seated near him. "General Var, your report."

The gray-haired officer rose and bowed differentially. "My lord, I sent a squad of men through Tor's Gate. They marched its length and returned. They spotted an abandoned encampment, but no troops."

Bahl's thin lips formed an icy smile. "That's a pretty gown. No point in staining it with blood. Take it off."

The room's heat and Yim's terror made her skin wet with sweat, so she nearly had to peel the gown from her body to remove it. When she stood naked and trembling before all the men, Bahl said, "Continue, General."

"Then I sent six men to scout atop the hills at night. Only one returned. He spied forces holding the high ground along the passageway. They were numerous and skillfully hidden."

Bahl addressed his general. "Blind those men who saw nothing and use them for sword practice." Then turned to Yim and patted the stool. "Brazen slut, don't you dress for dinner?"

The men burst out laughing as Yim quickly put the gown back on. As she sat down, she heard the general say. "Count Yaun, you owe me five golds. You wagered she'd piss herself."

Yim forced a smile. "General, he made that wager because he thought I'd act like him."

Even Lord Bahl laughed at that. It encouraged Yim to softly touch his hand, which felt unnaturally cold. "My lord," she whispered, "when you held my life in your hand, I fully felt your power."

Bahl said nothing, but he seemed pleased. Yim's mind was racing as she tried to understand him. He had enjoyed terrifying and humiliating her, but he had laughed when she made fun of Yaun. *Perhaps he's like a man who prides himself in breaking spirited steeds.* Yim decided to be arrogant and tart to everyone except Bahl. Toward him she would be submissive, fawning, and fearful. *At least the fearful part won't require acting.*

Yim sat upright in her stool to best display her body, a feat her damp, sheer gown made easy. She pretended to enjoy the men's lustful glances, while frequently gazing at Lord Bahl, as if to say, "I know I'm beautiful, but I'm yours only." Every time she looked at Bahl, she readily sensed the otherworldly being that possessed him. It was the source of his chill. Sitting close to Bahl in a skimpy gown, Yim was no longer hot, or even warm. As her nipples stiffened from the cold, she noted that the men who stared at them were dressed for winter.

Lord Bahl's chill extended to his features, which seemed as pale as quartz and as hard. He exuded an air of sinewy strength that left no room for softness. His eyes—so pale that his black pupils denominated them—epitomized both his coldness and his might. Yim was well versed in the arcane power that resided in some eyes, and she saw the forcefulness of his. Bahl's gaze would be dangerous to confront.

Peering at the other diners, Yim used her powers to view their inner qualities. Most of them were military men. They reminded her of Cronin's officers, though she perceived that they were far more hardened and ruthless. They were violent, but disciplined. Yim discovered no madness among them, which made her suspect that Lord Bahl had spared them that, finding rational officers more useful. Yim laid bare Count Yaun easily. He was sadistic, vain, and cowardly. The priest was an enigma. His face looked young, but his gray eyes belied that impression. His other qualities were impervious to her perception. Yim quickly glanced away, fearing that he could detect that she was probing him. Later, when she ventured another look, she found his suspicious expression disconcerting.

The meal was brought out. After Lord Bahl was served, the dishes and bottles were placed on the table for the diners to serve themselves. Yim was ravenous, but she neither filled her plate nor her drinking bowl, but left them empty and gazed at Lord Bahl like a dog begging from its master. Bahl ate awhile before he acknowledged the look. "Eat. Drink," he said in an indulgent tone.

Yim bowed her head and took food for her plate and wine for her bowl. Her memory of the charred leg caused her to avoid any meat, but fortunately there was some fowl. Her chill and terror made her gulp down the first bowl of wine, but she forced herself to sip from the second. The food and drink were good, an encouraging sign that Lord Bahl hadn't abandoned all human pleasures. As to whether he would seek pleasure from her, Yim still had no idea.

The meal progressed without Yim coming any closer to achieving her goal. She was afraid to appear too forward, for she realized that Bahl had to feel in control. Since he ate silently, the other diners were silent also. That provided Yim no opportunity for banter, sexual or otherwise. All she could do was try to appear alluring and hope for the best. The meal became a drinking session, and Yim still remained ignorant of her fate. When the drinking wound down, she decided that she must take a risk. Yim caught Bahl's eye and spoke to him in a tremulous whisper. "My lord, will you return me to the dungeon?"

Then Bahl's eyes traveled over Yim's body and took on an almost human look. "No, my little spy," he said after he finished his inspection. "Tonight you'll adorn my bed."

"My lord," said the priest, "that isn't wise."

Yim was surprised by the priest's tone. Even the general had been obsequious when addressing Lord Bahl, but the priest spoke to him as an equal.

"She's a slave and a whore," replied Bahl. "Surely no virgin."

"So you assume," said the priest. "I prefer to be certain." He regarded Yim. "Woman! Look me in the eye!"

Yim put on a meek expression as she obeyed, but she shielded her thoughts from scrutiny. After a moment, the priest frowned and turned to Bahl. "Something about her isn't right. I suggest you slay her."

"She's just a wench," said Bahl.

"If you *must* sport with her," replied the priest, "I insist you send her to Yaun first."

Lord Bahl shrugged and turned to Yaun. "Well, Count, it

seems the Most Holy Gorm has given you this wench for the night. You know what he requires. Tup her thoroughly."

"Yes, my lord." Count Yaun grinned maliciously at Yim, who was struggling to hide her shock. "I'll use her well."

"I know your habits," said Bahl. "Don't mar her."

"Never without your leave, my lord."

"Good," said Bahl, rising from his seat.

Yim rose with the others, her face a mask to conceal her despair. It had all been for naught. She had thrown away her single chance for love, endured pain and terror, and degraded herself so a sadistic coward might violate her. In the end, she would die and no one would be saved.

Yaun grabbed Yim's arm, gripping it so his fingers pressed on nerves. Then he squeezed until she winced from pain. "That was just a taste, you foul-mouthed slut!" he whispered. Yaun squeezed her arm again. "Follow at my heels and don't dare lag behind. We've a long night ahead."

THIRTY-FIVE

COUNT YAUN'S room was a large one on an upper floor of the keep. After Yim entered it, Yaun made her stand in its center as he shut and bolted the door. A blaze in the carved stone fireplace provided the only light. Its ruddy glow illuminated a large bed, stacks of valuables that Yim assumed were looted, a collection of shackles and other restraints, a pile of bloody rags, and a table covered with instruments for torture. The devices' shapes hinted at their gruesome uses, and when Yim saw them, she shuddered.

Yaun noted her reaction and smiled. "When Lord Bahl

tires of you—and he most surely will—I'll acquaint you with my playthings." He slowly walked over to Yim, grabbed her gown at the neckline, and tore it from her body. Then he grinned salaciously. "Stand like you did on the slave block." Yim lowered her hands to her sides and stared straight ahead as Yaun circled her. "My coppers bought you," he said, "but Honus denied me even a feel." Yaun reached out and grabbed one of Yim's breasts. "Well, where's Honus now?" Then he squeezed until Yim gasped from pain. "Answer me, slave!"

"I ran away from him."

"To your real master. To the man who bought you." Yaun squeezed Yim's other breast, causing her to moan. "Do you remember how much I paid?"

"Ten coppers."

"That's 'ten coppers, *Master*.' "

"Ten coppers, Master."

"And now you're secondhand goods. Did that Sarf use you often?"

"Every night, Master."

"Stand still while I see how worn you are."

Yaun's "inspection" was a brutal groping. As he pinched and poked Yim in ways that would leave no marks or in places where marks wouldn't show, she realized that inflicting pain aroused him. Thus she exaggerated her suffering, gradually escalating her wincing and moaning to writhing and screaming. The ploy worked, for Yaun eventually commanded her to undress him.

Yim obeyed, making sure she appeared abject and terrified. All the while, she steeled herself to attempt the one thing that might prevent her rape. She had conceived of it while following Yaun to his room. When her tormentor was undressed, she knelt on the floor before him, and bent down to kiss his feet in a slow, sensuous manner. Then she sat upright. "Since you're my master now, shall I perform the feat Honus taught me? You'll feel as if you're with dozens of women."

"Do your whore's trick," replied Yaun, "and pray it pleases me."

"It will, Master." Yim kissed Yaun's feet again, then sat on her heels.

Yim began her meditations, fearful she wouldn't complete them before Yaun grew impatient. Sure enough, she was only partway done when he said, "What is this? If you're just stalling, you'll regret it!"

When Yim remained silent to maintain her concentration, Yaun pinched her nipples. Still, Yim didn't react other than to grit her teeth. He squeezed harder before suddenly releasing them. "What's this?" he asked in an uneasy voice. "What are those moving shadows?"

Yim said nothing and kept her gaze forward, but she sensed that spirits were approaching. She knew they had arrived when Yaun gave a startled gasp. With the summoning complete, she turned to view what frightened Yaun.

The women were unclothed, as are all spirits of the dead. Yet when Yim glanced back at Yaun, he wasn't staring at their bodies, but at their faces. "I know them," he whispered in an awed voice. "I know them all!"

"Soon, I think you'll know them better," said Yim. She had recognized the woman who had suffered on the stake and who had not lived through the evening. The rest she had never seen before. Nevertheless, she knew that all the spirits shared one thing in common: Each had been one of Yaun's victims. The room was filled with them, and the air grew frigid from their otherworldly presence. The chill matched the spirits' icy hate. Even before they advanced, Yaun was backing away.

Unbound by the laws of the living world, the spectral women flew through the air and swirled around Yaun like a school of ravenous fish fighting over a bit of meat. The count fell to his knees and began to jerk and writhe. Yaun remained intact; yet by his actions, Yim assumed that he was suffering his victims' torments. She feared that he would scream, but only hoarse gurgles escaped his lips.

Driven by the vengeful spirits, Yaun gradually backed toward the fireplace. Then he entered it and cowered in the flames. His scorched flesh bubbled and fell away in blackened sheets. Yet he remained, immobilized by terror and whimpering shrilly, as the fire slowly consumed him. Apparently its torment paled compared to what his victims inflicted. As Yaun's writhing on the burning logs grew feebler, Yim put on the fur-trimmed cloak he had worn to dinner. He was still alive when she left his room.

Yim emerged into a dark hallway that was lit by only a few torches. She found a shadowed spot and leaned against the wall to regain her composure. She was shaky from her ordeal with Yaun and sore from his handling, but she knew that she had to act. Her doom would be sealed once Yaun's body was discovered. She had only one night to conceive a child, and first she had to find the father.

Looking up and down the hall, Yim tried to determine which doorway looked most opulent, reasoning that Lord Bahl would have the grandest quarters. Her greatest fear was that she'd blunder into the priest. *The one Bahl called the Most Holy Gorm*, she thought. *He already suspects me*. She studied the closed doors, but none stuck out. Eventually, she selected one because of its location at the end of the hall. Approaching it with her heart pounding, she softly knocked. The door opened. To Yim's dismay, General Var stood before her. "What are you doing here?" he asked. "Count Yaun's supposed to tup you."

"He did," replied Yim, "but he bores quickly when he can't hurt a woman."

"Aye, that's Yaun," said the general, betraying his contempt.

"So, I'm seeking my lord in hopes a man will finish what a boy had begun."

"Did Lord Bahl send for you?"

"No," replied Yim, trying to sound sensual and alluring. "But I'm certain he's waiting by his doorway."

General Var glanced in the direction of an archway. "Nonsense. You overestimate your charms."

Yim smiled sheepishly. "Well, I'd hoped he was waiting."

"Go back to Yaun. Lord Bahl isn't fond of surprises."

"I've been silly," said Yim. She cast Var a grateful look. "Thank you for the warning, General. When my lord tires of me, I hope he'll give me to you."

After the general closed his door, Yim rushed toward the archway. Beyond it lay spiral stairs leading upward. Although she wasn't certain they led to Lord Bahl's chambers, she thought the general's glance was a telling clue. Yim quietly climbed the stairway until she neared its top and saw that the door above was open. Then she paused a moment, licked her fingers, and used them to moisten herself. That done, she took a deep breath and entered the room. A blazing fire not only lit the chamber, it made it torrid. Lord Bahl sat in a chair before the fireplace, gazing at the flames that painted his pale skin and hair a bloody shade. He was still dressed as he was at dinner, in black velvet and gold, and looked comfortable in the heat. Bahl turned to gaze at Yim sharply. "What are you doing here?"

Yim slipped Yaun's cloak from her shoulders to reveal her nudity. "My lord, the count tupped me as directed, but since you forbade him to mar me, he soon lost interest."

"So?"

"I would fain please you, my lord. This body is yours, not mine." With those words, Yim knew that she had done everything she could. She had found Lord Bahl and offered herself to him. If the sight of her didn't provoke desire, no words could effect the trick. All she had left to do was wait.

Bahl didn't reply right away. He simply regarded Yim with an inscrutable expression as she stood naked before him. Finally, he spoke. "Come to me."

Yim walked slowly and sensuously toward the incarnation of evil, praying that she aroused him. Lord Bahl remained seated, and Yim didn't halt until her knees touched his. Then he reached out with both hands and his icy fingers explored her body. They brushed her neck, moved to cup her breasts, traveled over her flat belly, wide hips, and rounded buttocks to finish at the cleft of her womanhood. His touch chilled rather than aroused, and it didn't seem a true caress. Rather, Yim felt that he was examining her body as a man might touch a forgotten possession to refresh his memory of it. Again, there was another spell of silence before he spoke. "Lie on the bed."

"Yes, Master," whispered Yim. "Thank you, Master."

Yim went over to the bed and lay upon it facing upward. She stared at the ceiling, her lips forced into a smile as she listened to Lord Bahl undress. Upon hearing his bare feet padding on the stone floor, she turned to look. Bahl's torso was still dressed in black and gold, but his lower half was bare. To Yim, his erection seemed a dagger formed from flesh, a weapon he would plunge into her. She parted her legs to receive it.

There were no caresses or tenderness, only the deed. Lord Bahl pushed his way into her with the drive of an infantry assault. Yim wasn't ready for him—she could never be ready—and so it hurt. His pumping chafed, the stiff gold thread on his jerkin scraped her nipples, but the cold body upon her and within her felt the worst. It underscored the unnaturalness of their coupling, and Yim knew that something other than a man was violating her.

Yim fought to hide her feelings, but she was unable to fake pleasure. It turned out not to matter. The one time she opened her eyes, Bahl was staring at her blankly. *Is he enjoying this?* she wondered. She had no idea. His tupping was mechanical, and seemed to go on forever before the tempo of his thrusting increased. Then it became more forceful and spasmodic. Bahl gasped, thrust a few more times, and ceased moving. He lay atop Yim awhile before he withdrew and silently rolled over on his back.

"Were you pleased, my lord?" asked Yim, for it seemed prudent to inquire.

Bahl grunted and rolled over on his side, facing away. Yim lay perfectly still, wondering if it had been for nothing. She felt raw inside and ventured to touch between her legs. Her fingers came up bloody.

Yim shivered as she waited for Lord Bahl's breathing to assume the evenness of sleep. His unnatural chill had made her feel that she had been tupped by a corpse. Worse, Bahl's chill lingered in her despite the blazing fire. In fact, Yim grew colder as time passed. As her discomfort increased, it was accompanied by the disturbing impression that something alien had invaded her body. It felt like a taint of the vilest sort. The mere thought of her pollution made Yim nauseous.

Yim had no guarantee that she would conceive, but since Karm had directed her to Bahl toward that end, it seemed likely. Regardless of the night's outcome, Yim was certain that the malign entity within Lord Bahl had entered her. Apparently, it had left him to do so, for the man lying beside her was growing warm. Yim envisioned him waking sweaty for the first time ever in his overheated room and realizing that their encounter had been no ordinary tryst. Yim's only option was to flee. She waited until Lord Bahl slept, then slipped from his bed.

Having been preoccupied by her immediate goal, Yim had ignored the consequences of success. Suddenly forced to consider them, she saw that they could be as dire as failure. There was no question that Lord Bahl and the Most Holy Gorm would recognize her duplicity. Even if she became pregnant, she would be doomed if captured. Yim felt confident that Bahl wouldn't harm her as long as she carried his child, but her fate after delivery would be a different matter.

Yim doubted she would long survive the birth: There were many tales about the men who became Lord Bahl, but none mentioned a Lady Bahl. *And if my son's raised like his father, the destruction will begin anew.* To prevent that and to live, she must escape and do so before morning.

THIRTY-SIX

HAVING LEFT Lord Bahl's bed, Yim walked over to the cloak she had discarded and put it on. Then, after glancing at Bahl to assure that he still slept, she crept from his room. As she descended the winding stairs, the soreness and bleeding between her legs and her deepening chill evoked the violent consummation of her lifelong quest. Yim couldn't help but feel bitter upon recalling her first vision and how Karm had smiled at her. *I was only a child when she named me the Chosen.* Yim felt blood trickle down her thigh. *And this is what she meant by that!* Yim was painfully aware that the goddess had known where her path would lead. *Did the Wise Woman know also? Did the Seer? Did the Old Ones?*

Yim realized that she must shut such questions from her mind if she was to survive the night. She paused on the stairway to compose herself. It wasn't easy, but she managed. Then, after taking a deep breath, Yim entered the hallway and slipped into Yaun's room. The air inside the chamber reeked of burnt flesh, and an otherworldly coldness lingered, although the spirits had departed. Yim caught a glimpse of the blackened thing in the fireplace and quickly looked away. Then she began to search the room. She would need more clothing than a cloak, and her flimsy gown wouldn't do, even if it had remained intact.

Yim was rifling through Yaun's gaudy wardrobe, trying to find something suitable, when she glanced at the pile of rags. Among them was a woman's shift. Yim went over to it and discovered that all the rags had been women's garments. Examining them, she found that they were torn and bloodstained. Yim had little doubt how they got that way. After much searching, she found a homespun shift and a baggy gray blouse that weren't entirely blood-soaked. Both were ripped, but when worn in combination, the garments covered her. Then she found Yaun's plainest pair of trousers and pulled them on over the shift and blouse, using them to fill the wide waistband. The pants were too fine for peasant wear, but Yim hoped that it wouldn't be apparent in the dark. Taking a pair of blood-encrusted shears from Yaun's collection of torture instruments, Yim cut the fur trim from the count's dark-brown cloak. Then she cut a bloody rag and made a bandage to wrap about her head and hide her hair. All of the weapons in Yaun's chamber were conspicuously bejeweled. Yim took none of them, for her only hope to escape lay in blending with Bahl's ragged peasant army.

Thus attired, Yim entered the dim hallway. It was empty, but she could hear the footsteps of guards making their rounds. Yim listened. The sounds seemed to be coming from around a bend in the corridor. She sprinted for the stairway leading to the lower level, her bare feet making little noise as she ran.

The stairway exited in the dark banquet hall, where Yim was alarmed to spot three armored soldiers bearing torches. They were walking along the upright poles and inspecting the bodies impaled upon them. A dozen or more peasant troops followed behind them. "We're to take down only the ripe ones," said the leading soldier with a torch. "Use yer nose ta pick them out."

"Pah! They all stink ta me," said another soldier.

"Shut yer gob!" said the first. "Ye know a fresh corpse from a stale one."

The third soldier laughed. "Aye, we've made enough of them." The three halted before the blond woman skewered on a pole near the table's head and gazed at her lifeless form. "This birdie can roost another night," said the lead soldier. He moved to the next stake. "Phew! This bitch goes to the dump." He turned to the peasant soldiers. "Hop to it!"

Upon hearing this, the peasants moved to lift the pole out of its iron socket. As they struggled to do this, the soldiers with the torches moved farther down the row. Staying in the shadows, Yim reached the men just as they lowered the pole to the floor. None of them seemed anxious to touch the gray, stiff body, and that gave Yim the opportunity to seize an ankle. Then three men grabbed the other limbs to slide the body off the stake. Even free from the wooden pole, the corpse retained its bent posture, making it an awkward burden for Yim and the others who lifted it.

One of the torch-bearing soldiers shouted back. "Get it out of here!"

Yim helped bear the grisly burden out of the banquet hall, through the corridors of the keep, across the courtyard, past the guards at the gatehouse, and into a moonlit field filled with scattered encampments. Although Yim had passed through the field only once before, she immediately noticed a change. She no longer sensed a malign presence, and though she doubted the ragged men could perceive the change, they appeared to be reacting to it. The men seemed agitated. Many were up and pacing about, despite the late hour. Sleepers tossed and turned. They woke in increasing numbers as Yim watched.

The men who bore the corpse with Yim headed for a large pile of bodies in the center of the field. They halted when they reached the putrefying mound, and tossed the dead woman upon it. When they turned to head back to the stronghold, Yim dropped to the ground on the shadowed side of the pile and lay still.

"Where's that other bloke?" asked one of the men. "The one with the bandage."

Yim quickly pulled the cloth from her head before another man answered. "I don't know. He was just here."

"Maybe the stench drove him off. 'Tis enough ta gag ya."

"It never bothered ye afore."

"Nay, but tonight I smell it. Tonight I feel different."

"Aye, me, too," said another voice. "That lad had the right idea. I'll na go back either."

"But Lord Bahl . . ."

"Tup Lord Bahl."

There was a spell of silence, and Yim had to resist the urge to lift her head and see what was going on. Then she heard a laugh that had a hysteric edge. "Tup Lord Bahl. Aye, tup him. Tup him!"

"Hush! Ye dare na say that!"

"Why na?" said another voice, "I say tup Bahl, too. I'm weary of his shit. Are na ye weary also?"

"Aye, but . . ."

"Then walk away. Walk away with me. Spitting lasses on poles! What kind of thing is that? I'll be his dog na more!"

Yim heard yet another voice. It was filled with dismay. "What have we done? Oh Karm, what have we done?" Then she heard quiet sobbing.

Other peasant soldiers began to sob, and the sobbing spread. In the encampments, more men were awakening, and each wakening spurred additional ones. Soon it seemed to Yim that remorse was like a wind passing over the field, shaking each individual. The night grew noisy with lamentation. While grief was the dominant emotion, there were others also. Mingled with the men who wept were those who cursed or prayed or bellowed with rage.

When Yim lifted her head to peer around, the peasant army appeared transformed. No longer governed by a single will, it was falling into chaos. More and more men milled about. They seemed confused, as if suddenly wakened from moons of stupor. Their numbers swelled rapidly until Yim was in the midst of an agitated mob.

Yim hid her hair beneath the bandage and stood up. She was frightened and wary, for she feared that those who had been deepest under Lord Bahl's spell were still filled with hate and might never get free of it. Sure enough, she saw deadly frays break out as some men turned on their fellows. Furthermore, she knew that Bahl had soldiers who fought for him willingly and would remain loyal. It seemed likely that he would loose them on all deserting peasants. Before he did, she must get away.

As Yim began to flee, the chaos increased. By then, it seemed that no man was unaffected. The encampments scattered like overturned ant nests. Tattered soldiers were everywhere. Most wandered aimlessly in the dark, and many were dangerous. One huge fellow walked about swinging a gore-covered ax at anyone in his erratic path. Having just killed a man, he turned in Yim's direction. She darted from him and ran into someone else.

The startled man cursed and swung at Yim. She ducked, but the blow grazed her head and pulled the bandage from it. The man stared at Yim's long hair and beardless face. Then he grinned. "You're a lass!" Before Yim could get away, he grabbed her arm. "'Tis been a long time since I had a lass." He was reaching for her waistband when another man pushed him aside. Yim thought that she had been rescued until the second man grabbed her loose trousers and yanked them below her knees.

The skirt of Yim's shift tumbled down to cover her legs, and this seemed to briefly confuse her attacker. Before he could react, the first man grabbed his shoulder and pulled him away. The two began to fight. As they rolled on the ground and pummeled one another, Yim tried to run away, only to be tripped by Yaun's trousers. As she fell, she saw one of the fighting men draw a dagger. Then someone was attempting to tug off her pants. He was having difficulty because his right hand was mutilated. Yim tried to kick him, but the fabric about her ankles prevented it.

"Be still!" shouted the man. "Ye can't run with these about yer feet."

Yim let the man pull off the trousers. When she was free of them, he took off his battered helm, placed it on her head, and pulled her upright. Then he grabbed her arm and tugged her into the milling mob just as the fight ended with one man's death. The victor stood up and scanned the mob, bloody dagger in hand. The third man, still gripping Yim firmly, hurried her into the milling crowd. Yim didn't resist, although she was uncertain if he was her savior or her next attacker.

After dragging Yim farther, the man gazed about and then released her. "I guess we lost him," he said.

"Thank you," Yim said.

"I deserve no thanks," replied her rescuer. "I be a wicked man."

"Then why did you help me?"

"I've done terrible, terrible things." The man's eyes welled with tears. "I just want to . . . to . . ." He began to weep.

Yim gazed into those tearful eyes and saw what the man had done under Lord Bahl's sway. She also saw his anguish and remorse. It made Yim recall her vision of tortured men doing horrific deeds. Then she fully understood the depths of Bahl's iniquity. The man before her was as much a victim as the folk he had slain. Her heart went out to him, as it had to the wretched priest. Though Yim no longer felt that she was a Bearer or had any power or authority to do so, she touched the man's forehead and said, "I know what you did, and I forgive you."

The man looked at Yim first with surprise, then with reverence. It was reflected in his voice as he asked, "What be ye doing here?"

"Fleeing Lord Bahl."

"I've a mind to flee myself." He shook his head sadly. "Strange I never thought of it afore."

Yim's glimpse into the man's eyes had convinced her that she could trust him. "Then come with me. We'll flee together."

"Aye. I will."

"I'd be glad for your company," said Yim. "I'm . . . I'm Mirien."

"I be Hendric. I had a farm and family afore my count made me soldier. Mayhap I still do."

"Was your count named Yaun?"

"Aye, curse him."

"His deeds have done that. Now he's dead."

Hendric smiled for the first time. "That lightens my heart. Come, Mirien, I'll find ye some pants. They'll draw less notice than yer shift."

The two made their way among the seething mass of men, pausing only when Hendric stripped a corpse of its ragged pants. Yim managed to slip them on under the cover of her cloak. The darkness and the general confusion helped her do so without being noticed.

Even with Yim disguised, they were in constant peril, for violence sprang up without warning. Sometimes it was hard to make any progress without jostling someone or being jostled. Once, when Yim accidentally touched a man, he whirled with a blade in his hand and murder in his eyes. When Hendric killed him with his sword, no one paid attention. Everywhere, men were slain without apparent reason. The danger diminished only as the mob thinned out farther from the stronghold.

Eventually Yim and Hendric entered the ravaged countryside where the other deserters went separate ways. They seemed intent only on escape, and Yim relaxed. She discarded her scavenged pants, which had been too loose and long. Unencumbered by them, Yim walked more easily. She and Hendric fled until the sky began to lighten in the east. With the approach of daylight, Yim grew anxious again. "I think we'd better hide somewhere," she said. "Who knows what the day will bring."

Honus watched the sky lighten from atop a hill overlooking Tor's Gate. "General," said the officer beside him, "do you think Bahl will advance today?"

His mind elsewhere, Honus didn't reply.

"We've held position two days already, sir."

"What?" said Honus.

"The men, sir. They've held their ground for two days and three nights."

"I don't know Bahl's plans, only his habits," said Honus. "He's due to move out, and when he does, this is the only route he can take. We stay in position."

"What if we didn't kill all his scouts? Even if we did, won't he wonder why none returned?"

"Bahl will advance, even if he knows we're here," said Honus. "He's careless of his soldiers' lives. He won't stay an assault for their sake."

"But we'll lack the advantage of surprise."

"True, and it'll make a hard fight even harder," said Honus. "But would you rather go home and wait for Bahl there?"

"No, sir." The younger man was silent for a while before he asked, "Any news of your Bearer?"

Honus turned and glared at the man. "What does she have to do with anything?"

"Nothing, sir," replied the officer, shrinking from his commander's wrath. "Just making conversation."

"You're not here to talk. Go check the lines."

As Honus watched the man hurry off, his thoughts returned to Yim. *Why did she leave?* The question had been gnawing at him for two days, and he still had no answer. Her departure didn't seem forced; there were no signs of a struggle or the presence of strange footprints. It seemed that she had simply walked away. Honus's responsibilities prevented him from tracking her, so all he could do was ponder the significance of what she had taken and what she had left behind.

The neat pile of Bearer's clothes had unsettling implications, but the scrap of cloth disturbed Honus more. He clearly recalled the day Yim had come by it. *It's from the wedding gown that crazy woman gave her. Yim was angry that morning, and later she ran away.* Honus feared the scrap was a sign that he had angered Yim again. *How? She said she loved me. She said I must father her child.* Nevertheless, Yim had deserted him without a word. Honus feared that she had a change of heart, and left the scrap as a token.

Although Honus's conclusion made sense, he didn't believe it. Sometimes, he thought he rejected the notion only because he couldn't face the truth. Other times, he questioned his assumptions and wondered if he had missed some vital clue. Honus speculated on why Cronin's helm and cloak were missing. He wondered what Yim was doing, what she was wearing, and where she was headed. She was never far from his thoughts, even as he prepared for a bloody battle. With each passing day, he feared that Yim was farther from him and grew more despondent.

THIRTY-SEVEN

HANDS GRIPPED Lord Bahl and pulled him upright in his bed. He opened his eyes and beheld the Most Holy Gorm. Then the priest slapped him hard across his sweaty face. The blow came as a shock, but it paled compared to the specter of the priest's rage. Bahl had never seen Gorm in such a state, and it provoked a novel emotion—fear.

"Fool! You idiotic fool!" shouted Gorm, slapping him again. This time, Bahl tasted blood. "Where is she?"

"Who?"

"The bitch who stole your powers."

"No one did that."

"Pah! Don't you feel the change? Are you not weak and empty?"

With a surge of panic, Bahl realized it was true. "But she was a whore. No virgin."

"Then explain your transformation. You were nearly a god, but now you're just another mortal. You're only Lord Bahl's cast-off clothes. As of this morning, the true Lord Bahl resides in a womb. Where is it?"

"But this can't be! Yaun tupped her first!"

Gorm slapped Bahl again. "Don't argue with me! You forget who I am. As for Yaun, he's a cinder in his own fireplace. The girl. Where is she?"

"Why ask me? Your magic bones should reveal her whereabouts. They should have warned you before this happened."

"Their auguries have been muddled as of late."

"Then why blame me for this disaster?"

"Because it was *you* who tupped a virgin. Couldn't you tell the difference?"

"I've never tupped one before. How was I to know?"

Lord Bahl flinched as Gorm grabbed him, but the priest didn't strike him again. Instead, he gave a weary sigh. "We came so close. Not that it matters now. Get dressed and assemble the Iron Guard. Only them; your peasant troops are worthless. The Guard must find the girl and find her quickly."

"Are you sure she's fled?"

"She's fled. This was no happenstance."

"But who could have plotted such a thing? Only we know the secret."

"When we find the girl, we'll learn the answer. Now hurry."

Sunrise found Yim and Hendric in the burnt ruins of a hut. The blackened walls enclosed a collapsed roof, and the two hid beneath it. The small, cramped space between the charred rafters and shingles and the dirt floor was too low for them to sit upright. Yim lay close to her fellow fugitive and tried to rest, but it was difficult. There was something rotting in the debris and its stench was nauseating. Furthermore, Yim was not only cold, but thirsty, and the ashy air exacerbated the dryness in her throat.

"Hendric," Yim said, "since all the wells seem to be poisoned, do you know of a stream we could reach when the sun goes down?"

"I recall nothing of my march through here. It be only a horrid dream to me."

Yim sighed. "Well, we don't dare look for water by daylight."

"Why? Be dying of thirst any better than dying by the sword?"

"They won't slay me if I'm caught," said Yim. "At least, not right away. My fate will be far worse."

Hendric's voice reflected his sympathy. "Beed ye one of the count's women?"

"Yes."

"Then ye be lucky to be alive."

"I guess I am," replied Yim without conviction.

"If we escape, what will ye do?" asked Hendric. "Go home?"

"I have no home."

"I do, but I don't know where it lies. It be like I walked here with my eyes shut."

"A pass through the mountains lies close to here," said Yim. "It's called Tor's Gate. An army waits there to fight

Lord Bahl. If you throw down your arms and show you're peaceful, I think they'll help you find your way."

"We'll go together."

Yim imagined facing Honus, and the thought was unbearable. *I've been defiled!* Her love for him was as strong as ever, but her shame was equally strong. Although she had debased herself for worthy motives, she felt that didn't alter the result. "I can't," said Yim. "My path takes me elsewhere."

"But ye said ye have no home."

"I must find one. Someplace far away."

"I'd like to help ye if I can."

"You can't. No one can."

"Not even Karm?"

"Especially her."

The Iron Guard was aware of the change even before it assembled in the keep's main hall. Most of its soldiers came from families that had served the Iron Palace for generations. Thus they had heard tales of similar events. When the peasant troops had begun to desert en masse, rumor spread that the Devourer had forsaken their lord. Some of the oldest guards had been around when the same thing happened to the previous Lord Bahl. They warned their younger comrades that lean years lay ahead. The lord they served was no longer invincible, and the flood of plunder would dwindle to a trickle.

As General Var stood at the forefront of the Guard, he was in a black mood. *This time was supposed to be different*, he thought. *This campaign was to end with the Rising*. Instead of becoming general to the world's master, he would end his days serving a provincial lord. What heightened Var's rancor was the knowledge that—if the tales were true—he might have prevented the disaster. It was said that a woman always brought down the lord of Bahland. If that was true, then the agent of Bahl's downfall had knocked on the general's door last night. *I should have escorted her back to Yaun!* If Var had known what the girl intended to do, he would have strangled her on the spot. But it was too late for that, and he would have to live with the consequences.

When Lord Bahl entered the hall, he was visibly changed. His skin had assumed a more rosy shade. He had lost his confident stride; instead, he walked like a man with a hangover. Lord Bahl's eyes were different also. General Var puzzled over the change until he realized that Bahl's irises were more visible. They were gray. Overall, his lord looked diminished beside the angry priest who accompanied him.

There were many stories about the Most Holy Gorm. Var's grandfather had sworn that the priest hadn't aged within his lifetime. The general had once doubted that tale, but experience had proved it true. The years flowed over the man without leaving a mark. A priest named Gorm had served the first Lord Bahl in Luvein, and many believed that he was the same man who had just entered the hall. General Var was among their number.

It was the Most Holy Gorm, not Lord Bahl, who addressed the Iron Guard. His voice boomed out, echoing throughout the hall. "Know all of you that Lord Bahl has sired an heir and that the Devourer's grace has passed to this unborn child." He paused as murmurs spread among the assembled men. Then he silenced them with a frown. "The girl who bears this child is now a fugitive, and we shall not leave this place without her. Lord Bahl charges you with finding her. Be aware that the realm's future depends on your success.

"The girl you seek is about eighteen winters in age. She's comely, with dark eyes and walnut-colored hair. The man who brings her to us will be richly rewarded. Anyone who harms her will suffer such a fate that he'll come to crave death.

"Nothing is more important than finding this girl. General Var, organize a search and begin it at once. Keep me and Lord Bahl informed of its progress."

With that, the Most Holy Gorm left the room with Bahl at his heels. General Var watched them depart without any doubt where the true power lay. The previous night he had quaked before Lord Bahl, but that man had become an empty husk. *It was the Devourer that I truly feared*, Var thought. *Now its power resides in the priest. And in that cursed girl!* The general turned to lead his men in the hunt for her.

The noonday sun shone on the charred roof, turning the space beneath it into an oven. Yim's throat was so dry that it hurt to breathe. Yet she welcomed the heat; it kept her chill at bay. When she had summoned spirits from the Dark Path, she had experienced similar coldness. But while the thing inside her was from the Sunless Way, it was no one's departed soul. Thus its chill was familiar, but also different. Yim didn't merely feel cold; she had become its essence. Her chill was a state of being, rather than a mere sensation.

Then the cold within Yim stirred, and she suddenly cramped. The pain was so strong that she wanted to cry out. Fearful of being heard, she froze instead, breathing in gasps as she waited for the agony to pass. But it didn't pass. Instead, it coalesced into an icy presence as sharp and intense as a shard of glass deep within her. Yim had never felt anything like it. The sensation went beyond mere coldness; it felt as if a part of the Dark Path had settled in her womb.

At that moment, Yim realized that she had conceived. She knew her child would be a boy, just as she had known that the malign entity within Lord Bahl had left him to enter her. Yim's pain gradually subsided. While her overall chill diminished after concentrating in her womb, it didn't fade altogether. *It's likely to be permanent*, she thought, *at least until I bear the child.* She feared it wouldn't depart even then. While the cold was uncomfortable, it was bearable. Yim didn't shiver; it was as if her body sensed that shivering would be futile.

Yim's difficulties didn't wake Hendric, who had slept fitfully beside her throughout the morning. Yim had avoided dozing, since every time she drifted off, something foul invaded her dreams. It was the thing from Karvakken Pass and Karm's ruined temple, and it conjured up terrifying visions of slaughter. They seemed so real that Yim felt she was standing in their midst. However, the thing no longer sought to destroy her; she had become its vessel. What Yim feared most was that she'd fall under its influence. *Perhaps I'll murder this poor man beside me.* The thought had already flickered through her mind, a dark impulse that had arisen spontaneously. *Perhaps I'll surrender to that priest.* Yim felt as if she were walking in the dark, pursued by a lethal shadow. But the shadow was within her, so she could never escape it.

That dismal thought was interrupted by the sound of hoofbeats and tramping feet. Men were calling back and forth. Yim envisioned a line of them, stretched out evenly under the watchful eyes of mounted officers. *A search!* she thought. *A search for me!*

"Check the house," she heard a voice cry out. "It's a likely hiding place."

Yim listened in terror as the sound of boots on baked earth grew louder. Then she could hear them crunching charred shingles. "Phew!" said one voice. "Something's ripe in here."

"Aye, but that makes no difference. Be thorough."

Yim turned to Hendric, who had awoken, his eyes wide with apprehension. She raised a finger to her lips, then lay absolutely still. From the sound of it, the soldiers were kicking away the shingles to uncover what lay beneath them. The noise grew louder as the searchers approached Yim's cramped refuge. Then there was a crash and Yim felt debris falling on her leg. She glanced backward and saw sunlight shining on her ashy leg and foot. Then she lay still again and waited for the worst.

A hand grabbed her ankle. "Well, what have we here?" Yim's ankle was lifted and then quickly released. "Gah! I found that corpse. This leg's colder than a fish!"

"Come on, then," said a second voice before shouting, "Sir! There's nothing here!"

As Yim heard the men depart, she smelled the scent of Hendric's urine.

Honus watched silently as the men walked between the hills. His second-in-command whispered in his ear, "Should I sound attack, sir?"

"Not yet," replied Honus. "This puzzles me. They aren't acting like Bahl's troops."

"Could it be some kind of ploy?"

"Subtlety is not Bahl's suit. Besides, his peasant troops lack the discipline for subterfuge. Have a squad capture a few of them alive, and bring them to me."

The officer departed on his mission, leaving Honus to ponder the new development. It went contrary to what he expected. Bahl goaded his peasant troops to reckless madness, then used them in mass assaults. The men in the pass seemed neither mad nor reckless. They had the cautious and frightened look of deserters, although no one ever deserted Bahl's army. His grip was too strong, and the only escape lay in death. Puzzled, Honus was eager to question some captives.

A short while later, the officer brought forward three ragged men. They appeared to have come willingly, for the officer needed no soldiers to escort them. All three dropped to their knees when they halted before Honus. "Mercy on us, sire," said one of the men, his eyes rimmed with tears. "We've done terrible things, but 'twas na by our own will."

"Aye," said the second. "We've wakened from evil dreams

to find blood on our hands. We repent, though we know not what we did for certain. Mercy, sir. For Karm's sake, show mercy."

The third man bowed his head. "Slay me if ye will. I deserve no better."

"I believe that Karm is best served by forbearance," said Honus. "I won't take your lives. Moreover, I know something of your plight and the evil thing that gripped you. How did you break free of it?"

" 'Twas last night," said the second man. "I woke to find myself ruled by my own will. Until then, it seemed I dwelt in some dark place and watched another guide my hands. The things they did! Oh, Karm forgive me!"

"It was like that with me," said the first man. "I lived in Lurwic, and know not how I got here. I recall naught but nightmares."

"Has this happened to many?" asked Honus. "Or do you number among a lucky few?"

"All about us were affected," said the first man, "though not all turned peaceable. Some went mad with rage and slew all they could until they were slain themselves. Those who live think only of escape, but many are confused."

"And the Guard hunts us," said the second man, "and kills all it catches."

"Did any of you see a young woman on that night?" asked Honus. "She would have dark hair and eyes."

"I saw no wench," said the first man. The others said the same.

Then Honus turned to a soldier. "Take these men to the rear, and give the officer there these orders: He is to assist these men within our means, but to expect more soon. Perhaps a great many more. Keep them collected and question each about the whereabouts of my Bearer. If he hears of her, he's to report to me immediately."

After the solder left with the men, Honus's second-in-command spoke to him. "General, 'tis said that Bahland's might waxes and wanes. Could this be the beginning of its withering?"

"Perhaps," said Honus. "These tidings sound good, but I want to test them. Order the men to stay in position for the time being. Then assemble a hundred skilled fighters and bring them to me. I intend to reconnoiter beyond Tor's Gate."

It was afternoon when Honus led his troops past the opening of Tor's Gate. He had donned his chain mail and a helm, for even if Bahl's peasant troops had melted away, the Iron Guard remained. It had a formidable reputation that was well deserved. Honus advanced only a short way before it became obvious that the encampments about the stronghold were deserted. Judging by the number of empty tents and shelters, Bahl had assembled a formidable force. If it had surged through Tor's Gate, Honus's resistance would have been hard-pressed.

Many from that force lay slain, obviously cut down while fleeing. Honus could see their killers in the distance—the well-armored men of the Iron Guard. They were out in force, conducting a disciplined sweep. Honus halted his own men, waiting to see if the enemy would attempt an attack. If so, he planned to retreat and lure Bahl's troops into the ambush. Yet although his men were within plain sight, the Guard ignored them to continue their search. It made Honus wonder if they were looking for more than deserting peasants.

The enemy within sight greatly outnumbered Honus's party, and Honus had no doubt that there were additional troops within the stronghold. Therefore, he took care not to venture so far out that a swift assault could cut off retreat. He was judging the state of the stronghold's walls when one of his scouts reported: "General, I've found General Cronin's helm and cloak."

"Did you leave them in place?"

"Aye, sir, like you said."

"Then take me to them."

The scout led Honus to the base of one of the wooded hills that flanked Tor's Gate. There, behind a bush, lay Cronin's neatly folded cloak. The helm lay atop it. Honus was surprised to find Yim's sandals next to them. Honus motioned for the scout to stand clear while he inspected the surrounding ground. It had been disturbed by the scout's footprints and by other prints as well, but Honus made a careful survey. Eventually, his patience was rewarded. A dozen paces from the discarded helm, he discovered three faint prints on the dusty ground. They were made by a woman's bare feet, and they were headed toward the stronghold. Honus needed no other evidence to conclude that whatever had happened the previous night had been Yim's doing.

THIRTY-EIGHT

YIM WAS desperate for water by the time night fell. She had drunk a little wine the previous evening, but since then no liquid had passed her dry, cracked lips. When she crawled from her dusty hiding place, it was hard to see, for the moon had yet to rise. Yim had no idea if soldiers were about, but her thirst drove her westward in hope of finding water. Though Tor's Gate lay the other way, Hendric insisted on joining her.

"The clansmen will have water," said Yim. "You should go to them."

"Ye must drink, too," said Hendric. "So until ye do, I'll stay with ye."

"That's not necessary."

"Mayhap ye be right, Mirien. But I think not. So I'll not desert ye in yer need. And I'll say why: Ye knew my deeds and forgave them."

"Words," replied Yim. "Don't risk your life because of them."

"They be more than words to me. They gave me back my life."

Yim said nothing, and Hendric continued by her side. Although they found several wells, each of them was befouled, so they kept walking. Meanwhile, the horizon began to glow silver where the moon would rise. They were making their way through a broad field of waist-high grain when a nearly full moon climbed into the sky. By its light, Yim discovered they were not alone. The enemy had posted sentries, and three of them stood watch at the edge of the field.

"Soldiers!" whispered Yim as she dropped to the ground.

"Where?" whispered Hendric, who remained standing. "Oh, I see them. Keep down, Mirien." Then Hendric kept walking.

Hugging the ground, Yim heard the rustling sound of Hendric striding through the unharvested grain. Then she crawled away in a different direction, leaving as scant a trail as possible. She had traveled about thirty paces when she heard the sound of a noisy pursuit. The sentries, having no reason to be quiet, dashed through the field with their armor clanking. Yim froze until she realized that she wasn't their quarry. As the noise faded into the distance, Yim resumed crawling. Though she listened hard, she heard nothing that revealed Hendric's fate.

After a while, Yim began to fear that she might be making her way toward more sentries. She had no way of telling without rising to peer about, and that would be risky. Paralyzed by indecision, Yim remained still and listened. For a long while, the only sound was a breeze softly rustling the grain. Then she heard men's voices in the distance. Someone laughed. Afterward, the night turned quiet again.

Yim remained still until an impulse seized her to spring up and shout. She was nearly on her feet when she resisted the urge and dropped down. She lay in the dirt, still struggling with the inner darkness that tried to possess her. Eventually, she subdued it, though she was left trembling from the effort. *You and I have fought before*, she thought to her adversary, *and I've defeated you.*

As Yim recovered from her latest trial, she heard the fluttering of wings. Then a crow landed by her foot and gently pecked it. "Kwahku?" The bird responded by flying a few paces away and landing just within view. Yim crawled toward him, although it was the opposite way she had been traveling. Thus began a long journey on hands and knees through the grain. It was a painful way to travel, but Yim felt confident that she was moving toward safety. When she reached the edge of the field, a massive clump of brushes lay only ten paces away. Yet Kwahku waited a long while before flying toward them, making Yim conclude that there were soldiers close by. When the bird finally flew to the shrubbery, Yim dashed for their protection.

Soon afterward, the crow led her to a muddy puddle. Yim laid Yaun's cloak upon it so the cloudy water would seep through the cloth, which filtered out the worst of the silt. After drinking her fill of water, she donned the soaking cloak and followed her feathered guide on a long and erratic route that eventually led to a swamp. By then, morning was approaching, and Yim was in a state of near-total exhaustion. Nevertheless, she followed the bird and entered the black, reed-choked water where deep muck made every step an effort. She advanced far into the swamp before the crow reached a soggy hummock and finally stayed put. There, Yim collapsed and quickly went to sleep unmindful of what terrors might be waiting in her dreams.

* * *

Honus gathered his officers in his tent at noon for what he expected to be a contentious meeting. After Cronin and most of his staff had been slain, each clan had demanded representation on the general's staff. As long as battle seemed imminent, the arrangement had worked well enough. But Bahl's push into Averen had stalled, and as its threat diminished, so had the unity among the clans. Eager to get on with business, Honus addressed the officers as soon as all had assembled. "Lord Bahl has lost his grip over his peasant troops," he said. "They've deserted him, as well you know."

"Aye," said an officer. "And they're eating our scarce rations."

"Would you rather they pillage for their food?" asked Honus. "They're our foes no longer, but want can turn them against us."

"What of Bahl, General?" asked another officer. "Will he invade?"

"I think not," replied Honus. "My late Bearer studied him and his line. If he holds true to form, he'll retreat to the Iron Palace."

"Then why is he still here?" asked another man.

"I don't know," replied Honus, keeping his speculations to himself.

"I think Bahl's reversal offers a chance to attack him," said Havren, who had been one of Cronin's officers.

"It could be done," said Honus. "But if Bahl remains in place, it'll require a siege. Most likely a long one."

"We can na mount a siege," said an officer. "Winter's drawing nigh, and we have naught but tents for shelter and na great store of food."

"But our foe's weakened," said Havren. "This is the time to strike!"

"Aye, 'tis easy for you to say," said a man from Clan Mucdoi. "Na men have come feuding in *your* lands." He cast a baneful look toward an officer from the Dolbanes.

"Mayhap they had na cause," shot back the Dolbane man.

Honus silently watched the debate go back and forth. As the words grew more heated, any hope of consensus fell away. At last, he raised his voice. "Clansmen! Pause a moment! You called me to lead you in a desperate defense, and I reluctantly agreed. The trial you feared won't come to pass. At least, on that you can agree. Thus you have no further need for me. I'm a Sarf, not a general. My fate is to follow my Bearer, and that's what I'll do. Fight or go home, whatever you deem best. But if you choose to fight, then you must also choose a new general."

With those words, Honus strode from the tent. He had walked but a little way when Havren caught up with him. "Honus, please reconsider. Do it in Cronin's memory."

"His memory helped spur my decision," replied Honus. "Remember how Yim told him that fighting wouldn't defeat Lord Bahl? Well, she has been proven right. Yim earned us this peace, though at what price I cannot tell."

"How can you claim that Bahl's reversal is due to her?"

"Because I have faith."

"But now we can defeat Bahl for good!"

"Then act upon your faith as I shall act on mine. Yim didn't release me from her service, so I remain her Sarf. My obedience goes to her."

"How can you obey someone who's disappeared? You've na idea where she is. She could be dead for all you know."

"Yim lives," replied Honus. "I've tranced and not found her spirit on the Dark Path."

"Honus, please reconsider."

Honus regarded the young officer with comradely affection. "Havren, the clans won't unite, so forsake the sword and go home. A stretch of peace lies before you. Relish this gift."

"I know those are heartfelt words, Honus, and I'm inclined to heed them. But I suspect you will na do so. What are you planning?"

"To lay siege."

"Alone?"

"Yes, alone."

"Then I'll see that you have provisions," said Havren.

"I'd appreciate that," said Honus, "as well as your silence in this matter."

"But what do you hope to accomplish?"

"If I could read my runes, then perhaps I'd know."

THIRTY-NINE

YIM WOKE in the afternoon after a sleep filled with bloody dreams. Kwahku remained perched upon a skeletal scrub, so she went to forage for some food. Yim waded only a short way before she encountered a stand of cattails. She pulled up one for its starchy root, which she devoured on the spot. Although she rinsed the muck from it first, it was still a gritty meal that had a swampy taste. Yim ate another before the edge was off her hunger. Then she gathered and rinsed additional roots for a more leisurely meal.

When Yim returned to the hummock, Kwahku was gone. She wasn't overly concerned, for on their earlier travels together the bird often had flown off to survey the route. Having rest, water, and food gave Yim the energy to wonder for the first time where the bird was leading her. Before, she always had a destination. *Now I have none*, she thought. She questioned whether she should follow the bird, for it meant letting others make choices for her. *Probably the Old Ones*. Thinking of them brought back the bitterness she had felt after leaving Lord Bahl's bed. Yim still believed that the Old Ones, like Karm, had hidden the truth from her.

Just then, the crow swooped down. He landed by Yim's foot to peck it in an agitated manner. Then he cawed and took off to perch farther into the swamp. Yim was still hungry and continued to eat until Kwahku fluttered down to peck her again. Irritated, she shooed the bird off. Then she heard men's voices and understood the reason for the crow's behavior. The voices didn't come from a single place, but from a broad area. Yim had heard of hunts where men advanced in line to flush their quarry, and it seemed the best way to search a reed-filled swamp. Yim gazed with dismay at all her footprints on the muddy hummock. Then she heard splashing as a great many feet entered the water.

Kwahku flew off again, and Yim abandoned any hope of hiding her footprints; there wasn't time. She hurried after the bird, trying hard to leave no trail, for she knew that when her pursuers reached the hummock they'd know that she had been there. Spurred by desperation, she maintained a good pace and traveled swiftly. Gradually, the black water got deeper. In a few places, it nearly reached her neck. One such spot was choked with lily pads. Kwahku flew over it to perch on a clump of reeds. When Yim reached the clump, the water was only waist-deep, and she expected the bird to take off again. He did not. Instead he cawed and gazed down at Yim.

By the crow's actions, Yim decided that she was supposed to hide at that spot. She was in no state to question why she was obeying a bird; she simply squatted down until only her head was above water. Then she scooped up muck and smeared it on her face and hair. That done, she pulled a blanket of lily pads over her head. Then she waited.

The leeches arrived long before the soldiers. Yim could feel them, a subtle stealthy touch, followed by stillness as they fed. Nevertheless, she remained motionless. The leeches were driven only by hunger and meant no harm. The soldiers were another matter. Yim wondered what drove them so hard to hunt her. *Fear? Greed? Duty?* She also wondered who drove them, since their lord had lost his power. She suspected it was Gorm, not Bahl.

The advance was as noisy as might be expected from armored men walking in line through a swamp. The cursing was loud and abundant, which made Yim realize that the search was counting on thoroughness rather than stealth to catch its prey. *A line of men to make a human net*, she thought. *Will I slip through a hole?* The sound of splashing grew louder.

"A pox on this place!" said a voice. It sounded close. "It'll take days to polish my armor."

"Aye, curse that bitch!"

"She's here somewhere. So mark my words, we'll be here, too, until we find her."

The splashing became loud. Yim could hear the armor creak. When the water began to ripple, she gulped air and totally submerged. Yim held her breath until she felt her lungs would burst. When she rose to breathe, the sounds of the searchers came from behind. Gradually, they diminished.

Yim waited until all was quiet before she pushed aside the lily pads. Kwahku briefly alighted on a nearby pad before flying off in the direction from which the soldiers had come. Yim sighed and hurried after him.

Leaving took longer than Honus expected. Other officers besides Havren approached him and pleaded with him to stay. Although he patiently listened to each one, he remained resolved to go. But when Havren brought him a large sack of grain, he told Honus something that further delayed his departure.

"Honus, a deserter named Hendric has seen your Bearer."

Honus froze. "Where is he?"

"In the rear. He just arrived half-dead from thirst. I'll take you to him."

Havren led Honus to where the deserters had been

collected and took him to a haggard and ragged man who was hungrily devouring some cold porridge. Preoccupied by his meal, the man appeared startled when Honus called his name. Suspecting that Hendric had never seen a Sarf before, Honus kept his excitement in check and appeared placid. He bowed politely. "I'm told that you encountered a dark-haired woman recently."

"Aye, Mirien."

Honus recognized the name. *Gan's murdered sister!* He wondered if there was a message in Yim's choice of alias. "And she was young with dark eyes and shoulder-length hair?"

"Aye, that beed her."

"Then know that I serve this woman and am pledged to protect her."

Hendric regarded Honus suspiciously. "She said no one could help her."

"Perhaps that was true at the time, but no longer. When did you meet?"

"On the night Lord Bahl lost his hold on me. Mirien said she was fleeing him. We fled together."

"What happened next?"

"We hid all day in a burnt-out hut with not a drop of water. Last night, we went to look for some. There beed soldiers about, and I ran off to lure them away from her. I think I did, but I can't say for sure."

"And that was the last you saw of her?"

"Aye."

"Where were you?"

"In a grain field a half day to the west."

"Then you headed east to here. Why?"

"Mirien told me to come this way. She said there'd be help for me."

"Then why was she headed west?"

"She said she had to find a home. Someplace far away."

Honus felt stunned, though he hid it. "And was she well?"

"I could see no hurts, although she walked as if something pained her. And she said she had been with Count Yaun. He be hard on women. Exceeding hard."

Honus fought to control his rage, but his icy voice betrayed his feelings. "I think I know the man."

"He be dead now. Mirien said so. I beed glad to hear it."

"So other than her gait, she appeared unharmed?"

"Well, she beed cold. Unnatural cold if ye ask me." When Honus said nothing, Hendric asked timidly. "Be ye some kind of holy man?"

"No. I only serve a holy one."

"Be Mirien holy?"

"Yes. Why do you ask?"

"Because she said she knew what I did and forgave me."

"Then you've truly been absolved," said Honus. He turned to Havren. "When you return to your clan hall, would you take Hendric with you and commend him to Cara? He has done Yim and me a great service."

"I will, Honus," replied Havren. "Are you still resolved on your plan?"

"More than ever."

"But it seems Yim has other plans."

"She's alone and in danger. I won't rest until I find her."

Hendric looked confused. "Yim? Who be Yim?"

"A holy one oft has several names," replied Honus. "Yim is one of them. It seems that Mirien is another."

Yim crouched in a thick stand of reeds at the swamp's edge. There were bloody spots were the leeches had been, but most had dropped off by the time she had stopped fleeing. After she had plucked off the stragglers, there was nothing to do but wait for darkness. Though Yim suspected that she'd be traveling all night, she was too tense to genuinely rest. Heavy clouds had moved in, and they promised to obscure the moon. If so, it would be harder to follow the crow, but also easier to travel unseen.

After the sun set and light left the sky, Kwahku took off. When Yim had walked awhile, she perceived that they were heading toward the stronghold, and she thought she knew why: As the search for her expanded, a path toward its origin would be safer—at least if one had a sharp-eyed guide that could fly. The day's close brush with capture had dispelled Yim's ambivalence about following the crow, even if that meant that the Old Ones would determine her destination.

The journey that night was as difficult as Yim had feared, for the crow did not let up. The closer Yim got to the stronghold, the more imperative it was to move past it. Long after midnight, the ground began to slope upward. By then, Yim was so close to the fortress she could see the dim light from hidden fires reflected off the keep's stone walls. The mountain behind the stronghold rose ahead. Yim climbed it until the sky began to lighten. Then Kwahku led her to a narrow crevice in the mountain's rocky side. A film of water flowed down a portion of its wall, and Yim licked it until her thirst was quenched. Then she tumbled into sleep where the Devourer waited to trouble her dreams.

The sun had nearly set when Yim awoke. She found Kwahku standing near the opening of the crevice. Before him was a sizable mound of nuts, berries, and edible seeds. Yim had no idea whether it was the bird or other creatures that had gathered the food, but she ate with relish. Afterward, she licked more water from the wall.

"Well, Kwahku, where will you take me tonight?"

The bird cocked his head eastward.

"How about I fly tonight, and you walk? It's not easy climbing barefoot."

Kwahku cawed.

"No?" Yim rubbed her sore feet. "Oh well, at least you haven't given me your pack to carry." Yim scooped up a handful of berries, and the crow ate them from her extended palm.

Yim's quip about the pack made her think of Honus, and the thought of him awoke longing. Love for Honus had motivated Yim's sacrifice, and she was convinced that was the reason why Karm had bestowed her "gift." But the goddess hadn't reclaimed that gift, even after it had fulfilled its function. Yim still loved Honus deeply, although her love had become hopeless. *I must never see him again.* Her reason went beyond her defilement and even the fact that she bore Lord Bahl's child. Yim felt that she had become a host to evil and would endanger anyone she loved.

As Yim resumed climbing the mountain slope, she took solace in her belief that Honus would never face Lord Bahl's army nor endanger himself for her sake. "Karm," she said, "I pray for Honus, not myself. Please grant his heart peace. Let him forget me and find happiness with another. Do this for one who sacrificed all for you."

The night wind blew Yim's words aloft as it dried her tears. It was a chill wind, for autumn already gripped the mountain's upper slopes. Even on the plain below, Yim had seen the first signs of approaching winter, which came early and stayed long in Averen. The higher Yim climbed, the more distant seemed the prospect of capture. That focused her mind on her next dilemma. She was with child, and the only resources she possessed were a cloak, a torn shift, and a torn blouse. She had no means to make fire, nor any of the basics for surviving alone—no knife, no pot, and no water skin. In a land gripped by feuding and roamed by the Devourer's priests, she dared not seek help from anyone. It occurred to her that her destiny might be to die and take Bahl's unborn heir to the Dark Path. *Perhaps Kwahku's leading me to some precipice where he'll soar into the void and beckon me to follow.* At the moment, the prospect didn't seem so bad.

Kwahku did not take Yim to a precipice; neither did he guide her throughout the night. Instead, he flew a route that took Yim over a fold in the mountain that enclosed a high, wooded valley. Sheltered from the wind, the trees grew tall. The crow flew among them, guiding Yim to a spot beside an alpine stream. Yim drank its clear, cold water, which worked like an elixir on her. For the first time in many days, she felt a measure of peace. Coupled with it was the promise of dreamless sleep. Without even glancing toward the crow, Yim knew that he intended her to rest. Already drowsy, she found a pile of dry leaves. There, she wrapped herself in her stolen cloak to slumber, completely unaware that a huge bear sat nearby in the dark and watched her intently.

FORTY

As Yim slept in the hidden alpine valley, Honus began the second stage of his solitary campaign. The first stage had commenced while Yim was still hiding in the swamp. That was when Honus left the army bearing his pack for the first time. Haunted by longing for the woman who last bore it, Honus focused all his thought and energy on finding her. His first task had been to conduct a stealthy and lengthy reconnaissance. He did it in the guise of a peasant, hiding his face in a hooded cloak so as not to alert Bahl's soldiers that a Sarf shadowed them.

Honus's observations led him to several deductions. The first was that the Iron Guard was no longer searching for deserters. As a test, Honus had shown himself several times to Bahl's men while wearing peasant garb. Only once did it provoke a halfhearted pursuit. Thus Honus surmised that he search was solely for Yim and she was still at liberty. ince Honus could detect no preparations for a retreat, he ssumed that Bahl planned to remain in the fortress until Yim was found.

As long as Yim was at large, Honus planned to harass ord Bahl's soldiers. By that means, he hoped to protect her. With luck, he might even find Yim while on one of his forays. Furthermore, if Bahl's men captured her, he could attempt a rescue. Having formulated this strategy, he put it nto action.

It was past midnight when Honus silently crept toward hree of Bahl's sentries. Moving from shadow to shadow, is dark blue clothes and face made him nearly invisible. Meanwhile, his quarry showed the carelessness of armed nen who believed they had nothing to fear. When Honus eached them, he quickly killed two before they could draw heir weapons, and he easily disarmed the third. Holding his lade against the man's throat, Honus said, "Be still, and you may yet grow old. Why are you standing watch so far field?"

"Because I was ordered to."

"You're looking for someone. Why?"

"I don't know what ye're talking about."

"You've one more chance to talk. Why this search?"

The man said nothing, so Honus cut his throat. Afterward, he donned enough of the slain Guardsman's equipnent to pass for one of them in the dark. Then he disposed of the sentries' bodies in a nearby well. By the time dawn approached, the well contained eighteen more Guardsmen, but Honus was none the wiser about their mission.

None of the soldiers he had interrogated revealed anyhing. Honus speculated on whether this was due to discipline, fear of Lord Bahl, or disbelief in the possibility of nercy. Whatever the reason, by the end of the night Honus ad given up asking questions and simply slew all the sentries he surprised. He briefly had considered using torture to learn what he wanted, but rejected the idea. Yim wouldn't approve, and he was resolved to be guided by her wisdom. He retreated into hiding only when dawn approached, satisfied that he had embodied Karm's wrath and that twenty-one fewer men would be hunting Yim that morning.

A sniffing muzzle woke Yim. She opened her eyes to gaze on sunlight and a huge furry face. Yim had never been so close to a bear before, and she froze with terror. "Fear not," said a voice. "She's your friend." As Yim turned her head, the bear licked her face. Rupeenla sat on the ground a few paces away. She bowed her head respectfully. "Greetings, Beloved Mother."

At the sight of the faerie, Yim ignored the bear and sat up. "Beloved?" she said. "You've a strange way of showing it."

"You're angry," said the Old One.

"Does that surprise you? You knew, didn't you? You knew, and yet you sent me on my way believing I was going to my love."

"You were."

"But I had no idea what awaited me, and you did! I'm certain of it!"

"Knowledge isn't wisdom."

"Don't hide behind words!"

"I knew neither what path you'd choose, nor the ends of every choice. Should I have told you that you'd suffer or that you'd save your beloved from gruesome death? Both have come to pass."

"You could have told me something."

"I was constrained to silence," said Rupeenla. "I still am."

"Constrained by whom?"

The faerie bowed so low that her forehead nearly touched the ground. "Constrained, Most Honored Mother." When she raised her head, Rupeenla's large cat eyes were filled with such empathy that Yim was moved. "What you suffered! What you suffer still! I'm humbled by the depth of your love."

"That love was but Karm's ploy to lure me to Lord Bahl."

"Was your love for Mirien and her mother a ploy? For Hendric, Cara, Hommy, and Hamin? For all the ragged children and their worn parents? For the slain in Karm's temple? Love has always been your strength."

"I was speaking of my love for Honus."

When the Old One didn't respond, Yim gazed into her eyes and probed her thoughts. Some were veiled even from her, but Yim found no guile, only sympathy, love, and sadness. She looked away and sighed. "I forgive you. I hurt, and I'm discouraged. But you're right; what I did was my choice."

Rupeenla bowed again. "And I honor you for it."

"But that doesn't explain why you're here."

"To aid you."

"How?"

"Winter approaches, and foes search for you. You need a refuge."

"So you'll take me to Faerie?"

"No. What's in your womb must never enter the Timeless Realm," said Rupeenla. "This is a refuge of a different sort." She gestured to the bear. "This is Gruwff," she said, pronouncing the name like a short, hoarse cough. "Gruwff will take you as her cub and nurse you through your long sleep."

"My long sleep?"

"One that lasts till spring, like that of Gruwff's kindred. With a kiss, I can bestow that gift."

It seemed a perfect solution, for it would allow Yim to disappear for moons, perhaps long enough for Bahl to abandon his search. Nevertheless, Yim had a special reason to be daunted by the prospect of so long a sleep. "My dreams are no longer wholly mine," she said. "You know of the thing with which I struggle."

"I do," replied Rupeenla. "It's terrible and strong. It overpowered every woman who ever bore the child, but it hasn't mastered you."

"Not yet."

"Nor will it. That much I can say."

"So I might hibernate till spring, evade Lord Bahl, and find someplace to have this child," said Yim. "Then what?"

"Do what's necessary."

"Well, *that's* easy advice to give," said Yim. "It applies to every occasion."

"But you know what's necessary," replied Rupeenla. "Follow your instincts. Though the child will harbor the dark spirit that made his father so feared, he'll be your son as well. Care for him as your heart guides you, and good may result."

It had never occurred to Yim that she would regard a child who had been so traumatically conceived as her own, much less love it. But upon considering the possibility, she realized that she could. *He's innocent*, Yim thought, *although he'll be afflicted by what afflicts me now*. Yim thought how she might help her son overcome his inner foe, and thus vanquish it from the world. The idea gave rise to hope, the first she had felt since Karm's last visitation. Then Yim saw the truth in Rupeenla's words and perceived how love would be her strength.

Yim regarded the faerie. When she saw Rupeenla's serene but exultant expression, she knew that the Old One understood her thoughts. Yim smiled, and Rupeenla smiled back.

Hope was a tonic to Yim's spirit as she leisurely strolled about the sheltered forest. It was a relief not to fear pursuit, and she relished it. The high valley seemed like a lofty island of calm in a turbulent world, a place above mankind's dark deeds. The maples had put on festive gold, while the oaks were adorned in subtle reddish brown. The bright morning sunlight even took the edge off her permanent chill. In all, it seemed an idyllic place, and Yim drank in its peacefulness.

When Yim returned to the stream, she saw Rupeenla and Gruwff waiting for her, though Kwahku was gone. The Old One sat cross-legged on the ground before a large, flat rock that was piled high with nuts, berries, mushrooms, seeds, and honeycombs. There was even a plump hare. Then Rupeenla rose and pressed her lips to Yim's in a long and loving kiss. The faerie tasted of growing plants, long-weathered rock, still waters, and ancient earth. Yim didn't want the kiss to end, but it eventually did.

"Before you can sleep, Mother, you must fatten yourself."

Rupeenla smiled in response to Yim's thoughts. "Yes, I'll linger with you awhile. I'm honored that you desire my company."

Then Yim, Rupeenla, and Gruwff ate together, with Yim gorging herself at the Old One's urging. She even devoured part of the hare, though she had to eat it uncooked and tear its flesh with her teeth. It didn't feel unnatural in the presence of Gruwff, and the bear finished what she didn't. Then the three lazed in the sunshine. Yim enjoyed feeling stuffed, and even dozed a bit. While sleeping, she kept the Devourer at bay and dreamed she was brushing her hands over Honus's back as his runes spoke to her. "Someday you'll understand," they said. "Then all your trials will make sense."

When Yim awoke, she was surprised that she was hungry again, and pleased to see that the pile of food had been renewed. At this meal, Rupeenla only tasted a few berries, while Yim and the bear stuffed themselves again. This began a routine of eating and sleeping that persisted for days. It was a lazy life, for Yim had no need to forage. The ongoing feast was produced by a stream of animal helpers. Mice and squirrels brought the seeds, nuts, and berries. Skunks gathered mushrooms and roots. Owls and hawks delivered freshly killed hares. To Yim's special delight, woodpeckers flew in ample servings of wood grubs. The more she ate, the more she was able to eat.

Unlike Rupeenla, Yim couldn't converse with the bear, but she did gain some understanding of her growls and grunts. A short snuffing sound meant "Are you going to eat that?" A high-pitched grunt said "Try this, it's delicious." Moreover, Yim and Gruwff developed a rapport. When Yim dozed between meals, she nestled against the bear and often woke to find Gruwff's huge forearm about her waist.

By eating so much and so often, Yim quickly grew plump, and when the weather turned cold Rupeenla said, "Mother, I think it's time to leave with Gruwff for her den. Sleep with her pelt-clad." Then the faerie bowed deeply. "May I kiss you one last time? We shan't meet again in this world."

Yim responded by warmly embracing Rupeenla and kissing her. Afterward, Gruwff gave a long wavering grunt, and when Yim gazed toward her, the bear began to walk away. Yim turned to say good-bye to the faerie, but she was already gone.

Gruwff led the way out of the mountain valley and began to climb the mountain. She set an easy pace, and Yim followed her on the steep slope without too much difficulty. On it, a few stunted trees grew between long stretches of rock and brown grass. Higher up, there were no trees at all, and the slopes were already dusted with snow. From where Yim stood, she could gaze northward and see how sporadic hills gave way to a broad plain that exended to the far horizon. It seemed empty. *That's where I'll head in spring*, she thought. *I'll walk north and go as far as I can.*

The vista was hidden when the bear entered another fold in the mountain's side and descended partway down its interior slope. There, among scrubby trees, was a deep crevice in the rock. Gruwff entered it and disappeared. Mindful that Rupeenla had told her to sleep pelt-clad, Yim removed Yaun's cloak and her ragged shift and blouse to stuff them in a crack in the crevice's wall. There, she hoped they'd be protected from the weather.

After her clothing was stowed away for spring, Yim entered the crevice to find the bear. Soon she was cautiously groping her way in near total darkness. The floor sloped sharply downward a distance, but became level when the passage turned. Yim felt dry leaves and grass beneath her feet, and she could hear the bear's breathing. As she advanced, the covering on the stone floor became deeper. She bumped into Gruwff. Yim bent down and touched the bear's huge paw, then felt her way around the prone creature until she nestled against Gruwff's belly and pressed against her thick fur.

As Yim lay still, she felt her body grow quiet. Her heart beat ever less frequently, and her breathing slowed. Thought faded as she drifted into a state more deep and still than sleep. Time lost its grip on Yim as she slipped from awareness and entered a void.

Time passed in the world outside the den. The last leaves fell from the trees. The nights grew longer. Snow fell until it buried all trace of the crevice. Inside Gruwff's dark refuge, Yim glided through the changes in a state of oblivion. She felt neither warm nor cold. She was unaware that she had found Gruwff's teat to suckle at it like a cub. Her mind was at peace and empty of dreams, bloody or otherwise.

FORTY-ONE

HONUS SETTLED into the life of a lone wolf. Throughout autumn, he kept attacking sentries at night and observing the searches by day. He slept whenever and wherever he could, but never at any place successively. Eventually he caught a Guardsman who was willing to talk. The man described the subject of Lord Bahl's search as a woman eighteen winters in age, with walnut-colored hair and dark eyes. Pleased to have his deduction confirmed at last, Honus spared the man's life, although he was certain that his captive knew more that he told.

Honus's instance of mercy cost him, for the Iron Guard learned that a Sarf dogged them. As the cold deepened, Bahl's men hunted him as well as Yim. Honus became more cautious, but not because he feared death. Rather, he was painfully aware that he was Yim's sole protector. Lord Bahl's persistent searching both worried and encouraged him. He wondered what Yim had done to provoke such a massive effort, and feared that Bahl intended to wreak some terrible revenge upon her. On the other hand, the ongoing search seemed evidence that Yim was alive and remained nearby. Honus had no idea how Bahl could know that, but he suspected sorcery was involved.

Living in a depopulated and pillaged countryside, Honus depended on his foes for sustenance and winter garb. He wore a Guardsman's boots and heavy winter cloak. He captured the Guards' rations and horses and ate them both. Warmth was a perilous luxury, and he risked a fire only on the bitterest nights. The cold seemed to seep into him until he was cold-blooded and coldhearted. Honus became estranged from mercy. Whenever he dealt with a Guardsman, the wrath tattooed upon his face mirrored his feelings. He expressed his rage by meting out swift death. Honus wasn't cruel, but he was ruthless and efficient. Often during the snowy days and frigid nights, he imagined slaying all of Lord Bahl's men, so that Bahl would be forced to come out to fight man-to-man.

If rage spurred Honus, so did love. It was torment not knowing where Yim was and how she fared. Honus saw his suffering as proof of his devotion, and he bore hardship as an act of love. It was the only loving deed possible.

The sole happiness Honus experienced came from the memories of the dead. He had tranced infrequently after Yim had become his Bearer because she, like Theodus, hadn't approved of his habit of seeking joy upon the Dark Path. Moreover, with Yim by his side, Honus seldom felt the need. With her gone, the urge returned with renewed force. Trancing was a chancy business where so many atrocities had taken place. Honus frequently encountered them on the Sunless Way and was forced to relive their horrors. Afterward, finding a blissful memory felt all the more urgent. What Honus treasured most were moments of love and passion. After encountering one of those, Honus briefly felt warm and sustained. Yet soon the feeling would fade, to be replaced by emptiness and longing. Then Honus would trance again.

As the season dragged on, Lord Bahl ceased searching the area around the stronghold, and sent out foot and horse patrols that were often gone for days. That forced Honus to change his tactics. Since he couldn't follow all the patrols, he transformed from a warrior into a spy. He ceased harassing Bahl's troops. Instead, he observed their comings and goings, looking for any sign that might indicate that Yim had been found.

When the days lengthened with the approach of spring, Honus captured a horse and stabled it in a remote ruin. Although keeping a mount was risky and required time and effort, Honus thought it was prudent. If Yim was still in Averen, she would be more likely to take to the road with the arrival of warm weather. If she was captured, a horse might be required to save her.

Awareness came to Yim in brief episodes spread over many days. She would occasionally leave the dreamless void and enter sleep. Then, she would have a sleeper's vague sense that she possessed a body that dwelt in time and space. Then one day, she passed from sleep to wakefulness. Yim realized that she was in a cold den, lying naked beside a bear. When she lifted her head, the bear stirred also. Yim yawned. "Good morning, Gruwff."

The bear grunted, rose, and left the den. When Yim sat up, her body felt out of balance and wrong. Her hands went to her belly, where she was startled to feel a large rounded bulge capped by a protruding bump where her navel had been. Then Yim cupped her breasts in the dark and found them enlarged and tender. Having assisted the Wise Woman in birthing babies, Yim knew all about pregnancy's changes. But her transformation felt instantaneous, and so it alarmed her. Moreover, a pregnant woman's belly should feel warm, but hers was unnaturally cold.

Yim stood up. Unaccustomed to her body's new center of balance, she staggered clumsily to the den's entrance. When she stepped into the morning's watery sunlight, she gaped at herself a long while, despite the frigid air. Her breasts looked even larger than they had felt. They also drooped and were tipped with nipples that were dark and distended. Yet it was her curved abdomen that seized her attention. It seemed to dominate her body as a mountain dominates a landscape. Yim stared at it, trying to accustom herself to its appearance, but it looked too alien.

When the cold drove Yim to dress, she removed the clothes that she had stored in the crevice and discovered a nest of mice within them. She shook the creatures from her garments. Gruwff hungrily snapped one up while Yim surveyed the damage they had done. There was a gaping hole in the front of her shift and parts of her blouse had be gnawed and shredded also. The ruined garments would shame a beggar and only barely met the needs of modesty. Fortunately, there were only two fist-sized holes in the cloak. Yim quickly dressed, then stood shivering in the cold.

Yim took her shivering as a sign that her otherworldly chill had shifted to her growing child. She still felt a vestige of it, but her discomfort seemed mostly due to the weather. High on the mountain, spring was more a promise than a reality. Broad patches of snow still covered much of the slope, snow that Yim would have to walk through barefoot to reach the lowlands.

Gruwff turned to look at Yim and then gave a long cry before heading down the slope. After going a short distance, the bear stopped and turned to gaze at Yim again, giving her the impression that she was supposed to follow. Yim did, and the bear led her down the mountainside. The long and grueling descent was especially difficult, because Yim was unsure of her balance. She feared her clumsiness would send her tumbling down the steep slope at any moment, and it caused her to lag ever farther behind. For some reason, the bear didn't slow down, and after a while, Yim followed only tracks in the snow. Yim felt deserted as well as awkward, cold, and ravenous. She was so miserable that she burst out bawling. Yim recalled all the moody mothers-to-be that the Wise Woman had tended and realized that she had become one.

The bear descended the mountain using a route completely different from the one she had taken to the den. It was less direct, and veered sharply to the east. When Yim reached the lower slope and could no longer discern Gruwff's tracks, she was far from Bahl's stronghold. Yim had spied no dwellings from the higher elevations, and she saw no trace of humanity closer up.

Yim continued down the ever-gentler incline and entered a forest where the trees had leafed out and the air was milder. Slumping on a fallen log to rest, she was too exhausted and hungry to appreciate the change. Yim had never felt so hungry in her life, and her hunger had a keen and desperate edge. *I must feed more than myself now*, she thought. At that moment, she felt movement inside her womb, a reminder of the other life within her. It made the baby seem less abstract, and its needs more immediate. Yim rose wearily to complete her descent into the lowlands where she might forage for food.

As Yim traveled through the forest seeking mushrooms and spring greens, she caught no sight of Gruwff. Certain that the bear was also hungry, Yim wondered if the creature was having better luck at foraging. Her efforts had yielded little, for it was still early in the season. Then Yim heard a hoarse bellow and saw Gruwff in the distance. The bear lifted a limp hare from the ground, shook it once, set it down, and bellowed again. As Yim started in Gruwff's direction, the animal turned and lumbered off into the woods. When Yim arrived at where the bear had stood, she saw no sign of her other than the freshly killed hare. It seemed like a parting gift.

The hare was still warm when Yim lifted it to gnaw at the soft hide at its neck. She spit out several mouthfuls of fur before her teeth penetrated the skin. Then Yim pushed her fingers into the hole to rip it wider. Warm blood spilled on them, and Yim succumbed to a sudden compulsion to lick it off. When she tasted the blood, she instantly craved more. The urge felt stronger than hunger or thirst. Without an instant's hesitation, Yim raised the dead creature high and drank greedily from its throat. The blood flowed, warm and strangely intoxicating. It dribbled down Yim's chin and onto her clothes, but she gave it no heed. When the flow lessened, she squeezed the small corpse to wring out the last drops. When no more came, she dropped the drained hare and shook like a drunkard who had emptied the last bottle. She craved more, but there was none to be had.

Yim trembled awhile until the craving passed. Then she was ashamed and horrified by what she'd done. She stared at the fresh stains on her rags, feeling perplexed by her unseemly desire and the strength of it. Her fear that she couldn't trust herself resurfaced. A dark spirit remained within her, ready to bend her to its needs. The gory evidence of its power marked her face, hands, and clothes. Yim resolved to be more wary of its presence.

Despite her chagrin over what she had done, Yim was still ravenous and in need of sustenance. She devoured the hare with more delicacy than when she had drunk its blood, but with equal thoroughness. Someone whose need was not so great would have been appalled at the sight. When Yim finished her meal, there was little left. Not a shred of flesh remained. The bones were cracked for marrow, and the skull was smashed for the brains. The liver and the heart were gone, leaving only offal, shattered bones, and a torn hide. Yim rose from her meal feeling satisfied and went searching for a stream where she might drink. When she found one, she also washed as a nod to civilization, although her hands had been licked clean already.

When Yim had looked for water, she also had looked for Gruwff and Kwahku, although she expected to find neither. She sensed that the Old Ones could no longer help her. Yim couldn't say how she had come to that conclusion, but instinct told her it was true. She was on her own, and she felt that was the way it must be.

Yim spent the night buried beneath a pile of leaves. Upon rising with the sun, she didn't bother to brush them from her rags or tangled hair. Yim drank from a stream, then began to walk. Existence had been reduced to two imperatives—travel unseen and eat. She hoped they were compatible. *A new phase in my life*, she thought. *My feral one*. First, she had been a lonely girl preparing for a great task. Then she had been a slave. Next, a holy one. *And soon I'll be a mother*. Throughout it all—stringing them together like beads on a necklace—was Karm's will. Yim's resentment toward the goddess had dulled to resignation. Karm had achieved her purpose and disappeared like Gruwff and Kwahku. Yim expected no more visions. *How can Karm speak to me when the Devourer's always listening?*

Feeling abandoned, Yim tried to tell herself that she didn't care. Yet it stung. Karm was the only mother Yim had ever known. The goddess had been often unfathomable and always unpredictable, but that had only spurred Yim to strive to be the perfect daughter, obedient and diligent. Old habits made Yim wonder if she might earn the goddess's love and gratitude by turning Lord Bahl's child from evil. *Then the goddess could return to my life!* Despite everything that had happened, the concept had appeal.

The immediacy of hunger soon drove such speculations from Yim's mind. Chancing upon a deep brook, she tried to catch a fish with her hands as she had seen Honus do on several occasions. Unfortunately, Yim lacked his patience and skill. Then she foraged an unsatisfying meal of woody mushrooms. She ate these while she walked northward. As the sun rose higher in the sky, Yim continued to walk and forage. The walking sharpened her hunger faster than the foraging dulled it. By noon, she felt famished, and the pangs in her stomach increased as the day wore on.

Eventually, the forest thinned and frequently gave way to fields that had either been burned or abandoned with their crops unharvested. She foraged through one of the latter and found the remnants of last year's plantings spoiled and inedible. Later, Yim ventured into an abandoned farmhouse to look for anything useful, but it had been thoroughly pillaged, and she left as empty-handed as when she entered.

Toward late afternoon, Yim spied a man tilling a small plot outside a hut. He was the first person she had seen. Yim considered approaching him, but she worried that there might be a price on her head. Thinking how readily desperate people betrayed strangers, she decided to endure her hunger and pass the hut unseen. Before the sun set, she encountered three more inhabited huts among the many ruined ones. Yim avoided them all, suspicious of people who had survived when all their neighbors had not.

As night fell, Yim found a large patch of musk cabbage. The thick, ribbed leaves were newly unfurled and an enticing shade of glossy green. The plant was named for its odor, which was reminiscent of skunk. Yim held her nose and gorged herself, then suffered from cramps and belching for most of the night. It was a cold one, which the chill from her womb made even worse. When she rose at dawn, Yim was bleary-eyed and nauseous. Nevertheless, she stumbled northward.

Yim made poor progress on her second full day of travel. Several times, she had to make wide detours around a settled place. Her nausea eventually cleared, but the hunger pangs that replaced it were scarcely better. They stabbed her as they sapped her energy. On all her travels, she never felt so tired, not even in Luvein. Yim stopped early to gouge a rotted log with a stout stick in an effort to find wood grubs. Instead, she fell asleep, stick in hand, and awoke shivering in the middle of the night.

Yim began her third day of travel with a growing sense of desperation. She had come to realize that her long hibernation and her growing child had depleted her body's reserves. Moreover, pregnancy placed increased demands on her, and the foremost among them was the need for nourishment.

Early spring's always a time of want, she thought, *and I'll need more than greens and mushrooms to survive*. Seeking charity seemed her only option.

Thus as Yim continued north, keeping a sharp lookout for anything edible, she also looked for a refuge. Fearing betrayal, she cautiously observed any habitation she encountered. They were scarce in the war-ravaged region, and her instincts warned her away from every place she came across. Each time it was only a vague feeling—the way a man walked or how he held his hoe like a weapon—but Yim heeded the slightest twinge of unease. So much was at stake. Yet hunger fought with caution, and each time it was harder to walk away.

The sun was low in the sky when Yim spied the modest hut. Nestled in the folds of a low rise, it seemed off the beaten track. As before, Yim hid and observed the dwelling from a distance. For a long time, the only sign of habitation was smoke rising from the hut's chimney. Then two barefoot girls scampered out. Neither seemed over six winters of age. They went over to a large mound of earth that was covered with overlapping boards that formed a kind of crude roof. The girls lifted several of the boards, and began to dig in the uncovered mound with their hands. Its earth was obviously loose, for the girls scooped it up easily.

Yim had seen such mounds before; peasants used then to store roots. After the girls had gathered a small pile of them and were putting the boards back in place, a woman emerged from the hut bearing a crockery bowl. Yim watched as the woman examined the roots the girls had gathered. She liked the way the woman pretended to be astonished, as if the children had discovered fabulous treasures. The girls' laughter floated across the field, a heartwarming and inviting sound. Yim made up her mind. She rose to place her fate in a stranger's hands.

FORTY-TWO

IT WAS only forty paces to where the woman and the children stood, but it seemed a much greater distance to Yim. She traversed the empty field silently and slowly, feeling slightly dizzy as she walked. Once the strangers saw her, they stared. Yim felt their eyes, but she was too exhausted to read them. Besides, she had surrendered to passivity and felt incapable of evading whatever the woman chose to do.

"Kuvri! Wreni! In the house!" said the woman.

"Mama," said a tiny voice, "what's wrong with her?"

"She's seen troubles. Now go!"

As her daughters ran into the hut, the woman turned to watch Yim's approach. When Yim was a few paces away, the woman spoke. "Why are ye here? What do ye seek?"

"Kindness."

" 'Tis a rare thing these days. Why leave home to seek it?"

"I have no home."

The woman glanced at Yim's bulging belly. "Well, ye had a man. Where's he?"

"Slain in the feuding."

"The feuding's been over since fall."

"Tell that to those who killed my husband and burned our home."

"And how long have ye been wandering?"

"I've lost count of the days. It seems forever. Do . . . do you wish me to leave?"

The woman regarded Yim silently awhile before answering. "Nay. 'Twill na please my husband, but come inside. By the circle, ye're a sight."

Yim felt a chill when the Devourer's token was invoked, but it was too late to do anything except hide her unease and hope that the woman's faith was as mild as that of Devren's household. Indeed, the woman seemed kindly. When Yim started to waver on her feet, the woman steadied her, and that simple caring act caused tears of gratitude to flow down Yim's filthy cheeks. The woman noticed and spoke softly. "I'm Taren, dear. What's yer name?"

"Mirien."

"Ye do na speak like folk from here."

"I'm from the north, but my husband was from Averen."

"Was he a Falken man?"

Yim assumed that Taren was referring to a clan. Considering the recent feuding, the question seemed a loaded one. "I don't know," replied Yim. "We never talked about it."

Taren's look reflected disbelief, but she didn't question Yim's reply. "And when did ye last eat?"

"I found some mushrooms this morning."

"I mean a proper meal."

"There was a dead hare. I ate it raw," said Yim. "That was three days ago."

"Oh, poor dear."

Kuvri and Wreni were excitedly waiting in the hut, and both began talking at once. "Mama! Mama! Who is she?"

"Is she dying?"

"Is she having a babe?"

"Is she a beggar?"

"A bandit?"

"Will Da be mad?"

"Girl, girls, give me some rest!" said Taren. "This is Mirien, and she's na going to die or rob us. Na will she have her babe for at least a moon. And asking for kindness is na the same as begging."

"And Da?" asked the elder girl.

"We'll find out when he comes home." Then Taren led Yim to the only mattress in the one-room hut. It was made from coils of straw bound with cord. A tattered blanket lay atop it. "Rest, Mirien. I'll warm some porridge."

"Thank you, Taren. Kar . . . uh . . . Bless you."

Taren didn't reply. Instead, she poured some water into a pot that apparently contained some cold porridge, stirred the mixture a bit, and set the pot on the fire. By the time it was ready, she had to wake Yim. Taren guided her guest to a bench at a rude table, placed a wooden bowl before her, and ladled some porridge from the pot. The porridge was lumpy and watery, but Yim savored it. The two little girls, apparently unaccustomed to strangers, watched her with wide-eyed fascination. Yim tried to eat daintily, but because she had no spoon, she was forced to lift the bowl and sip. When the bowl was virtually empty, Yim succumbed to her hunger and scooped the last bits up with her fingers, much to the younger girl's delight.

Yim hoped that Taren would refill the bowl, but she took it away. "Best na eat too much at once," she said. "And there'll be evening sup when my husband comes."

"Is he planting?" asked Yim.

"Nay, he's found other work. Why na rest some more?"

Yim gazed into Taren's eyes to perceive her thoughts. She found no deceit there, but she detected apprehension. *Her husband worries her*, Yim thought. *Should I be worried, too?* Yim realized that, whatever the answer, she was in no position to leave. Besides, it was nearly dusk. She lay down on the straw mattress, where despite her anxiety, she drifted off to sleep. Yim didn't wake until she heard Kuvri and Wreni outside the hut. "Da! Da!" one cried. "There's a raggedy lady inside!"

"She's going to have a babe, Da," said the other in an almost pleading tone.

"Taren!" shouted a man's voice. "What's this the girls tell me?"

Taren rushed out of the hut. Then Yim heard Taren's low, tense voice mingled with a louder, harsher one. She rose quickly to brush her ragged clothes with her hands and arrange them so they weren't revealing. Yim had just finished when she heard heavy and rapid footsteps. There was no question whose steps they were.

A red-faced man stormed through the open door and glared at Yim. His mouth opened, but no sound came out. Instead, the man simply stared as his expression underwent a transformation. Surprise briefly flashed across his face to be replaced by excitement that he attempted to hide. "Welcome, lass. Welcome to my home. My woman says ye've traveled hard."

"I have, Father."

"Nay, nay. Call me Kamish. And bide with us till your strength returns."

Just then, Taren entered the hut, her face pale and taut. Kamish beamed at her. "My dear, ye were right. 'Twould be cruel to turn the lass out. Cruel indeed, and I'll na do it."

Relief and surprise lit Taren's features. "I'm glad, husband. I truly am."

"Good," said Kamish. "Then 'tis settled."

When the evening sup was served, Kamish was in a cheerful mood. He wasn't a talkative man, but his good spirits put his family at ease. As the meal was being cooked, he had sent his daughters to get more roots for it and had insisted that his wife shave some smoked meat into the simmering pot. Surmising from Taren's reaction, the latter was a rare treat. If the meal was supposed to be festive, dread spoiled its savor for Yim. Unlike the good-hearted Taren and her innocent children, she wasn't fooled. A single glance into Kamish's eyes had confirmed her fears: Tomorrow, he'd betray her.

Yim tried to sleep wedged between her two hosts on the family bed. Kamish had insisted on the arrangement, though it meant his children were banished to the hut's dirt floor. They weren't happy about it, but they were too frightened of their father to complain. Yim was frightened also. *What will Kamish do to me? March me off to Lord Bahl? Tie me up?* Her only hope lay in convincing him that she was unaware of her peril. She had done her best during the meal and its aftermath to appear thankful and relaxed. *Was he fooled?* It seemed that she'd have to wait until morning to find out.

Yim's first hint that she had succeeded came when Kamish woke before dawn. Although Yim had been long awake, she pretended to be asleep as she listened to him quietly dress. When he left the house, she dashed to the board where Taren prepared food and grabbed the knife that lay upon it. Then Yim returned to the mattress and feigned sleep. Taren woke soon afterward and rose to place her sleeping daughters on the bed. Yim continued to listen for signs of Kamish's return as Taren moved about the hut.

Time dragged on until Yim finally decided that it was safe to rise. Taren smiled when she saw that Yim was awake. "Good morn, Mirien."

"What work does your husband do?" asked Yim.

Taren seemed puzzled by the sharpness in Yim's tone. "What?"

"You said he doesn't plant. So what does he do?"

"He guides soldiers. They pay him in grain."

Yim revealed the knife she had hidden and brandished it. "I'm sorry, Taren. I truly am. But I need food."

Taren stared at the blade, confused and terrified. "Mirien, what . . ."

Yim waved the knife menacingly, though she felt terrible doing so. "I mean it, Taren! Give me grain and roots, and do it now!"

"Why?"

"Your husband will betray me, so I must flee south. I'll need food for that. And a flint and iron. I don't want to hurt you or your children, but I'm desperate."

Taren started to tremble. "I'll have to dig the roots from the mound."

"Then just the grain. All you have."

"Please," said Taren. "My children."

"Then keep some, but hurry!"

As the panicked woman rushed to comply, Yim felt relieved that Taren's children still slept and wouldn't witness how their mother's kindness was being repaid. While Yim watched Taren, she struggled with her own rising panic. She had no idea of where to go or how she could evade capture. Her only strategy was to appear to head south and then turn north as soon as she was out of Taren's sight.

Taren took a sack of grain and poured some into an empty kettle. Then she held up the sack. "Is this enough?"

"Fine, fine," said Yim. "Now the flint and iron."

Taren got those items, put them in the sack, and advanced toward Yim. "Please, 'tis my only knife."

"I'm sorry, but I need it more."

Taren held out the sack, and as Yim reached for it, Taren lunged for the knife. Yim slashed wildly and sliced Taren's bare arm. The woman shrieked from pain, waking her daughters. The girls began to cry in terror at the sight of their mother gripping her gashed arm. Blood was already flowing between her fingers.

Yim was sickened by what she had done. But what disturbed her even more was that she had felt a sudden thrill when the blade struck flesh. Feeling pleasure at another's pain ran counter to her entire being, and yet she had. Yim felt far guiltier than when she had drunk the hare's blood and far more tainted.

"Go!" shouted Taren. "Go! Whatever ye did must be vile and wicked!"

Then Yim fled the hut, her deed, and the children who wailed for their wounded mother.

FORTY-THREE

YIM RAN as fast as her condition allowed, which wasn't very fast. After she entered the woods and was screened from view, she turned eastward. A rise lay due north. Its heights seemed a logical place to flee, but Yim didn't feel up to climbing. She was already tired and hungry, and the day had just begun. Moreover, she was so heartsick and discouraged that every effort seemed daunting. Thus she plodded east, attempting to hide her trail, but too listless to do a good job.

By midmorning, Yim rounded the eastern end of the rise, and was able to head north. She traveled only a short distance before the woods ended. Yim stood at their edge and gazed at the open country beyond. It had been farmland until the recent invasion, a place principally marked by low stone boundary walls. None of the huts or other buildings stood intact, and most had been reduced to little more than blackened rubble. The fields and meadows were reverting to weeds, but the process had begun only recently, so they offered little cover. There were a few places for concealment—orchards, woodlots, and ruins—but Yim would have to cross open ground to reach them.

Yim saw that the route ahead would involve alternating safety with exposure. *It'll be a journey best made by night*, she surmised. The sack of grain meant she could forgo searching for food during the day, at least for a while. Escape seemed feasible, and that gave Yim a measure of confidence. *All I need now is a place to hide and rest until tonight*. Yim supposed that she could hide in the woods, but they were open and the undergrowth was still thin and new. It looked too scant to offer real concealment. Yim scanned the landscape ahead and spied a blackened hut with a collapsed roof. She had escaped detection before in just such a place. It wasn't close, but she could hurry. Yim decided that she would, and rushed into the weedy field before her.

As Yim ran, she felt the exhilaration that comes from action. She was speeding toward safety, albeit more clumsily and slowly than she would have liked. Still, as she neared her goal, it felt like the completion of a significant first step. The burnt hut was near when the soft slap of her feet upon the ground was accompanied by another sound. *Hoofbeats!* Yim turned, and her exhilaration became despair. Armed men, accompanied by Kamish, were emerging from the woods. Among their number was an armored horseman who was galloping toward her. He was already far ahead of the advancing foot soldiers.

Yim stopped running. The hut was no longer a meaningful goal. She dropped the sack of grain. It would not sustain her. Only the knife was of use. She had no hope of overcoming an armored and experienced opponent, but she could use the blade on herself. Turning to face the oncoming rider, she parted her cloak. Her rags barely covered her, and a rounded expanse of flesh was visible beneath the holes. Grabbing the hilt of Taren's kitchen knife with both hands, she pointed its blade toward Lord Bahl's son and herself.

It seemed such a quick way to end it. A single stab would seal her fate and end Bahl's line. Yim pressed the blade's point against her skin with trembling hands. The spot began to bleed. *Just one thrust*, she told herself. *One easy motion*. But it wasn't as easy as she thought. Yim struggled to summon her will to do it.

Unnoticed, the horseman dismounted. "My lady!" he called in an urgent voice. "I beg you, please forbear!"

Startled, Yim glanced at the man. Both of his hands were

raised and empty, as if he were surrendering. "Please, my gracious lady, don't harm yourself! Your sufferings are ended. We're here only to protect and aid you."

"I'm no silly thing to be so easily snared!" said Yim, raising the blade to plunge it in.

"You're the honored mother of my future lord," replied the man, his face earnest. "I'd sooner die than harm you."

"You won't harm me," said Yim, raising the knife even higher. "I can do that myself." She drove the blade downward.

Yim expected searing pain. What she experienced was a flash of steel, a ringing sound, and a jolt as the knife flew from her hand. She saw it spinning off into the field as the soldier sheathed his sword almost as quickly as he had drawn it. Yim was stunned by the swiftness of it all. *He's as fast as Honus!* Then the soldier seized her.

Yim struggled as the man wrapped his armored arms about her, but she did so halfheartedly. The soldier, for his part, was as gentle as he could be while still restraining her. "My lady, calm yourself. We mean no harm. Your safety and comfort are our sole concern."

By then, the soldier's comrades arrived running. Soon, more hands restrained Yim, albeit gently. Her cloak was taken so her wrists could be bound behind her back. The rope was soft and smooth, but the knots held fast. Yim's filthy, tattered cloak was replaced by one like the soldiers wore. A man raised a silver flask. "Would you like some honeyed wine, my lady?" When Yim nodded, the man delicately held the flask to her lips and wiped her chin when she was done.

"She's a lady?" Kamish asked one of the soldiers, his voice reflecting his incredulity.

"Aye, for certain."

Kamish smirked. "Well, she does na look it. When do I get my gold?"

"When the wagon comes for her."

"When's that?"

"Soon enough. You won't wait long."

A tall soldier whose armor was more finely adorned than the other men's approached Yim. "I'm Captain Thak, my lady. You'll be my charge awhile. I regret that I must have you walk a little longer until we reach a suitable campsite. There, we'll erect a pavilion where you can repose in comfort until transport arrives."

"Transport to where?"

"Why, to the Iron Palace, the seat of your son's domain."

"Perhaps I'll have a daughter," replied Yim.

The captain chuckled, "Nay, nay, my lady. It's always been a son for six generations."

"And don't call me 'my lady'!" snapped Yim. "Call me 'Karmamatus.' "

The captain's face reddened. "That doesn't suit," he said in a curt tone. Then he turned solicitous again. "Would my lady like some bread and cheese before we depart? It's soldier's fare, but mayhap you've not dined well of late."

"Some food would be good."

"Then I'll have a man feed you."

A soldier arrived with coarse stale bread and a chunk of cheese so hard that he required his dagger to break off pieces. He wouldn't untie Yim's hands, despite her promises to behave, but fed her like a pet bird. Yim ate bits of bread and cheese, washing it down with sips of honeyed wine, until she felt full. When she was done, the soldiers marched her northwest until they reached the bank of a tiny river. The soldiers halted there, and as they began to set up camp, the horseman galloped off. Yim had little doubt that he had left to bear the good news to Lord Bahl and the Most Holy Gorm.

Yim's "pavilion" proved to be a tent too low to stand in. Inside, a few blankets had been spread upon the ground. Yim had to enter it by awkwardly walking on her knees. Captain Thak followed after her. "Lie on your back, my lady."

When Yim complied, she saw that the captain held a stout wooden rod that was about as long as an extended arm. At either end were iron hoops with a hinge on one side and a lock on the other. He grabbed one of Yim's ankles and locked it inside a hoop. Yim spoke as he secured the other ankle. "So this is how you treat 'your lady.' Am I to wet myself? I'm with child and make water often."

"A man shall tend to that business," replied Thak. "He'll feed, dress, and bathe you also. But don't worry, I'll blind him first."

"How barbaric!" said Yim. "Since it pleased Lord Bahl to show me naked, my modesty needn't cost a man his sight."

Thak grinned. "I was at that dinner. But then you were only a whore, not the vessel for the heir. Lord Bahl's will is plain in this. The man must lose his eyes."

"I'd rather wet myself."

Thak allowed some of his contempt to show. "So well you might, but you'll be treated as a lady regardless."

A short while latter, a soldier groped his way into Yim's tent. He wore no armor, nor bore any weapon. As Yim feared, his head was circled with a bandage that was bloody about the eyes. After he touched Yim's ankle, he bowed in her general direction. "Greetings, my lady. My name is Finar. 'Twill be my honor to serve ye." He groped outside the tent until he touched a pot of steaming water. Finar pulled it inside and closed the flap. "Captain Thak said ye need a bath."

While Yim waited to be taken to the Iron Palace, she led a life of anxious idleness. Finar was always by her side, and she gradually adjusted to his obtrusive presence. The man seldom spoke, and he was as morose as might be expected of someone blinded so he could catch a woman's urine. The soldiers found Yim better clothes somewhere, and she wore a clean shift that was well made and almost new. She dined on the finest food that the men could obtain. It was mostly plain fare, but abundant and vastly superior to raw hare and musk cabbage. She ate from Finar's hand, for her wrists were always tied behind her back.

Yim felt that her existence likened to that of a lamb being fattened for a feast. All her pampering was for a purpose. Despite her courteous treatment, Yim had no illusions that she was valued; she was only the vessel for something that was. That was why she was bound night and day, so she could do nothing to jeopardize Bahl's precious heir. *And after I deliver him, then what?* Yim gazed at her growing belly. She wouldn't have to wait long to find out.

It was the rider's haste that first alerted Honus. Good soldiers conserved their mounts, driving them hard only in times of need, and the Iron Guardsmen were good soldiers. Accordingly, Honus's curiosity was piqued, but he didn't jump to conclusions. Instead, he continued to observe the stronghold. The rider could be warning of an enemy's advance, the imminent arrival of fresh troops, or Yim's capture. Lord Bahl's response would be telling.

The rider had arrived late in the afternoon, and Honus noted nothing unusual during the rest of the day. It wasn't until the following morning that a wagon was driven out of the stronghold. It looked like a supply wagon that had been modified by the addition of a tentlike structure over its bed. By observing the ease with which the two horses pulled the vehicle, Honus surmised that it wasn't heavily laden. Despite its seeming lack of cargo, the wagon was well guarded. Two dozen foot soldiers marched behind it. A mounted guide led the way, accompanied by two mounted officers. Judging from the gilt armor of one of the officers, Honus thought that he was probably a general. However, it was the presence of a priest in the party that seemed most significant.

Honus had never seen the priest before, but he seemed an important person. He rode a magnificent black horse; his black robes and cloak appeared richly made even from a distance; and the iron pendant of the Devourer hung from an elaborate gold chain. The priest's inclusion in the company made Honus conclude its purpose wasn't military. The wagon and its accompanying troops headed east, the opposite direction of the Iron Palace. *Could Yim have been captured?* wondered Honus. *Is the wagon meant for her?*

Honus wavered over whether he should trail the wagon or continue observing the stronghold. He had few facts upon which to base a decision. All he knew for certain was that a wagon had departed accompanied by troops and a priest. As he speculated on what that signified, Honus worried that if he broke his watch he might miss what he had waited all winter to observe—a sign of Yim's whereabouts. Yet it was also possible that he had just witnessed that sign, and inaction would doom Yim. If the wagon was intended for her, he had no assurance it would return to the stronghold.

When evening fell, Honus had yet to determine what to do. Though the wagon's tracks would be easy to follow in a landscape emptied by warfare, he knew he shouldn't postpone a decision for long. Honus pondered the matter while he made the long trek to tend his stolen horse. He had stabled the steed in a derelict manor house beyond the swamp. The structure was little more than four partial walls, overgrown with vines. Honus visited it only under the cover of darkness, and he reached it a little after midnight.

Honus approached the structure cautiously, for he never knew if its secret had been discovered. When he reached the ruin, he peered through an empty window to check its interior before entering. Someone stood in front of the makeshift stall. Honus could barely make out the person's form in the darkness. He ducked from sight, and crept to another window for a closer view.

Honus slowly advanced without a sound, but when he raised his head, the figure had moved to within a few paces of where he stood. The form before him was that of a dark-haired woman with equally dark eyes. Honus cried out "Yim" in a voice that conveyed alarm, for she was spattered with blood from head to her bare feet. It made her white gown look dark.

The woman shook her head. Then she began to fade as she raised a bloody arm to point eastward. She continued to grow ever more transparent until she vanished altogether, leaving only frost upon the ground to mark her visitation.

Honus immediately knew that he must follow the wagon. The fact that Karm—he felt certain that the woman was the goddess—was covered with blood mystified him, but he pushed it from his mind. His long, lonely vigil was over. Honus fed his horse, saddled it, and led it into the night. He had no intentions of riding in the dark, but he wanted to be far from the stronghold when he rode off in the morning. Honus believed that his whole life had been preparation for the task ahead, and he approached it with single-minded intensity. The odds were overwhelmingly against him, but he had the assurance of a man whose defining moment had arrived. Karm had sent him eastward to manifest her wrath, and he would do his utmost to fulfill his role.

FORTY-FOUR

YIM SPENT four dreary but anxious days within the tent, waiting for something to happen. All that she could do was rebuild her strength in preparation for the trials ahead. At least the soldiers cooperated in that endeavor, and she was no longer famished or exhausted when more men arrived. At first, her ears gave only hints of what was going on. She heard hoofbeats, the rumble and creak of a wagon, and the tread of many booted feet. When the commotion stopped, she strained to overhear conversations, but they took place out of earshot. Then the camp grew quiet as if everyone had cleared out. After a spell of silence, Yim heard approaching footsteps. A man's voice said, "I want to speak to her alone." Then Yim heard Captain Thak's voice. "Finar, out of the tent!"

Yim's attendant departed, and a moment later the Most Holy Gorm entered. He was furious, and he glared at Yim so venomously that she thought he would hit her. Then she watched him restrain his rage. Instead of striking out, he raised her shift to uncover her bulging belly. Clasping it with both hands, he smiled when he felt the chill within her womb. "It's there."

"What's there?" asked Yim.

"Don't play the fool with me." Gorm removed his hands and gazed at Yim. They locked eyes, and Yim immediately sensed him probing her, seeking to expose her secrets. She veiled her thoughts and began an assault of her own. She held nothing back, but bent her entire will toward wrenching the truth from Gorm. The suddenness and strength of her assault caught her adversary off guard, and Yim was astonished by what she briefly glimpsed. Then Gorm resisted, and his thoughts were hidden from her. Afterward, Yim and the priest engaged in a silent struggle that was motionless, but nevertheless intense.

Gorm broke off the contest first by looking away. "You have some power," he said. "I expected as much. What you did was no happenstance."

"I was only an ambitious whore who hoped to bed a lord."

"Ha! The transparency of your lie. A virginal whore would be quite a novelty. Was the Sarf behind your deed? Tell the truth for once."

"Pull down my shift, and I will."

"All right, *my lady*," said Gorm, putting a sarcastic edge to his reply. After covering Yim, he said, "Well? The truth."

"Karm sent me. I have visions."

"The goddess sent a mere girl? Why not a Sarf?"

"Because she's wise."

"Why not say 'weak,' for that's the truth of it. Force requires power."

During Yim's brief glimpse into Gorm, she had noted his pride and thought she might goad him into revealing something useful. "Curious words to come from one such as you, a mere priest . . . a hanger-on . . . Bahl's shadow."

"You understand nothing," retorted Gorm. "I'm the real power behind Lord Bahl. I created him."

"Then it was your beard that fooled me," replied Yim. "I thought you were a man and not Bahl's mother."

"Do you imagine that's what you'll be? The mother of the next Lord Bahl? You're but a container, one of no value."

"Well, you can't be important either. My visions concerned only Lord Bahl. What tiny part do you play?"

Gorm laughed mirthlessly. "You're trying to goad me into saying something I'll regret. It's an old ruse, one I've often encountered. You can't imagine the depth of my experience. I witnessed the Orc Rebellion. Traveled beyond the Eastern Reach and tutored the first witch king. I was there when Luvein fell. You and I may talk, but don't presume we're equals."

Yim had discovered Gorm's true age when she had probed him, but she feigned astonishment. "But that would make you centuries old! How can that be?"

"Because I serve a truly potent master," said Gorm. "My long life and youth are but some of the benefits."

"But what price was exacted for such favors?"

"I might ask the same of you if visions were truly boons," said Gorm. "But look where they've led you. And Karm's devotees call visions 'gifts.' Ha! The goddess is stingy, and gives only those things that suit her purposes. I should know. I once studied to be a Seer."

"You studied in the temple?"

"One in the north," replied Gorm. "It's long gone now. In those days one could present oneself for training, and I wished to learn how to prophesy. What I discovered is that magic doesn't come from learning. All power derives from the nether realm. A Seer's ability is a gift from Karm, not the result of learning meditations."

"That's no great revelation."

"Yes, only basic knowledge. The crucial matter is this: What's the point of glimpsing only what Karm wishes you to see? I wanted to learn things that would benefit me. So I left the temple and sought instruction from another source, a man who'd discovered a means to prolong life. It involved sacrifices that captured the victims' souls before they reached the Dark Path. By that means, my mentor extended his years."

"And that's what you did?"

"No. The process was flawed. The man looked like a sun-dried corpse. His most useful lesson was that Karm is not the only source of magic."

"He taught you about the Devourer?"

"I devised that name when I created its cult. At first, I knew it only as a being upon the Dark Path. It's the wellspring of all sorcery, a thing that bestows power upon those who satisfy its needs."

Its need for slaughter, thought Yim, keeping silent to appear ignorant. "And what did you do with that power?"

"I devised a set of magic bones by coaxing a bit of the being from the Dark Path into them. It was a perilous thing to do, but it gave the bones the power for augury. Using them, I became a counselor to mighty men. But I sold the bones to a mage."

"Why would you do that?"

"I sensed a new role for myself. I took the Devourer for my master and became the man who advanced its cause through other men. They suffered the risks; I reaped the rewards. I fully realized the possibilities when someone destroyed the bones and their power entered the mage."

"I'd think that you would have preferred it enter you."

"Far from it," said Gorm. "The mage was burnt and maimed. But he gained the power to control others' minds. Unfortunately, that power quickly destroyed any mind it ruled. The mage was a failed experiment that I eventually ended. Yet it set me on a path of experimentation that led to the first Lord Bahl, a man whose spirit contained a bit of the Devourer. Bahl became the means for my master to act directly in this world."

"Why unleash such a thing?"

"Because when it rules the world, I shall be its viceroy."

"Just a fancy word for 'servant.'"

"An eternal and omnipotent servant." Gorm smiled at Yim. "What has your service to the goddess gained you? You're a prisoner who'll bear the child of your foe."

"At least I've stopped that foe."

"You've not stopped the Rising. You've merely postponed it."

"The Rising?"

"Yes, Karm's little harlot, the Rising," said Gorm. "Bloodshed will usher it in. Upon that day, the Devourer will overwhelm Bahl's flesh to rule the living world forever."

"If this rising is so certain, why hasn't it happened already? There have been many wars and many Lord Bahls."

"It nearly happened with the first Lord Bahl. The slaughter at Karvakken Pass almost caused it. An invasion of Vinden would have made it surely so. But Lord Bahl raped a woman and lost his powers. At the time, I was unaware of how readily the Devourer forsakes one human body for a new one. It sees us as overly fragile. But my greatest error lay in slaying the woman after she delivered the child."

"Why did you do that?"

"For revenge. She'd ruined my plans."

"She ruined them unwillingly," said Yim. "She was raped."

"Regardless, she still ruined them. Yet I came to regret my vengeance. Though the child possessed his father's powers, they were greatly diminished. I didn't understand how things worked."

"And how do they work?"

"Wouldn't you like to know." Gorm grinned. "But I've told you all I intended."

In a final effort to provoke Gorm, Yim flashed a mocking smile. "But I've learned far more than that. I'm not as helpless as you think."

Gorm merely shrugged. "Empty words. From now on, you'll be like all the other mothers."

"No I won't. I've heard they were docile."

"There's something to be said for ignorance," said Gorm. "Their lives at the Iron Palace were contented."

"But short."

"No shorter than yours shall be."

"I understand what's within me," said Yim, "and I don't mean the child. I've faced your master at Karvakken Pass and within the ruins of Karm's temple. It's an abomination. I didn't surrender then, and I won't now."

Gorm regarded Yim with astonishment. "So, it was you! You're the foe who entered the temple! You're the one who enraged my master!"

Yim saw no advantage in denying it. "Yes, I stopped a second massacre, one that would have slain all the priests in the Black Temple. It seems your 'god' doesn't care who dies. The thing you call 'master' is ravenous and evil. You're a fool to worship it."

"You're a greater fool to worship Karm," replied Gorm. "See how she's abandoned you."

"My story's not yet finished. Don't pretend you know its end."

"But I do," replied Gorm. "The mothers always die."

"Despite your grandiose plans, your story will end likewise, for the Devourer craves death. It's only a being formed from the memories of slaughter. It'll turn on you. It has no loyalty."

"Neither does fire. It burns the careless, but that's no reason to forgo cooked food and warmth. The Devourer is a well of power, and I've learned how to harness it."

"If you believe that, you're deluded," replied Yim. "It's *you* who has been harnessed."

"You're a mere girl," said Gorm. "And a helpless one at that. You're bound, shackled, and under guard. You'll say anything in desperation."

"Even the truth!"

"I've heard little of that from you." Without warning, Gorm slapped Yim savagely across her face, leaving the mark of his hand and a trickle of blood flowing from her lip. He smiled, seeming pleased for the first time. "In the Iron Palace, you'll learn to speak more honestly. I look forward to that."

Gorm left the tent, and Yim was alone awhile before General Var entered. By then, the camp had turned noisy. The general smiled when he saw the blood on Yim's lip and the mark on her cheek. "So, you and the Most Holy One had a little chat. By the Devourer, I'd like to do what he did!"

"What? Inquire about my health?"

Var clenched his teeth. "I wish I'd strangled you that night."

"Well, do it now," said Yim. "Be my guest."

Var scowled. "I'm sorely tempted, but I'd rather live. Besides, I so look forward to the suckling." He grinned at Yim's confusion. "Haven't heard of it? Well, I witnessed the last suckling when my lord was but a lad. You'll see your son only twice—when you birth him and when you suckle him."

"You obviously know nothing about nursing."

"Oh, your son won't suck from your tits. He'll have a wet nurse for that. You'll provide a more substantial meal. They'll lock you away until he's a strapping lad. Then there'll be a ceremony atop the highest tower where the Most Holy One opens your neck and the boy drinks."

"My blood?" said Yim in horror, recalling what she had done to the rabbit.

"Every drop until you're white as snow. A most invigorating meal. It transforms him." General Var smiled maliciously. "I may not strike you, but it pleases me to tell you that. It'll give you something to contemplate during your imprisonment."

Yim gazed into the general's eyes and saw both his pleasure and that he had told the truth.

After General Var departed, Finar was led back into Yim's tent. When the flap was briefly opened, Yim saw that the soldiers were striking camp. She didn't ask her attendant what was going on, because she knew he wouldn't talk. His loyalties lay elsewhere, and she was certain that he had been ordered to keep silent. Instead, she asked him to wipe her face, not bothering to tell him that he was cleaning blood from it.

As Yim waited for the next stage of her journey to begin, she contemplated her conversations with the Most Holy One and the general. Gorm had confirmed what she had already suspected—that he was the power behind Lord Bahl. Most of what he had told her was interesting, but not particularly useful. However, there was one thing that intrigued Yim: It was the possibility that the creation of Lord Bahl could never be repeated. It seemed to her that after the first Bahl had lost his power, Gorm would have produced a replacement if he had been able. Instead, he stuck by Lord Bahl's weakened son and nurtured his descendants until the line produced a Bahl whose power equaled that of the original. *Perhaps the Devourer can leave the Dark Path only once*, thought Yim. It was merely speculation, but it would explain her treatment. *I'm bearing something irreplaceable.*

Additionally, Yim had learned the name of what the Old Ones had feared so much—the Rising—and had come to understand its nature. It threatened to transform the world into a nightmare realm ruled by cruelty and death. Yim couldn't imagine why Gorm would work to achieve such a thing. *Who would want to live forever in such a place?* Madness seemed the only explanation. But Gorm's madness was a thoughtful and patient one, and despite racking her brain, Yim saw no way to prevent his scheme's fruition.

From what Gorm had said and from Var's taunting, Yim saw how her death would fit into the process. Upon conception, the Devourer had entered her child and her, and apparently it would remain in both of them even after the child was born. *That's why the second Lord Bahl's power was diminished*, thought Yim. *That's why my son must consume my blood: It will make the Devourer whole again.* It would be a gruesome way to die. Moreover, it meant that the Devourer would leave her only upon her death. Until then, she would never be free of evil.

What Yim had learned only served to heighten her despair. She saw no way to use the information. Gorm had been right: She was helpless. Regardless of her bold words, she feared that Gorm had also been right when he said Karm had abandoned her. Yim felt her suffering had bought the world a bit more time before darkness fell, but it would fall nonetheless.

Captain Thak entered the tent and unlocked the shackles about Yim's ankles. "Up, my lady. Your transport has arrived."

Yim left the tent, enjoying standing upright for the first time in days. As she gazed about the dismantled encampment, she saw Gorm gallop off. Yim suspected that he wouldn't return. Then two soldiers grabbed her upper arms and led her toward a wagon. It seemed an ordinarily supply wagon—one light enough to be drawn by two horses—with a wooden frame added to support a tentlike canvas covering. When they reached the vehicle, one of Yim's escorts climbed into its rear and lifted Yim inside.

As the second soldier climbed into the wagon, Yim looked about. A mattress took up most of the wagon's interior. Yim noted a shallow chamber pot, a water skin, and a few blankets in addition to the mattress. She also spied manacles and chains fastened to the wagon's sides. "Sit on yer bed, my lady," said one of the soldiers.

Yin sat down, and the soldiers locked her ankles in iron manacles that were cushioned with velvet. Afterward, they untied her wrists and placed them in manacles also. When they were done, they hoisted Finar up before departing. Yim lay upon the mattress in a spread-eagle position. The chains allowed her some mobility, and she immediately tested its limits. She could sit up, but not stand. She could move her legs a degree, but not enough so her knees could touch. Her hands were so restrained that she was unable to touch any part of her body. Thus she would remain dependent on Finar for all her personal needs.

Yim flopped back on the mattress. It was stuffed with feathers and extremely soft. She suspected that was more to prevent self-injury than to provide comfort. "Well, Finar, this is our new home," said Yim in mock cheeriness. "I wonder how long we'll dwell here."

Out of habit, Finar turned his head toward the sound of Yim's voice as if he could regard her with his eyeless sockets. Then he shrugged.

FORTY-FIVE

LOVE, WRATH, and faith combined in Honus to produce a single will. Not a bent blade of grass, a footprint, or a clump of horse dung escaped his notice. Everything instructed him, and he followed the wagon's trail with certainty, which was not to say that he followed it swiftly. Honus knew all the maps of the region and had trekked over much of it. Thus he knew where best to strike. Bahland lay to the west, just north of Averen. The Iron Palace overlooked a bay on the faraway seacoast. The rolling plain that lay ahead was still called the Western Reach, though it no longer belonged to the Empire. The region was a lonely place, for generations of war had stripped it of folk. Honus planned to trail the soldiers at a distance until the empty sea of grass lulled them into complacency. Then he would fall upon them.

On the beginning of his journey, Honus stopped at several farmsteads for provisions. He didn't request charity in Karm's name, although he felt it was for her service. Instead, he demanded what he needed in the certainty that no one would dare refuse. He was loath to do so, and it felt like stealing to him. Though his actions were driven by necessity, they still troubled him afterward.

Thoughts of Yim troubled Honus far more. He was certain that he would find her, but he had no idea what he would find. Hendric had told him that he saw no hurts, but he also had said that Yim walked as though pained and that she had an unnatural chill. The chill particularly worried

Honus, for it might be a sign of some spell. Yim's behavior added to his concerns. It seemed that she was fleeing from more than Lord Bahl. Honus feared for Yim, and all the apprehensions that had tormented him throughout the winter were sharpened by the prospect of seeing her again. It was a testament to his discipline that he was able to push them from his thoughts and focus on his goal.

Honus's examination of the soldiers' trail allowed him to determine the pace and manner of their advance. It was hard to ascertain the exact number of marching men, but he saw signs of three horsemen with the party. They didn't serve as scouts, but rode alongside the foot soldiers and the wagon. That allowed Honus to trail the wagon fairly closely, keeping just beyond eyesight and matching his pace to that of the marchers. Honus shadowed the men for five days before he decided they were sufficiently isolated. Then he made the first move.

The moon was in its first quarter when Honus tethered his mount at dusk and followed the soldiers' trail by moonlight. He spotted their encampment as the moon neared the horizon. Using stealth perfected by long practice, he made his way toward it. The ground undulated gently and Honus halted on one of the low rises to observe the camp. He made a careful count of those in it. Thirty-four enemies were visible. There was a small tent that probably sheltered an officer or two. The common soldiers slept on the ground surrounding the wagon under the watch of three sentries. The horses were tethered nearby in a lush patch of grass. Another sentry watched over them. Honus could see no sign of Yim. He sank into the high grass and waited for the moon to set.

When the sky was lit only by starlight, Honus advanced toward the sentry that guarded the horses. What little noise he made blended with the rustle of the night breeze. The man appeared relaxed, lulled by the quiet of the empty landscape. His head dipped occasionally as sleep nearly overcame him.

He didn't see the blade that severed his throat. A hand covered his mouth, so he died silently as Honus eased him to the ground.

After donning the dead man's helm and cloak, Honus walked over to the horses. He stroked each beast and fed it a treat before quickly and mercifully slaying it. He regretted the killings, but they were essential. Without the animals, the soldiers could move no faster than they could march and no horseman could summon aid.

Honus retreated to watch the encampment for signs that his handiwork had been discovered. When all remained quiet, he crept toward the sleeping men. The sentries there were no more alert than the one who had guarded the horses, and Honus was able to join the sleepers. Wrapped in the slain Guardsman's cloak, he lay upon the ground and blended with the slumbering soldiers. Whenever the guards were looking the other way, Honus used his dagger to cut a sleeping man's throat. He took six lives that way before a guard noticed a pool of blood about one man. Honus didn't wait to find out what would happen next. He leapt up, drawing his sword as he did, and decapitated the surprised sentry. Honus grabbed the falling sentry's sword, plunged it into a soldier who had just wakened, and dashed off into the night.

As Honus hurried to where he had left his steed, he could hear the noises of confusion arising from the camp. *Nine slain*, he thought. Honus was well aware that he was still outnumbered by at least twenty-five to one and the enemy had been alerted to his presence. Next time, they would be waiting for him. When Honus reached his horse, he rode off into the night, knowing that his enemies could only pursue him on foot.

Honus waited until midmorning before he returned to the enemy campsite. It was deserted, as he had expected, but he was surprised to find the wagon missing. Its trail showed that soldiers pulled it. Honus found it a puzzling choice, but one that played to his advantage. It would slow the soldiers' advance and tire them as well. Honus assumed that Yim was in the wagon, and he feared that she might be hurt. The whole matter baffled and worried him.

By studying the encampment awhile, Honus learned what had happened in his absence. He found the corpses of nine men. They were laid out in a neat row. That seemed to be the sole dignity afforded them and a sign of a hasty departure. By studying the trail left by the soldiers, he noted that a pair of men had diverged from the rest. By the length of their strides, Honus surmised they were a pair of runners, gone ahead to get reinforcements. *They must be unaware that I have a horse*, Honus thought. He rode off to intercept them.

Honus took a circuitous route in order to bypass the marching soldiers, for he wished his horse to remain a secret. After riding ahead a fair distance, he had to find the runners' trail before he could track them. As he feared, they had split up to make pursuit more difficult. It indicated that they suspected only a single enemy had attacked them. It took Honus a while to find the men, and he offered each a chance to save his life by talking. Both chose to fight, but neither was a match for a Sarf. Honus pulled up turf to hide the bodies so that vultures wouldn't betray the runners' fates. Then he rode off to prepare for more combat.

On the night of Honus's first attack, Yim had known when the first soldier died. The malign spirit inside her exulted like a hungry dog that was fed a scrap. Its pleasure was unseemly and foul, but so intense that it woke Yim. Instinctively, she understood what had happened, and she fought against any feeling of delight. Afterward, she lay awake in the quiet dark, sensing when each man died. Only the last two deaths were accompanied by sounds—the first by a wet crunch like a cabbage being split and the second by a moan.

Afterward, Yim heard the din of confused voices as sleeping men awoke to discover that death had visited them. Chained inside the wagon, Yim could see nothing and was forced to form her impressions of events from snatches of talk. There was a great deal of cursing. Then she heard Captain Thak bellowing orders, and General Var shouted orders also, but only to the captain. Torches were lit. Discoveries were made. Yim knew about the dead soldiers, but she didn't know about the slain horses until Thak let out a string of obscenities in response to the report. Peppered throughout all Yim heard was a word that gripped her attention—"Sarf."

"The Sarf's back, plague his blue hide!" cursed one man.

"Aye, 'tis that cold-blooded prick for sure," said another. "Did ye see what he did to poor Fatar?"

Yim had no doubt that the Sarf was Honus. It seemed that he had been plaguing Bahl's men for moons. The idea that he had found her aroused a range of contradictory emotions. Honus's persistence showed devotion that stirred Yim's love. It also brought her hope. Yet she was fearful that he would die for her sake. She had prayed to Karm that Honus would forget her and find happiness elsewhere. Obviously, the goddess had ignored her plea. Meanwhile, panic warred with love and hope, for Yim dreaded a reunion. She doubted that Honus knew she was pregnant with Lord Bahl's child. *How will he take the news? The last time we spoke, I said he was to be the father.* Yim also worried that Honus might have misunderstood the meaning of the token she had left behind. It was easy to imagine his resentment over her desertion.

But most of all, Yim despaired over what she had become. She felt that she was no longer the woman whom Honus loved, but someone befouled—a host to something vile and evil. Yim was terrified over what it might cause her to do if she let down her guard for only an instant. Additionally, Honus was a deadly man. His deeds, however nobly intentioned, fed the evil thing inside her.

Hope, despair, love, shame, and terror fought within Yim, and she could no more resolve the conflict than she could save herself. Chained and helpless, she was unable to act. All she could do was wait, and waiting was agony.

Yim saw Finar stir. "My Sarf's come to save me."

As usual, Finar didn't reply.

"I know your loyalty lies with Lord Bahl," Yim said, "although it was he, not I, who had your eyes plucked. While you serve me grudgingly, you still serve me, and I'm grateful. When my Sarf returns, I'll have him spare you."

"Ye know not the Iron Guard, my lady. They'll fight to the last man. So 'tis no good to spare me, a blind man is a waste. Don't speak of mercy. My life's saved only by yer Sarf's death."

The day passed. When the moon set, Honus moved like a shadow in the dark and just as quietly. There were more guards that night, and fear kept every man alert. They bore torches made from dry, twisted grass. Honus halted outside the circle of the light cast by one and watched it slowly burn down. When the flame neared the sentry's hand, he picked up a fresh torch to light it. Then Honus attacked, striking at the narrow spot between the Guardsman's helm and his chain mail. He seized the dead man's torch as it fell.

Dressed like the man he had just slain, Honus held the torch aloft to keep his face in shadow. The helm also helped hide his tattoos as he approached another guard. "What are ye doing away from yer post?" asked the man in a hoarse voice.

"I need another torch," replied Honus.

"Yer not . . ."

Honus's blade cut him short. *Thirteen slain*, he thought. He took the dead man's broadsword and began hacking his corpse, while still holding the torch up high. "The Sarf!" he shouted hoarsely. "I got him! I got him!" As the two closest guards came running, Honus dropped the torch and snuffed its flame with his foot. Then he turned and surprised the two oncoming men. Seven sword strokes and it was over.

Fifteen. Honus charged into the sleeping men, interrupting dreams and lives. Some of the soldiers, exhausted from a long day of pulling the wagon, sat up sleepy and confused to be caught by Honus's blade. Other soldiers, energized by terror, bolted up with sword in hand. The darkness added to their confusion, and one killed a fellow soldier before Honus relieved him of his head. Within the chaos, only Honus was prepared and focused, a deadly acrobat performing a well-practiced routine. With each stroke, he felt closer to Yim and more convinced that he manifested the divine wrath tattooed on his face.

Honus lost count of how many he had slain, but not his grasp of tactics. When the alert and armored guards rushed in from their posts, Honus retreated into the moonless night, satisfied that he had wreaked sufficient havoc. He easily lost his pursuers, found his horse, and rode off to sleep.

Yim had felt each death during Honus's raid as a jolt of malign joy. It was tiring to fight off an inner foe that grew stronger after each successive jolt, and Yim felt barely rested when Captain Thak shook her awake in the morning. He had exchanged his officer's armor for that of a common Guardsman. His expression was hard and angry. "Sit up!" he barked.

Yim sat up, and the captain unlocked the manacles that restrained her wrists. Then he tossed something on her lap. "Put this on." It was a Guardsman's armor, consisting of a long-sleeved chain-mail tunic that was reinforced on the shoulders and chest with steel plates. Made for a large man, it gave Yim a boxy shape when she donned it. Afterward, the captain bound Yim's wrists behind her back. Next he drew his dagger and roughly trimmed the length of her shift so it extended just below her knees. That was the same length as a Guardsman's cloak. Finally, the captain unlocked her ankles. "I'll help you out of the wagon," he said. "Thanks to your friend, you'll walk to the Iron Palace."

Yim gazed about the encampment. Eleven bodies lay in a row. General Var was handing out small glass vials of brown liquid to the soldiers. "Paint this on your sword and let it dry before you sheath it," he told the men. "Nick yourself, and you're dead."

While the general gave out poison, the captain tied a leather noose around Yim's neck, apparently intending to use it as a leash. He placed a Guardsman's helm upon her head, covered the armor with a Guardsman's cloak, and grabbed the dangling end of the leather noose. "Now, my lady, you're dressed for your little stroll."

Finar called from the wagon. "What about me, sir?"

"You'll slow us down. I left the water skin in the wagon." He walked over to one of the dead soldiers, took his dagger, and gave it to Finar. "Use this if you want to end it quick," he said. "Otherwise, there's plenty of fresh meat if you can stomach it."

General Var walked over and regarded Yim. "Well, she looks less like a woman, but not much like a soldier."

"She'll walk in the center," said Thak. "Out of view."

"Keep a tight rein on her," replied the general. Then he took the leather strap from the captain's hand and pulled it upward until Yim was forced to stand on tiptoe. "Don't think you're winning," he told her. "There's no escape. You'll either walk to the Iron Palace or I'll kill you myself."

FORTY-SIX

YIM TROD over the prairie hemmed so tightly by soldiers that all she saw was their bulky, armored bodies and the grass beneath her bare feet. They were already cut and bleeding, but she didn't complain, for she sensed the men's grim mood. Honus's relentless assaults had gripped their imaginations. When Yim gazed into the men's eyes, she saw fear. It had nothing to do with numbers; there were fourteen of them against one Sarf. Moreover, their blades were poisoned. Nevertheless, the previous night's slaughter has sapped the soldiers' morale, and they saw their foe as something more than a man.

The soldiers' mood did little to encourage Yim. Desperate men were dangerous and reckless. She was late into her pregnancy, and they were pushing her hard. The pace was determined by the men's anxiety rather than her ability to sustain it. Her heavy disguise made walking all the more strenuous. Whenever she lagged a bit, Captain Thak tugged on her leash.

Finally, Yim could stand it no longer. She let out such an ear-piercing shriek that even Thak stopped dead in his tracks. Yim screwed up her face in pain, moaned, and shrieked again. "I must lie down," she said in an agonized voice. "Who knows about birthing babies?"

The question had the desired effect. The men looked at one another helplessly. Thak let go of the leash, and Yim lay on the ground. She curled on her side, gasping and moaning like a woman undergoing labor. She had witnessed enough births to make her imitation perfect, though she doubted any of the men had the experience to appreciate her artistry.

General Var stomped in frustration. "You're not due for another moon!"

"I know. It's too . . . early," said Yim between gasps. "I might . . . be mis . . . carrying . . . or having . . . false labor." Then Yim continued her performance, and the men backed away to give her air. Captain Thak untied her hands, and she grasped her belly and moaned. When Yim decided that she had made her point, she gradually relaxed. Even when she lay absolutely still, the men let her rest. Yim imagined that each one was thinking of what Gorm and Bahl would do if they brought a dead infant to the Iron Palace. Not wanting to push her advantage too far, she gave a deep sigh after a while and said. "I think it was false labor. I feel better now."

The march resumed soon afterward. Yim's hands were bound again, but the men set a gentler pace and Thak went easy on the leash. Nevertheless, by the day's end, Yim was walking in a state of nearly senseless exhaustion. When the march halted for the night, she was fed, and then her ankles were securely tied. Yim lay upon the ground and quickly fell asleep.

The jolt that came whenever someone died woke Yim. She listened but heard nothing. *Honus is at work*, she thought. She assumed that he had killed a sentry. For a long while there was only silence, then Yim heard swords ringing in the dark. "The blades are poisoned!" she shouted.

Someone struck her hard in the face before slapping a hand over her mouth. "Get me something to gag her with," she heard the captain yell. Soon he pushed a foul-tasting rag into her mouth and bound it in place with another strip of cloth. While that was going on, Yim listened for some sound of Honus. The fight had ended shortly after she had shouted, and the clang of swords was replaced with the quiet rustle of men running through grass in a deadly game of tag. One runner sped toward the soldiers, all of whom were awake. They stood in a circle around her, blades drawn and facing outward.

Yim caught a flash of movement against the sky and heard the soft whistling of a sword spinning through the air. A man gave a startled cry that rose in pitch as he tumbled to the ground writhing in pain as the sword blade's poison took effect. Yim heard the whistling sound again. Two men fell this time. It was gruesome to watch them expire, though part of Yim relished their agony with obscene delight. Afterward, the night grew quiet.

Knowing that she faced a long, hard march in the morning, Yim tried to sleep, but her heart was pounding. All her turmoil resurfaced, no more resolved than it was when exhaustion had clouded her thoughts. Mingled with her opposing emotions and coloring them like a vile tint was blood lust. It repelled her as always, but it gave her insight into Lord Bahl and his master. *The need for death is so strong*, she thought. *This is what will grip my son.*

Yim had no idea how long she lay awake, encircled by anxious men who pointed poisoned steel at the night. When sleep finally came to her, it was deep, and she didn't wake until the sun had cleared the horizon. Yim was surprised that the soldiers hadn't roused her, for they customarily rose at first light. Curious, she struggled into a sitting position and peered about.

Five corpses lay nearby. Three of them were twisted into grotesque shapes with matching expressions that told of agonized deaths. Yim was surprised to see only seven men in camp. She glanced about and noted that Captain Thak was missing. So was one of his men. When General Var saw that Yim was awake, he said, "The bitch is up. Feed her."

When a soldier came over and removed Yim's gag, she said in a hoarse voice, "Can I have some water, please."

Var grinned. "Mouth a little dry? I've half a mind to cut out your tongue. Another peep like last night, and I will."

Yim looked at him and saw he wasn't bluffing. "I'll behave."

The general scowled and looked away.

A soldier fed Yim a meal of bread and water. Afterward, he untied her ankles and escorted her to where she relieved herself, then led her back to the other soldiers. From what she overheard, they were waiting for the captain's return. It was midmorning before Yim spotted him striding toward camp. He appeared to be kicking something as he walked. The tall grass prevented her from seeing what it was until he arrived. Then, with one last forceful kick, he sent what remained of a head sailing into the pile of corpses. It had been so mangled that Yim couldn't tell if it was tattooed.

"Anyone else want to desert?" asked the captain, staring at each man in turn except for the general. "By the Eater, I'm worse than any Sarf! Put a helm on the bitch and move out."

Yim marched at the end of Captain Thak's leash in the center of a square of men. The general strode behind her, and the six remaining soldiers formed two flanks of three. Yim walked with a sense of dread. Instinct told her it would end that day, but she had no idea what that ending would be. The day grew hot as the sun rose higher, and marching quickly became a wearing grind. The helm felt like a little sweaty cage. It muffled her hearing as exhaustion dulled it. Thus she heard the hoofbeats only an instant before the attack. There were three rapid sounds, and then Yim saw the rear of a galloping horse. Honus was leaning far over in the saddle, a sword extended. As he righted himself and sped away, two men fell to the ground in convulsions.

"Curse the sneaky bastard," said a soldier. "He's using a dead man's poisoned sword!"

"I warned of this," said Captain Thak.

"Shut up!" said General Var. "Have the men re-form the flanks." Then he muttered to Yim, "Don't gloat, bitch. Remember my promise."

The march resumed as soon as a soldier hid his two dead comrades' poisoned swords. The sun scorched everyone until even the men dragged. Yim stumbled ever more frequently. One time, the helm fell from her head. No one replaced it when she recovered, much to her relief. As the soldiers advanced, the plain's undulations became more pronounced. Low hills alternated with low valleys in monotonous repetition that wore Yim down even further.

Yim and her captors had just descended a hill and were heading to the next one when Honus appeared on its summit. The soldiers halted and gazed at him. Yim gazed at him also. The rage needled on his face no longer seemed a mask. Like the soldiers, there was trepidation in Yim's eyes, but there was also love.

Honus walked down the hill with an easy stride. "Captain Thak," he called out. "Finar wishes you to know that water skin you left him was empty. We talked a bit. I offered to return for him, but he declined. A good soldier to the end." Honus shook his head mournfully. "He made two last requests. That I end it quick for him and that I return your gift." Upon the word "gift," Honus's hand flashed with dazzling speed. Yim heard a wet-sounding thump, and the captain released her leash. He stood quivering for a moment before he fell in a twisting motion to lie faceup. A dagger's hilt protruded from his mouth.

Then all the men, except the general, charged Honus. He met their assault with his own, one that seemed a fluid dance. The soldiers looked ponderous in comparison. They swung at empty air while Honus darted in and out, employing his blade with deadly precision. None of his motions appeared wasted, not even those that didn't slay. Each stroke was followed by another in choreography that always climaxed with a killing thrust. Yim watched, having never seen Honus move so quickly or with such assurance. He was death personified, beautiful and appalling at once.

The four Guardsmen became three, then two, and then one. As Honus fought the remaining soldier, Yim felt a sharp and heavy blow to her kidney. General Var had stabbed her with all his might, and though the chain mail that Yim wore stopped the blade, it didn't blunt the force of the blow. Yim crumpled to her knees, her eyes clinched tight from pain. Perhaps the general thought he had mortally wounded her or perhaps he was distracted, for she remained in that position for a long moment before he seized her hair. Yim felt a hand tug her tresses back and down so that her exposed neck arched upward. She opened her eyes and saw a dagger moving toward her throat.

Then the hand upon the dagger halted and the hilt slipped from its grasp. General Var's head tumbled to the ground. A fountain of blood showered Yim as her hair was released. Then Honus knelt before her.

FORTY-SEVEN

YIM GAZED at Honus through blood and tears. Never did he look so lovely or so terrible. She was stunned speechless. She didn't know what to say, what to tell, or even what she thought. Her hands were tied, so she couldn't embrace him. All she could do was weep.

Honus seemed equally confused, as if recovering from a spell. Rage briefly lingered in his face. Then it softened and his eyes became tender and sad. "Oh, Yim," he said softly. "What has happened to you?"

"I obeyed Karm's will, and now I'm with child."

Honus gazed down at her bulging belly, as if noticing it for the first time.

"Will you untie me?" asked Yim, feeling that Honus needed prompting.

Without a word, Honus removed Yim's cloak, cut her bonds, and pulled the armored tunic from her. Yim remained kneeling, for the general's blow still pained her terribly. Honus seemed astonished by her appearance. *He didn't know*, she thought.

Honus cut a bit of cloth from a soldier's cloak, wetted it using a water skin, and knelt to wash General Var's blood from Yim's face. Then he kissed her with almost timid delicacy. "Nothing matters except you're safe," he whispered. "Throughout the cold moons of winter I dreamt of this moment."

The touch of Honus's lips evoked memories of joy, something that Yim had believed was gone forever. When he kissed her again, she responded passionately. Starved for his love, Yim communicated her hunger, and Honus's kisses became less delicate and more fervent. They embraced as pent-up desire blossomed and overwhelmed them. For a while, their world consisted only of each other, and they were oblivious of the dead surrounding them.

It was Yim who broke off the embrace to rise unsteadily to her feet. "Let's leave this place. I want to get far from the sight of slaughter."

"Yes, Karmamatus."

"Honus, please don't call me that. It's no longer fitting."

"Why?"

"I'll speak of it later. Right now, I just want to get away from here."

"All right, Yim. I'll get my horse. Do you think you can ride?"

"Cara taught me a little about it," replied Yim, "but I'll need help getting into the saddle."

Honus walked off to get his horse. When he was out of view, Yim relieved herself in the tall grass and was startled to see blood in her urine. She decided not to mention it. Then she climbed over the low hill so that the corpses were no longer in view. There, she eagerly waited for Honus's return. It had taken only a few kisses to convince her that she loved him as much as ever. She was certain that Honus felt the same way, although she bore another man's child. *Of course, he doesn't yet know who fathered it*, Yim thought. She suspected even that would make no difference to him.

Yim craved a measure of peace, a time to be with her beloved after so much suffering and horror. "Is that too much to ask?" Yim said aloud. "Can't I be happy for a little while?" Yim wavered over what to do, then surrendered to desire. She knew it wasn't prudent or fair to Honus, but she couldn't help herself. "Just one day," she promised, all the while knowing that it would make doing what was necessary even harder.

When Honus returned with the horse, he had already adjusted the stirrups for Yim. He helped her climb into the saddle before taking water skins and provisions from his slain foes. After he placed those things in his saddlebags, he grasped the reins to lead the horse. "Aren't you going to ride?" asked Yim.

"That saddle won't fit three," replied Honus, gazing at Yim's rounded belly. "So, where shall we go?"

"Someplace peaceful. Someplace where we can be alone."

"With Bahl's men dead, half the reach would qualify. But I know of a river not too far from here. This time of year, it might even have some water in it."

"Oh Karm bless you!" said Yim. "How I'd love a bath."

Honus looked at her with a twinkle in his eye. "And I'd be honored to bathe you."

Yim felt her face flush with excitement. "What's your horse's name?" she asked quickly.

"Vengeance."

"What a horrid name." Yim stroked the animal's neck. "That's not your real name, is it?"

The stallion neighed.

"He says it's Neeg," said Yim, wavering the vowel sound. "It's the same as his sire's."

"His former owner neglected to tell me that," said Honus. "Guardsmen are a closemouthed lot. But when did you learn to speak to animals?"

"I didn't. I've only picked up a few words. But I spent the winter with a bear."

Honus looked up and grinned. Then he saw that Yim was serious. "In its den?"

"Yes, hibernating. You see, I was faerie-kissed."

"Like that girl and her mother?"

"Yes. I stuffed myself and snoozed till spring." Yim gazed down at Honus's gaunt face. "I think you had a less easy time."

"After you deserted me . . ." Yim winced at his choice of words, and Honus apparently noticed, for he paused before continuing. "After you fulfilled Karm's will, I met a man named Hendric."

"So he made it safely to your camp?"

"Yes. He spoke of you. He said you were fleeing Bahl. He told me other things, too. That you . . ."

"Let's not talk of that now," Yim said quickly. "How did you survive the winter?"

"Lord Bahl was searching for you, so I made things difficult for him. His Guardsmen became my prey." Honus's voice hardened with the memory of it. "I lived off them and watched for signs of you. And now I'm here due to Karm's grace. She sent me to you."

"You mean you had a vision?"

"Yes, my second one involving you. Karm also sent me to the dark man's castle, although you said I was only dreaming."

"I had to keep my secrets then."

"But now you don't."

Honus spoke those words more like a plea than a statement, and it tore at Yim's heart. "I won't keep secrets from you, Honus. I swear. But after what I've been through, all I want is to forget awhile. To be at peace and to be with you." She reached down to stroke Honus's cheek. "How I've longed to do that."

Honus gazed up at her and smiled.

The river Honus spoke of was mostly a ribbon of wet sand, but he followed its bed until he found a stretch of water. It resembled a long, winding pool. By the time they reached it, a low sun painted the grass in greenish gold. Reflecting the rose and blue of the sky, the pool reminded Yim of Faerie and also of the morning when love was a revelation. After Honus set up a rudimentary camp, Yim shed her clothing and waded into the pool, hoping that her new body wouldn't repulse Honus. She called to him. "You said you'd bathe me." Honus's smile showed Yim that she needn't have worried. He quickly undressed and joined her.

Both custom and belief forbade full intimacy after a pregnancy showed, but caresses were permissible. Yim needed Honus to wash more than dirt away; she wanted to be cleansed of the repellent memories of Yaun's and Bahl's groping. She saw Honus's concern when he first touched her skin and felt its chill. But then his hands began to work their magic. Strong, yet gentle, they spoke to her. They said, "I love you. I accept you. I grieve for your hurts. I want to give you joy."

The water was warm in the pool. Yim and Honus lingered there until the sun slipped from the sky. When they left the water, they didn't dress, but let the breeze take the wetness from their skin. By Karm's grace or by some strength of hope and will, Yim's mind was truly at peace. She didn't dress, enjoying the way Honus looked at her body. She felt his eyes upon the fullness of her breasts and belly, and once again recalled the life within her wasn't only Bahl's child, but hers, too.

They ate, kissed, and caressed, then lay down flesh-to-flesh upon Honus's cloak to sleep.

A chill woke Yim. She left Honus's arms, rose, and pulled on her shift. Then she wandered off to relieve herself. Her urine appeared black in the dark. Yim hoped that Honus wouldn't find its stain. He had been worried about the darkening bruise on her lower back. If he knew the full extent of her injury, it would make tomorrow all the harder. When Yim lay back on the cloak she shared with Honus, he put his arm around her and gently kissed her neck.

Although Yim had no cause to rise early, she did. Honus had grain and a pot, so she made porridge, enjoying the old routine from her former life. While they ate, she asked, "Honus, what lies to the north?"

"The Western Reach extends all the way to Lurwic, or what was once Lurwic."

"Is all of it as desolate as here?"

"Only the southern portion is completely empty. There are villages and homesteads farther north, though Bahl has preyed on them."

"And north of that?"

"The Empty Lands, though some dwell there."

"And north of that?"

"The Grey Fens. A desolate place south of the Turgen River."

"And north of that?"

"No one ventures beyond the Turgen. It's too wide and swift. Why do you ask?"

"Because I must go there."

Honus shrugged. "I took Theodus to places just as wild."

"You won't be taking me, Honus. I'm going alone."

Honus stared at Yim, speechless.

"I said I'd keep no secrets from you, and I won't. The child I bear is Lord Bahl's. Karm chose me to mate with him."

Honus's face fell.

"Karm visited me on the night I left you, and told me I must go to Bahl. Everything that happened was directed toward that purpose."

"Even our love?"

"Especially that."

"Then I'm meant to be with you."

"You don't understand. You live because Lord Bahl lost his power. He lost it because it passed to his unborn son. I gave myself to him to save you."

"I don't care whose child you bear. If you can love it, so can I."

"But Bahl was host to the Devourer. It was the source of his power. And now I'm host to it. I'm no longer holy, if I ever was. I'm befouled. You must flee me."

"I can't."

"There are things more important than you or I, and this is one of them. You've faced Bahl's army, but not Bahl himself. I have and know he's far more than an evil man. The Devourer within him was poised to transform the world into a place of everlasting horror. It nearly succeeded. That evil has now passed to Bahl's son, and the world's only hope is to turn this child from his destiny. It's a task that I must do alone."

"Why not just kill it?"

"You can't solve everything by killing, though as a Sarf, you might believe so." Yim could see her words hurt Honus, and though it tore at her, it didn't sway her. "The child's not our foe. It's the evil within him, and that can't be overcome by violence. Violence nurtures it."

"Then how can you defeat it?"

"Through love."

"Then why do you reject mine?"

Yim saw that Honus was searching for some sign that she would relent. Knowing that she dared not give him one, Yim gazed back at him dry-eyed and firm. "I don't reject your love, but I must forsake it. All my life I've followed Karm's path. It's never been easy. But now that I see its end, I'll make this sacrifice to reach it."

"I can help you by protecting you and your son."

"I'm sorry, Honus, but this child will be drawn to death. He can't grow up around you. I must go to some distant land, somewhere apart from wars and warriors."

"Even if you find such a place and raise your son there, if the Devourer is within him, how can you hope to turn him from evil?"

"The Devourer is also within me now. If I can resist its evil, perhaps my son can also."

"Yim, don't you love me?"

The devastation in Honus's voice nearly shattered Yim's resolve. But she persevered. "I'll love you forever. That love is Karm's gift. But my child will need my love more than you. So it's Karm's will that we part. Honus, that night in the temple, you swore obedience to me. I hold you to that oath. I'm leaving, and you mustn't follow."

Honus, who had been so formidable, looked utterly defeated. "So Karm granted us love, always knowing she'd snatch it away?"

"Yes."

Honus was silent for a long while, a man seemingly drained of all feeling. Then emotion returned to him, and he stood up, his face reddening. "Such cruelty! To play with lives like that! It makes Karm no better than the Devourer."

"Don't say that!"

"Why not? Perhaps you can forgive her, but I can't. Karm took me from my parents. She decreed that I should train to kill. For what? So she might break your heart and mine? So we might end our days in bitterness?" Honus drew his sword and slashed at the heavens. "I gave my life to Karm! But now I repent and hereby curse the day I stepped into her temple!"

Honus drove the blade into the ground with such force that it was half buried. Then with a violent kick he snapped it and flung the hilt away. "I renounce Karm forever!"

"Honus!"

"I'll obey your will, but not hers. I'll take but two water skins. The rest is yours. Go north if you will. I'll not follow. May Karm give you solace. I'll seek mine elsewhere. And when folk gaze upon my face, I'll say it shows my hate for Karm."

Yim stood stunned and heartbroken as Honus grabbed two water skins and dashed up the hill. In his haste, he didn't even bother to take his cloak. Yim climbed the hill and saw him running through the vast expanse of grass. She remained there, wiping her tears so she might see him for the last time. Honus's form grew ever smaller until it disappeared from view and Yim was alone.

FORTY-EIGHT

YIM WEPT. There was no one to see or care, so she gave sorrow free rein. It ruled her for a while. Then the resolve that allowed her to send Honus away resurfaced. She had given up the one she cherished most, and she was determined that it would not be in vain. Yim shouted to the empty plain. "The world won't fall into the abyss! My child will know love, not hate and death!"

Yim almost smiled at her bravado as she prepared for her journey north. She inventoried her supplies and found all the basics—a flint and iron, a knife, a pot, a wooden bowl, a healing kit, and a spoon. There was ample grain, some roots, a loaf of stale bread, and a bit of cheese. She had her shift, which she washed in the pool and laid upon the grass to dry. She also had Neeg for transportation and companionship. Lastly, she had Honus's threadbare cloak. She picked it up and pressed it to her face, cherishing something that smelled of him.

Yim packed the saddlebags, donned her damp shift, saddled Neeg, and after much difficulty, mounted the horse. Her bruised side was painful to the point that it hampered her as much as her extended belly. The stallion stood so patiently through her clumsy efforts that Yim had the impression he understood her plight. Yim sensed a rapport between them. It made her wonder if Rupeenla's kiss had given her more than the ability to overwinter with a bear.

By noon, Yim was riding north. Neeg bore her gently, as if he knew that every jolt pained his rider. Yim's kidney hurt so much that she was nauseous. Riding would have been pleasant if not for that. Instead, it was an ordeal made worse by the need to dismount often and spray the grass with bloody urine. Each time, climbing back into the saddle was a struggle in which the skill gained by repetition was offset by Yim's increasing fatigue and pain. By late afternoon, she could no longer manage the feat and slumped to the ground. Neeg nuzzled her, seeming to offer comfort.

After resting awhile, Yim rose and removed Neeg's bit so he might graze. As she did, she gazed into the animal's large brown eyes. "You don't need a bridle and reins, do you?"

The stallion gave a snort.

"I thought not." Yim threw the bridle away. "I'm hurt, Neeg, and I don't know how bad. Bad enough that you might have to find the way north. Can you do that?" Neeg just lowered his head and began to graze. "Great," said Yim. "My first day alone, and I'm already asking my horse for help. Perhaps he could make porridge also."

Yim removed Neeg's saddle and saddlebags, drank some water, and forced herself to eat some bread. Then she spread Honus's cloak on the ground and lay upon it. Though the otherworldly chill never left her, Yim detected the onset of a fever. It produced warring sensations that were both unpleasant and wearing. Yim lay on her good side, staring at the grass—it looked like a forest so close up—while her body alternated between hot and cold. Though it was still light, she drifted toward sleep.

Yim's last thoughts were of Honus. She wondered where he was and what he was doing, thinking, and feeling. She felt that she would be asking those questions for the rest of her life, and the answers would always be the same—"I don't know." That didn't prevent Yim from guessing. She worried that he was trancing to seek memories of happiness on the Dark Path after being so disappointed by life. She wondered if such memories could be found in so empty a spot, if the ground she lay upon had at one time been home to folk with their measures of sorrows and bliss. *If so, will Honus chance upon their joys or their tragedies? I'll never know.*

Perhaps Neeg had understood everything Yim said to him. Perhaps the Old Ones worked some charm. Either way, the horse acted differently the following morning. He gently nuzzled Yim at dawn and persisted until she rose, feverish and bleary. Yim drank some water, colored the grass with a pinkish stream of urine, munched some bread, packed the saddlebags, and lifted them onto the stallion. She felt drained by the effort, and was worrying how she would ever manage the saddle when Neeg knelt on the ground. Yim had the impression that he wanted her to climb on his back. She did so easily. Then the horse rose, and without any direction from Yim, headed northward at an easy pace.

The rest of the day was mostly a haze to Yim. Somehow, she managed to stay on the horse. That was her sole contribution to the journey. There were times when the fever made her forget where she was headed or why. Neeg took charge. He chose the route and anticipated all of Yim's other needs. In the late afternoon, he stopped for the day by a shallow pool where Yim found some relief by bathing. They spent the night there.

The next day was worse for Yim. By midmorning, she became delirious. Then she felt that she was headed in the wrong direction. In her mind's eye, she saw a huge castle perched on a cliff overlooking an expanse of water that reached to the horizon. The castle was either made of iron or plated with it. The oiled metal was black and had a sheen that reflected the blue of the sky and water. It was a compelling image, and Yim knew it was a real place, a place she must reach at once. She even knew where it lay.

"Neeg!" Yim cried out. "You're going the wrong way! Head west! Head west!"

The stallion continued on its northward course.

"Head west, you stupid beast!" Yim began to sob. "Why won't you listen to me?" She grabbed the horse's mane to use as a rein and wrench it westward. The horse resisted, and eventually Yim's efforts spent her strength. She slumped on her horse's back, sobbing with frustration. Images of the iron fortress gradually faded as she slipped into gruesome dreams.

The following day, Yim's fever broke and her urine was a paler shade of pink. She felt drained and weak, but clearheaded. When she tried to recall the previous day, nothing came to her except the disturbing feeling that the evil within her had briefly gained the upper hand and only Neeg had resisted it. Yim cooked porridge for the first time since she had made some for Honus, and when she had eaten, the horse knelt so she might mount him. Then she rode off with a fuller appreciation of the expression "horse sense."

Yim's journey northward fell into a routine in which one day blended with the next. That was partly due to Yim having lost her edge. Although her illness gradually abated, it left her weakened. Whenever she overexerted herself, she grew dizzy. Once, she even fainted, something she had never done before in her life. Yim told herself that she'd get better, but feared it wouldn't happen until after her child was born.

Neeg chose the route, for Yim had come to trust the horse as she had Kwahku. She never encountered another person on her journey. Whether that was due to the land's emptiness or intention on the horse's part, she never knew. The result was the same either way; no one marked her passage. The land changed slowly over time. It grew flatter. Trees lined meandering streams. Occasionally, they encountered ruins.

Yim noted personal changes more than those of the landscape. The child grew larger and more active within her womb. Her appetite returned with such a vengeance that she began to forage to supplement her provisions. Her breasts swelled further, and she sometimes found a thick yellowish fluid on her nipples. Her ankles and fingers swelled. When the shape of Yim's belly changed, she knew that her son's head was pointed toward the birth canal. That was when she began to experience sharp sporadic pains in her lower back. Then Yim knew that the baby could come any day.

It was then that Yim entered a vast, boggy region of tea-colored water and broad stretches of grayish green reeds. *This must be the Grey Fens*, she thought. It was a landscape so flat that it was dominated by the sky. The fens' monotony was broken only by occasional clumps of trees that grew on patches of slightly higher and drier ground. Those were few and widely scattered. There were no roads or dwellings, and for the first time, Yim questioned where Neeg was taking her. Still, she let him take her onward, for she had no alternative; the horse was in charge.

After they entered the fens, the route Neeg took was no longer straight, for much of the ground was treacherous. A patch of greenery might be growing in soil or upon a floating mat of vegetation. If it was the latter, a step would plunge through seemingly solid earth into murky waters. Yim found that out the hard way several times. By means Yim couldn't understand, Neeg seemed able to distinguish the driest route, although little in the fens was completely dry. After a while, Yim felt she had entered a maze that she might never leave.

Yim traveled ever deeper into the fens. On the morning of the third day, she spotted something new. Near the horizon, huge outcroppings of gray rock jutted from the reeds like mountain peaks poking above a layer of cloud. The outcroppings reminded Yim somewhat of home, and she was pleased when Neeg headed in their direction. Because of the boggy ground, the horse's approach was indirect and it was a long while before Yim was close enough to see wisps of smoke rising from some of the larger outcroppings.

Toward late afternoon, Yim felt pains in her lower back. At first, she thought they would go away as had the previous ones. It was only wishful thinking. Instead, the pains began to come more often and their intensity increased. Neeg picked up his pace without any signal from Yim. Although his more jolting gait added to Yim's discomfort, she understood the importance of haste. She didn't want to give birth in a bog, but time was running out.

The limestone outcropping that lay ahead resembled a tiny mountain. Trees even grew on its sides. To Yim it seemed a haven, but one that might be out of reach. Although it was near, Neeg didn't head straight for it. He took a serpentine path instead. Yim assumed that he was choosing the most solid way, although she saw little that distinguished one patch of the fens from another. As the frequency of Yim's pains increased, the horse sped faster. He also seemed to be taking more risks, for sometimes he chose to splash through dark water and muck. The jostling was excruciating when combined with the increasingly wrenching contractions. Yim gritted her teeth, and grabbed Neeg's mane so she wouldn't fall.

Yim knew far better than most first-time mothers what was in store for her. She had attended many births. But holding a moaning woman's hand while she suffered through the process and being that woman were quite different things. Yim was discovering how different. She was actually surprised when her water burst, soaking her legs and Neeg's flanks.

The horse responded with a burst of speed that approached a gallop. Yim found the bouncing nearly unbearable, but the outcropping, with its promise of dry ground, was close. Neeg headed straight for it, with Yim gripping his mane and holding on for the sake of two lives.

Then the ground beneath the galloping horse seemed to suddenly explode. Reeds and moss rose up in a spray of dark wet muck as Neeg splashed forward. Yim nearly fell over the horse's head as the bog grabbed her running steed. Still, he made progress, forcing his way forward. The floating vegetation closed around Neeg's legs, giving Yim the impression that he was sinking into the ground rather than wading through water. As he advanced, the ground seemed to rise higher. Soon Yim's feet were immersed in water.

As Neeg drew closer to rocky ground, the water became deeper until it lapped against Yim's calves. A sulfurous stench of decay assaulted Yim's nose and her legs felt less wet than enclosed in muck. Neeg still advanced, but far more slowly. Yim could feel his body straining with the effort. With each step, he sank deeper. Soon, Yim could no longer see her horse's legs, and her legs were submerged ever deeper in wet, rotting vegetation. Neeg's progress was measured in ever-shorter distances until he halted altogether. By then, only his head, neck, and upper back were visible. The rest of him was swallowed by the bog. The horse began to shriek. It was a loud and terrifying cry, the voice of despair. As Yim heard it, another contraction hit.

Yim tried to control her breathing and manage her pain, but there was too much going on. Neeg was shrieking. She could feel his powerful body struggling beneath her. But the bog was stronger and winning the contest. Neeg remained in place, slowly sinking. Soon Yim would have no dry place to sit. She looked about. The surrounding bog appeared deceptively dry and solid, as if she were sitting in a meadow. *I can't stay here*, she thought. *I'll have to jump*. The idea was daunting. Even if she could manage, she had no idea where a safe spot lay. *Perhaps there are no safe spots, and I'll sink without a trace*. As Yim had the thought, she realized that she was sitting in water.

Yim was forced to wait for a contraction to subside before she could attempt a leap. By then, only Neeg's neck and head were visible, and when Yim rose shakily to stand on his back, she was ankle-deep in soupy water. The horse stopped shrieking and lowered his head. It seemed a sign to Yim that she should jump, and she did.

Yim's leap was neither a graceful nor a long one. She landed on what seemed dry ground and her legs immediately disappeared into it. Yim flung her torso forward, but she wasn't well shaped for the maneuver. Still, she managed to grab some plants. They pulled free from where they grew, leaving black, wet holes where their roots had been. Yim's lower half was totally submerged in water and her toes touched nothing solid. Neeg began to shriek again, and there was a doomed quality to his cries. Yim feared that she was doomed also.

Swim! thought Yim. *It only seems that I'm on land*. She laid her face and torso against the soggy ground and fluttered her feet, sensing more vigorous kicking might suck her downward. Gradually, Yim's body assumed a more horizontal position. Then another contraction hit her. Yim gasped from the pain. *Float! Float until it passes*.

Between contractions, Yim "swam." It looked like a combination of swimming and crawling through rotting muck, plants, and murky water. It was painfully slow and exhausting at a time when Yim needed all her strength to give birth. She was so caught up in her ordeal that it was awhile before she noticed that Neeg's shrieking had stopped. When she turned her head, she saw no trace of him, just plants on seemingly solid ground. Mourning him would come later, if she survived.

Then Yim's kicking toes touched something firm, and she realized that she had reached the bog's edge. She groped with her feet and decided to risk trying to stand. The idea of sinking into muck and being trapped was terrifying, but time had nearly run out. Yim's contractions were following one another in rapid succession. She stood up, and ooze immediately gripped her ankles. Yim panicked and nearly fell on her face before she pulled free and made a step.

Each step was a struggle until Yim reached firm ground. Then, caked in muck, she staggered forward. Her efforts to escape the bog had left her spent and dizzy, but they had also distracted her from the pain of her contractions. Once she was safe, they were excruciating. Yim felt the urge to scream, but she didn't dare. Instead, she made it to a small tree, leaned against it, and assumed a squatting position. Pulling up the muddy hem of her shift, Yim pushed some of its fabric into her mouth. When the next contraction jolted her, she bit down hard. Her legs were shaking and everything was growing black. *No!* she thought. *You can't faint. Not now. Push! Push!*

It was nearly dusk when the two women walked up the path with the catch from their traps. Frogs, strung like beads on a cord, dangled from the women's hands and kicked helplessly. Then the younger woman cried out. "Mam, a body!" She rushed to a tree that grew near the path.

"Who is it?" called her mother.

"A stranger. She must have strayed into tha bog. And she has a babe! I think they're both dead!"

The other woman hurried to join her daughter. In all her life, she had never gazed upon a stranger's face. Setting the frogs upon the ground, she knelt to place her ear against the stranger's wet, muck-covered chest. "Her heart beats, Rappali, though 'tis faint." She regarded the afterbirth on the ground. The umbilical cord had been chewed through. "She just gave birth, tha poor dear."

"And her babe?"

Rappali's mother touched the still newborn boy lying on the stranger's lap. " 'Tis cold and dead." Then the child moved. "By tha Blessed Mother! 'Tis alive!"

Rappali picked up the child. "Aye, 'tis unnatural cold. 'Twon't live long. We must name it afore it dies."

" 'Tis a mother's task, Rappali."

"There's no time, and unnamed spirits haunt tha bog forever."

The older woman nodded. "Aye." She touched the child's forehead. "We name ya 'Froan,' which means 'frost' in tha old tongue."

At the sound of his name, the tiny boy opened his eyes and seemed to gaze at the one who had spoken it.

"By tha Blessed One!" exclaimed the older woman. "Those eyes! How pale they are!"

"Aye," said her daughter. "So faint tha pupils liken ta two black holes." She shuddered. "They pierce me ta tha quick!"

FORTY-NINE

The Most Holy Gorm paced atop the highest tower of the Iron Palace. From there, he had a commanding view. To the west, he could see the bay, enclosed by high rocky cliffs, and the sea beyond. To the north, east, and south as far as the eye could see was Bahland, Lord Bahl's domain. Gorm gazed upon its scattered villages and towns, aware that their inhabitants were watching the palace for omens. Its iron was no longer being oiled, one of the first economies for the lean times that loomed ahead. Soon the palace walls and towers would begin to rust.

The folk of Bahland had a term for the stretch of years when their lord diminished to an ordinary man. They called it "the browning." They still obeyed Lord Bahl and feared him, but not to the extent they had when their lord was in the fullness of his power. Then he could sway their very thoughts, and they trembled in fear of his displeasure. Even during the browning, folk were mindful that a new Lord Bahl would rise to supplant his father and always acted with that in mind. The Most Holy Gorm had taken steps to insure that they believed the time ahead would be no different.

Only Lord Bahl and the Most Holy Gorm knew that there was no heir within the Iron Palace. There were rumors, but it could cost one's life to repeat them. Several loose tongues had already been pulled out, and the men who had found the empty wagon and General Var's headless corpse had been quickly silenced. Thus only two men knew for certain that the heir had vanished and his trail had gone cold. Even the magic bones were unable to augur where he had gone.

Another man would have given up, but not Gorm. He was old enough to have learned that lost things had a way of being found. Moreover, the child would want to be discovered. Not soon, but soon enough. All that was necessary for Lord Bahl's return and triumph was time, and time was something the ancient sorcerer had in ample supply.

END OF BOOK TWO

The Shadowed Path trilogy will reach its conclusion in the final volume, coming from Del Rey.

ACKNOWLEDGMENTS

LIKE ANY endeavor, writing a book is never a solo effort. These people aided me, and I'm deeply grateful for their help. Richard Curtis was with me from the onset with advice and encouragement. Betsy Mitchell, as always, was an insightful guide. Gerald Burnsteel, Carol Hubbell, Justin Hubbell, and Nathaniel Hubbell provided the fresh perspective of careful readers. Finally, Deana Eaton Jones spurred me onward with her enthusiasm.